The Education of Miss Emlyn Gwen

Morgan L. Potts

The Education of Miss Emlyn Gwen
Text and illustrations © 2021 Morgan Potts
Wyrd Road, LLC
Edited by: Enchanted Ink Publishing
ISBN: 978-1-73-1

The Education of Miss Emlyn Gwen

Text and illustrations © 2021 Morgan Potts

Wyrd Road, LLC

Edited by: Enchanted Ink Publishing

ISBN: 978-1-7364299-1-4

DISCLAIMER: This work contains gore, sexual violence, mental trauma, and scenes of torture.

Glossary- page 440

Gilla: A person forced into servitude.

On Martials:

One generation after the founding of Kymbri martials as we know them became a popular item for high patricians. They were the new fashion, a status symbol. However, they had practical use—protection and loyalty. A guard that could not be bought by your opposition or intimidated into submission.

It might seem an odd thing to arm a gilla, but in your research you will find that at many points in history, gilla were used as guards. To our ancestors this was nothing new, never causing more than some banal gossip among the high class. So we must ask, what made martial gilla so special?

During the fifty-odd years after Rome's fall, before the rise of the Mithran cult, travel was perilous for patricians. Brigands would kidnap and put-up ransom if not outright sell them. In response, many patricians began training trusted gilla to fight and stay near them most hours of the day. Eventually this turned into an institution unto itself.

In our recent past, general knowledge among the lower class would have you believe that the Gwen's were the first martials, this is partially false. Gilla called martials already existed. Examples of this can be found in the Kymbrian archives. In my opinion, the martials who came before were a version in a less refined form. It was Oghan Gwen who created the idea of martials that would last for over a thousand years and invades our modern consciousness whenever we hear the word.

Oghan was never a gilla himself, but he was the steadfast servant of his lord, Delwyn Chronister. The two grew up together, and according to manuscript entries found within the walls of the Chronister estate, Oghan's loyalty to his lord was inspiring. There is no reason to dispute this. All one has to do is look at the education he created for his son,

Milo, and refined with his grandson, Feryn, and granddaughter, Feryl, to see the truth in this. He raised his grandchildren along with his lord's grandchildren, carefully prodding them to become close friends before revealing the truth of their gillary. Many other patricians took this basic model and produced their own bloodlines for martials. Most of the big martial bloodlines do not go further back than this time.

As time marched on, martials became less important. An expensive anachronism with little relevance beyond representing the status of a few high patricians. Now we view them as a romantic symbol of a bygone era. "Loyal as a martial" has become a phrase signifying trust between friends and valuable employees. Films, music, and a multitude of plays have been produced glorifying this particular type of gilla.

Should we look upon them with pity, disdain, or admiration? Perhaps a bit of all three? It is not for me to judge this bygone institution, but we cannot deny the cultural impact they have had upon us.

—Excerpt from *The Cultural Significance of Martials*

Bloodkin in Peristyle

Growing up from a raised soil bed were dozens of tulips reaching for a worn, moss-covered deity incapable of ever bending down to pluck them from the muck. Yet they seemed to strain for his touch as the sunlight beamed through their faintly translucent petals, making it look as if the stone feet were striding atop a pile of gold. Camilla thought it to be a fitting sight for a proud, cracked marble God.

Camilla Chronister, formerly of the Rhydderch clan, wondered at the meaning of this image. She was never a religious person. Oh, she held a belief in them, but her concerns left little time to commune with the Gods. She decided to leave the meaning behind the natural order to the druidi priests. Camilla had real concerns of the here and now to contend with. Followed by a long coach ride back to Londinium.

She leaned on the iron armrest, casting her deep blue eyes over the quaint country garden made up of a dozen flowerbeds neatly shaped into little squares. Each space held not only a different kind of flower but also separated colors. Those spaces were lined with small arched fences painted white, and between them were rocky paths of brown stone laid out like a grid.

She spotted a little gilla boy. The boy was about seven years old by the looks of him. He was dressed in what amounted to a dirty potato sack, no shoes, with unkempt hair freckled with sandy dirt. He stood at the edge of an idyllic stream with small toes digging into the mud. The boy was staring out at the Dé Ard statue surrounded by the golden tulips. It did not take long to realize why he looked so eager. He was almost jittery with either want or need. Camilla knew what it was; he wanted to play.

Her daughter Sylvia ran around the statue. Her black hair and the skirt of her flouncy yellow dress flowed behind her. She was looking for someone, so she slowed for a moment before her fae-like features perked up. She had found her quarry.

"I'm gonna get you, Tabby!"

Another little girl popped up from behind a nearby bush. This one had chestnut hair and wore a white version of the other's dress. Sylvia's best friend and soon to be martial if everything kept going right.

"Nuh-uh! I'm faster!"

The future martial possessed stronger features, was a full inch taller than the other, and ran from Sylvia like a shot. Camilla smiled at this and did not expect Sylvia to gain in her chase.

She glanced back at the boy. Being a gilla of his caliber, he was not allowed into the garden. Camilla knew he had snuck out to play with the two girls last night. A game of marbles no doubt, since that was the only game she allowed them to bring. Assuredly the boy must have marveled over the fact that they were truly made of their named substance. She had decided he would not be punished, and she would say nothing to his mistress, since he seemed starved for playmates, and children needed someone else their own age to romp around with, gilla or not.

Sylvia tripped and fell, but she put her hands up in time to save her face from an embarrassing accident.

"Be careful, Sylvia!" yelled Camilla.

"I will, Momma!"

By the time Sylvia was back on her feet, Tabby was doing a little victory dance as if she were a savage from the new lands. It struck Sylvia as amusing, and she could not help but giggle as the chase continued.

Camilla smiled again and turned back to look at her midday tea companion sitting on the peeling white iron bench across from her. Eneddia Chronister was a cousin, four times removed. When it came to the mainline Chronisters, Camilla had married into it. Married to Eneddia's brother, to be perfectly on point. Her sister-in-law could claim stronger blood, especially being the oldest, but that no longer held any bearing. Eneddia was cut off, disowned, minus the name.

Camilla herself wore a white dress bedecked in embroidered swirling patterns of blue. It sported a high collar that sloped down into a plunging neckline where blue lace fanned out from the end. It framed a necklace showcasing the house emblem: an eagle with a dead she-wolf in its talons on top of an eight-spoke wheel surrounded by gilly flowers. The sleeves of the dress ended at the elbows, where the same blue lace flowed out in the shape of a pleated bell. On her upper biceps were four gold bands, buffed to a shine. Her black hair was done up in such elaborate braids that it took the help of two gilla to accomplish.

Eneddia was not so lucky in her attire. She was decidedly plain, wearing a white dress with capped sleeves. Her light brunette hair was pulled severely back, done up in a bun and stuck through with two long red pins.

Hatred was evident behind Eneddia's eyes. The woman was never any good at hiding this, at least not from Camilla, who prided herself as being no fool. Any pathetic move Eneddia tried to make was leisurely countered, and this visit was no different.

Eneddia avoided her cousin's eyes and looked to the martial, Stella, standing beside the short bench like a sentinel. Camilla and Stella had known each other since they were children; one could say they were best friends. At eleven, Stella was made into a martial, Camilla's personal gilla. These types always carried a revolver and a killing knife to protect their owner. Their eyes were fierce and often described by people as cold and dead. So it was a mistake for Eneddia to look the martial in those pale blue eyes for too long. The hooked raptors beak of a nose did not help either.

She quickly looked away and out over the garden at the two girls.

"I swear, Camilla, they are much too close! You should separate them and show the girl her place!"

Camilla took a moment to finish sipping her tea before putting the cup back on its saucer.

"Ened, dear. This is how we make martials. Stella and I went through it. All Chronisters and Gwens, their cousins and so forth, have been through it, for how long . . . ?"

She gestured, and Stella wasted no time in responding. "Since the naming of the great nation of Kymbri, Mistress."

A female gilla stood a few feet away, as still as any statue. The girl wore a light type of livery, or what Eneddia considered livery: a cheap low-thread linum dress tied with a coarse rope around the waist. The gilla girl came close to dropping the tea tray, where many delicate pastries were perched in a circular pattern. A pattern now disturbed by the gilla's sudden movement.

Stella gave her a disapproving glance, making the girl back up a few steps. Most low gilla had an understandable fear of martials. They were practically overseers in households lucky enough to still have them.

Camilla continued, "I am truly sorry that your martial died young but doing it this way breeds loyalty and devotion. They will both know exactly where they stand when the time comes for her to be broken; it will be hammered home to both quite intensely, I *assure* you. Perhaps you're questioning this age-old tradition through some silly middle-class paranoia? Jealousy perhaps?"

Now that would raise her ire. Eneddia screwed up her face, showing how deep it cut. Camellia had been told that Eneddia considered her disownment unfair, seeing it as a product of preferential treatment. It was not that Eneddia was less favored than her younger brother, Andreas. The gross thievery and causing the death of two bloodlined gilla . . . this was what ultimately ousted her. But she would never see the reasoning behind this decision, or if she did, then she thought unreasonably upon it.

"Well, I don't see why you clothe her as grand as your own daughter."

Camilla shrugged and leaned back. "That is part of the process, dear sister."

Oh, how Eneddia hated being called sister. Judging by the barely perceptible twitch under her left eye it still rose the same ire. Eneddia forced a smile to spread across her face as if the ends of her mouth were being controlled by an unseen puppeteer. "You should have her stay here for the night; she'd sleep in the barn wearing only a potato sack! She'll know her place by morning."

Camilla only nodded, not taking it as a serious statement. Eneddia would never have the backbone to go against her, at least not blatantly, but she wanted to push to see the ghastly woman's threshold for rage.

They both took a sip of tea. The air was thick with invisible warfare and violent subterfuge. This did not affect Camilla in the least. She was relaxed, calculating her next move. However, Eneddia lifted away from the bench backrest, full of muscular tension and close to breaking out in a sweat.

Only Andreas was invited to visit, but he had no flair for this kind of thing. He wanted to rail against his sister, tell her exactly what he thought. Camilla had talked him down and convinced him to stay home. Instead, she brought the girls with her knowing that it would frustrate the woman. Eneddia hated children as much as her neglect and depravity for her gilla. Not only that, Camilla showed up the night before she was supposed to, catching her off guard.

Money was the reason she was asked to come, though Eneddia sure as Hades would never admit it upfront. She always waited till the last minute when she had exhausted all your time and patience. If she had even half a chance, she would waste every kint of the Chronister fortune.

A fortune Eneddia's father worked so hard to obtain. Augustus Chronister was responsible for putting the family in high standing once again after generations had come and gone with no power behind the name. Too much was at stake to let this vile, depraved woman have even one fenni. The long-awaited question would present itself any minute now.

As Eneddia handed the tea and saucer to the gloved serving girl, she hung her head in apparent shame. An insincere shame, Camilla noted. She knew it was coming then.

"I must talk to you about—"

"About money, yes? I thought that was the reason for this visit. Not seeing your dear niece. Not to enjoy a nice day in the country." She said it in such a calm voice that the rage sliding its way into Eneddia's eyes told a different story behind that oh so very sad face.

"I'm still part of the family! I only want what I'm owed!" pleaded Eneddia.

"You forfeited your inheritance a long time ago when Augustus cast you out. You should come to terms with this, dear."

The dam of anger broke and rampaged across Eneddia's face. "Just say it, will you! You . . . condescending, pompous . . ." She stopped herself and sighed in exasperation as if she were blowing out pent-up steam. Camilla sat back, smiling in satisfaction. She had to admit, there was a little bit of triumph in making her lose her decorum.

Eneddia sat back and gazed at her lap for a moment before once again looking into Camilla's eyes.

"My husband is dead, and it's only me now. I have nothing left. Please, sweet sister."

Ened was never poor, not even close, but the woman was hemorrhaging money according to the official records that Camilla was able to obtain before driving out here. The poor dear hid her losses well in a physical form, but not well enough in her records.

Camilla moved her head around, exaggerating the motion, looking about again at the well-maintained garden. "It looks as if you're doing well for yourself, Eneddia."

"Well, I mean—"

"Before we left the city, I took it upon myself to look at your public financial records. You are losing money at an exorbitant rate, yet your estate looks lush. Last night I counted twenty gilla. Twenty! Not counting the male child born on your estate, or the one on the way. Do you even have breeding papers for them? Breeding pens are illegal. The Roman remnant taught us why they needed to be, but you know that. You never cared for ethics, or societal decorum, dear sister, only what you desire. How many kints have you already made on advanced orders, or perhaps we're talking about dracs?"

The insinuation of being a gilla breeder made Eneddia's entire face flush red. She pursed her lips.

No, Camilla did not believe her sister-in-law was doing such a thing, but something was amiss here, and she wanted to get to the bottom of it if at all possible. She studied Eneddia, who was glaring daggers at not only herself but Stella as well. Camilla hoped she was not planning anything stupid. She let out a low sigh. Of course she was probably considering whether her hired hands could overtake Stella. An unlikely prospect. Martials were known for their speed and dead aim.

"Momma, may we please have some tea?"

Camilla had no idea that her daughter along with her daughter's friend approached. An idea formed. An idea that might drive Eneddia over the edge.

She smiled down at her daughter. Sylvia was standing next to her best friend, Emlyn, who she liked to call Tabby for some odd reason. Camilla never asked her about this but suspected it had to do with a cat the girl saved. They would have to do something about that cat soon, but still it was a cute name. The best pet names for martials were the ones with a story attached.

Sylvia was breathing heavy after chasing Emlyn around for the last hour. She never could quite catch her, which was only expected. Martials were bred to be a little stronger, a little faster. Camilla was glad the girl had developed these traits. Yes, Emlyn had what it took to become a perfect martial. She should know since she grew up with Stella and with all that the training entailed. Plus, keeping gilla was quite a fascinating, if not pleasurable, pastime for her.

"Of course, darling. That was a very nice way to ask." As Camilla said this, she waved the serving girl's gloved hand away from the teapot and poured it herself. She handed the porcelain cup and saucer to Sylvia, who grasped it gingerly.

"Be sure not to chip the cup."

Camilla glanced at Eneddia, who was staring at Emlyn so intensely that it looked as if she were trying to set the girl on fire using only her mind. The girl was visibly shaking with mounting fear under the fierce gaze.

"What about Tabby?"

Camilla smiled at her daughter's consideration. She knew this was a good chance to subtly teach her where Emlyn stood, so that when the breaking came, it would be an easier rite of passage. Also, Eneddia might burst.

"Tell Emlyn that it is okay if she helps herself." She put the teapot down on the table near Emlyn. She looked at the girl and waited, anticipating the reaction.

Looking over at Camilla, Emlyn's fear seemed to melt away. The girl reached for the teapot. Camilla leaned back, staring at Eneddia, wondering what her response would be. Not good, judging by her eyes attempting to bore a hole through the girl.

"How dare you touch that!" Eneddia slapped Emlyn's hand away, stood with a violent ferocity, grabbed her wrist, and lifted the girl to her toes. Emlyn looked shocked and uncomprehending over what was happening.

"Gilla should not touch anything so refined without gloves!"

Emlyn's voice wavered. "I'm not a gilla!"

Eneddia squeezed the girl's wrist harder, too hard. Sylvia burst out into tears as she screamed for her aunt to stop.

Camilla was worried that the woman would give up the ruse. It was much too early to reveal Emlyn's gillary, and she had no intention of losing the girl's prospects as a martial. It was a long and delicate process, a waste if Eneddia said the unthinkable.

She quickly stood and almost glided to her. And she gripped the raging woman's bicep.

"Eneddia, let her go." Camilla put as much steel into her voice as she could muster, and it seemed to work. Eneddia looked at the hand. Then looked blankly at her before finally glancing back at Stella, who was undoubtedly ready to pounce. She looked at Emlyn who was on the verge of tears.

"You're hurting me!" Emlyn said weakly.

"Let her go, Aunt Ened! You're hurting her! Let her go!" screamed Sylvia.

She released her grip, and Emlyn collapsed on the ground. Sylvia immediately rushed in to comfort her friend as Stella's knife made a notable click when the guard hit the edge of the steel sheath.

The teacups were broken. The steel teapot lay on the grass; its contents flowed out of its spout and soaked down into the earth.

Camilla comforted her daughter while Stella checked Emlyn's bruising wrist.

"You'll be fine. A perfect opportunity to learn to use your left," said Stella. Emlyn received no comfort. Martials were not treated kindly by their parents. It ultimately made it easier during the breaking. The girl sniffed, holding back the tears, then nodded in assent.

Camilla kissed her daughter on the forehead as Sylvia's sniffles subsided. She then rose to her full height and stood there like a hurricane would have no chance at knocking her over. Her ire seared like a heated knife toward Eneddia, who had the decency to appear sorry for what she had done. This dreg of a woman almost gave it away, and if she had, then Emlyn would have been ruined. All the work they had accomplished so far would have been unraveled and set aflame. A sacrilege most profane, for there were few higher reasons for one to become cursed by the Gods.

Camilla paid no attention to Eneddia as they left. More than willing to let her wallow in failure. Camilla hoped beyond anything that the woman of bile and ugliness would stay out of their lives for good. That the next time they heard of her would be through the obituaries.

Chapter One

It was rare for Emlyn to walk on the streets alone. So it came as a marvelous surprise when her mistress signed a pass, placed the note in her hand, and told her of a very special piece of property that needed acquiring. She thought about that slight twinkle in the mistress's eye and knew this gesture was a reward, a reward she longed for but never desired out loud. She could not help but smile as her black pointed boots clicked on the elaborate herringbone brick leading into Iria Park.

Though Emlyn's heels produced an echo, the sound was soon drowned out by a bevy of noise as if life itself was hiding behind every corner. The colors seemed vibrant. The sounds of small birds mingling with crowds of people were sweetly acute. Even the overbearing heat of the sun could not keep her from enjoying the splendor of it all. She breathed it in, savoring every detail. Being able to walk out like this by herself with a nice juicy red apple in hand, bought from a market vendor who had no trouble selling to the whims of a gilla, was such a rarity. It was a glorious day to be walking uptown in the overcrowded, wondrous city of Londinium. The shining capital of Kymbri.

Two fully clothed female gilla walked toward her. One was clearly not of the isle. She understood that other lands used different words for it and some of those words had come into fashion. But gilla was a wholly Kymbrian word and had different views and expectations.

As the two got close, they both noticed her. Their alarm was evident, and they almost jumped out of the way as if she were a viper slithering on the walk, ready to strike at their shivering heels. Emlyn paid no mind to their unease. Low gilla being frightened of her was nothing new. She glanced back and noticed that the two possessed the criminal brand on the back of their right shoulder, and for a quick moment she tried to guess at their transgressions. Something petty most likely, and were unfortunate enough to be caught one too many times.

Further down the winding path, the heads of a dozen monoliths appeared above the treetops. The wide concrete walkway went straight through the middle of these giant marble statues, giving the passerby the feeling of being surrounded by Godhood. She studied the statues portraying a myriad of popular Gods and Goddesses in three rows. All of them clean to a fault besides the bird droppings dripping down over their heads and shoulders.

She smirked. "The birds must have a good laugh reanointing the Gods every morning. Poor druidi," she said under her breath. She then thought, *People say it's good luck for a bird to cac on your head, so the Gods must be lucky indeed.* She would never dare to say this out loud for fear of their retribution.

Hundreds of melted, burnt-out candles lined the bases of these statues. Emlyn's smirk curled further up, and she thought the birds must have cac'd them out too. At the feet of the statues were altars of various shapes and styles based on which God they sat in front of. Some were ornate, others were disheveled. Others were gaudy with trinkets, a scant few were next to bare. Each had a bowl upon them, many with a few dozen copper fennis. But not a lot, it was still early in the morning. The bowls would be full of fennis and kints by night's end, all going to the nation of Kymbri to fuel further public works.

Emlyn tossed a fenni onto the simple wooden altar of the God Under the Hill, a lesser God that gilla, servants, and the downtrodden tended to pray to the most. He was the servant of the father, Dé Ard, and the all mother, Dé Brigantia, which included most of her aspects. This particular representation had him in supplication, on his knees, head down, with palms held above his shoulders. Emlyn kissed his smooth stony feet and prayed for an increase in her ability to protect her mistress. Not that she needed much protection. Emlyn could count on one hand how many times the mistress had stepped a single foot outside of the house since the breaking. Calling Sylvia a recluse was an understatement, and since her mistress so rarely left home, it went without saying that it made Emlyn a recluse as well.

Two children—a boy in his best suit, looking like a man in miniature, and a girl in a long, short-sleeved peach dress and white floppy hat—chased each other around the monoliths. In fact, many kids were wandering around with no supervision. Most were poor, but there seemed to be no division among them. Play was the most important business of the day. They had no notion of divisional lines quite yet.

Every so often the girl would turn around with a stick and point it at the boy. "You'll never catch me, Admiral Phossus!"

In response, the boy would take out his own stick from the side of his belt as if it were in a scabbard. The boy yelled, "You'll never get away with this, pirate scum! As long as I live, I'll chase you to the ends of the earth!"

They clashed in mock battle, breaking character every so often to laugh. Emlyn decided to watch; it made her smile warmly to think back to when she and the mistress were this age.

He hit the girl's shoulder.

"Ow! That hurt! No fair!"

The boy pointed his stick in the air. "Ah-ha! I have struck down the great pirate Merri-Grew!"

Both of them noticed Emlyn watching and promptly stopped in their tracks. Their faces showed awed confusion, probably not used to seeing her kind wander about in such a manner, much less with a gun and a large knife at the hips. The boy opened his mouth to say something, but the girl pushed him forward and they returned to their revelries, seemingly forgetting about her.

Emlyn continued on her way with her hand resting on the round silver pommel of her knife. She wanted to whistle, but that was not expected of a martial. Her ilk was supposed to be calm, collected and alert, not given over to wanton frippery. She kept from showing that joy.

She came upon a large crowd gathered around a newly cleaned and polished wooden platform big enough for a small play or group of musicians. The crowd looked like a gaggle of agitated ducks. The picture Emlyn created made her want to laugh. It was an image her mistress would find humorous, so she locked it away for later.

She stood in the back as her station dictated, flat boots pressed firmly on the dewy grass, waiting for the auction to start. She made a study of the people around her. Women used their fingers to make a passageway into their high satin collars while frantically waving large lace fans. Some simply used their hats, or if they were too poor for a hat, then using makeshift fans folded with cheap paper seemed to do just fine.

Any man in the crowd with more common sense than decorum left their jackets and long vests at home. Emlyn found the pools of moisture under their arms amusing, though not out of place, but knew better than to show such emotion. Deference was key; it was always key when it came to her kind. This did not stop her from thinking about how lucky she was, having to stand in the back under the canopy of trees. As lucky as the children weighing down the old, fork-limbed oak some yards behind her. Her station as a high gilla, a martial, demanded clothing that breathed, clothing one could move around in, that allowed swift action. She thanked the Gods for the practicality needed for her station, and she thanked them silently for the lack of a heat stroke.

Emlyn put a finger inside the steel band encircling her neck. It was her collar, locked onto her since she was fifteen, made of high-grade steel and burnished as to not attract too much attention. She moved her collar around all the way to the thin part, keeping the beads of sweat from gathering. She walked her fingers down to feel the engravings on the attached flat circular tag sitting at the hollow of her neck. The band was loose, but not loose enough to fit over the head. Just enough to get a shirt collar underneath or to be readily controlled. Collars held a surprising amount of weight so that the wearer would never forget what they are. Not that Emlyn needed a reminder of that, she breathed it. To her it was just the way things were, the way things had to be for society to stay on course.

Forget the stoics' talk about how we all breathe the same air and all that jab and bunk. If that were true, then a man pushing an excrement cart is the same as a high patrician, she thought while producing a slight sneer.

Emlyn composed herself and stood straight. Taller than most of the women in the crowd, she had no trouble seeing the platform. The auctioneer was late. The crowd showed up excited, whether they were buying or not, for auctions tended to be entertaining affairs. Now everyone just wanted to go home and cool off. For now, they seemed stuck here waiting on an auctioneer who had little care for their time. Worst of all, even with flavored ice stands nearby, the children standing at the sides of their parents started to grow more restless than the adults. A low whining sounded to her left.

"Momma, nothin's happening. Can we go?"

"Hush now!" said the mother. She was trying to keep herself and her daughter from being audible above a whisper, but the girl failed to get the signal.

"Please, Momma! I'm bored!"

The girl's father looked down at his child. "Listen to your mother, or I will use my belt when we get home. Understood?"

Without turning her head, Emlyn side-eyed the couple and noticed a short man—well, short compared to herself. The man's much shorter wife held the hand of their daughter. All three were dressed richly, but the make, stiffness, and quality of thread pegged them as low patricians.

This was their first auction. The tell was in their wide eyes, trying to take in everything around them yet not noticing any of the details. Like puppies seeing the world for the first time.

She took another bite of the apple, focusing on the rest of her surroundings with precision.

The auctioneer finally came into view, followed by a young female gilla. He was the portrait of a satisfied man. His once magnificent rose red shirt was stained with sweat. He climbed the stairs to the platform, breathing deeper with each creak of wood. Despite an obvious limp coming from his right knee, he made it to the podium with minimal difficulty. At least not enough to fully embarrass himself.

The auctioneer pulled on the right side of his long white tweed vest and brought out a cylindrical flask as an advert auto came roaring by. It was piled high with wooden signs. The large speakers poking out from the sides like ears blared with announcements concerning such things as Clackway soap, Steelbor ovens, and Vitruvius aweloncell autos.

Few looked in the advert auto's direction as it passed by. Autos were rare, only afforded by those with means, low and high patricians, a few merchants and statesmen, or higher equites. However, the advert auto was a usual sight. Emlyn was used to hearing its static voice wafting through the windows daily. She guessed it served its purpose, for when you need one of those items, your thoughts would turn to the adverts.

The portly auctioneer finished taking a swig, replaced the cap, and put the flask back into his pocket. He gestured toward his gilla with a sausage-like finger, signaling for her to escort the merchandise up.

A diversity of naked commodities aligned themselves side by side on the platform. They were fed seemingly well. Most gilla were from within Kymbri. Authorities were very strict on which non-Gaelic were allowed on the isle; of course, bribery went a long way, and smuggling was rampant.

Jeers from the crowd rang out over the quality of the shivering merchandise.

"Where's the seasoned property?"

"Can we buy that clothed one?" said one, pointing at the auctioneer's gilla.

"Sell 'em cheap!" said another.

The auctioneer's voice bellowed out, making the crowd go silent. "This is what's selling today! I know they look nervous, and they are indeed new to their condition! But they very well and fully know what is expected of them!"

It was plain as day how new they were to their predicament. The display of emotions on their faces was amusing. Emlyn smirked and took another bite. To a few special kinds of buyers, they would be of interest. Even new and untrained, they could at least gain thirty full kints—a quarter of a year's salary for a working man with a decent job.

They would either learn or find a red slit at their throat, though in today's age it would be an unnecessary waste of kints to do something so drastic. Gilla were becoming rare. A change of thought, mainly due to the cost of upkeep, and stoic ideologies permeated the isle. This kept the possibility of gilla rebellions to a minimum. It was the reason gilla came mostly from criminal stock, hence their loyalty was consistently questioned. Then there were the few from the streets, looking for steady meals and housing. Those types tended to think of being a gilla in a good house as a lifetime "job" until they found out they truly had no rights. She guessed a constantly growling stomach could push anyone to accept another extreme. At least the ones who did it for that reason tended to be more grateful.

The auctioneer snapped his fingers, and the first was led forward. A young man with strong, broad shoulders, though not very handsome, stood straight, head down, with muscles rippling from his shivers. The girl lifted his chin, making him look over the crowd. Emlyn thought that he was a good strong pack mule type, and she made a bet to herself that he would be used for some sort of farm work. Maybe fixing the machines which needed a strong hand. The auctioneer gave every relevant detail about the man: weight, height, education, so on and so forth. Then an older gentleman near the front raised his hand.

"Forty kints!"

Another hand shot up, gaining the auctioneer's attention.

"Forty-five!"

The young male ended up selling for sixty full kints; not bad, not bad at all. Emlyn recognized the man's new master as Dylan Arwel, an owner of numerous mills and bakeries across the city and surrounding countryside. The gilla looked strong, but Emlyn doubted his muscles would be put to use more than his mind. She had seen Arwel almost jump out of his skin when the gilla's education was mentioned. His fate would be that of an accountant, and no one would pay a bit of attention to his counterfeiting past. She shrugged. Every so often her ability to read someone turned false.

The next one was a boy of thirteen; this surprised her. She knew children could be gilla. By the Morri she had been raised as one herself. But she did not know that any children were auctioned off like this. Then again, how would she know? Auctions had been only viewed in passing from the window of a moving carriage when she was very young.

The boy ended up going to a high-end courtesan for thirty full kints. She looked to be a former pleasure gilla judging by her movements and of course her beauty that came from such breeding. Likely earned her freedom early, for she only had a line or two within the creases of her eyes. Emlyn narrowed her eyes and studied the woman. She might be working on her own or working for her former masters. Her fan was ornate and bedecked in jewelry, and she had her own gilla in attendance, so business must be going very well. It was telling that the boy had the same color hair as she. Emlyn had heard of pleasure palaces contracting their former gilla to scour auctions so that they could freshen up their bloodlines. And one thing they looked for were certain hair colors. She was sure that was exactly what was happening here, just . . . she never expected they searched for someone this young.

Those two were exceptions in the group of twenty. As each gilla was sold, their history was explained. Most were petty criminals who were caught one too many times and given one of three choices. Prison, where there was more than a fair chance of dying from unsanitary conditions if you were not shanked first for your share of maggoty bread. Exile to the southern colony was the second choice, where you would have to contend with murderous savages, where survival skills in an unfamiliar land were a must. Then you had gillary, where there were at least two square meals a day, a roof over your head, and a more than even chance that you would end up in a patrician house.

Only one of the new gilla had been poor with nowhere else to turn, finding the workhouses less appealing than their current condition.

Emlyn was having fun. She never had the experience of being auctioned off and was glad for it; she was of a rare breed, a martial. A type of high gilla, born and bred to protect, serving one highborn mistress or master. The skills of a martial had almost become mythical due to their rarity in these times where they were needed less and less with each generation. Now only high patricians could front the cost and time of their training and upkeep. She was proud over the thought and took another bite of the apple as her quarry was brought to the front.

The last girl stood stock straight. She had a small, slender build, well curved and cold yet fearful ice-blue eyes, eyes that had seen far too much for her age. Her blonde hair was shorn and uneven, with no real care for the scalp. It was the cruel cut of a woman who got caught sleeping with a supposed enemy. Emlyn wondered how beautiful the girl's hair would be if allowed to grow out.

"Here we go! Our last property of the day! A pretty thing, is she not?"

Someone in the crowd whistled in enjoyment of her beauty.

"You might not be whistling, good sir, after you hear what I've got to say about this lass!"

The crowd forgot the heat and became silent, giving their full attention to the auctioneer. The man let the silence sit in the air for a few moments before he coughed, clearing his throat. Emlyn remembered what she had been told about the girl, so she made no indication of surprise over what he said next.

The auctioneer walked over to the girl, reached around her, grasped her right arm, and spun her about so that her back faced the audience. On the left shoulder blade, just above where he placed his hand, was a brand in the shape of two bars joining together. "She's a criminal! One who would rather be gilla than in prison!"

"So what?"

"Not another!"

"What'd she do?"

"A good question, sir, a very good question! This former low patrician of Leon is a traitress!" He moved his hand away from her shoulder, showing a horizontal line underneath the criminal brand. "Caught making love to a Zarmatian soldier! And doing so willingly!"

Zarmatia was not technically an enemy, but to say there was animosity between them and Kymbri would be an understatement. Dealings with the large country east of the Skaldanes had been peaceful of late. After their Zarcon was ousted from power, a republic replaced it, and talks were ongoing between the two nations. But old animosities do not die so easily. Despite the facts, the crowd still gasped and went into an uproar. Several expletives were thrown at the girl, as well as a tomato; it bounced off her skin and burst upon hitting the planks of the stage. The girl stared at it. Perhaps she saw it as an apt metaphor to a former life. As the girl stared, her tears fell in beautiful droplets near the guts of the tomato.

The girl's lips moved, and Emlyn paid close attention, but she was too far away to read them. Whatever she said, it caused the auctioneer to cuff her with his heavy fat hand. Her head went sideways, but she stood her ground and spit out a string of blood before standing straight again.

Emlyn admired her for taking such a strong slap. The girl's resilience would bode well for her prospects as a gilla.

Emlyn raised her hand, the apple still clutched in her palm.

"Three half kints!"

The auctioneer stared at her for a moment, mouth wide open. He snapped it shut.

"We have a starting price!" He looked down at the stage and mumbled his annoyance. He perked back up by standing straight and puffing out his barrel chest, putting confidence into his demeanor. "Think of all the fun you could have, beating her for the terrible deed of treason!"

The girl winced.

"Four half kints!" offered a man from the crowd.

"Come now! Only serious bids!" pleaded the auctioneer.

The crowd laughed.

"She's untrained!"

"She's a former low patrician, good sir! I assure you she is aware of etiquette!"

It became obvious that he hoped, since the payback angle did not work, that the girl's beauty would carry past her being a so-called traitor. He was getting worried. She could almost smell the sweat that poured off him, and she felt slightly sorry for the man, but the cheaper the purchase, the better.

A little boy perched on his father's shoulders gave his opinion. "She's probably lazy then!"

The entire crowd, including Emlyn, roared with laughter. Maybe a hundred or so years ago that would have been a good price, but not now; a gilla would have no redeeming features for the price to be that low.

"Two *full* kints!"

On the verge of fury, the auctioneer had to swallow his rage when he spotted a man with his hand raised near the front. A well-to-do fellow who knew how to dress practically on such a hot day, decorum be damned. His sleeves were rolled up, and his white shirt was unbuttoned down to his chest. His hair was pulled severely back, and he moved with the flair of a magician. The gilla standing beside him held his jacket, but she was not allowed the same comfort, being clothed from head to toe.

The auctioneer's face turned to glee. This man was not unknown to him, nor was he unknown to Emlyn, as he had once visited the Chronister house to learn about martials.

Training houses used to be a surefire moneymaker, but now there were not enough gilla to pump out. Strangely, Hornbow's house somehow kept growing, even though he trained only a few. People were willing to pay a premium for his quality rentals.

Emlyn remembered him as a jovial fellow who had given her a lollipop—cherry, if she remembered correctly. When she was a little girl and unaware of her gilla status, she rarely received treats, so the man's face had stuck with her. She had not had a notion of his occupation then, but Emlyn did remember his sad eyes, which she later took as unwarranted softness. She wondered if the gilla with him was Kittie, a contractor that this man trained. She had many fond memories of Kittie and would delight in seeing her again. She was unable to tell if it was her or not due to the wide-brimmed hat the woman wore.

"Galan Hornbow! Why so low?"

"If there was profit and more than a crumb of potential! But she's a traitor! Imagine how that will look in her histories, and you can't get rid of that brand! No, I'll take her for two full, and *that* is it!"

The auctioneer whined, "Come on, Galan."

But Galan did not make a move.

"Okay then! Two going once! Two going twice!"

"Five full!"

Galan glanced back at Emlyn. She did not know if he recognized her—she expected not. Hornbow rolled his eyes before raising an outstretched hand in the air. "Five and a half!"

The auctioneer wiped away the sweat from his brow. "Fine. Do I hear six?"

The new-money father standing with his family leaned his head toward his wife. "We need a nanny. What do you think, dear? Buy the girl on the cheap, then have Mr. Hornbow train her up? Our neighbors need not know she's a traitor."

"That's a wonderful idea, Ergist!"

"Five and a half going once! Five and a half going twice!"

"Six!" said the new-money man.

"Six! Do I hear seven? Anyone?"

The wife smiled and grasped tighter to her husband's arm, while their daughter clapped her hands, jumping in glee.

"Going once!"

"Eight!" Emlyn dropped her hand and took another bite of her apple. The family looked over at her in disbelief.

"Mommy! She can't bid, can she? She's a gilla!"

"Nine!" Hornbow looked back at Emlyn, eager to know if she would dare to bid again, but Emlyn was nothing if not obedient to her mistress.

"Ten!"

"Eleven!" countered Hornbow.

"Fifteen!" responded Emlyn.

Emlyn pretended to not notice as Hornbow stared at her.

"Galan?"

He looked at the auctioneer and smirked before shrugging.

"Fifteen going once! Going twice! Sold! To the . . . Whom do you represent, gilla?"

"Chronister, Master!"

"Sold to the Chronister house for fifteen kints!"

Emlyn tossed the apple core to the ground.

"Winners! Please pay and collect your new property on the right side of the stage! In an orderly fashion if you will!"

Emlyn made her way through the crowd, showing respect to every master and mistress she passed.

In a sudden jolt, she was almost knocked off her feet. Transferring the momentum to her left leg then slamming her foot down hard was the only thing that kept her from crashing to the ground. If that had happened, she would have humiliated herself, and her owner by extension. Emlyn looked at the man that ran into her; he was on his knees scrambling to pick up a myriad of packages.

He was quite agitated. "Watch where you're going, missy!"

He was not bad looking. Shaved face, close-cropped dark red hair, and a tailored vest and shirt that fit a triangular frame, under which she could tell was a body of well-kept muscles. She swept away a twitch of a smirk and was about to apologize when she noticed the man's collar. Then she peered down to his pistol and knife. Before she could scan her surroundings for his master, fingers wrapped around her own collar and tugged, forcing her face-to-face with another man. He had to be the owner. His gilla was handsome, but the master was far above the charts. Surely blessed by Dé Áine. A young, chiseled face, and a wisp of a moustache jutted out from under his nostrils, ending in points just under the dimples. The style reminded her of an old Egyptian khopesh, perfectly curved and sharp. And his eyes were just as sharp and alert. She cursed inwardly, wondering how this could have happened, but kept her features deferential.

"Apologies, Master."

Using his free hand, he moved a length of Emlyn's chestnut hair away from her collar and read the tag. "Emlyn Gwen, property of Sylvia Chronister." He said it slowly, in a tone that was heavy and loud. It was his intention to get the attention of anyone passing by. "Martials should never be so clumsy! Look at the mess you've made of my property!"

Emlyn obeyed the underlying command in his voice and looked to where he directed. His martial was still gathering packages. Some of them seemed fine, but others had their brown paper wrappings torn, and one slender rectangular package was soaking wet.

"That one is now a broken bottle of Don Delguise nine thirty-two! Broken!" He emphasized the word. "Do you know how much that wine cost me? Maield! Hurry yourself!"

Maield rushed faster to pick up the rest of the packages as the master turned her tag around and laughed.

"Her mistress gave her a pet name. Tabby!"

Maield laughed along with his master. This irked Emlyn, as it could be interpreted as a slight insult toward her owner.

"I have never understood women's seeming need for giving their female martials pet names!"

He released her collar, and she almost stumbled back. He eyed her up and down in appraisal. "You're strong, and a pretty trup. Just enough to be pleasing to look at, but not distracting. Exactly what is expected of good breeding! What do you think, Maield, should I petition Lady Chronister to have Emlyn breed with you?"

Maield stood at attention and gave her the same appraisal. "Gwen is a very respectable martial family, Master. I would be delighted to breed with her."

The master pointed a finger at Emlyn and made sure everyone could hear, as if he were making a proclamation. "Very good! Go tell your mistress, Sylvia Chronister, that Lucius Donsill wishes to have his martial, Maield Caldivin, bred with her martial, Emlyn Gwen! Ask your mistress if that is appropriate recompense for the dishonor you have done me!" The proclamation was made and heard by many.

CHAPTER TWO

Sylvia's bright, almost iridescent blue eyes glinted with mirth. She threw her head back, sending her sable hair flowing down the back of the chair. She let out a bellowing laugh with a sweet and infectious edge.

The sarcasm that bubbled up inside her was difficult to keep down, so she let it pour out as a smirk threatened the delicate mole just under her left cheek.

"Truly now. Is that all?"

Emlyn mirrored her smirk. "I'm afraid so, Mistress."

She stood a few feet away from Sylvia's brilliant white desk in the middle of a room of white borders and eggshell walls dotted with family portraits and framed photos of various properties.

The desk was strewn with papers, making the surface hard to see. Pure chaos until Sylvia would eventually get tired of the clutter and organize. The only thing that had order was a fruit bowl full of apples, sitting dangerously close to the corner.

Sylvia crossed her legs, barely noticeable beneath the sleeveless white dress and many layers of flouncers. The only color in her outfit was a wide blue satin sash situated high on the waist.

She put a finger to her temple as she leaned back in the chair. Something playful was dancing across her mind.

"Do you approve of this . . . Maield Caldivin?"

Emlyn cupped her chin, feigning deep thought. Years ago, she had met a few Caldivin martials at the only high patrician "gathering" her mistress had ever attended. A type of vacation resort where a lot of betting took place, mostly by pitting martials against each other. She defeated a Caldivin in one of those unarmed combat competitions. She remembered her well, a smaller girl with deep red hair, same as Maield's and around the same age. One heck of a left hook. But Emlyn had persevered, knocking her out in the second round. Nonetheless, the Caldivins were upstanding martials.

She answered her logically. "He would be an ideal match, Mistress. But this is not about what he and I want."

Sylvia's playful look rose with a raised eyebrow. "Oh? What do you really think, Tabby?"

Emlyn took a few steps to the desk and snatched one of the red apples from the fruit dish before making her way to the grilled, ground-to-ceiling windows. She looked out beyond the courtyard and over the walls. This was a tease, so she decided to further the tease by taking her time in responding.

The buildings in the immediate vicinity were similar in style to the Chronister house. Insulae, famed in old Rome and its territories for housing the urban poor, now remade into gaudy, ornate mansions that could span entire blocks. The Chronister insula covered two of those blocks. It rose to three stories on all sides except the more substantial right, where a fourth was added many years ago.

Half of the estate remained in disuse because Sylvia believed there was no point in its upkeep. She had no mind for guests or parties, viewing it all as a waste of time and money. She and her mother, Camilla, had a heated argument over it when the decision was made some years ago. Camilla was a romantic at heart, a true adherent to the ways of her generation and respectful of what came before when there was a purpose in interacting with high society. Sylvia could not see it that way. Eventually they learned to stay clear of the subject after testing and pushing at each other's boundaries. They were both oaks with firm roots. Oddly enough, Sylvia saw the need to keep the garden in all its splendor, even expanding upon it by tearing out the rooms on the west side, leaving only the boundary wall. The reasons being that you could see it out of every interior window and that it was one of the first areas encountered when the inventors and businessmen came by for a chat. Mainly, Emlyn suspected, its purpose was to attract birds. Sylvia had a particular fondness for them, all of them. Even the flying rats known as pigeons gained her admiration.

She glanced down into the expansive garden where the head gardener, Fagan, fought back some bushes with his shears. Not too far away, in front of one of the many fountains, his assistant, Olier, played dice with one of the housemaid gilla they had named Lemon due to the almost constant sour look on her face. The top gilla, Strawberry, sat next to him; in fact they sat very close, almost cuddling.

Good, Olier deserves a reward as much as Strawberry's earned a treat.

Her eyes lingered out the window for a few seconds more before turning and leaning roguishly against the sash. The light flooding through gave her somewhat of a silhouette.

She took a bite of the apple.

"It's the start of a marriage proposal."

She stated the obvious, Sylvia just wanted to gauge her reaction, but Emlyn remained composed in her loose manner.

It was true, marriage proposals between the high patricians tended to start with an offer to breed martials, though in this particular case, it was done in a very unusual manner. Embarrassing a martial could look very bad indeed, but knowing that Sylvia had many suitors, Lucius calculated the best way to get her mistress's attention. Emlyn was sure that it worked. She thanked the Gods that no breeding would occur until the marriage was consummated.

A warm smile spread across her mistress's face. "I concur. Now, let us speak of this Mira girl. You've put the collar on her?"

Emlyn nodded.

"Did she cry or break down?"

"She cried after hearing the snap. If she broke down, I would have personally beaten her."

Sylvia tapped her finger on her lips rapidly.

"Good. Please send her in . . . but give her the lecture first. Loud enough for me to hear."

Emlyn performed a martial bow, right fist over heart, bent at the waist ever so slightly.

"As you will, Mistress," she said in a playful tone.

* * * * *

The girl from the auction sat on her knees, naked as the day she was born. Her eyes were downcast, studying the twisting blue patterns of leaves and vines embroidered in the rug typical of the current Kymbrian corraí style, always in motion and swirling. She was shaking and swore she could feel the shivers all the way down to her bone marrow. The weight of the collar made it worse. She had no idea how anyone could get used to it, and it seemed to always be cold to the touch. The shivering earned her a slap across the top of her head.

"Cac, girl! Compose yerself! Ya don't want yer mistress to view ya as a nervous nell, and whatever ya do, dun't be a cumber!"

The girl looked back at a much older, frumpy lady. She had no collar, so the woman was a servant, not a gilla. She was known as Ms. Cord, and she was placed in charge of the girl until summoned. Cord was in her fifties and looked as if she belonged in wild Erie. She wore a stained white apron over a lavender dress. Both were given a fine dusting during the creation of some cherry pastries. The apron had a slightly sweet smell wafting from it, comforting in a way. It reminded the girl of a favorite kitchen maid who used to sneak her similar confections before going to bed. She missed that maid.

She had a few souvenirs in the form of bruises on her back end from a large wooden spoon, a punishment for accidentally dropping some of the dough for the pastries on the floor. Even after a few hours it felt as if the Kymbrian black hound had taken a bite from her rear. It was difficult to sit back.

"Cumber, what does that mean miss?" she asked, truly curious. It was a word that patricians did not use and hence she was unfamiliar.

The cook roughly grabbed the girl's hair near the scalp, forcing her gaze forward. "It means dun't be brainless, and I never gave ya the okay to call me anything other than mistress, but if a good girl ya be, I might let ya call me ma'am!"

In the lands of the pan-Gaelic—Kymbri, Erie, Gallia, and Gaelland—gilla called all free women mistress, and all free men master. Other honorifics were allowed upon quality of service and gaining trust.

She kept her head forward and down like she was supposed to. Eyes studying the sloping, whirling patterns of the rug.

She had to admit, helping the cook in the kitchen took her mind away from meeting the mistress of the house. Technically there were two mistresses of the house, the mother, Camilla, and the daughter, Sylvia. As soon as she was released to the cook's care, she became a fountain of questions about her owners, which was only right. She found out that the mother had largely retired soon after the husband, Andreas, died, relegating herself to the affairs of the family estates and of the extended family. Thus, she gave Sylvia the lead in handling the family's outside investments in technology, government, and religious functions, along with a few yearly charity events. This also included buying new gilla and selling off the ones who were no longer useful. But according to what she'd overheard, Mistress Sylvia was as reclusive as they come and rarely dealt in anything other than the family business of being the money that backed various inventors.

She did not look up as the heavy mahogany door before her creaked open. Beads of sweat formed. She swallowed, keeping the fear down, not letting it overtake her. This moment seemed important. To mess it up could be dire, heavy punishment or put up for resale. And based on what she'd sold for, resale would lead to a situation even worse than this one. A woman's voice, deeper than average, smooth but commanding, came from the doorway.

"Look at me, girl."

She tilted her head up slightly and was looking at the face of the woman who bought her at the auction. She understood by listening to the conversation during the paperwork proceedings that this was Emlyn Gwen, martial to Sylvia Chronister.

When learning that she was in the company of a martial, to cut and run felt like a good idea. She did not understand this type of specialty gilla. Of course, when she was hiding in Leon as a patrician, she had seen a few, but always stayed well away.

The woman's dead eyes unsettled her. Where she grew up, martials were just stories told to frighten children. Keep them from fraternizing with gilla too closely. Hence, unlike Kymbri, the aristocrats of her homeland tended to not have any gilla serve them directly. It was easy to pretend that they did not exist. Emlyn was everything those stories described, an imposing figure with a thousand-yard stare that could humble any assailant foolish enough to stand against her. The masters that owned them fed them disobedient children—she did not think that part was true, but that stare, she had it. It was difficult to look very long into the woman's cold, brown, almost amber eyes. She could not take it any longer and diverted her gaze. She was shivering again.

Emlyn put a finger under the girl's chin and tilted her head back up. The martial did not look happy. "When I give you a command, I expect you to follow it! When anyone in this house snaps their fingers, I expect you to stand at attention and be ready to receive instruction! Understood?"

"Yes."

"Yes what?"

"Yes, ma'am!"

Emlyn nodded in cold satisfaction. "You have chosen gillary over the traitors' prison. So, understand that your new mistress, Lady Sylvia

Chronister, took pity on you and risked scandal by accepting a traitress into her house! You should be grateful!"

Mira shot her head up, and the words flowed out like a jumbled mess. "Yes, yes! I'm grateful! Very grateful!"

"I thought you knew how to address me?"

Mira bowed her head quickly and flushed red in embarrassment and fear. "Yes, ma'am. Sorry, ma'am! Please forgive me!"

Emlyn smirked and nodded. "Very good! I went over how to formally thank your mistress. Do you remember, or should I go over it again?"

"No, ma'am!" she said, affirming that she did indeed know.

"Then I suggest you do what I told you to do when you step through the doorway!"

"Yes, ma'am! Thank you for the advice, ma'am!"

Emlyn looked over at the cook and nodded. "Thank you for bringing her, ma'am."

"How 'bout that! I'm impressed! Ya managed to stop calling me mistress after I had to say it, what, few thousand times? Again, Emlyn, just call me Ms. Cord." Ms. Cord slapped Mira upside the head again. "Yer girl here did well, as well as any low patrician would in a kitchen I suppose. Dropped some dough, but I gave her a right paddling. Put the fear of the Morri in her I did."

Mira groaned, suddenly embarrassed. She could not help but think that she was not purchased out of pity but for the inherent hilarity of a treacherous low patrician turned gilla kneeling to kiss their feet. She knew the Chronisters did not have to worry about scandal. They were one of the greatest, most well-known patrician houses in all of Kymbri. They set the trends. Even so, she could not mess this up and reminded herself that even being made fun of constantly was better than death.

You have to accept this new life, she thought.

Emlyn nodded ever so slightly toward Ms. Cord, which let the cook know she was good to go back to the kitchen.

"Well, Emlyn girl, tell the mistress that dinners at six. Boiled veal, spiced shallots, and Garum, and I am not making anything different! No way, no how!"

"I'll be sure to tell her."

The cook nodded, then walked away toward the kitchen downstairs, leaving them alone. Emlyn looked the girl over and smiled in approval.

"She cleaned you up well. Listen, girl, here is some advice, and I want you to pay close attention, so hear this well: Just because you chose gillary over a traitors' prison does not mean that you're any less likely to die. If you are in the least bit displeasing, then a quick slit to the throat will be your fate."

The girl gulped and fought down the urge to touch her neck.

Emlyn bent down next to her ear, letting what she said sink into the girl's mind before continuing. "However, you do have a chance here. Rejoice in service. Rejoice in the attention of your mistresses. Now go."

Mira shot up onto her feet like lightning had suddenly zapped her. "Yes, ma'am! Thank you, ma'am!"

"Hurry!" barked Emlyn.

Mira walked briskly into the study, trepidation apparent with every move she made. She spotted Mistress Sylvia sitting at a pristine white desk with neatly stacked papers on top. The dozens of paintings, of ancestors, battles, old land holdings, and other property, lined the walls. They loomed in, telling a resplendent and deep history. The people in the paintings seemed to stand beside her mistress, shrouding her. Though the girl's own family had a very deep history, just with more portraits and more land, the sight still had its effect. She always thought specters lived within the paint of family portraits, and as a little girl that thought terrified her. It terrified her still. She stopped walking halfway between the door and her mistress, as she was instructed to by Emlyn earlier that morning.

She stood for an uncomfortable minute and knew that her mistress was drinking in every inch of her body. She was used to men doing it, but a woman? It was strange. All of this was strange.

The formal greeting from a new gilla in Kymbri was much different than the one from her homeland. Such a greeting did not exist back home. Even though Emlyn scared her, she was grateful for the martial's thoughtfulness in providing the information on how to perform this action.

Sylvia beckoned her forward. The girl sank to the floor and slowly crawled on hands and knees, keeping her head down.

"Faster."

The girl obeyed, stopping just as a pointed pair of leather boots came into her vision. More sweat formed and landed on the carved vine pattern flowing down, ending in little bunches of leaves and flowers on each side. There were no laces, not even silver snaps, but delicate pearl buttons ran every inch of the way down the middle. The boots were recently polished. The strong, sharp odor made her wrinkle her nose.

"You know what to do. Do you not?"

"Yes, Mistress." She knew how, but she didn't want to. It was humiliating, but what other choice was there?

She bent forward and kissed each boot lightly. With her hand, she made sure to wipe away any trace of where her sweat fell, then, keeping her head down, she crawled backward to where she originally knelt, before leaning back on her heels.

"Thank you for purchasing me, Mistress."

"Ah, very good!" She laughed. The mistress drummed her fingers against a knee. "When you were a *low* patrician, your name was . . . Mira Sauden. Am I correct?"

"Yes, Mistress."

"Look at me."

The girl did as bid and tilted her head up.

"You know that your name means nothing now. You are no longer part of that family, *any* family. But I think I will let you keep Mira. Just know that I can change it at any time if I deem it necessary."

"Thank you for my name, Mistress."

"We are in need of a kitchen gilla, so you will be working closely with Ms. Cord. Keep in mind that everyone in this house is above you, even the other gilla. Visiting gilla shall be treated as your superiors. Other than what Ms. Cord requires of you, there will be no fighting for favor here. We are not wild beasts. You shall have nothing without my or my mother's permission. Do you understand me?"

"Yes, Mistress!" She hated the thought of being under the cook's thumb. Ms. Cord had already proved to be a hard, unrelenting overseer, but at least she might be well fed.

Looking on the bright side was the way through this cave. There was food at hand, rich food. The mistresses would have little to do with her, and she was . . . not dead.

Sylvia snapped her fingers. Mira sat straight at attention. "I have an errand for you to run, Mira. I want you to go to the kitchen and ask Ms. Cord for two bottles of Don Delguise six twenty-two—then I want you to wrap the bottles with brown paper and take them to Lucius Donsill's residence at thirty-one Cerrick. Tell him, or his martial, that I regret the clumsiness of my martial. And that the proposal to breed our properties is generous, but I must decline. Ask him to please accept these two bottles of what I understand to be his favorite wine."

Mira listened earnestly.

"Mistress, shall I clothe before I leave?"

Sylvia's eyes narrowed, and her words had a harsh bluntness that made Mira wince. "No. You have not earned such a boon."

Shock spread across Mira's face.

"Pay attention!" Emlyn's command rang in her ears.

Mira somehow knew that if her mother and father were looking at her from the afterlife, they would be shedding tears. The shame came to her then. Even after all she had been through. She could not help but fixate on the floor in an attempt to hold it all back.

Now, why now? After all the shame I've already encountered? she thought.

Emlyn grabbed her by the hair, knocking her away from the shame for a moment. She was lifted to her feet and cried out in pain. Mira slowly opened her eyes and investigated Emlyn's face.

"You should be thanking your mistress for letting you run this important errand!"

"Yes, I—"

Emlyn thrust an envelope at Mira's chest, and as she grabbed hold of it, Sylvia spoke. "That is an invitation to the Wellspring Ball as my escort. Make sure he receives it. Now hurry, gilla!"

Emlyn tossed Mira toward the door, making her stumble and almost fall. Mira blinked, barely comprehending what had occurred.

"Y-yes, Mistress!" Mira responded. Then she ran out of the room and down the hall, barely holding her emotions together.

* * * * *

As soon as Emlyn shut the door, they both burst out laughing. "Did you see her face, Tabby?"

Between gasped breaths, Emlyn managed to respond. "Yes, Mistress."

Sylvia wiped away her tears. She was laughing so hard she failed to notice that Emlyn had brought her a glass of water, poured from a white pitcher on the corner side table. She took the glass and drank half and handed it back. Emlyn finished it off, then went to return the glass to its place.

"This is proving to be quite amusing," said Sylvia, sitting back in her chair. "I wonder what my ancestors would think of owning a patrician."

"She's a low patrician, Mistress."

Yes, low patricians might be lumped in the same group, but high patricians were a category unto themselves. Almost an entirely different social structure, a structure that Sylvia had no interest in and almost loathed. Though she could not gather much animosity toward other high patricians, or much of anyone for that matter. People just did not fall on her mind. She had spent years making herself and the insula fortress-like. But perhaps it was time to loosen up, just a little. For Emlyn's sake. For the sake of her own blood. To finally attempt to erase these old feelings that she had for her old friend.

Sylvia looked down and bit her lip, suddenly worried. She gathered herself to ask, "Do you think I was a bit harsh with her?"

Without missing a second, Emlyn responded, "Not at all, Mistress. She was a low patrician; she needs to know what it means to be a low gilla."

Sylvia agreed with a nod of her head. They were always the best of friends in their adolescence. But ever since then, Sylvia had a certain sorrow clinging to her like a dark aura. A sorrow brought on right before moments like this, this game they played, and she could feel a game coming soon.

"If I may be so bold, Mistress?"

Sylvia raised an eyebrow. "You may."

Emlyn cleared her throat and continued, "It looks bad to send a low gilla to apologize for my failing. But if you sent me, that might seem weak. He might think you too submissive to bother with. But you make up for the possible insult by offering two bottles of a better vintage, showing off your greater access to the finer things. Finally, you offer an invitation to an exclusive ball, showing your influence again, and your interest in him being a suitor, which rebuffs his direct offer to breed martials, and hence, his marriage proposal."

Sylvia clapped, very much delighted by her most trusted confidant. "That was very astute, Tabby! Bravo!"

Emlyn took a grand courtly bow, bending at the waist. "I'm not nearly as astute as my Mistress."

Sylvia responded with a smile and a nod. "The man is bold. He got what he wanted, my interest, though I question his method. If he had miscalculated, even slightly, and embarrassed you, then he would have embarrassed me. Intriguing, is it not?"

Emlyn dipped her head. "As you say, Mistress."

Emlyn grabbed the apple from where she left it on the side table and took another bite as Sylvia gave a playful smile.

"I know you, Tabby, you are not clumsy in the slightest. So since I do not believe Mr. Donsill's accusation, I will not punish you."

Emlyn bit into the apple.

"However, you took that apple without permission."

Emlyn stopped chewing and put her free hand to her mouth in mock surprise. A laugh threatened to come out. She had trouble keeping the apple mush in her mouth but managed to hold on.

Sylvia's grin deepened and became mischievous. She shook her head, knowing exactly what was happening. It happened often, the tease, the game. The bending of the rules with a martial. It was a delight. She was the mistress of this house, so why couldn't she have some fun every once in a while with a female gilla? Her most . . . loyal gilla. A twinge of guilt crept in, but she crushed the feeling, obliterated it as she narrowed her eyes and let lust conquer her.

"You minx. Strip for me. Now!"

Emlyn could not hide her grin and decided to further the tease by turning to face the window. She took the last bite of the apple, tossed its core aside, and started unbuttoning her blouse. With demurely cold eyes, she looked back over her shoulder at Oliva.

She shimmied the blouse down from her shoulder blade and then did the same with the other side. It fell to her waist, exposing her perfectly curved back.

She looked over her shoulder again. Sylvia had not moved from that swivel chair but sat back with tension circling in her eyes. She bit a nail in barely controlled frustration. Emlyn could tell, even under that layered dress, her mistress's legs were spreading ever so slightly, inch by inch.

Sylvia's right hand moved slowly from her thigh toward her sex. "If you have in mind that I am coming to you, then know that your notion is backward."

Emlyn slipped out of her boots and quickly, but still elegantly, shimmied her skirt down in the same manner as her blouse. She turned to face her owner.

Sylvia studied her. Seeing her nude was nothing new, but it was always thrilling to see a taut, well-built woman naked and ready to please her desire. The fact that it was Emlyn made it so much sweeter. She loved her. A notion locked away in her mind and never shared. She was certain no one else knew, and hoped no one would, not even Emlyn herself. It would be ruinous.

The martial's every movement was calculated, controlled, like the methodical tension of a panther stalking its prey. Letting loose the reins and allowing Emlyn to venture out for an errand did wonders for her protector's mood.

"Crawl to me, tabby cat."

Emlyn lowered herself with an easy grace to the floor as Sylvia spread her legs wide and lifted the many layers of her skirt. She made a short whistle.

"Come here. You know what to do."

Emlyn crawled achingly slow to her mistress's fully spread legs. She looked up into Sylvia's eyes. Sylvia searched those eyes, hoping she would recognize something warm and alive, but what she sought could not be found. It did not reverse her own mood; her excitement was too hot, too high to disperse so easily.

Emlyn disappeared under the skirt and flouncers.

"Go on, take your punishment. Oh!"

Emlyn found the spot and went to work.

"Ah! That's a good girl!"

She grabbed Emlyn's head through the skirts, keeping the martial exactly where she wanted. She arched her back, pushing her sex further onto Emlyn's practiced tongue. The slow lead-up and her Tabby under the skirts was delightful, so delicious. Tabby always knew how to pleasure her, and she made it interesting each and every time they played this game. She needed this. "Such a good girl!"

The door suddenly burst open with a ka-thrump. Sylvia sat up, surprised, and pushed Emlyn's head downward as a very fanciful flurry of a yellow-and-white lace dress flowed like cascading flowers into the room. A carefully maneuvered, large hat covered in red florets pushed through the doorway, as if they were supplicants reaching up to a statue of Dé Brigantia. This woman of graceful movement and assured confidence was Camilla, Sylvia's mother.

She had a brisk gait, only loping when her black enameled cane clicked on the floor every few steps, which did not diminish her ability to own a room with her presence; in fact, it seemed to enhance the effect of supreme, steadfast will.

Her own martial came into view, heeling on the left. Emlyn's mother, Stella, stood two inches taller than her daughter if you could believe such a thing. She was much more dour and imposing than Emlyn, with those seemingly never blinking ice-blue eyes that were more terrible than the fields of amber Sylvia was used to. She was glad Emlyn had not inherited that long face and hooked nose.

"Good morning, darling!"

Sylvia looked around like someone stuck in a burning building, desperate for an exit.

Camilla looked around the room, then inquired, "Where's Emlyn? She's supposed to be with you."

Wide-eyed, Sylvia bit her lip and went through dozens of possible responses, landing on one. "I—uh, sent her for a bath!"

So obvious, you idiot! she thought.

She waited for her mother to say something about how terrible it is to lie, followed by a treatise on how the Gods punish liars. A particular story from her youth about what happens to lying children came to mind, a dreadful tale about a wolf sniffing out the lies and gobbling the child up. But a rebuke never came.

"Splendid! Keep her hygiene up!"

Sylvia looked her straight in the eyes. She was surprised. It seemed like her mother was in an overwhelmingly good mood, so it could be possible that she missed the lie, could it not?

"Um, of course, but why do you say that?"

Stella placed an extra seat next to the desk. Camilla sat down and adjusted her leg.

Camilla looked over the desk, over newspaper clippings of a recent series of murders before spotting a stack of unopened envelopes.

"You need to start taking a serious look at these bachelors!" She took the top envelope, read it, then waved it to the side, keeping it up for Sylvia to see. "You're twenty-five, practically an old maid. It is past time to marry, and there are plenty of young men who would suit this family. You cannot ignore them any longer."

She tossed it back toward the pile. "And when you come to a decision, make sure you pick one with a martial, so that our future heir will be safe."

Sweat started to break out on Sylvia's face. Her patience was quickly wearing thin. She kept her smile up. "Families who want nothing more than to steal our money."

Camilla gave out a long sigh of exasperation. "You're paranoid, darling. I understand that paranoia comes with money. Paranoia can be useful to help you keep it. But it can also get in the way. And a good example of that can be found staring back at you in the mirror." Camilla sighed again and looked at her daughter with caring eyes. "I know you do not want to hear me say such things, though it must be said. You have to put it down and take the chance. You're intelligent, so put the paranoia aside and use your reason."

Sylvia looked down at where Emlyn should be and nodded her assent.

Camilla continued, "I've got some good news for you!"

She stared at her mother, wondering what it could be, hoping she would just say it quickly and leave. Sylvia gave a sudden twitch of her legs, cursing inwardly, and hoped the odd movement went unnoticed.

"I know it is early for a natal present, but time is sensitive with this."

"Mother, what are you talking about?"

"I want you . . ." She pointed to the stack. "And one of your suitors to accompany me to the theater next Tuesday evening! Julius Peneton and Alma Minceed are starring in . . ." She dramatically flourished her arms, her fingers rolling out. "*A Gail to Shore!*"

Sylvia blinked a few times. "Is that not . . . opening night? It was sold out when I asked—"

"Daaarling! We're Chronisters! Nothing is *ever* sold out!"

Except the few people who have now lost their seats, Sylvia thought. Her mother never cared for such consequences. Besides, tickets were a fortune anyway. So the monied hoity-toity did not truly miss out when the ultra-rich took their frills.

"Sounds like fun! I, um . . . have a suitor in mind."

Her mother winked. "Keeping secrets from me?"

Sylvia hoped that did not mean Emlyn being between her legs. "Uh, he made his proposal this morning."

"Well, well, you never cease to amaze! Would he be amicable?"

"Yes. I . . . believe so."

"Splendid! Just splendid!" Camilla looked a vision of relief but suddenly winced and rubbed the back of her neck, a pain that had bothered her ever since the auto accident a few years ago. Her hand got replaced with Stella's palm, who continued to massage. "Ooh, that feels good."

She sat for close to thirty seconds, letting her martial's palms do their magic before continuing. "Well, I must go. Elps is laid up in bed after refusing to show any respect to Stella."

She tapped her martial's hand, signaling her to stop, while Sylvia responded with a type of sarcasm her mother approved of. "Yet he lives."

"I'll be gentle. After all, he's just some poor boy from the stints. I'll instruct him on martials and how to interact with them. Better yet, I'll have Stella do it." She laughed. "He will think facing down the black hound to be preferable!"

She stood up and turned to leave. Sylvia was able to breathe deep for only a second before Camilla whirled back around. "Before I forget!"

"Y-Yes?"

"That Miltin fellow, what did you think of him?"

Sylvia responded swiftly. "A blowhard who was faking his ambition to gain our patronage. Don't worry, Mother, I investigated him thoroughly."

Electricity was changing the world, like a frightening wave coming to swallow everyone whole—and electrify them for good measure. The Chronisters anticipated the wave, riding it all the way to the top, but there was no shortage of charlatans trying to get into the family's coffers. Her father certainly did not raise a fool. Yes, they were just money men, financiers to geniuses, but he made sure she could talk shop, and more importantly, understand the jargon. Having known what she was talking about helped pinpoint Deleran S Miltin as a fraud.

She made certain he got what he deserved. Performed research and found that he conducted similar grifts all over Kymbri, and with Emlyn pointing a gun at his head, she forced him to declare himself a gilla and kiss her boots. Then, after doing the paperwork, she gave him away to a woman, as it had seemed fair and just to do at the time. She had second-guessed herself afterward, of course, but then she thought of the schemes he would have pulled if she hadn't. Besides, the man would have hurt her family's reputation. So of course he needed to be taught a lesson, a permanent lesson.

"You have the eye! Oh yes! Your father would have been very proud of you!"

Stella lingered behind as Camilla walked out of the room. The older martial looked over her shoulder at the messy pile of clothes and the apple core nearby. The answer to the mystery was obvious. She looked down at Sylvia, who had not bothered to move from her chair. The face of the young mistress stared back at the martial, cracking a nervous smile while the soft wrinkles of her forehead contorted in worry.

Stella shook her head and rolled her eyes. She knew exactly where her daughter was. Then she turned on her heel and quickly caught up to Camilla.

The door slammed shut, allowing Sylvia to lie back and blow out a sigh of relief. She looked down at her lap. Was Emlyn still there? She was very still. But then the skirts rustled. Sylvia methodically pulled back each layer of fabric, finally revealing a face of barely controlled hilarity.

"You need a bath!"

They both started to giggle, and it went on and on, rolling into laughter.

CHAPTER THREE

"You're gripping it too hard. If you're going to keep that stance, spread your fingers on the hilt and grasp it lightly, but not too lightly," Stella said, trying her best to explain through annoyance.

Emlyn let out a frustrated sigh. She did not need to be treated like some amateur. It was as if she were a six-year-old again, an ignorant child, and it infuriated her. She should be used to this treatment. It was par for the course when it came to her mother, but Stella always could twist the knife just right. She banished the feeling to her gut, only showing it through gritted teeth. Despite trying her best to hide the emotion, it did not go unnoticed.

"What are you so angry about, girl?" asked Stella, brimming with sarcastic menace.

They were a few yards away from each other in ready stances, knives forward, practicing their movements down among the brilliant, well-maintained grass of the courtyard. Bordered like a frame by dozens of arches, this large area was gargantuan compared to most other insular gardens. Second only to perhaps the Teyrns' garden in grandeur and size.

They stood under one of a few dozen elms and aspens, whose leaves were already turning to amber. Among their branches were tattered white-and-rose ribbons, the last remaining vestiges of a Mayday ritual some months ago. It was proper to let the ribbons fall away. After they fell, they were gathered and burned at the altar of the mother Goddess Dé Brigantia.

Emlyn breathed in and out, unwilling to glance away from Stella. Both were rooted to the ground like stone. Staring at each other with their heavy breathing moving their chests up and down in discordance.

There was more than enough room, but they were practicing on the same spot where an important time in Emlyn's life took place, most commonly called in patrician circles "the breaking."

Her mother was standing in front of that shed: the breaking shed. That haunted place so prevalent in her nightmares. She always tried to avoid that spot if at all possible. One day it would be her duty to put her offspring through the same trial, give them the same nightmares. It was ten years ago, but memories of her torment still seemed fresh.

Being near the grayish, rotted boards always made her muscles tense and her throat dry up like a cracked desert. She thought that perhaps practicing in this spot was some kind of lesson her mother was attempting to impart. Whatever that lesson was, she did not want to comprehend.

Her hands tightened around the silver vine grip that wound its way up the onyx handle and a bit over the guard—a true work of art and function.

Her fingers loosened. In a split second she flipped the knife, holding it poised with her thumb and index finger.

She threw. The blade spun like an auto wheel. Her mother dodged by throwing her shoulder back. With a resonating thud, it stuck in the old rotted wood of the shed with a loud ker-thunk.

"You never throw your knife! Never!"

Stella rushed her.

Emlyn drew out her revolver, making a turn as she got near. They were not supposed to use a gun during this exercise, so Emlyn flipped the revolver, holding it by the barrel. As she completed the turn, the butt of the gun came down onto . . . nothing but air. For a second Emlyn was confused, then Stella ended her daughter's confusion with a swift knee to the stomach. She let loose her breath and saw red spots racing across her eyes. It felt like an Olympian threw a discus into her gut. With legs shaking, she rasped a cough before falling to her knees.

Stella grasped Emlyn by the neck, taking her to the ground with such force that every corner of her vision spun clockwise. She felt Stella's weight, then felt the cold steel at her throat just above the cold steel of her collar. She opened her eyes and focused on her mother's unblinking gaze, then focused on the blade pressing itself against her jugular.

Stella cried out in unrestrained frustration, "You're too slow! Always too slow!" She took a breath to calm herself. "Though I applaud your use of the gun as a club—fatal, if you had managed to hit my cranium . . . but it's never quite good enough, is it, girl?"

Emlyn felt the edge of the cruel blade press down. She still held her gun, but Stella's knees were pinning her arms. If this was a real combat situation, she could have angled it to shoot a thigh, though the recoil would be killer. But like always, Stella would have a counter to it. There was always some trick up her sleeve, and Emlyn would be forced to begrudgingly admire it. She looked into those unloving eyes again.

"I know what you were doing with Sylvia!"

For a moment longer they stared at one another. Stella was trying to read her.

"I was only doing as I was instructed. Would you've not obeyed?" Emlyn asked, rasping.

The blade pushed harder against her neck. But she remained perfectly still.

"Yes, I would, but I have noticed many other incidents too, even though you think I'm blind. So I'll give you this warning, blood of mine: it is unseemly for a Master or Mistress to use their martial in such a way!"

Emlyn grasped Stella's fist wrapped tightly around the knife handle.

"You taught me to be a gilla! You have what you asked for! So if Mistress would like to use me in that fashion, then she is well within her rights!"

"I taught you to be a martial. Being a gilla is incidental."

Stella let Emlyn push her blade away. A small irrigation of blood wound its way to the grass.

"A Master, or Mistress, should not seek to pleasure a martial," stated Stella.

Emlyn smirked as she rose to her feet. "That was Uncle Erill's favorite saying."

"And you clearly haven't been paying attention! Take heed to those words; your uncle was a wise man!"

Emlyn got to her feet, put her gun back in the holster, and brushed the dirt and grass away from her skirt.

Stella breathed in and spoke flatly. "We are not for sexual pleasure. We are bred for one purpose: to protect our masters from all threats. To protect them even if the result is our own death; this is your duty. To die protecting our masters is the ultimate loyalty. To die in your duty gives honor to your ancestors. *That* is our lot. Providing pleasure is for other gilla."

Emlyn rolled her eyes as she took out a handkerchief to dab the blood from her neck. "I know that."

"I will say it as many times as it takes so that it sticks in your head."

"So what do you want? Do you want me to tell my Mistress no?"

Stella sighed and restrained her anger by running a hand over her slicked-back hair. "No. Of course not."

"Then what should I do?" asked Emlyn with genuine interest.

"Remind her of decorum. Tell her about tradition. Remind her of her duty to marry a man. Say all of this subtly. Ween her away from you and toward a low gilla if you have to."

Emlyn turned her head down, spying her blood on the grass, and breathed out. The sons of Dé Brigantia, Delwufnr and Feal, were lovers to everyone they came across. So a love between two women, or two men, only raised an eyebrow for most. She did not want to say no in the way her mother wanted. But it wasn't fear of angering her mistress that would stop her; it was deflecting a pastime that she knew Sylvia enjoyed on a daily basis.

Everyone knew, it was something that went unsaid. High patricians using their martials in a sexual manner happened every so often. But gratuitous use of a martial, who is in your presence most hours of the day, your personal confidant . . . it could be a scandal. Making the patrician look as if they cannot keep their desires under control. That they see something other than a gilla. It was a big reason it was preferred that women have female martials, and men, males. Did the mistress see her as something more than what she was? Even though Emlyn was almost exclusively used to handle her mistress's desires, she didn't think the reason was more than familiarity. Still, best not to risk such actions that would invite so much shame to the house.

What she personally felt about it did not matter. She was a gilla, after all; her wants did not count. Her will belonged to her mistress and her alone. But Stella was right . . . it was unseemly. It looked terrible to patrician society, and her mistress needed to start paying attention to these sorts of things. Sylvia needed to take courting more seriously . . . go out more often. Meet people. Do the duties given to patricians.

It was unusual for Emlyn not to respond quickly; in fact, she looked like her mind took a little vacation. Stella stared at her, arms crossed. She grew impatient, which was never a virtue of hers when it came to other gilla, not even her own daughter. No, Stella was the taskmaster. A harsh unrelenting overseer, she had a job to do, a tradition to follow, and even though her daughter made it to, and through, the breaking, she would never cease that training. For any lapse could spell death to their owners as it had for her partner, Briar, and his master, Andreas Chronister.

"You are soft, just like Briar."

Emlyn whipped her head toward Stella, her mind suddenly present again. "Is now really the time for that conversation, Stella?"

Her father and mother never got along. They bred as they were supposed to and planed the education of their children to continue the traditions. But nothing was in the cards when it came to love. Not an unusual thing among martial partners. Emlyn was sure that fact hit hard with her father, Briar. He always had a romantic flair with other gilla. But Stella was as cold and rocky as a mountaintop.

"Whether you can admit it or not, he is the reason you're like this!"

Emlyn walked toward the shed and twisted her knife out of the wood along with a few rotten chips. She did not want this argument again. Her mother could not let it go, could not let go of the Olevanti way and accept the Gwen outlook. To be honest, neither outlook included sexual liaisons with owners, but since the Gwen style was much more loose in what a martial was allowed to do, Stella always blamed the Gwen "hogwash" for any failing in her. Or perhaps it was because her father, Briar, somehow convinced everyone to hold off on her breaking until she was fifteen instead of the customary ages of ten, eleven, or twelve.

Emlyn marched past Stella.

"Emlyn, where do you think you're going? We're not finished!"

"You can go ahead and keep thinking whatever you like—my namesake being tainted, that I'm such a disappointment. I truly don't mind being your black sheep!" said Emlyn without stopping or looking at her.

"Emlyn, stop!"

She paid no attention and stormed past the shade of the trees along the rock path that cut through into the peristyle portion of the garden. She rounded past the circular fountains that surrounded marble statues of Dé Brigantia and Dé Ard. Stella kept yelling for her to stop. Emlyn drowned out her mother's noise by tightening her fists. She passed under the archway bordering the garden, then into the building proper.

Once inside, she leaned against the wall. The green wallpaper harbored a vine-and-leaf pattern in an old triskele style that swirled around her like the byways of memory. She started thinking of her father.

He was never easy on her. Far from it but he knew when to place a hand on her shoulder and give her a warm heartening smile. Those few moments meant everything. It was always that smile that brought her back to him whenever she was angry or hurt. Stella, on the other hand, was nothing but ice that had never once melted.

Emlyn produced her own smile in response, at the few happy memories.

* * * * *

This was the only moment to say goodbye. It was a few months past her breaking, and she was waiting for him in the hall that led to the side exit. She made sure the carriage outside had all the provisions her father and the master of the house needed for the trip. Even though it was not part of her duty to do so, something just felt . . . off about this, and the unease in her gut was worrying.

Emlyn fidgeted by lacing and unlacing her fingers as Briar came down the stairs and into the hall. His shiny black knee-high boots clacked on the marble tile. He stopped a few feet away upon noticing her and stood straight to his full, taller than average height. His eyes took on the look of surprise, and the frown he held slid easily into that familiar warm smile that no amount of moustache could hide. His inviting demeanor complemented the warm orange overcoat like a flame against the cold outside.

"You . . . came to see us off?"

"Just you, Papa."

He stepped in a little closer, but she stepped back. "I'm sorry," she said.

She looked to the ground and swallowed. During the breaking and for a time afterward, she would have given anything for a kind touch. But now, any touch not from her mistress brought so many unpleasant memories.

He slicked back his chestnut hair and did it again when an errant strand refused to cooperate. He sighed. "It's okay. We waited too long. So what you're feeling is my fault. I'm just glad you're talking to me."

She eyed his collar, hidden during the first fifteen years of her life. It seemed so new to her and not something her father had worn since he was a child. For most of her life, Stella and Briar managed to hide this bit of jewelry; she bet they felt relieved now. She had never felt their collars under their clothing upon hugging them. Then again, hugs were not a common occurrence. But collar or no, after her breaking it was Papa who attempted to bring her to a semblance of familial normalcy. No one else bothered beyond entrenching her into the Gwen martial tradition. Not even Grandmother Cali, who Emlyn once adored, would look upon her with the same warmth she once had.

"This is the first time you're leaving since . . ." She looked down and hated the feelings saying it out loud brought up. "My breaking."

"Ah." He waved his hand. "Don't worry, it's only a dispute. Every few months, like clockwork, one of the master's clients becomes incensed at a clause or two when they finally take a closer look at the wording. We'll be back in no more than half a day."

"Briar!" Coming down the stairs and into the hall was the master of the house, Andreas Chronister, Sylvia's father, resplendent in a gray overcoat, red cotton vest, and a black Alban bonnet cocked to the side. Upon the hat was a metal pin of the full Chronister emblem consisting of an eagle striding a dead she-wolf on top of an eight-spoke wheel and surrounded by gilly flowers.

"Did you grab the papers?"

Briar turned to him. "Yes, Master." He moved his hand, showing the papers secured in a folder tucked under an arm.

Andreas looked at Emlyn. "Emlyn, should you not be with Sylvia right now?"

"Yes, Master."

"Then go to it, girl. She is wondering where you've got to."

She put her fist on her chest and bowed. "Right away, Master."

"Emlyn?"

Emlyn turned to her father, who was smiling hopefully. "Yes, Papa?"

"Will you talk to me when I get back?"

She took a moment before nodding.

Briar's face lit up. "We'll be back soon."

Emlyn bowed to them both, turned on her heel, and walked past Andreas. She stopped at the top of the stairs and turned to look down at them.

"Is that wise, old friend?"

"I know how my ancestors did this, but I . . . She's my blood. I shouldn't have insisted on waiting so long." His voice sounded dry.

Andreas looked up at him seriously. "Briar, she has turned out fine. She looks like a martial, fights like a martial, and is loyal as a martial. She will be a credit to your bloodline; so, for once, stop fretting about it." He put a hand on Briar's shoulder. "Now come. Let's get this over with. I want to be back in time for the next Cened meeting."

The uneasy feeling in her stomach was still there, and it would stay there for the next few days, until they heard of the attack on the carriage and the word that her papa had been killed.

Chapter Four

Mira did not try to escape on her way to the Donsill residence. Her mind
was still set on accepting this new life. Plus, she was naked as a babe,
besides the heavy collar she wore of course. But when Lucius Donsill
accepted the gifts with surprise and graciousness, she thought she was
clear to leave, and if she had, then she might have come back still
accepting her fate and not in this hated torment she found herself in. Her
relief didn't last long when he ordered her inside and offered her to his
martial, Maield. She had no idea what to expect, but being held against a
desk and teased with the martial's phallus had never crossed her mind.
He never entered her, but it was threatened over and over again. And
she would tense up in fear with each threat. What made it especially
terrible was Donsill sitting back in his chair in studious fascination, as if
he were conducting an experiment on some animal. She had to share
every humiliating detail with Emlyn, who only nodded with no
expression whatsoever besides a serious frown.

Mira stared at the blue tiles. Polished to perfection, each shown
with her own distorted image. She hated that damn expanse of squares
with every fiber of her being. She spat on its sickening blue surface and
rubbed it down with a large hard-bristle brush, making sure the grout
shone bright. It gleamed as brilliantly as its neighbor sitting uniform to
its twin, waiting to get up and march away any minute. She honestly
wished they would do so. Maybe these superstitious people would label
it black magic and put her out of her misery. She was tired . . . so very

tired and could use a good rest, but no, she had to scrub the damned tile floor over and over and over again. Every movement made her feel worse, like flesh scraping against freshly burned skin. And as she scrubbed, she wondered why she was more upset about the damnable tile in this moment than what happened to her earlier at the Donsill residence.

After she had prepared the food, she scrubbed the floors for the next several hours. She would not receive supper until Ms. Cord was satisfied, and Ms. Cord never seemed satisfied.

She looked down at the long skirt she now wore. It was ankle-length and sheer as a lightly frosted window. It left little to the imagination, that was for sure. But just the act of receiving something to cover herself felt good, for a few minutes at least. Emlyn had awarded her with the skirt after hearing about the Donsill residence and clarified that earning clothing on one's first day was unprecedented.

She admonished herself for being joyous at this, over something so simple and idiotic. It made her forget, for only a moment, about what happened with Maield. But she did not want to fall into that deep pit where she would lose herself like a few other gilla she had known in this damnable country.

Mira thought about all the expensive, refined clothes she had owned, clothes that covered everything. What happened to her over these past two months to get excited about a simple skirt?

Being constantly naked for so long was what happened, she surmised, and it was best in this situation to take and appreciate a victory while one could. She cursed under her breath. Then returned to her scrubbing and once again quickly became irritated at the bristles scraping against the tile.

A bell rang at the door leading to the street. Mira peered around the leg of the prepping table. She could see the shadow of someone with broad shoulders on the other side of the four milky glass squares.

Ms. Cord opened the door, and a man stood there, studious and broad. He looked to be in his forties. His short scraggly beard followed the contours of a well-worn smile. His bearing: the very definition of an Erie rogue. He held a big jute gunny sack propped easily over his shoulder. Ms. Cord had a look suggesting that she was very familiar with this man.

"Hello, Cordi!"

"Neuan boy! Come, come! Get out of that muck for a spell! Ya know where to put the potatoes!"

He crossed the threshold in giant steps, almost ungainly with the weight of the sack. "Aio, don't mind if I do!"

Neuan dumped the potatoes in the bin under the bottom shelf of the vast walk-in pantry, past the butchery tiles that Mira was cleaning. When he came back out, he spotted Ms. Cord setting some tea down for him on a small rectangular table with only two chairs near the door. Cord sat opposite with her own cup of tea. Hers was a white porcelain cup decorated with a gold rim and painted violets flowing down the side. He smiled pleasantly and went to the table, completely ignoring Mira as he passed her.

"How's Adela doing? She done with that Nica boy? Skinny good-for-nothing brosthun is six weeks to a workhouse, sure as rain!"

Neuan smiled as wide as any man who was able to get rid of an unworthy suitor for his daughter's hand. "Nodens he's not! Made sure his trip to the steel screw was an easy slide!"

Ms. Cord laughed, her belly rolling in response. "No time for a Mithra's lover to love in a workhouse, eh, lad?"

Neuan sipped his tea; his smile broadened. It was pure tea from India, the best tea by most accounts and the Chronisters could afford the best. After two years she had forgotten how it tasted. The cream was certainly from Kymbri. Cord mentioned that she bought it from one of the many farms not far outside the city limits.

Ms. Cord took time to enjoy Neuan's delighted facial display.

He relaxed his posture, finally throwing off the anxieties of the busy city street and looked at her wonderingly. "When are you getting out of this place an' coming back to Lolainn's to down a pint or two like we did back in the day?"

She gave a knowing smile. "When our ancestors leave Tech Duinn to come drink with us. When the good folk abandon the miller. Perhaps when the Kymbrian black dog comes for me. No, I'm too busy to leave for such a frivolous thing. I got all I need right here."

"Come now, you can't be fine staying around these gilded pig-haves!"

Her smile faded, and her eyes glowered at him. It was over the line. His eyes widened in realization. Cord had always wanted to work in a high patrician house. Since she got the job, she'd never uttered a single negative word about her employers.

He coughed within the silence. After a moment, Ms. Cord moved on.

"I'll give ya the word."

He put his hands on the table and leaned in.

"About, oh, seven days ago, Terisus Cardew sat down with me employers to ask for fundin'."

"Cardew Electric, being backed by Chronister money is nothing—"

"May the Morri take ya! Let me finish!"

"Okay, okay. What did he want funding for?"

Ms. Cord relaxed and went on like nothing happened. Neuan had his warning, and she did not like dwelling on faults. She leaned back into her chair and continued.

"New sky-ships ta replace the ole Imperators."

"I heard Gallia were making their own Imperators."

"Gallia? That's a rib tickler! No, some new, superior version. But I know not when they start. Ya should get yer boys an' see bout joinin' the crew."

"Gods!" exclaimed Neuan, sitting back in his chair. "Just five or so years ago, the first Imperator took flight."

Cord leaned forward, placing her arms on the table. "We movin' along right fast. Go an' get yerself a proper job. Make yer daughter into a proper lady so no dingy cumber takes her hand."

He rubbed his chin. "I hope security is better this go-around. I'd hate to face down a horde of gilla . . . It's worth the risk I think." He took a sip of his tea. "We're getting ready for another war, sure as bleeding rash!"

"Goes without sayin', lad," said Cord.

Neuan leaned forward. "You know the Cened were discussing extending gilla status to prisoners of war."

"Roses and thorns! The last thing we need is aggressive, filthy foreigners as our gilla!" She spat on the tile, showing her contempt.

Mira's heart started racing with fear at the statement of foreigners as gilla, but the snap of the cook's fingers rang loudly in her ears. They paid no mind to her as she cleaned the tile of Ms. Cord's spittle.

"I'm with you, Cordie. They're at a premium. Best to keep it that way, or it'll be like old Rome all over again. Two shit gilla for every citizen! Then where's the work? Poof, I tell ya!" He stroked his beard in thought. "I don't think it'll actually happen. Atyress Aurelia made an impassioned speech against it. Dyed-in-the-wool stoic that one."

"Which Atyress is that?" asked Cord.

"Trelauni. She proposed that we allow runaways to come forward and be given their freedom as long as they give two years of military service."

Ms. Cord snorted. "Cumberwhirls!" She crossed her arms under her chest. "It's bunk if I ever did hear! Yeah, we might be going to war, but nothing else changes besides a draft!"

"Perhaps. Times like these I'm glad I've no son."

They spent awhile drinking down the rest of the tea and engaging in idle small talk until Neuan set his cup down on the tablecloth, missing the saucer. Ms. Cord cringed but refrained from correcting him.

"I must be going."

She placed a hand on his wrist. "Before you go."

Everything went silent, and it took a few moments for Mira to realize that no one was speaking. She could feel two pairs of eyes examining her. She looked up. They were grinning down at her, and the only thing that went through her mind was *No, no, please no!* But she did not dare say that out loud.

"How long has it been since you've had your way with a gilla?"

He rubbed his chin, looking up in thought. "Hmm, a few months."

She beckoned Mira to come closer to the table, then made a motion for her to remain on her knees. She patted Mira's head, stroking her hair like a dog. She could keenly feel Ms. Cord's fingers go over the scar tissue from when it was so cruelly shaved.

"Well, I got a perfectly good, fresh gilla here for you ta dingle yer bobber in. Go on, have a go at her." Ms. Cord's hand took Mira's trembling chin and guided her up to where her entire head was above the height of the table. Then she produced a wooden spoon, one the cook seemed to always keep with her. The same one that was used to beat Mira earlier in the morning. "Open yer mouth."

Mira did so, and she shoved the handle of the spoon between her teeth.

"Close. Good girl! Now don't drop it, do you hear?" She squeezed Mira's chin.

Tears ran down her face as she gave a curt nod. She wanted a way out of this. Now not even begging would help, which no longer seemed humiliating. She wanted to beg to not have this man use her, even if it would have led to a beating.

"Hm, really that's not necessary. It's been a long day. I'm tired."

Mira felt a wave of relief. But Cord was having none of it. "A nice bout with a gilla is exactly what you need to relax, lad."

He thought and Interest began dancing in his eyes, and it frightened her, making her more acute to the pain she was in.

Neuan grabbed her by the hair, pulling her to her feet. She winced but did not fight back as he led her to the prepping table.

"Not there! Dun't want her sweat getting in the grain."

Instead he took her to the tiled wall where the meat would often be hung. He pushed her upper body forward, making her grunt as she barely got her palms up on the tiled wall in time to keep from falling face first into those familiar, damnable squares. There was no preamble. No warm-up. He just entered her as a ravenous dog takes a bitch.

She ran through a litany of thoughts. Sounds of olive seeds hitting a can pelted the walls of her mind. Her family owned an olive farm in the southern regions. She spent all day beating down the olives and crushing them. It was work mostly performed by her brothers; she was only seven at the time and could do very little. The evenings were spent popping ripe olives in her mouth and spitting out the seeds into a can. Her brothers made a game of it; she never won.

She remembered those terrible lonely days in the snow, waiting for letters from Father. Then the train barreling through a haunted landscape, and the days spent cold and wet hiding in woodlands, relying on the hospitality of strangers. The smell of the snow mingled with the bark of the surrounding forest. Nostalgic now, but it was frightening at the time.

Her hands almost lost their grip. The ability to escape within her own mind was taken away. Like how her freedom was snatched from her grasp through no fault of her own. She bit down harder on the spoon.

Neuan finished. He moved away from her, turning before she collapsed. She curled up on the spot upon the cold tile, unable to control the shivering.

Mira did not want to go on. How could she go on? She was better than some worthless gilla, damn it all. The spoon fell from her mouth with a long trail of spittle. Ever since that day on the train, everything had swirled down a whirlpool ending in a devouring maw. She could not imagine it getting worse than this.

There was a snap of fingers, and before she even knew she was doing it, Mira was on her knees ready for instruction. Looking about the room, she realized that Neuan was nowhere in sight. It was just Ms. Cord watching with a gleam in her eye, studying and smirking. The cook's finger beckoned her over.

"Why dun't ya come up an' sit a spell, eh?"

It seemed to take forever to stand, having to adjust herself with every inch of gained height. She fought to keep the shivering down and to not utter a moan or scream with the pain. Eventually she was able to stand straight and looked around, just to make sure Neuan was truly gone. She made her way over to Ms. Cord and gingerly sat down in the chair once occupied by the man.

She kept her eyes downcast so as not to commit any faux pas that would invite further anguish. No looking directly in a master or mistress's eyes unless invited to do so.

"Well, you're not stupid! A bleedin' idiot would have complained, looked me in the eyes and asked why, why me? I think you've figured that much out at least, eh, lass?"

Mira nodded. She understood . . . at least what Cord wanted her to understand. Having been a patrician, she needed to know her place on the lowest rung of the ladder. To be shown that she was property, that she meant nothing. Not that it sat right with her in the least.

No, she would not give up and accept this, not now. She would make it back to her homeland one day and take her rightful place. That was something to hold on to.

They will not break me to this insanity. I will escape. A nasty spoon attached to a mean old bitch of a cook will not stop me, she thought, gritting her teeth.

"Oh-ho, lass! Yer gonna be a feisty one! Ya can try, thrash yourself against me, but sooner rather than later you'll tire yourself or break."

Ms. Cord had a genuine smile as she poured tea into the cup Neuan had used. She put the saucer down in front of Mira, then put the cup on top. Mira just stared at it.

"Go on and have yourself a wee drink."

Mira was able to force enough control over her quivering appendages to not spill the tea everywhere. If one drop fell onto the table, then it would mean another beating. But that did not matter as she bitterly stared over the rim into Cord's amused eyes.

CHAPTER FIVE

The sun was bright, and no clouds obfuscated its golden eye. The only relief for those who dared to step from their homes was by retreating into shops or under the shade of umbrellas. Despite the overbearing sun, Emlyn was determined to enjoy the day. She breathed deeply. A block over sat the tanneries, and the scent of curing leather mixed well with the scent of fresh baked bread wafting out from the open windows of the nearby bakery shops. Standing on a platform in the middle of the crossroad was a marble effigy. This statue showcased Dé Ard, standing gigantic, bearded, and proud atop an equally tall cylindrical base. He held a censer full of burning incense perched on his palm. The light breeze, which did nothing to lessen the heat, sent the woody aroma in her direction. It all swirled about them, making one hell of a grand stew. It made Emlyn straighten as she hustled down the old street. Mira knew, as she watched closely, that Emlyn was happy to be out of that stuffy house.

Mira begged for sandals before they left, but to no avail. The eroded cobblestones made many rocky protrusions that needed some fixing. Mira tripped more than a few times, producing sore and red toes. She was always well balanced, it was her only physical act of prowess. But being able to catch herself each time did not stop her from cursing or save those delicate toes from burning and bruising. This was expounded by the inability to keep up with the pace of Emlyn's longer legs. No mind was paid to her near nakedness. No one saw it as odd, and she became accustomed to it.

The only article that covered her slightly was on her back, where a few dozen packages were secured by a net attached with straps buckled over her shoulders and around her waist. It was a heavy load weighing on her back that was only becoming more difficult to handle with each stop they made. She doubted her strength would hold fifteen minutes from now, much less an hour or two, with the sun's rays beating down and making her sweat a river. She thought Emlyn would have no problem carrying these packages with her stature, but the martial carried nothing that would encumber her assured gait. Mira narrowed her eyes, burrowing her gaze into the back of Emlyn's head. Emlyn was a gilla like her and seemed much more suited to this kind of work. But among gilla, martials were close to royalty, as sad as that seemed.

At the statue, Emlyn stopped, and so too did Mira. The martial glanced at the girl almost as if she knew what Mira was thinking, and perhaps she did.

"We will stop at the Waapole pub, up the street from here. They'll give you water while I pick up the wine."

Mira moistened her lips at the mention of water.

"Mira?"

"Yes, ma'am?"

Emlyn had a kindness in her eyes, and the smirk was not one of smug satisfaction but of pity.

"If you do well and you do not drop any of the packages, then Mistress will let you wear a blouse."

Mira's face lit up at the news.

Emlyn turned on her heels and went on walking while Mira kept heeling. She continued speaking. "Eventually you will perform your duties with zest. Not due to the promise of a reward."

Mira scoffed at the notion.

They reached a large three-story building sitting on the corner just beyond the marble Dé Ard statue. There was a wide wraparound white-washed porch enveloping it like an uncomfortable hug. Like many buildings, there was a garden on top poking out like a grassy head of hair. Jaunty string music emanated from inside. Standing on the porch was a crowd of middle-class men with only a few wives, girlfriends, or whores mixed among them. The men engaged in lively conversations about their work, possible futures, the rosy past; but for the most part they prophesied war and its prospects for glory.

Ignored by the crowd, they both squeezed their way past and through a cloud of stinking pipe smoke. In front of them were swinging doors with carved images of prancing deer. The hinges gave out a sight squeak as they pushed through.

Mira looked about at the lively pub and noticed that the inside was as full as the porch. Smoke and the smell of beer wafted through the air, with a hint of sweet perfume. It made her eyes water.

The people here were in heated debates of good nature for the most part. A few serving women sauntered around the tables, talking the patrons up in hopes that they'd buy more alcohol or the services of a prostitute. Above was a balcony with prominent steps leading up to it. The area supported ten whores by the looks of them; only one had a noticeable steel collar. They tried their best to solicit the men below to pay for their carnal services. A few gave quick flashes of their breasts before pulling their bodices back up. Then they rubbed their thumb and index finger together in the universal sign for payment.

A citarra was being played by a man in the corner. Next to him sat a young, slight woman holding an electric krutto, a bow instrument with its origin somewhere in Gallia. A very popular instrument at that. The woman's light brown hair flowed down, framing an aquiline face. Another man was playing a drum, but it was the electric instrument that really got Mira's attention. They were very expensive. The bar seemed flushed, so it would have the money to afford it. The woman belted out a long note in a sweet tone. As a result, the instruments changed course into another song.

Mira was enraptured. Emlyn turned to watch them play. It was intricate and bawdy. The type of song one would hear at a bar, but in truth, it was stolen. It was a well-known song amongst gilla in the city, about Bakers Street, about how a man was cheated out of his freedom and sold to a ship.

Everyone clapped in concordance with the woman's sweet voice and repeated the chorus with her. It was quite good. Emlyn smiled, amused that the free would make such a happy commotion over a song like this, and wondered if they would sing the second part. The first part was exact, but part two was a real killer. It was about the new gilla killing his ship masters, then being caught and hung upon the mast. But instead they went into another song. It only made sense that they would neglect to sing of such a thing. Gilla uprisings were terrifying to the free. Lucky for them the gilla population in Kymbri was kept low, leaving little chance to effectively rebel.

Emlyn snapped her fingers, making Mira stand at attention. She motioned for her to follow, then headed for the bar.

A burly bartender was cleaning a glass, or so it appeared by the movement of his elbows. His back was to them, but Emlyn could see his face in the mirror that was hanging above the back of the bar. His shiny bald head made her think that his hair must have run completely away from the top to settle in a thick community on his jaw. He kept it well trimmed though, as trim as the long black vest and white undershirt he wore.

"My apologies, Master."

He spotted them through the mirror, and without turning around, he whistled. A male gilla, fully and impeccably dressed, came through the curtains that concealed the back rooms. The bartender shook his head back and forth at him and whistled again. This time a young female gilla came out. She was clothed but her blouse was down, revealing full breasts, which got some attention from the patrons. Either the girl's owner ordered it down or a customer commanded it. He jerked his head for the girl to come over. As she got into arm's length, he grabbed her upper bicep and growled, "Cover yourself!"

Visibly frightened by his cadence, she did so, snapping the buttons of the loose-fitting blouse back in place before daring to look up again into his irritable face. Again, he gestured with his head, this time toward Emlyn. The girl put on a smile, doing her best to look cheerful. She was good at that, but not good enough to pass a martial's scrutiny. The girl was supremely unhappy. The bartender went to help a free patron asking for a pint, leaving them alone.

"I'm so sorry, ma'am, Waapole's does not service gilla."

Emlyn furrowed her brow. "Your owner knows well that I am not here for myself. If I were, he would have barred my entrance. House Chronister and I suspect gilla of other houses conduct business for their owners on these premises. Am I correct?"

"Oh! Um . . . well, yes!"

Emlyn put a hand on the bar. "My mistress has come to understand that you possess bottles of Gaelyn of Isle. If she was not mistaken, then she requires your vintage, if you please." She gestured toward Mira. "And this one needs water."

The bar gilla bit her lip. "Um."

"What is it?" asked Emlyn with growing annoyance.

"I'm . . . truly sorry, uh, can I see your tag? It's just that I gotta dot my i's and all."

Emlyn let out an angry huff and mumbled about how high-bloodlined gilla should not have to do this for low gilla, but they both leaned over the bar anyway, meeting halfway. She lifted up the tag. The girl struggled through the words, mouthing them slowly as her eyes scanned. Then she released the tag and moved from the counter, motioning for Mira to follow her. Mira took a step but decided against it;

instead she looked at Emlyn with a worried face that was asking for permission.

"Go on."

Mira did as she was told and happily followed the other gilla to a thick ceramic cylinder sitting on a short table next to the bar.

Loud cheers emanated from the seating area. Emlyn turned around in time to see a stout, well-dressed fellow with a peacockish strut climb the stage. He reminded her of an Hesperian perfume salesman, minus the bit of sun touch.

His magnificent bushy moustache wiggled as he spoke with a measured melodic tone, emphasizing his words. "Brothers and sisters of Kymbri! My name is Derban Kimball, and as you know, I am running as the representative of this district!" Applause broke out. Kimball let it subside before continuing. "I am here today not to get your vote—no, I am here to discuss the rumors that we all have been prone to let slip from our lips since the Cened meeting just a week ago." His eyes were stern as he gazed over the silent crowd, who were now giving him their full attention.

"No one has been able to say it over a whisper, but that will not make it any less of a fact! War! War is on our lips!"

As his melodic tenor rose to reflect the gravity of the subject matter, everyone murmured. Kimball put his hands in his pockets. "Most of these rumors talk about war with Zarmatia. My friends, this is a falsehood perpetrated by those with little understanding of the political realities we face! Over a year ago, the Zarmatian revolution occurred. This was successful in rooting out their backward aristocracy! Since then, Kymbri has been in talks with their new republic. Those talks are still going well."

There were a few boos from the crowd. He paused, head down in thought before looking back up. His voice turned grave as a sadness spread across his face.

"The Mithran dogs have anexed territories of the Haemus! They talk of encroaching into the territories of our Hesperian allies! And Gaelland along with Gallia, our friends, who both border the Mithran theocrats, are gathering their forces! If hostilities further ensue, then we must become involved in supporting our allies! Make no mistake, my dear folk, if given the chance, the Mithrans will overtake us! If we stand back and watch the carnage on the continent from afar, then they will chew at our land like the dogs they are until they swallow us whole!"

He let it sink in. "So you will have to ask yourselves: Do you want your wife and your children to live under the customs of Mithra? To be made to worship the bull? To deny your own Gods? To become gilla for the Mithran machine? For that is exactly what they seek for all the world to adopt! For us! The Hesperians, Zarmatia, and all those who oppose Mithra's ways! Help the effort! March for your country! Give to the drive!"

As the crowd applauded, he put his palm up to calm them. "Tomorrow the state will start asking for volunteers to join our glorious army!" There were no cheers and no clapping at this, only silence.

"If you join, then ten full kints are yours every month starting as an infantry man, along with a sign-up bonus of thirty. Then three hundred after rendering your time served! And to every man in my district who writes his name, I'll personally hand them a barrel of the finest mil milis!" Now this got cheers and applause, even whistles.

"It is my hope to see you all tomorrow and to see your signatures in commitment to the coming fight."

Emlyn clapped with the rest of the crowd. She noticed only a few kept from doing so enthusiastically. When the clapping died down, she turned her head to see what was taking Mira so long. But the girl was nowhere to be seen.

Emlyn burst into the room of the gilla who had watered Mira. The girl dropped the basin she was carrying on the floor, spilling the soapy liquid onto the hardwood. "Oh! Oh no!"

The girl took a wash towel from where it hung on her belt and bent to the floor to clean the mess. But Emlyn grabbed her hair before her knees touched the wood and forced her against the wall.

The girl screamed at her, "Why'd ya do that for?"

Emlyn put a knife to her throat, right under the collar. It surprised the girl. She of course did not understand how another gilla was allowed to carry a knife meant to kill people, but Emlyn saw the girl's eyes dart to the revolver seated in its holster. A detail that the height of the bar had concealed earlier.

She understood. "Nooo! Please! Whatever I did, I'll make it right! Right as rain! Yes?"

The blade pressed harder against the girl's throat. "What did you do with her? Did you take her? Sell her to a ship?"

The girl was on the verge of hysterics. "Oh, Gods! No! What're ya talkin' 'bout?"

"The gilla who was with me!"

The girl closed her eyes as her waterworks started up. "I-I left her there and went straight back here to wrap your bottle, but Master needed a basin . . ."

A man coughed behind Emlyn. She looked over her shoulder. It was the well-dressed male gilla, blocking the exit and ready for a fight judging by the affronted stance. Emlyn removed her knife from the girl's throat and put it into the sheath, letting the girl fall to the floor. She turned on her heel to face him and patted the onyx butt of her revolver.

"Do you think you're good enough to take on a martial, boy?"

The fight drained from him as he looked at the knife, then the gun. He realized what he was doing and made the smart move as she expected he would, backing away from the exit.

She rushed through the bar and pushed out the swinging door, stopping in the middle of the porch. She looked around and spotted a man standing in front of the steps. He was the only one not engaged in conversation. A cane hung from the crook of his elbow while he tried and failed to get his lighter to work.

A lighted match appeared in his vision. He bent down a little more, putting the end of the cigarette within the flame, and sucked in, making oxygen light the paper. He looked at Emlyn and removed the cigarette from his lips, blowing out the smoke into her face. She made no protest and no movement.

"Nothing like a good old reliable match." He studied the end of the cigarette a moment before looking back at her. "You look distressed, gilla."

She gave a quick martial's bow. "I am sorry to bother you, Master."

"Nonsense. Tell me, what's gotten you in this state?"

Emlyn did not want to say anything. This man had an odd way of holding himself. She must have been in too much of a hurry to see it before her approach. His way of dress stood out from the crowd. It was much more upscale: shiny brown boots, cream pants, tan brocade long vest, and a red shirt. His short, light brown hair swept up in the front into a duck curl that complemented the well-maintained straight goatee and jutting moustache. This signaled a man of some importance. At least more so than the other men on the porch.

"Master, did you see a low gilla exit the pub?"

He looked Emlyn up and down with a well-practiced appraising eye. Then pumped his thumb over his shoulder toward the left, on the street from which the pub got its name. "That direction."

She did a slight bow again. "Thank you for your help, Master."

As soon as she stepped onto the street the man spoke up. "I believe I'll accompany you."

She wanted to show some sign of exasperation, but she locked that away and turned, performing yet another bow. "As you wish, Master."

The man followed Emlyn ten yards behind as she slowly walked down the street. She opened her senses, focusing on anything that could lead her to Mira.

"Why is this girl so important? You could leave her to a gilla catcher and pick her up later at affairs."

"She belongs to my Mistress, and she carries packages that the house requires," Emlyn responded, barely taking her attention away from the task at hand.

"Oh . . . so it's not just to protect yourself?" He smiled playfully.

Emlyn could sense that no answer was required and decided to ignore the comment.

A muffled scream resounded, and she focused on its direction. They stood at the entrance of a long, dim alleyway, and from there she could hear . . . something. A voice certainly, though faint and talking to someone. It would not hurt to take a look and see what it was about.

"That way," she said in a whisper.

When they entered the alley, Emlyn heard more than one voice echoing off the old stone walls. She crouched low and put each foot in front of the other, the ball of the foot first, before rolling the rest down. She instructed the man to do the same so they both could approach in silence.

An alcove was visible further up to the right from where they were; the voices were coming from there. As they approached, the voices became clearer. Emlyn put her hand on the grime-covered stone and peered around the corner. Mira seemed to be in a panic, talking to two cutthroats. The girl tried to open a old green door off to the side, but it was locked. With enough force it could be kicked in, but Mira did not have the strength. If Emlyn decided that running was the best option, it would be a good way out. Strewn about in front of the door were various potted plants with dead stems sticking out from dry, packed soil. The place seemed to be a flower shop, or rather it used to be.

Mira tried to speak in her light and squeaking singsong voice, but what came out sounded to Emlyn like the most discordant coloratura she ever heard.

"No! Please, Masters! Let me go! Please, I beg you!"

"Come 'ere, lil gilla. Do as we say, hen!" said the man standing to the right of Mira, clearly drunk out of his gourd. He rubbed the spittle away from his chin. Their grasp of Kymbrian speech left much to be desired.

"We're your masters, so be a gud lil thin', put that stuff on the ground, an' lower yerself wit 'em."

Emlyn poked her head out from around the corner a little further. The two men backed Mira slowly into the corner of the alcove. A man with patches of dirt on his sharp, hooked-nose face stood in front of and to the right of Mira. The other, a confident barrel-chested man with a patchy beard, stood with his back directly toward Emlyn.

"I—um, I'm not allowed!" pleaded Mira.

"Oh, that dun't matter none, yer a low crimey gilla. No one cares."

Emlyn managed to sneak up and insert herself between them and Mira in a fluid motion like a ghost suddenly making its appearance. The men stepped back, startled, but did not take long to recover.

"Good sirs! We are property of Chronister! If you—"

"Bunk!"

Emlyn unbuttoned her blouse enough to show her collar and tag in full. Then patted her gun and knife hilts. She made sure to move her hands away from the weapons right after so as not to incite violence, to not be held liable if something did happen. A rule she might have ignored if the man that came with her was not watching.

"Masters! Do not take me for a low gilla! You are speaking to a martial of—"

The man with the sharp face interrupted her. "Ya got a mouth on ya, fer right!"

His friend hushed him, then looked back at Emlyn. "Jus' the criminal then. Yer mistress wouldn't care 'bout that any."

Emlyn put out her arms in a halting motion. Mira shrank back, trying to hide herself behind Emlyn.

"To touch Chronister property in a lewd manner would be a great insult to my mistress! That cannot be allowed!"

"Well, girlie, there's two of us, one of you, an' we got guns as well!"

The two men moved back the edges of their coats, revealing holstered pistols. Emlyn drew out both her knife and revolver before they had a chance to release their coats. They took another step back. Mira instinctively backed away into the corner of the alcove. If she could have melded into the stone and come out the other side, then that would have been perfect. She grabbed the straps of the harness and bent down, trying to get as close to the ground as possible while not dropping any packages.

"I advise you, Masters, to turn around and visit the brothel up the way," Emlyn proclaimed in a concerned and slightly begging voice.

The eyes of the barrel-chested man shone with rage. "No gilla tells me whadda do!"

He lifted his gun out of its holster. The motion seemed achingly slow. She wanted to shoot him, but the one who followed her was watching. Like the bar girl said, "Gotta dot my i's." Emlyn stayed put as the barrel finished its agitated ascent, the hollowness of its length trained at her head.

The boom echoed through the alley. Mira put her hands over her ringing ears and missed seeing the bullet bury itself into the brick to the right of Emlyn's head. Emlyn, in the blink of an eye, ran up on the man and bashed his forehead with the butt of her gun. She hoped it was enough. He fell fast with a thud, bringing up swirling dust.

The drunken sharp-faced man held up his gun with shaking hands. A cane came down on his wrist, and the shot from his firearm rang out at the same time. The bullet slammed into the dirt at Emlyn's feet. In an instant she placed a toe under one of the ceramic pots, then lifted it off the ground and catapulted it right into the cutthroat's face. A few ceramic shards lodged into his cheek, and his clothing took a shower in the old dirt. He landed on his knees, wailing and carrying on like a banshee. He tried to pull out one of the shards but was unable to, resulting in more screaming echoing off the walls.

She looked at where the bullet had struck, then up at the man who followed. He was inspecting his cane for damage.

"Thank you for your assistance, Master."

"Is that some sort of power martials have? To know if they will be shot or not?"

Emlyn knew it was sarcasm, but it was also a compliment on her skills. She used her hand to wipe the bit of blood off the butt of her revolver before placing it back in its holster.

"Not at all, Master. His hand was shaking. That told me he had little training, not to mention the angle of the barrel was off."

"So, plain old body language. Impressive."

She bowed to him once again, this time with added respect with a closed fist over her heart.

The sharp-faced man, now more sober than he had been, tried to sneak away while nursing his wrists, but the cane turned him around and pressed him against the wall.

"Stay right there." The follower shoved a handkerchief in the man's mouth.

A voice suddenly rang out, "You! Gilla! Hands in the air!"

Emlyn obeyed, and she cursed inwardly. Thoughts on all the ways this could play out crossed her mind as a uniformed municipal peacekeeper, abbreviated to peacer by most people, walked toward her. He had his pistol out, its barrel pointed directly at her. His uniform was buttoned down a few inches, matching the uncaring look of his long-disheveled hair tied at the nape of his neck.

This man was young, a babyface itching for a fight. A man who relished the power he had. But his posture was tense, making him seem nervous under the surface bravado. If the peacer determined that she did not have good enough cause to harm a free man, then her execution was in order. Immediate execution. The alley was the worst place she could be in this situation. She was now thankful that the strange man with the cane had followed her and hoped he would not let her down.

"Hold back, peacekeeper! This gilla was well within her rights to protect her mistress's property!"

"It looks more like murder to me!"

Emlyn looked at the man she bashed and realized she must have hit harder than intended, for he was dead as dead can be. Her nose wrinkled, unused to the sudden stink of released bowels.

She stared at the body, her first kill, and one that was purely by accident. A gross miscalculation. The officer brought her out of the daze by putting the barrel of his gun near her forehead.

"Peacekeeper! She is within rights! I stand in witness, or do you plan to do away with me as well?"

The peacekeeper had a murderous itch, as if it was the one thing he wanted to do most in life. To know what it would be like to shoot a high gilla, but reason caught up with the man and he thought better of it. He slowly released the hammer of the gun.

"Okay . . . you're coming with me."

Emlyn peered over his shoulder at another peacekeeper quickly walking into the alcove. This one was of higher rank. He had the wisdom of age upon him, bald on top and a white-as-snow moustache curved upward. His bluish-gray uniform was well pressed. The cut made him look stately with a dozen gold buttons trailing all the way up to his neck. Three green stripes outlined by silver encircled his left bicep, signaling that he was a superior peacekeeper. Just under a decanus, who were responsible for a full team of peacers, around eighty. Each decanus oversaw different regions in the city, six in all under a high decanus.

"What's going on here, Silas?"

The murderous peacer turned, startled.

"Superior Filch! This gilla murdered a free man!"

His superior looked over the body. "Did you notice, Silas, the gun near the body? The martial has her gun holstered." The superior bent at the waist, curiously looking into the face of the bashed man.

"No, but—"

"This is Doma Scaunon. He's a known thug. It's obvious that the gilla was protecting her owner's property." He nodded toward Mira, who was still crouched in the corner, shivering.

The superior known as Filch walked up to her and grasped her tag.

"Ah, Chronister." He released it.

Emlyn slowly lowered her hands, but she could not pull her eyes away from the dead man.

The superior looked at Silas. "You see? When Scaunon could not obtain what he wanted, he resorted to force, and well, poor Doma finally ran out of fate's thread."

He looked around and finally spotted the man with the cane. "Why Mr. Colmane! Were you involved in this mess? Trying to catch a gilla perhaps? Or were you working on the murder case?"

Colmane pointed his cane at Emlyn. "I was assisting this martial in the recovery of her mistress's property, Superior Filch, nothing more. We ran across these dregs trying to steal that gilla away, aiming to do harm when they had no permission to do so. She was within rights, and I am willing to stand as a witness."

The peacekeeper rubbed his chin in thought. He went up to the sharp-faced man, who had not moved one muscle since Filch's arrival.

"Ah, Mr. Plat. Didn't have money for a brothel? Thought you could get it for free instead, eh? You've had four warnings this month alone. You've only wiggled your way out because Decanus Vigus likes your stories, but it's past due that you stand before a magistrate." He let it sink in before adding, "And I'll personally suggest you be given the three choices."

"No, please! Filch, think! If ya put meh in, all me stories will be lost!"

Filch tsked. "Find paper in a prison colony. Write on toilet paper in the can. Perhaps your future master will loan you a pen so you can write your broken speech. I don't care which."

Plat moaned, not relishing the threat of choosing prison, gillary, or exile. Filch turned Plat around and cuffed his wrists together.

"What about the gilla, sir?" asked Silas.

"Let her go."

"But—"

"Colmane knows what he's on about, so do it!" said Filch with growing impatience.

"High-gilded pig-haves," Silas mumbled a little too loud.

"That's enough, Silas! I don't want to hear one more word!"

Before they left, Silas bent down and looted the dead body and found a few fennis in the dead man's vest pocket. They kept the downtrodden Plat between them as they went and disappeared around the corner.

Emlyn and Colmane had no intention of staying with the body. The stink of feces had grown strong, and the peacekeepers would have it picked up in an hour or two. He wiped the length of his cane on his arm sleeve.

"That was quite a show!"

"Lady Chronister might wish to reward you for protecting her property."

"Nonsense! I need no reward! But yes, we should go and see your mistress. Which means an auto ride in my Vitru Frig. What do you say to that, eh? A reward for you I'd expect!"

Emlyn smiled in eagerness. A Vitruvius Frig was nothing to joke about. It had a sleek design and was the latest in their electric line, the newest version of the lead acid battery, and it could achieve an astonishing thirty kilometers per hour, though there was a speed problem next to steam, and it was considered suitable only in towns and cities. Still, they were rare and expensive. And the quicker they could get away from the body the better.

"I'm so sorry! They forced me out here!" yelled Mira.

Emlyn turned toward Mira and considered the poor girl as she walked up to her. Mira's body language was set on flight, but there was nowhere to go.

As Emlyn got closer, a look came over the girl like she was about to be eaten by the most horrible of creatures. Emlyn bent down and put her lips near Mira's ear, whispering, "I know what you've done. I know that you were not brought out here by those men. You tried to escape."

The girl's face turned white.

"Don't worry. I'll keep that to myself, but I will be watching you closely."

The pristine yellow open-topped auto was parked by the walkway on a busy street called Hetton, not too far from the pub. It was a curvy auto with silver trim that gleamed in the sunlight, all in a style that Emlyn was unfamiliar with. Trends in art and fashion were something few gilla had to pay attention to. Though it screamed expense, and she wondered, if Colmane was not the dalarwain of gilla affairs, then how in the world could he afford such a machine? Looking at his expression as his roamed over it, it was obvious how much pride he had in this auto, and she figured it was no easy expense.

Mira was putting the packages in the trunk as Emlyn and Colmane stood on either side of the girl.

"After you sort the packages, make room for yourself."

Mira looked at her, shocked. "Ma'am?"

"It is unseemly for an unclothed gilla to ride next to a master."

* * * * *

The wind blew through Emlyn's hair, taking the heat away for a moment. She closed her eyes and leaned back to bask in the pleasure of it. The wheels hit another bump, and she knew that her charge was not having a swell time in that trunk. Served her right. Fitting punishment for trying to escape, a lenient one too. She could have been beaten and whipped, but then Emlyn would've suffered a whipping herself for losing the girl.

"She's a beauty, is she not? Drives like a charm!"

"As you say, Master."

"Do martials learn how to drive?"

"Yes. We're taught in case the driver is out of commission."

"I see. I must confess, I know little of martials. One does not deal with them in the gilla-catching business."

Emlyn smiled at that. "With all due respect, Master, I would expect not. There is no equal in loyalty to their owner. A martial who willingly escaped would be a scandal."

"You think it's impossible?"

She crossed her arms. "Unthinkable."

He frowned and kept his eyes on the road. "Interesting. I always had the notion that a soul yearns to be free. I suppose it comes from my profession. Seeing so many try to escape, it's inevitable to come to that conclusion."

A friend might have responded, but Emlyn said nothing. She knew the statement invited no response.

"I noticed your quick draw. I dare say that it was faster than a professional shootist, and I've seen my share. How did you learn to do such a thing?"

This was a direct question. No matter how much she wanted to refrain, she had to tell him, and so she recited it as best she could manage.

Chapter Six

-Laced with Truth-

BANG!

The shot rang across the rolling green hills, scaring the black gile birds from the trees. They flew east, dozens of little black dots with wings, squawking and carrying on.

Andreas sat on a stump watching the pests fly off. He breathed out a longing sigh as they disappeared beyond the tree line.

Andreas Chronister had three children—two boys, one girl. Cassius was the oldest, or he was before the red sickness took him, along with Briar's only son, Thom. The other son, Vantalis . . . He had held the babe upon his birth and felt his last heartbeat. It was a memory Andreas did not like to dwell upon. No matter how much they tried, he and Camilla had no luck in producing another child. So he'd placed all his hopes on his daughter, Sylvia.

Today, out on the old ancestral estate, manned by a skeleton crew and retired martials, they were shooting. Well, Briar and Emlyn were shooting. He had hoped Sylvia would have a fondness for hunting gile. Some girls do, it was considered a patrician sport after all. It would have been something splendid that they both could share, but Sylvia most certainly did not enjoy hunting. As soon as he raised the small-caliber rifle at any gile, she would go into hysterics about how innocent they were. How we had no right to shoot them. Even after he explained how giles became nuisances to country landowners, she still refused to the point of tearing up and made him promise that he would never shoot another animal. So here he was, a man who would rather give up a passion than see his daughter cry.

He winced at the thought of her weeping over Emlyn in a few years. Then again, Briar was pushing to wait for another five. But prolonging the time of the breaking would be a very risky experiment. He had heard of a few martials turning out better for it, but Emlyn was no soft brain and eventually would have questions. Questions that would become very hard to answer. And could they really keep lying to them for a few more years?

Why does this all seem so much harder with a daughter? He shook his head, dislodging the light brown curl at his forehead, and flipped to the next page of the morning newspaper.

Camilla did not come along with them on this trip, as she had a previous date with a few friends. She was eager to show off Bootsie to them for some unfathomable reason that he had no intention of understanding.

Bootsie was lithe and feminine in mannerism despite being fully male. Fully clothed, one would think he was a rare androgyne. Now that would be worth showing off. The poor creature was apparently being beaten up in the middle of the street. The homeless were easy targets for the perpetually bored and irascible. Finding the scene distasteful, Camilla had Stella pummel the ruffians. But before they could leave, the boy threw himself at her feet, declared himself gilla, and begged to serve her house. She agreed. Gods bless her romantic soul, not many patricians would do such a thing. Too much paperwork to give someone shelter and a full belly nowadays.

Kittie came out of the woods, with Sylvia trailing behind her like a duckling keeping up with its mother. His daughter, upon seeing him, jumped up and down, waving. He stood up from the stump and barely had time to wave back before she was right there before him, hopping about like some kit given sugar.

She talked on and on about all the wondrous sites she'd seen in the woods. She found a clear stream where Kittie informed her of fool's gold and of fae who loved to roam the waterways. She spotted numerous types of birds and a cute hedgehog that Kittie warned her not to touch.

"Kittie knows so much! Are all gilla smart?"

"Some are."

"Why is Kittie so smart?"

The gilla blushed.

"Well, she was born to a professor."

"Oh." Sylvia stopped jumping about and looked at Kittie wonderingly. "Daddy, why didn't she escape while we were in the woods?"

Andreas looked at the gilla, whose eyes became big as saucers. He wanted to ask Kittie what was said between the two but thought better of it. It might betray his daughter's trust.

He sat back down on the stump so he could be face-to-face with his daughter and decided that this was as good a time as any to explain such a thing.

"I'm going to be very honest with you, princess, and you need to pay very close attention, okay?"

She nodded.

"Good. Every civilized country possesses gilla. Many are made gilla by convention or law—"

"That's what we do!"

"Correct. Most of our gilla were criminals. It is viewed as an acceptable punishment. It might seem cruel, but many do find some measure of peace. Our family treats them well and values them. Remember to be good to them, and you will have their loyalty."

Sylvia looked up again at Kittie. "But Kittie was not a criminal!"

"No, she was not. Some people do it for a roof over their head and for regular meals. Others do so because of some ridiculous romance stories." He was at a loss for why Kittie became a gilla. Since she was under contract, he did not actually own her. He thought that asking such a thing would be stepping on Hornbow's toes since she was rented out to him as a gesture to prove a point. It was a secret that Hornbow refused to tell until the term of service was up.

He decided to change the subject slightly and let his daughter come to her own conclusions on the ways people become gilla. "Do you know how to tell if someone is a gilla?"

She shook her head.

"First, there is the collar around the neck with a tag." He gestured for Kittie to come near them and kneel. He made her lean forward by grasping her tag and pulling. "The tag will show who the gilla belongs to. The tag can be removed easily, but the collar cannot since the band has a special lock."

Kittie leaned back on her heels as soon as he let go of the tag.

"A gilla will often have a house brand to signify who they belong to."

Kittie shimmied her arm out of the right side of her blouse and showed Sylvia two circular brands on her back shoulder. The first one had an ornate cage within a circle, which showed where she was trained and was an uncommon mark nowadays. While most would use their initials, Hornbow used names of birds to refer to his gilla. As silly as it seemed, Andreas had to admit that it made the man stand out from the gaggle and was one of the reasons he took the bet between Hornbow, Kittie, and himself. Even if gilla were not Andreas's area of expertise.

The brand right below that one was simplified. The full Chronister mark was an eagle and a dead she-wolf at its feet showing that the family had fought with Lucanis against the Romans. The wolf lay on an eight-spoke cart wheel, signifying their influence in industry. Around the wheel were the heads of gilly flowers, symbols of opulence, charity, and life. The one used on their purchased gilla was broken down to the wheel and gilly flowers for the convenience of other marks. Only their martials received the full mark, or if a gilla became bloodlined.

He continued, "There is nowhere to run for a gilla; the collar will immediately place them back in servitude. If a brand is discovered, then they would need a paper signifying freedom."

Sylvia's face was downcast. He knew it sounded harsh to her young ears since she adored Kittie.

He put on his best smile. "Besides, Kittie loves serving us. And watching after you of course. Though I'm not too sure she likes the weight of that hunk of metal." Andreas bopped Sylvia's nose with his finger, and she giggled. Kittie's nervousness turned into a weary smile.

BANG!

Another shot rang out.

Andreas took Sylvia's hand, and the three of them went to see the Gwens fifty yards away, shooting at a few dozen glass bottles. Looking at the targets, it was apparent that Emlyn had not hit a single one so far. The six-shot revolver she held pointed at the next bottle. She closed one eye and stuck out her tongue like a lopsided dog. Briar bent down to whisper in her ear.

"Open your eyes and put that tongue back in your mouth. Stand straight. This is your last bullet. If you miss this shot, then I will put the gun away and we'll go home. I know you don't want that, so breathe in. Now when you let the breath out, all soft and easy like, shoot."

She was rarely allowed to leave the house, so she concentrated on the tall thin bottle across the gully. It was of emerald-green glass that had contained olive oil at one point. She focused on a reflection upon the surface, swirling and shimmering in the sunlight.

Sylvia cheered for her friend, but it seemed drowned out like a low static hum from a musicura box. She let her breath out slowly, just like Papa told her, and squeezed the trigger as if she were petting a puppy, soft and easy.

BANG!

The glass shattered into hundreds of tiny emerald pieces. Sylvia jumped and hooted in celebration while Emlyn massaged the slight pain in her arm due to the recoil and then looked down at the gun in amazement.

Briar patted her shoulder. "Very good!"

She looked up into his face, eager in her exuberance. "Can I shoot some more, Papa? Please?"

He bent down and had her head between his hands so fast that she tensed up. The sudden fear melted away when he wrapped his arms around her in a hug.

After a few seconds, he held her by the shoulders away from him. His warm smile made her stand up straight and smirk. Her eyes brimmed with pride.

"You got that fire! I can see it there!"

"Emlyn."

She turned toward Andreas.

"Good girl." He tossed her something, and she snatched it out of the air with her free hand. That move seemed to impress Sylvia, and she clapped again, giving a little jump. A shiny red apple sat in Emlyn's hand. She smiled.

"Emlyn, what do you say?" said Briar.

"Thank you, Mr. Chronister, sir." She bowed as best she could with her hands full.

Yes, Kittie subtly taught the girl well. That was her purpose, after all. A teacher. Not only in the basic things like literature and math but also subtly teaching Emlyn how to be a gilla.

They would have to keep this charade up for another four years or so, if he went with Briar's idea, that is. If the behavior of the girls permitted. Andreas wanted Emlyn's transition, from mock freedom to her true gillary, to be as smooth as possible, and this was a method the family used since the grandchildren of Delwyn and Oghan.

For two more hours, Emlyn fired shot after shot at the bottles. With every dozen shots she would improve, ending up missing two out of six.

Afterwards Briar put the onyx-handled revolver back in its case, he found a nice, soft grassy spot and taught her the basics of tumbling, treating it like a game. Emlyn was exuberant over this, purely because she found herself to be very good at it. Sylvia joined in and found that she could not do it quite as well and soon gave up. For the next two nights, they would stay on the estate, and Emlyn would shoot, tumble, run in the woods, and continue her studies under Briar's strict supervision.

* * * * *

On the last day, they were at the carriage, packed and ready to depart. Emlyn carried herself with supreme pride. The swagger in her gait carried her in a way that the girl imagined the legendary Hesperian Tolido pistoleers had walked. This was based entirely on the descriptions she read from those cheap fenni novels that were lying around the house.

As Emlyn pretended to twirl imaginary pistols, Sylvia bounced around pleading for Emlyn to save her cousin from those Zighan miscreants who absconded with said victim, three horses, and a goat Tuesday last. As the two played, he was reminded of when he and Briar were no more than chest high. Running around, pretending to be Lucanis and his right hand, Jaker, fighting against the Roman remnant.

Emlyn would be a fine protector for Sylvia. She had gotten this far with flying colors and was always steered into the proper direction with no hint of conspiracy or hidden machinations. She thought that all this was to entertain her, just spending time with her family.

He watched as Briar patted Emlyn's head before bending down to kiss her on the brow. His martial was always the sentimental type. Not even his breaking changed that, nor did the wars in north Libya.

As soon as the girls were settled in the back seat of the carriage, Briar opened the passenger door for his master. Andreas looked into his gilla's eyes for a long moment and, for the hundredth time, noted the difference in them.

As boys those eyes were alive, now they were deadened. Such a shame to lose so much passion. If there was any passion his old friend still possessed, it was placed on little Emlyn. Oh sure, if you asked Briar what his passion in life was, he would say, "To protect my master" or something equally silly. The truth was there in the lines his face produced when he looked at the girl, and it was always there underneath those terrible eyes. Martials tended to keep their distance from their offspring because they needed them to be tough, and it made it easier during the breaking to step away and let it happen. He couldn't fault Briar for this. Briar's son died from the red sickness not long after Cassius. They were just two fathers being protective of their daughters, their last of blood.

Briar gave a nod that said it all. He was proud, even jubilant, over successfully proving that his daughter had everything it took to become a martial.

Andreas mulled over a thought. *The best charade is the one laced with truth.*

CHAPTER SEVEN

Dusk came in splendid red and gold, layered on top with a hazy dark purple. The black iron streetlamps ebbed to life, illuminating the area as the Vitru Frig turned onto Verndi Street. The tires screeched to a stop and idled at a set of large metal doors located at the back of the Chronister insula, the only entrance big enough for an auto to fit through.

Emlyn jumped down from the passenger's seat and grasped the door's warm metal handle. She pulled, putting her whole body into it. It slid back, giving out a metallic moan. As she pulled, the other side automatically slid away. She signaled Colmane to drive under the archway, then rushed inside and directed him to park within a small concrete area right next to an immaculate garage housing two shiny blue autos. One was being waxed by Donnon, the driver, who only paid enough attention to admire the Frig before returning to his work.

Flowers of the pheasant's eye lined the parking area next to the enormous garden. Arches bordered it, held up by roman columns with triskele motifs except on the west side, where so many trees stood that it was impossible to see the end. Between the arches and trees were various shrines and water fountains sprouting up from peristyle features.

Emlyn jogged through the garden, into the side entrance, and almost ran into Strawberry carrying dirty plates and a coffee carafe from the dining room. The girl wavered, trying to steady the items, and apologized to Emlyn's back racing up the stairs.

Sylvia had an out-on-the-town dress on, a rarity but a welcomed sight. It was a shimmering white and like a sash, embroidered red flowers fell from the right shoulder to the hem of the flowing skirt. The sleeves ended at the elbows with intricate lace dangling from the ends. She was putting her gloves on as Emlyn stepped into the room. Sylvia did not move, only peered at Emlyn through the mirror.

"Emlyn, where in the Dé have you been?" she said, annoyed and slightly angry.

Emlyn bowed. "Forgive me, Mistress. There is someone here to see you. He's waiting down in his auto."

Sylvia turned around and narrowed her eyes at her. "Where have your mannors flown to? Invite him in, make sure he's comfortable, then come back up here and inform me what is going on."

* * * * *

Mira was sore from the bumpy trunk ride but so very glad she did not have to lug that weight all the way back to the house. *Looking on the bright side. That's the way of it.* The thought did nothing to dent her determination to escape.

Her mind teetered on various memories, cold days within that little cottage under the shadow of the stone belt. Also of the friendly Gaelland man who taught her to speak Kymbri, along with Kymbrian axioms and mannerisms.

Thoughts of her previous life did her no good. All it brought was a melancholy state and a meeting with the cook's spoon. So she turned her mind to remembering the little songs that she heard the gilla sing while going about their chores. She tried to remember some words and ended up humming a few pleasant melodies. This really helped pass the time with all this drudgery and left her in a better mood.

Oblivious to Colmane's attentions, her mind was on getting the task done quickly, and then supper, which was a nice creamy chicken and potato soup. Once she realized he was looking her up and down like a hungry wolf, she tensed up, gritting her teeth. She only had a few more packages to deposit from the trunk to the pantry, so she steeled herself, sure that she would be allowed to retreat to the kitchen afterward. Soon enough she was finished. Mira was about to dismiss herself when Emlyn reappeared.

"Master, if you would please follow me. Mira, you will follow as well."

Mira paled as she took her place behind Colmane. He glanced back at her more than once as they walked on the stones of the garden path and into the house, and she shivered, fearfully uncertain. Then they went into a green-tinged, ornate room. It was used as a waiting area with no more than a green couch, two green chairs, a coffee table, and a ready table sitting under the white-curtained window. A few landscape paintings bordered by gilded frames hung on each wall. It was small, used for non-patricians.

Emlyn gestured for Mira to kneel on the floor as Colmane sat on the two-seat couch with wonderfully green upholstery, almost velveteen to the touch. His arm rested over the golden side support with his hand angling near Mira's head.

"My mistress wishes to apologize to you, Mr. Colmane. She expected no guests today and was caught unaware by this turn of events. In the interim, Mistress Sylvia has given you permission to use her gilla, Mira, in any way you see fit, within reason of course, until the mistress is ready to make her appearance."

He dipped his head toward her in understanding. "No apology necessary, but do thank your mistress for the gesture."

Emlyn nodded and performed her martial bow.

Mira's gaze followed Emlyn making her way out past the archway leading to the steps. She wished that the martial would come back right now and tell this man that the mistress changed her mind, and then send her off to the kitchen. No such luck as the sounds of Emlyn's boots ceased clicking on the hardwood floor. There was no color in her face left to drain, and she could not bring herself to look over at the man beside her.

"You're such a pretty thing."

His fingers wormed their way through her short hair.

"I'm very partial to blondes, you know." He grabbed what little hair he could and wrenched her head back, making her squeak out in pain.

"I would own you if I could. Perhaps after my purpose here is resolved, I will be able to buy you from Lady Chronister."

Living in this house was bad enough, but she was sure that living with this man would be far worse. Emlyn had to be punishing her for trying to run. She regretted that attempt. It was poorly thought out, a spur of the moment response that had no chance of paying off in hindsight. Now, because of that, she must endure this man.

He moved his hand from her hair down to the back of her neck, holding her still, and put his thumb against the soft part of her throat. She froze, holding her breath, and did not doubt what his intentions were. He moved his finger lightly across her throat to her collar. He fingered the tag.

"You know, I only have one gilla, and she is not nearly as pretty as you."

She let out another squeak. "Please don't . . . Master, don't."

He violently grabbed her neck and brought her face-to-face with him.

"You whelp! What kind of place is this?"

"Mr. Colmane!" interrupted Sylvia, standing resplendent under the arch doorway. "She's not a house girl, she is a kitchen gilla. Would you disparage how my cook uses her because it does not fit your own methods?"

He let Mira go. She immediately crumpled to the ground and shivered. Colmane stood to greet Sylvia with a bow. "Of course not, Lady Chronister. My apologies if I've overstepped my bounds or offended you in any way."

She looked at Mira for only a second to determine damage before casting her gaze upon him. Sylvia studied him for a moment, taking in his mode of dress. A professional in his field but not one to waste money on flippant finery, unless one counted his hair in that category. He looked to be a man who kept his cards close to his chest. A man who liked to stand apart from the crowd, who felt apart from his class.

"My Emlyn offered her to you on my behalf, and I am sure my cook would not take offense. Besides, this girl" —she gestured toward Mira— "is just a low gilla."

He grinned and nodded. They proceeded to make each other's acquaintance in the typical fashion, with the mistress offering her hand for Colmane to kiss before giving his full name.

Emlyn came in and shooed Mira away. She fled through a narrow door in the corner, more glad than ever to be sent to the kitchen.

Emlyn went to another door on the other side of the room and grasped its handle. Sylvia came behind her and bid Colmane to follow. An automatic electric light flicked on as soon as the sliding door finished its journey into the wall. For a moment it seemed that it was still daylight outside. The brightness of the peach walls was close to overbearing. Peach velvet couches begging to be reclined on sat in the middle flanking an oval, white marble table.

She flared out her skirts and sat, hoping this would go quicker than she expected. Once Sylvia was situated, he too sat. The wall behind Colmane was a painting, a mural of a peach orchard finished some years ago. It always made her happy to look at it, for it reminded her of better times when she was a child, before she was made aware of certain realities. In the corner, above the artist initials, was the title: *Caul Orchards*.

He glanced at Emlyn standing straight with her hands behind her back, next to a small liquor cabinet close to Sylvia's side of the couch. She too looked over at the martial standing as still as a statue, but Sylvia knew better. Emlyn's muscles were primed for movement, ready tension, only deceptively relaxed.

"I have to admit, I was becoming worried when Emlyn failed to arrive home on time."

She looked across the low marble table at him. "I am glad to hear that she successfully protected my interests."

He leaned back, taking a less protected posture. "Yes, I was quite impressed with her skills."

Sylvia kept her face neutral. There was not much she could gather about him, and Emlyn had offered little help. Money seemed the likely culprit though. "Tsk, how rude of me! A guest in my house, and I've neglected to offer a beverage? Tell me, Colmane, what is your mode of drink?"

"Spiced rye if you have it." As soon as he began the sentence, Emlyn poured it in a short glass and set it on top of the table upon a coaster. The quick, smooth movement made him sit back and catch his breath.

"That was quite impressive."

"Emlyn has the ability to read body language. In all probability, she knew you were a spiced rye man when she first greeted you."

He took the glass off its coaster and sipped it, savoring the faintly sweet taste. Sylvia let him savor it as she studied him further. He looked young, with thick, solid tawny hair and bright blue eyes, but the lines around his mouth spoke of encroaching middle-age.

"What does it take to teach a gilla such a thing?"

Sylvia accepted a half glass of red cordial. "A skilled gilla, well, I suppose one could probably pick it up in a rudimentary way. I'm afraid you will have to ask my mother about such things. She is more knowledgeable than I when it comes to these creatures. I can only say with certainty that martials are trained extensively to pick up minute details." She swirled the liquid in her glass and sipped.

His eyes widened ever so slightly, showing that this was information he was fishing for. He wanted to ask something but was not sure if he should. Maybe he thought it impolite, but it certainly had something to do with Emlyn. A picture was starting to come together. Instead of playing it out, Sylvia decided to help him along. She had no time for polite back and forth.

"It is my understanding that you helped Emlyn fend off some men of ill notion?"

Colmane shrugged. "True, though I'd say she had it well in hand."

"Your humbleness is to be admired, but helping to protect my property deserves some reward."

He turned his head to the side and rubbed the stubble on his chin as if lost in thought. "Well, my profession is gilla catcher. I don't know if you've heard of me—"

Sylvia cut him off. "Of course I have. Your investigations are fascinating, and I know that you're in the running to be the next dalarwain of gilla affairs. I can promise you my support if you wish."

She had seen his investigations into runaway gilla numerous times, and a few of those investigations produced free people helping to hide them, people of the stoic notion. Then there were these recent murders.

He bowed his head slightly in respect and was more than a little flattered. "I am humbled indeed, but while I'd appreciate your support, I have something else in mind."

Sylvia rested an elbow on the armrest and put her jaw against her fist. "Please, go on."

He continued, "For the last few weeks, my mind has been focused on a number of . . . murders."

She leaned forward, her interest piqued. "You speak of the murders on the front page of late? Multiple homicides . . . by the same person?"

Surprised at the genuine tone, he showed his palms while spreading his hands apart, inviting her curiosity. "Possibly, there is the same pattern to all the killings. The first murders were of gilla, not a big deal in the public eye. However, I noticed that the tags were missing. Their owners insisted that they had not touched the bodies before I arrived. Upon further investigation I found that these gilla had failed in some way and were being readied for sale."

He looked down in thought. "Recently it has become a more serious matter. Now, this is not in the paper yet, but the last murder was of a freeman, killed in the same gruesome manner. The police believe this is the same killer, and there is a theory, a strong theory, that the killer is gilla . . . or a freeman. I was the expert brought in to consult and . . . I'm conducting my own investigation."

"I read that Inspector Hwyfar Nary was put on the case."

Colmane drank the rest of his rye. "In a way I am pitted against him." He looked over at Emlyn. "It would be a help to the case if I could borrow the expertise of your martial."

Sylvia's face contorted in confusion. "You want my Emlyn to help track down the suspect? Why, so you can win this . . . race against Hwyfar?"

"No." He looked down again, considering his words carefully. "I have a hunch that the killer is, or rather was, a high gilla. I am loath to admit that my knowledge of high and bloodlined gilla does not extend very far. Having backup who knows more about the subject and whose eye for detail is just as deep as my own would be a tremendous help."

"If that is true, then surely it must be some entertainer or someone from a low brothel!" she said wonderingly.

"True, they are vulgar creatures, but I believe any type of gilla can be put on the table and inspected."

She looked over at Emlyn, then tapped her own rose-colored lips three times; the movement made Emlyn walk out of the room. It was a way to silently tell her to go and get ready. As the martial left, Sylvia stared at her backside a little too long, and she knew that Colmane noticed. She cursed inwardly before turning back to him, smiling warmly, but Colmane held an odd grin, and she knew that he knew. Sylvia admonished herself, and paranoia bubbled to the surface. He had no proof of course, but rumors, rumors can kill. She forced the feeling down.

"Of course you can use Emlyn in your investigation, but I want you to do something for me in return."

"Name it."

Sylvia gave a wry smirk. "Make sure my involvement is known."

* * * * *

Sylvia did not want to come across as impatient while talking with Colmane and hoped that she did not seem as such. Now she and her mother were late for the theater. She let Emlyn perform the final touches on her hair and pinned up the last few strands herself before rushing out to meet Camilla in the hall. Her mother was sitting prettily in blue upon a simple chair with her arms outstretched, hands resting on the pommel of her cane. Stella stood stout and dour next to her.

"Is everything okay? Who was that man?"

"Just a commoner."

Donnon, the servant driver, was asleep in the back seat when they came to the garage. Camilla banged the silver pommel of her cane against the auto, startling him awake. He cursed. Upon seeing who it was, he quickly made his profound apologies. Sylvia couldn't blame him for falling asleep since she was the one who made them all late and could only smile at his words before Camilla berated him on his language, declaring that they should not be seen in public with a driver who had no control over his tongue. Donnon deepened his apologies, making Camilla harrumph before helping herself into the auto. When they were all situated, she told him to go fast, and he replied with a curt, "Yes, ma'am!"

Stella and Emlyn sat in the back with their mistresses and did not say much on the way there. Only enjoying the night air and the small amount of coolness that the breeze created. Sylvia wondered at her martial, her old friend. She had killed someone earlier. Was she thinking about it, was it bothering her?

Stella demanded that Emlyn undo the ponytail and braid it. Emlyn shook herself out of her thoughts looking confused, and searched for an explanation from her mother. Stella sighed and informed her daughter that this was also special for her.

"From now on, you will keep your hair braided."

"Why?"

"It's tradition. While your mistress is courting, you'll wear it braided until their wedding. Shows that your mistress is spoken for and hence *you* are not available for breeding offers."

Emlyn only stared disbelievingly at Stella and blushed as she worked her hair into a braid. Emlyn had a few offers over the years, especially when it became clear that the mistress of the house was not courting. Sylvia remembered all the times she read them. They offered a ludicrous amount of kints, and an old name like Gwen in their own martial's bloodline would have been worth the expenditure. Still, despite how polite these letters were, she only felt disgust before tossing them in the fire.

Sylvia had paled at Stella's comment and looked the other way. She too had never heard of this tradition. That was when Camilla decided it was the right time to ask.

"So, darling, will you tell me the business you had with that man? He looked well put together to be just a commoner. A new business opportunity perhaps?"

"He will be the new wain of gilla affairs in a year or so. Wanted Emlyn's help with an investigation."

Camilla looked shocked. "You did not."

"I did."

"What in the high one's grace convinced you to do such a thing? Martials should never leave their owner's side."

"Why not let her use the skills she was taught for the greater good of the city instead of standing around in the insula every day doing nothing?"

"Protecting you is nothing? It's bad enough you stay inside and let her run your errands instead of using a low gilla or servant for the job, now you want to lend her to a low-class catcher?"

Sylvia waved a hand and sighed in frustration. "She's not me. She needs to get out and—"

Camilla interrupted her. "She's a gilla. Her comfort is immaterial. She exists for you and you alone, not herself, or anyone else for that matter, and it is best that you call off this . . . loan."

An angry huff escaped from Sylvia's lips, and she looked over at Emlyn, who was conveniently staring out at the passing buildings as if they were the most interesting things in the world. She wondered what she was thinking, what she felt after hearing that. But asking would be a violation of what they were, and Emlyn would just clamp down on her martialhood, making the wall between them even thicker. It had happened before when she asked about such personal, inner thoughts. And she could only curse the breaking for putting the wall up in the first place. An old hatred against what the world had made of them, against Kymbri, against her mother and father, crept up, clawing into her mind like a splinter. She breathed deep and reminded herself that it was a child's notion and that the world is as it is and there was no changing that. So the splinter of a thought vanished into nothing, and the shadow that had fallen over her gaze lifted.

"Of course you're right, Mother, you're always right. She's my martial and nothing more." She continued after seeing Camilla's relief, "But I will not rescind my loan."

Sudden tension straightened Camilla's back. She hit the bottom of her cane against the floor. "Whatever could be your reasoning?"

Sylvia looked into her eyes for a moment. "It is a high-profile murder case. Loaning Emlyn's skills is a service to Kymbri, and it makes our house more famous and more well liked."

Her mother frowned, and her eyes were distant in thought. "That . . . could be true, but it is unheard of."

Sylvia interrupted her. "If you worry about what your tea companions think, I would ask, Mother, that you keep our current reputation in mind."

The only thing the people heard of the Chronisters in the last eight years was Sylvia's reclusiveness. "I would also ask you to remember that you put me in charge of our outside affairs."

Camilla looked affronted. "I am your mother and have every right to counsel you."

The auto pulled up to the front of the crowded theater, and the conversation ceased. Above the entrance, big round bulbs surrounded signs with big bold letters exclaiming "*A Gail to Shore*! Starring: Julius Peneton and Alma Minceed! Opening Night!" There was a line of low patricians being barred from entering until thirty minutes before the show, while high patricians could enter any time they wished.

Camilla seemed transfixed by the dazzle, but Sylvia wanted to go hide in a dark corner where no one could find her. Back to studying contracts while discussing them with Emlyn. Oh, the things she could be doing with Emlyn instead of this.

The tires of the auto gave out a long droning squeak as it came to a halt next to the curb. Lucius Donsill stepped up to the auto and smiled, genuine in his appreciation of the long, sleek aquiline auto in carriage style. The body gleamed with electric blue, bordered by silver trim. The motor was partially exposed and covered in chrome with a few golden bits and pieces, designed to catch the eye.

He took a step forward, greeting the four women with such a charismatic grin that he could charm the trousers off the Teyrn. The move was too abrupt for Stella, and she placed a hand on the hilt of her knife. She tensed, ready to leap.

Emlyn thought that her mother's willingness to allude to pulling a knife was gratuitous at best, paranoid in the least. Maield stood behind his master's left shoulder, looking like an unyielding tower. He ignored Stella's movements as his sentinel eyes glanced at Emlyn for just a moment, but enough for her to discern his interest. She smirked in response just enough as to not betray the stoic countenance expected of a martial out in public.

"Good evening, ladies," Lucius said, opening the auto door in lieu of Donnon, who scrunched up his face at being blocked by Maield from performing his duty. Camilla placed her hand in his, and he led her down the two steps from the auto to the sidewalk. Her heels hit the ground with a clack. She ran her eyes over him, and they danced with approval. "Donsill I presume?"

He took her hand and kissed it. "At your service, Lady Chronister."

Impressed by his etiquette, she let out a sigh that sounded almost like a slight giggle. "Please, call me Camilla! Sylvia, why did you not tell me how handsome he is? He's a fair pleasure to look upon!"

"My apologies, Mother. It must have slipped my mind."

Lucius helped Sylvia down from the auto next, making the same gestures. His eyes drank her in.

"Sylvia, you are Dé Áine incarnate!"

Sure enough, she was well put together in her long white dress reaching the floor with frills cascading down the back. It complemented her black hair, pulled back into a large bun held in place by a silver net. Strands came out from underneath, falling in waves that resembled a river at midnight, ending abruptly in the middle of her shoulders.

She recognized him. Lucius was no stranger to the city, having made his residence here five years ago. He attended every society function he could, where he'd encountered Sylvia during one of her rare sojourns at an unveiling of a new public shrine. She had not seen him since. Of course, that was not surprising, seeing how going to any function whatsoever made her stomach churn.

Sylvia dipped her head slightly, making a few strands of hair fall forward. "It is good to see you again, Lucius."

She wondered if he spent time looking for her at other patritional events. After the incident between Lucius and Emlyn, Sylvia did her research and uncovered that he was career military, discharged to take over his departed father's printing business, lucrative but cutthroat.

"Ah, I'm flattered you remember me."

She smiled up at him. "You will find that I have an optimal memory."

He was at least six foot. A golden brown, sharp moustache jutted vigorously out to the sides with a matching goatee pointing straight down. He wore a black long vest, embroidered with an old-fashioned triskele pattern instead of the modern corraí vine style, probably done to impress her mother. A red scarf sat smartly on his long white shirt. He put his hand out. "Shall we?"

She did the same, placing hers in his, noticing his well-maintained nails.

She kept her head down and frowned. She would just have to endure this. They walked right through as the doormen didn't even give them a second glance, but the people waiting to get in gave them stares of hatred and envy.

* * * * *

"Everything is true to the order."

Maield eyed the tray with exaggerated uncertainty. Perched on top were two drinks: a Derg rye straight and a white wine. The servitor grew impatient and breathed out a frustrated sigh.

"I'll take that, sir," Maield declared in a low but confident voice.

The servitor made no move to hand the tray over, and it looked as if the much smaller man was going to refuse until Maield's intense hazel eyes caught his vision. The man shivered and shoved the tray into

Maield's hands, then marched down the hall as fast as his legs could take him.

Maield closed the door with his foot and made his way to his master and the two mistresses looking out from the balcony box at the continuing play. He made a light cough to let them know he was there. It was polite to serve free women first before one's own master, so he handed the wine in its stemmed glass to Camilla, who paid no attention to him. He skipped Sylvia since she had ordered nothing. Then he handed the glass of rye to his master, who nodded at him before returning his attention to the play and once again becoming rapt by its players.

Sylvia shifted on the red cushion, trying to get herself into a more comfortable position. The play was nothing special in her eyes. However, her mother, along with Stella, were leaning on the rail of the balcony enraptured by the performance. If her mother got any more interested, she swore the old woman would fall from the balcony. The thought amused her before it brought horror. Of course, she would not actually want that to happen. If mother died, well, Emlyn would be the only person she could count on. She glanced back at Emlyn, who was standing next to Maield at the entrance and watched them converse.

"Your master played a risky game," Emlyn said in a whisper.

"It worked, did it not? Credit to your mistress for her reaction."

Emlyn looked at Maield and dipped her head slightly in thanks.

"You played your part well. Did you break the bottle, or was that a coincidence?"

"It was the first package to fall."

She smiled at that.

He chanced a glance at her. "What do you think about this?"

Emlyn raised an eyebrow, expecting him to explain.

"I know you're keen to my meaning . . . about our owners being together."

She shifted her weight from one foot to the other. "Too soon to tell."

"Humor me."

She took a moment to look up at him, at his stout shoulders, the perfect posture displaying confidence. His dark red hair swept to the side and curled at the end. His perfectly aligned clothing was not much different from last time. Simple, as all martial attire. Long brown vest, white shirt with its stiff collar going under and over the gilla collar.

She considered her own look: light brown ankle-length skirt, white blouse, its sleeves ending at the elbows with a bit of lace. The neck of the blouse opened just below the collarbone and flared out, then swooped up and around her neck, leaving her collar sitting on bare skin. She thought they made quite a pair.

She placed her gaze forward again, looking at the back of Master Lucius's head. "Okay . . . well, your master is very handsome."

Maield smiled and gave out a low snort, making Emlyn grin, promoting her to go on.

"Mistress has a lot of pressure on her to wed. He fits with . . . what is required. If it happens, I just hope she will be happy."

His face fell in concern. "Is she not? Happy, I mean."

"Most of the time she is, but . . ." She frowned, lost in an unhappy thought. "She has so much on her mind. Keeping up with the contracts, researching, approving investments, managing properties, keeping up with holidays and family functions that she never deigns to attend. I think merging our houses would be most welcomed. It would lift some of the burden off her back."

They both put their eyes forward. A few seconds later he glanced at her again. "Where does that leave us?"

"I don't know. Where does that leave us?" she said playfully.

He chuckled. "If it does happen, then we will be bred, and I for one would prefer it if we genuinely liked each other. Not only because I think it would be better for our offspring."

Emlyn looked down, trying to hide a deep blush. "Huh . . . we'll have to find out."

Sylvia watched the two banter for a while out of the corner of her eye. She could not hear what they were saying, but the blush lighting on Emlyn's face spoke volumes. It caused confusion and anger to sprout. She could not understand her sudden jealousy over seeing the two martials interact. It was wrong of her to think in such a way. *This is the way of things: two high patricians get married, their martials are bred, and life moves on*, she thought. She calmed herself and let her heartbeat subside.

She turned back to the play and pouted her lips as Alma Minceed, in the role of Julia Potis, lamented in her loneliness. Sylvia could relate to the loneliness, albeit in a different manner. Julia's fear was palpable as the casualties from a recent battle came in the form of a letter. She hoped against hope that her husband's name was not on the list . . . It was. Her wail seemed to break every heart in the theater, and Sylvia doubted there was a dry eye in the place, besides her own.

She heard sobbing beside her and looked at her mother drying her eyes with a silk handkerchief. Sylvia had to admit that Alma's acting was impressive. But the story was not as exciting as she hoped it would be. War was a tiring subject, though she understood the sudden obsession with it over the last few years. You could not escape a heated discussion of war at any society function. Not even a funeral was free of such dreaded talk. War with Zarmatia, war with Mithra, even fear of the Tengra trying after five hundred years to invade from the east despite being on friendly terms now. War always led atrocity. No, Sylvia wanted none of that, not even in a story, which had a habit of stoking the fires.

She felt a hand brush the top of hers. Donsill had an almost comically gigantic grin on his face. She forced a smile, hoping it looked genuine.

Well, she thought, *he's not bad looking, certainly a pleasant sort. Who am I to judge this man so soon? He is as good as any and fits Mother's criteria . . . and this is expected of me.* Thinking that felt like she was thrown into the water and drowning and her stomach churned because of it.

The red curtain fell for the final time. The clapping was unanimous, and even Sylvia joined in on the celebration of skill, despite her feelings on the play. She leaned back, relieved that it was over. When the actors came back on stage to receive praise, her mother stood and continued clapping. It reminded her of a skinny walrus banging it's flippers together.

If my mother was a walrus, then what would that make me? She stifled a giggle, then chided herself over such a childish thought.

As soon as Camilla finished her exuberance, Stella handed the black and silver handled cane to her mistress. Knocking the point of the cane on the floor, Camilla declared that she must meet the actors, that they deserved more than the paltry wages they undoubtedly earned. Lucius noticed Sylvia's unease at the notion and offered to escort her back to the car. Camilla seemed slightly upset about this at first but quickly realized the benefit of a little alone time between her daughter and, who she hoped would be, her future son-in-law.

Donnon pulled the auto up to the curb, but Lucius and Sylvia, being the only ones outside, took their time walking up to the passenger's side. Donnon tipped his hat to her. "Whenever you're ready, Mistress."

She nodded to the young man, then turned to face Donsill.

"Thank you, Lucius. Truly." She gave him a warm smile.

He returned the gesture. "I have to say, it appeared that you were not having the least bit of a good time."

She acknowledged this with a nod. "I regret to say that the play was not as satisfying as I thought it would be. Minceed was . . . brilliant. She was the one worth watching on every account. I could truly believe that she lost a husband."

"Oh, I agree, but that is exactly what one would expect from a former gilla who grew up in the theater."

Sylvia's eyes grew wide with interest. "Really now! High and bloodlined! I had no idea!"

"The girl is free now, of course. She stopped doing roles for the skin shows to pursue a serious career, adopting the Minceed name while doing so."

"I suppose that is not common knowledge?" asked Sylvia.

"No, and if you care for her career, you'll keep it that way. It is believed that she's a distant Minceed cousin."

"So the Minceeds adopted her into the family. How generous of them," said Sylvia in all seriousness.

"True to gossip, she has no bounds. I wonder what she could have sacrificed to Brigantia to make the Minceeds free her and increase her fortune in such short order," said Lucius.

She shrugged. "She's married to the oldest son. Perhaps they read one of those horrendous fenni romance stories."

Lucius laughed. "I would have no doubt!"

"It proves fascinating how one can rise, does it not?" Sylvia asked, lost in thought.

Lucius shrugged. "Or fall."

This caused her to snap out of the heady revelry of rare romanticism. She raised an eyebrow. "What is your purpose with such words?"

"When someone rises as briskly as she did, they walk on a tightrope. One small breeze could bowl her over. If she knows what is best for her, then she'll keep walking carefully. At least until she can produce a suitable heir for the Minceeds, of course."

"Come now, let us not hope for ruin on the girl. A talent such as hers counts greatly." She pointed at his chest. "You, sir, assume that producing an heir is the main intention for her freedom. I will assume pure, raw talent, and consider love."

"Forgive me, I mean no offense. Talent it could be, but love would be absurd. I know this because the previous wife was barren, and due to that sullied divorce, every patrician house has become unwilling to give their daughters up for his consideration."

She was impressed at his information on the matter. She shifted side to side, finally putting her weight on both feet, making her feel more grounded.

Her lips formed into a mischievous grin. "Let us bet on it, Lucius."

He mimicked the smile while leaning an elbow on the Chronister car. "The price?"

No high patrician would refuse an enticing bet.

"One thousand full kints that she does not get knocked down before producing an heir."

He rubbed his beard once to contemplate the offer.

"I have a slightly different price in mind."

He leaned in, and she did the same until his lips were next to her ear. She put her hand up, covering her mouth in curious wonderment as he finished telling her what he was thinking.

"Yes, I believe that can be arranged. My compromise is that there will be nothing before the bet is done. If I win, I get the thousand. The time limit is half a year. Is this acceptable?"

Lucius bowed slightly. "We have reached an accord."

Sylvia gave him a nod in acknowledgment as his auto, driven by Maield, pulled up. He took Sylvia's hand and kissed it as Maield opened the door for his master.

"Until we meet again, my dear Dé Áine." He tapped Maield on the shoulder, and the auto jaunted down the road. Sylvia noticed the blush in Emlyn's cheeks and felt jealousy creeping up again. She suppressed it until it subsided. But her severe frown remained as a pounding started at her temple.

* * * * *

Sylvia sat heavily onto her favorite white chair, relishing the feel of the blue velvet cushion. It had been a long night, and exhaustion threatened to overtake her. She worried about Emlyn, the conversation with Colmane, and the date with Donsill. She would have preferred instead to stay in and consider the merits of this new switch invention proposed by Cardew Electric. She let the proposal fall, and the papers hit the floor and caught the breeze from the fan running at full speed in the corner, sending them across the room.

Her eyes were heavy, and she squinted as the pain from the headache throbbed. Despite her body begging for rest, sleep would not come anytime soon. So she rested her arms on the flowing ornate supports and swished her legs up on a matching stool before trying to bury herself further into the cushions. She tried her best to get away from the pain. Turning her head to the side, she put a finger on her temple as her brows furrowed.

A glass of water with a tablet at its bottom, fizzing aggressively into its surroundings, appeared before her. She took the tall glass, feeling the nice cool moisture on its surface, and mixed gratefulness into her pained face. "Thank you, Tabby."

Emlyn moved to her mistress's feet and undid the delicate ivory buttons on the boots before grasping the intricately carved leather, inching them off at a glacial pace so that Sylvia would barely notice the act. She put the boots to the side of the stool and placed her hands on the intrinsic muscles of Sylvia's white-stockinged feet. As Emlyn kneaded and pressed in with her thumbs, she methodically lowered the knee-high stockings down below the knee and over her mistress's calf. Emlyn had a lot of practice at this, and her skill produced a delighted moan from her mistress.

Sylvia looked at Emlyn. It was a perfect angle to watch such strong, knowing fingers at work. They were almost hypnotic. She started to relax as she sank further into the chair. It was late, long past the time to retire, but she found her eyes closing inch by inch despite the headache. She kept watching those fingers move rhythmically as she drank the fizzy water and thought back to when she and Emlyn were at the age of seven, when she had seen Stella doing the same thing.

She only fought for a moment to keep her eyes open before they closed like falling shutters.

CHAPTER EIGHT

-TABBY-

"You find it?"

Emlyn, feeling exasperated, yelled back at Sylvia from beyond the bushes, "No!"

"I'm sorry, Tabby!" Sylvia yelled from the clearing, feeling rather guilty for what she had done. Emlyn ignored her. She was angry and thought that Sylvia was being a sore loser.

She did not want to play this game, a simple game of catch that became heated over time as they tried to make each other miss the ball. She knew that her best friend, smaller and slower than she, stood no chance. Upon realizing this, Sylvia would become angry, and she certainly did just that. But it did no good to dwell on this since Emlyn had to find the ball before her parents found out and scolded her. Perhaps worse if it was just Stella doing the scolding.

Emlyn made no response. No, sir. No way. No how. No time to respond in this search; she was still angry.

Instead, someone else did the responding. "Is this what you're looking for?"

Emlyn looked up at black pants tucked into calf-high boots.

The knees bent, and a hand with the yellow ball they had been playing with rested on the palm. She tried to take it, but the hand kept it beyond her reach. She looked up at the hard face of Cassius Chronister, the only son. She scowled.

"Now that's not how someone like you should react," he mocked.

She did not understand what he could mean. Cassius was thirteen and had just returned from a visit to relatives living in the high country. Emlyn's older brother, Thom, studious and plain-looking, stood straight as an arrow to the right of Cassius.

A few months ago, Emlyn and Sylvia were forced to stay with a friend of the family, and it turned out to be a vacation at a peach orchard. They had such a fun time on Uncle Caul's estate getting to know Sylvia's very distant cousins. But when they returned, Thom and Cassius had vanished. And for a whole month their parents would give them little explanation.

When the boys came back, Thom was no longer a talker. He used to have a way with conversation that could steer it in any direction he desired. He had no problem conversing with her, telling her jokes and wondrous stories filled with adventure in faraway lands. Those stories thrilled her and made her ache to experience them.

Now it was gone. He was missing a spark that made him . . . *him*. Instead it had been replaced with an unsettling quietness that made her stay as far away as she could. She missed him, who she considered the real him, not the creature he was now. It seemed like a fae copied his image and her real brother was locked up in some otherworldly prison.

Cassius tossed the ball gently to her, and she caught it. "You had better get up off your knees, girl, before you dirty that pretty dress."

She did so, coming up to her full height just below his chest.

"Good girl."

She cocked her head to the side, raising an eyebrow and wondering why he was talking to her this way. He was so kind before that first trip. Now he treated her no better than scum on the bottom of his boot. When he looked at her, there seemed to be some sort of sick joke resting right behind the surface of his grin. A joke that she knew deep down involved her in one way or another.

"Just like a dog—"

Thom placed a hand on his shoulder, interrupting him.

"Right, right. Forget I said anything, Emlyn." He bent down to her height. "Fancy playing a game, little Emlyn?"

She looked hopeful that maybe they had not changed so much after all, but she responded with more than a little caution. "Really? We can play?"

He smiled. She knew then that it was just a mask and became uncertain of their intentions. She took a few steps back.

"Let's play where's Emlyn's cat?"

She blinked a few times, uncomprehending of the intent. Then it fell on her, and the thoughts it produced were terrible indeed.

"W-what'd you do with Lady Baxster?" Tears started forming in her eyes.

"Now is not the time to cry, little Emlyn, time is sensitive."

Emlyn's tears continued to well up.

"Suck it up, Emlyn."

Hearing those commanding, cold words that she was used to hearing from her mother now coming from Thom startled her. Making her suck back the tears and the snot that was threatening to come out. This was not the brother she once knew. No, not at all.

Sylvia came through the bushes to stand next to her. She looked Emlyn over, noticing the remnants of the choked-back tears. Sylvia crossed her arms and sneered up at her older brother.

"Why're you making Tabby cry?"

He smirked with assured confidence. "You two pay too much attention to that . . . pet."

Emlyn looked over at Sylvia; the tears threatened to boil over. "T-they hid Lady Baxster!"

Sylvia looked at her brother again with a mixture of anger and concern. "She has babies!"

"Yes, well, you'll have to find them too." Cassius laughed.

Both of the girls bit their lips and looked at each other, sharing fear between them.

"Go! Shoo!" He spread his arms as if commanding a dog, so they ran, with Cassius's laughter following in their wake.

* * * * *

The girls burst into the nursery area connected to Emlyn and Sylvia's bedroom, breathing heavily, eyes wide with fear and utmost urgency. They called for the cat but heard no response, no meow or even the little squeaks of kittens. They looked under and behind everything that could be moved, but only found some fur and the cat bed shoved under the blue and white patterned sofa.

They did not have to say anything to each other. Their emotions were there to read in every movement. Without speaking, they both thundered into their bedroom and turned the once pristine room into an area of maximum clutter.

The two girls searched the entire wing that housed Emlyn's family, barring her parents' room. No signs of life appeared except for Emlyn's grandmother, who had seen nothing, and if Emlyn could believe anyone, it was the warm smile and inviting face of Grandmother Cali.

At their wit's end, panic permeated the air and manifested across their faces. Goosebumps rose as the fear of what might've happened started dripping into their minds, and even though it was the last resort, it was time to bother their parents.

The insula was huge. It took a long time to search around the dozens of rooms being diligently cleaned by servants and gilla. They did not impede those people, for the girls were threatened with fearful punishments if they did so. They both came upon Sylvia's mother in the garden next to a water feature dedicated to a statue of the Dé Morri, Goddesses of fate and war, and death.

Sylvia came up behind Camilla, who was sitting upon a wooden folding chair. As Sylvia came around, she noticed Stella rubbing her mother's feet. She thought she spotted a glint of metal upon Stella's neck but was distracted by Emlyn running up from behind. She looked back and the glint was gone. It left her mind when her mother looked over at her with concern.

"Sylvia, darling, what is wrong?"

Sylvia stared back at her mother and found it hard not to cry. She could not find any words, but before she could squeak out, Emlyn took over. "Lady Baxster and the kittens are missing. Cassius and Thom . . . they hid them!"

Camilla sighed and moved her feet, which signaled for Stella to stop. She sat her bare soles on the ground and turned, locking eyes with her daughter.

Stella looked at Emlyn evenly and spoke as if it was a chore to do so. "It was mine and your father's wish that your pets be done away with."

Emlyn's face drained of color. "W-why?" she said in a whine.

Stella's entire demeanor became stern. "You're too old, and you're spending more time with that cat instead of focusing on your studies. Do not dare cry over this, girl!"

Emlyn held her emotions back by biting her lower lip. Instead they seemed to be directed and transferred to Sylvia, who burst out crying like a broken dam. Camilla picked her daughter up, putting her on her lap, hugging and soothing her. "Shhhh, it's okay. How about some honey candy?"

Emlyn stood there, hands behind her back, fingers bouncing, lacing and unlacing. She bit her quivering lower lip even harder to keep the flood back. She could taste the iron of blood. She watched Camilla carry Sylvia away, and even though she wanted to follow, she remained glued to the spot. Emlyn could feel her mother's unyielding gaze upon her. She focused her attention on the ground, having found it too difficult to look into that face.

"Look at me, Emlyn."

Emlyn did so hesitantly and found her anger slowly building.

"We indulged you for far too long. You should have never had any pets. Damn your father for allowing it, and damn me for going along with—"

Emlyn's anger boiled over. She clenched her fists and dug her nails into her palms. "Why are you so mean!"

Stella's eyelids almost disappeared as her brows furrowed. She stalked toward Emlyn like a charging bear defending its territory, bent only on her destruction. Emlyn backed up a few yards and turned to run, but her ankle twisted. She squeaked and fell hard on her knees. A rock scuffed one knee, making her yelp in pain. She turned in time to see Stella bearing down. In response she put her hand up in a feeble attempt at protection.

Stella stood over her with a fist raised in the air, ready to come down upon the girl with terrible force. From between her raised arms, she stared out at her mother. The anticipation of the coming pain ebbed away. Time seemed to slow, and it became clear that Stella was making no motion. She wondered if this was to make her lower her guard for the strike. To her surprise, and what little relief she could gain, Stella lowered her fist.

"You should be ashamed for letting your clothes get stained! Now get up and go change them!" Stella turned on her heel and walked in the opposite direction.

Emlyn blinked a few times, unbelieving that her mother was not going to strike. She waited until the sound of Stella slamming a door resonated across the garden.

Her terror ebbed away at a snail's pace. She placed her hands on the wet grass and tried to lift up, but when she moved her feet, pain shot through her ankle, making her teeth grit. She collapsed back on the ground and started crying. Not for herself, she was used to this treatment. She cried for Lady Baxster: a little tabby cat she had saved on a roof a few years back.

She remembered playing in their shared bedroom. An insistent meowing emanated from outside the window. They looked at each other, and together they went to peer out of the glass. They were on the fourth floor, looking out over the steepled roof protruding before them. Water hit the glass panels like knuckles rapping violently on a door.

They narrowed their eyes for a better look through the dense rainfall. At the end of the long roof sat a pitiful-looking kitten, drenched and matted. Sylvia convinced—no, begged—Emlyn to climb out the window and save it. Emlyn was always more athletic, even at that age. So she gathered up her nerve and climbed out onto the wet, slick roof into the pelting rain. The rain hit hard, almost stung her skin in an unrelenting bombardment. She kept her eyes away from the ground, going slow, repeating to herself, "Go slow. Forget the rain." Her hands were careful to grasp the tiled spine of the roof inch by excruciating inch. When she reached the kitten, it hissed, warning her away. She put out her hand, and as she came close to grasping it, she got bit. She hissed at the pain but recovered quickly and focused. Emlyn narrowed her eyes, then lifted her wounded hand and waited for the right moment . . . there! She snatched the kitty by the scruff of the neck before it could react.

There was no going back with just one free hand, so she put the cat's scruff in her mouth, keeping a firm grip, and headed carefully backward, slow as a snail. It took so long that her teeth started to hurt.

Sylvia jumped up and down, clapping and giving whispered cheers for their safe return. Upon seeing the kitten in her mouth, Sylvia was thrilled and barely able to keep her squeal of delight down.

From then on Sylvia called Emlyn Tabby. Her brother Thom loved the story. Her father was deeply disappointed for putting herself in such danger, but when she asked to keep it, he agreed. For almost two years she took care of Lady Baxster. Not too long ago she met a feral and produced four cute little healthy kittens whose eyes were already open and curious about everything. She loved chasing them about and bringing them back to their mother. Every day Emlyn would go to the kitchen and Ms. Cord would hand her a saucer of milk to feed them. Cord had said that she would like one when they grew up to keep the rats away from the pantry.

Briar found her in the garden. She hoped he had no harsh words. He just shook his head, picked her up easily in his arms, and brought her to the kitchen.

Ms. Cord shooed everyone out upon seeing him, put her hands on her hips and then looked at her sympathetically. "Ah, Briar. What happened to the poor lass?"

"Knee scraped and twisted ankle."

She took a look at the offending knee and tsked. "Bit more than a scrape. Sit her down in the chair."

She was seated in one of the two chairs flanking the small kitchen table near the outside door. As Ms. Cord searched around in a small hanging medicine cabinet, Briar went to one knee and looked into Emlyn's eyes.

"Emlyn, I could not let you keep Lady Baxster any longer. I should have taken her away from you that night. I thought of it as a reward, that you deserved it." Her lip quivered, causing him to quickly follow up. "You can be sad that your cat is no longer here, but you have no reason to worry about her safety. I made sure she and her kittens went to a suitable home."

"Really, Papa?" said Emlyn, hopeful yet disbelieving. "Everyone makes it sound like they did something terrible to her."

She caught a smirk appearing on his face, but as soon as she blinked it was gone.

"I will have a talk with Cassius and Thom about teasing you, and your mother . . . you know how she is."

"An' you should know better than to antagonize her," said Ms. Cord.

Emlyn looked down at her bruising ankle and felt guilty. "I'm sorry for talking back."

Ms. Cord handed Briar two different bottles of healing cream and a roll of bandages.

"There is no reason to be sorry," he said as he applied one of the creams to her knee. She seethed, taking in the pain. He wrapped the knee, then gently started on her ankle. How could her papa be so kind when Stella was so mean? Camilla was so nice to Sylvia. Why could she not have a mother like that? Emlyn had no luck in figuring out why. Papa only ever said that it was her way.

Sylvia bounded down the stairs like a wild squirrel loosed in the insula.

"Stop running before I give ya another spanking!" yelled Ms. Cord.

Sylvia skidded to a halt after seeing Emlyn. Kittie hurried down the stairs, trying to catch up to her ward. She bent over, hands on her knees, trying to catch her breath. "How did you get so fast, little one?"

Upon seeing Briar, Kittie stood up straight and blushed. "I-I'm sorry, sir."

Briar grinned, truly smiled. "Don't worry yourself, sweet."

Hearing the word *sweet*, Sylvia drove her hand into her skirt pocket and brought out a piece of honey candy.

"Is it okay if I give Tabby some candy, Mr. Gwen?"

He nodded.

She rushed to Tabby and gently handed her the candy. "I snuck a few into my pockets," she whispered.

This bit of mischief made Emlyn smile.

Sylvia rocked back and forth on her heels. "Is it bad?"

Emlyn thought for a moment. "No, I'm used to it."

Sorrow for her friend contorted her face. "I'm sorry."

"She's bad enough to be bedridden for the next few days," said Briar as he gathered her up in his arms again. He looked at Kittie and smiled. "Meet me in my chambers later tonight?"

Her cheeks took on a rosy color. "Yes, of course, love."

He carried Emlyn up the steps. Sylvia followed closely behind them. Emlyn looked over her father's shoulder, then down at her friend and grinned.

"Got good news about Lady Baxster."

CHAPTER NINE

Emlyn wiped the sweat away from her forehead. High or low, her kind could not wear hats nor take advantage of a parasol, for those items were status symbols of a higher class. But exceptions were made on estates or during travel. This did not fit either option. She kept her head down because of the blinding sun, preventing her from surveying the surroundings properly. She cursed the building she leaned against for not having an awning. In fact, none of the buildings had awnings. It seemed a crazy thing not to have during this oppressive summer.

She could see the well-maintained bright red bricks of the walkway and hear boots clicking and clacking by. She made a study of the boots, determined rich from poor and when they were last cleaned. All of them slowed down when they came near to stare at the gilla possessing a revolver and killing knife before moving on with their own matters.

She sighed and whispered to herself, "Another scorching day in paradise."

One pair of shined boots of a deep walnut brown stopped in front of her. "You've been waiting a while I see."

Her gaze started up the boots to the plain black tucked-in pants. A red leather belt wrapped around a brown long vest that was decorated with yellow embroidery resembling leaves blowing in the wind. The pattern made her long for a cool breeze. His brilliant white shirt had its sleeves rolled up with the open collar unbuttoned down to his chest. The pit of the shirt showed little sign of sweat, telling her that he'd recently stepped out into this heat. She continued up, resting her eyes on the freshly shaved face of Colmane, a look she thought suited him more than the sharp goatee.

He brought out a heavy white cotton handkerchief from the inner pocket of his vest and tossed it to her. "Make yourself presentable. You represent not only your mistress but me as well. Make sure your conduct is satisfactory."

She wiped her face with the cloth. "If my behavior is unsatisfactory to you in the least, then my mistress will see fit to punish me." She did not hand the handkerchief back since he made no move to accept it. No accepting soiled rags from a gilla.

"Then we have an understanding." He turned. "Follow me."

They walked through a group of children who splashed and laughed in a few large wash tubs lined in front of an apartment block. They passed small vendors hocking finger foods and trinkets under shady trees before coming to a corner and turning.

Her gaze rested on the Lucanis Basilica; it was hard to miss and drew one's eye. It was where representatives throughout Kymbri held a Cened a few times a year to air grievances and propose new laws. This group was mostly made up of high patricians, landowners, and royalty. The meetings could last up to half a year depending on the severity of whatever situation happened to occur, or to support a new Teyrn.

The basilica had a shining emerald dome perched like a hat on top of white stone with a brilliant marble facade that could blind if the sun hit it just right. At the start of the dome was a gold band filled with swirling images and representations of the war of two wolves, the battle that all seemed to agree was the beginning of their great nation. The building was flanked by brilliant white towers piercing the sky. They had no edges but instead were just smooth, ending in a point. Heads of traitors used to be placed on top. Now such a thing was considered too barbaric, but if you looked closely, one could still see the bloodstains.

She walked along but could not keep her eyes away from the splendor. She had only beheld it once or twice, and the last time was a particular incident when she tried to run away a week before her breaking. She did not get very far, having been talked down by a druidi priest.

As the basilica overtook the sky, Colmane turned down an inviting alleyway. They passed under yellow arches onto a path made up of red bricks in repeating circular patterns. The alley opened up into a large area full of grass and trimmed hedges, and from here the path became lined with smooth, straight columns resembling tall mushrooms with small yellow heads. The columns held up a canopy above them full of vines and lush vegetation. The resemblance to a man's phallus was intended and difficult to ignore.

At the end of the path sat a circular building made of white marble, five stories high. Each story had modest-sized windows, and many windows on the top floor possessed small balconies. Ledges circled around the building at ten-foot intervals, almost like ribs. Its top was also decorated with vegetation. This was a blonde palace where certain pleasure gilla plied their trade. One might believe the ancient gardens of Babylon held a similar resemblance. Emlyn was certain that was the intention. She had a dislike for pleasure gilla. She had never met one, but she learned about them. Like martials, they had their own rituals, training, and outlook as well as bloodlines that went even further back than her own. And like martials, they were very concerned about those bloodlines. But they had no loyalty to their owners. Instead their loyalty went to their large families, who kept each other in line and hence could operate independently from their masters.

As she brushed a hanging vine away from her face, Colmane seemed to sense her questions. "Another murder occurred last night within this establishment, and it had the same modus operandi as the previous killings. I want you to see it. To roll that eye of detail of yours over the crime scene and see what you can find."

Emlyn nodded, noticing the lack of solicitation under the green canopies. A murder in a collared harlots' place of service could do that. It made an unusually quiet atmosphere, antithesis to the surrounding architecture full of virile life and vibrance.

The door was closed and covered by half-cylinder concrete tiles, but this was just an illusion. The tiles slid up into each other at a reasonable speed like a stage curtain rising at the beginning of a play. It was meant to make the customer feel as if they were entering another world, but Emlyn and Colmane thought nothing of it. Even less so for Emlyn since she knew how it worked, knew when they stepped on the stone that activated the machine and could hear the hum of the electricity coming from below.

They walked into the wide-open oval foyer lined with white-and-yellow floor-to-ceiling columns. Fans whirled at the top of the structure, sending air tumbling down onto the two visitors, who took it like a man who had walked across a desert grasping his first glass of water.

"We're closed. The Collared Peacock is down that-a-way. It's cheaper fare but decent." The man was sitting behind a desk in the middle of the foyer, pointing without looking up. His stocky build and platinum blonde hair stood out, even though his face was buried in the morning newspaper.

"I prefer a certain amount of . . . class."

The man looked up, recognizing the voice. "Mr. Colmane!"

He hopped up from his chair and came around the desk to greet him with a warm handshake. The man's face was close to perfectly proportioned. Emlyn imagined the shining face of Ard Belenus as a good comparison.

"I did not expect you to return so soon! Four hours seems hardly enough sleep!"

"After seeing what happened to that poor lad, I'd rather get this investigation over with quickly so we can all get a good night's rest."

"True enough. The thought of someone willing to do that, stalking the streets, it—"

Colmane interrupted, "Scares the mind?"

The man nodded. "Yes, quite." He looked over at Emlyn. "Hardly seems your type."

Colmane glanced back at her, taking a moment to respond. "She is the martial of Sylvia Chronister, on loan to me for the investigation. Refer to her as Emlyn, or Gwen, if you must."

"Very well," said the proprietor. "Martials, we don't see them much, but not *too* uncommon. We get our share of high patricians of course. When they do bring a martial, we tell them to wait in the library, but since we are closed, the children are running amok in there with that jib of a teacher. So the parlor room will have to do, I think."

"You misunderstand me; she will be accompanying me to the scene and beyond. The fact that she has an eye for the details should suffice for reason."

"A martial in pleasure quarters? Preposterous!" He waved in dismissal.

Colmane clasped the man's hand with both of his. "Listen, my friend. She's coming with me, so suspend your traditions for the circumstance for a while, eh? And restrain yourself from going to the papers, at least for a time. I do not need that distraction."

He released the proprietor's hand. The man held up two full kints. He turned them over, inspecting the quality. "Anything you desire, Mr. Colmane." He pocketed the coins.

Colmane nodded and patted him on the shoulder. "Good man." He nodded at Emlyn, signaling her to follow.

They climbed the marble stairs past a statue of Venus Áine standing atop the short column that acted as the start of the banister. The old Roman Goddess was often equated to Dé Áine, and Londinium still had a strong cultural streak remaining from that dead empire.

Voices could be heard coming from above, making Colmane stop in his tracks.

"Oh, Briganti," he said under his breath.

The two strangers came into view, and upon sighting Colmane, they grinned and then hurried down to meet him. The older man in front had a long peppered beard wrapped in golden rings. The man behind him had the typical look of a peacer: flat-billed hat and short bluish-gray uniform.

"Gilla catcher!" He held out a hand.

Colmane hid a sneer. "Inspector Nary." They grasped each other's wrist in a cold greeting.

"Has a pleasure gilla absconded? Another Merri-Grew perhaps?"

Colmane did his best to come across as even "I am here for the same reason as you."

"Ah, that. There is nothing to see really. The killer was in a hurry and left nothing behind. You know the rest, of course, but check for yourself if you must. You know . . ." He gave a dramatic pause. "You should be working under me on this."

"I will not."

"Then you should stay in your realm, catcher. Go find those twins. That will gain you the notoriety you so desperately seek. Excuse me."

Colmane and Emlyn stood against the banister, allowing the inspector and peacer to pass by.

"Farewell, gilla catcher!" Nary said, flippantly waving a hand.

Emlyn looked at Colmane and could hear him grinding his teeth. She knew who Hwyfar Nary was, the wain inspector, and a high patrician. She was unsure if he recognized her, though, and had no idea whether it would be a bad thing if he did.

Colmane furrowed his brows. "He believes that I have the resources to chase a group of gilla pirates around pan-Celtia?" He swallowed. "People like that should take a wrong step off a high bridge."

They stepped onto the fifth floor. The door on the right, just off the stairs, was guarded by a scowling uniformed peacekeeper. Colmane smiled at him, getting a nod in response without any hassle. His menacing eyes stared at Emlyn's weapons as they passed into the room, but he made no attempt to stop her.

The door creaked open; Emlyn's eyes widened in surprise. While she was used to brutality, this was a few steps beyond barbarity. The body was sprawled out, legs apart. The arms were laid out straight from the sides exactly in the middle of the room. The ribs were splayed open like some hand of a giant skeletal figure in the midst of escaping its ghastly confines. It made Emlyn think of some of the grim sacrifices portrayed in an especially gruesome crime book. Blood had pooled out from the body onto the rug beneath, which soaked it up to the point where you would think the rug had always been red, not yellow. Barely anything remained completely untouched by blood. It contrasted grotesquely with the virginal white of the room. It looked like an accidental painting, as if an artistic butcher opened shop in an opulent mansion.

As they approached the body, it became clear that the heart had been taken out and stuffed in the mouth roughly.

She noticed the angle of the bones and remembered the description from one of the newspaper articles mentioning how the ribs were broken at the spine, angled straight out like wings. These ribs were angled in multiple directions with most broken off at the ends.

"He was trying to get to the heart as quickly as possible before anyone came back. He might not have paid for the room yet?" She gritted her teeth and sucked in. "I'm sorry for speaking out of turn, Master."

It did not escape her notice that since they entered the room, Colmane's eyes had not left her.

"Nonsense; speak freely. Your opinions could be a great help to the case. Look around, take notes if you must, just don't disturb anything."

She nodded assent, then proceeded to cast her eyes around the room. "From what I know of pleasure palaces, every floor from the second on up are bedrooms. The most spacious and comfortable ones are at the top, which contain the senior and best-earning gilla. Who resides in this room?

"Thacia Trill-Mercer."

Pleasure gilla were high gilla due to long bloodlines. Like martials, they were allowed more dignified names and surnames. Unlike martials, they took the name of the family that owned them, in this case the Mercer family, who had owned the Trill for many hundreds of years. It was theorized that the Trill were an original tribe of Caledonia subjugated and sold when Rome ruled half of the island over fifteen hundred years ago. As it was, the Trill-Mercers were considered top-of-the-line golden-haired courtesans.

"Obviously we are not looking at a murdered gilla." She bent down next to the body, reaching her hand out to the collarless throat.

"Be careful," said Colmane.

She felt along the dead man's clammy neck, drained of so much blood that it resembled the color of snow. "The neck has abrasions, not from choking but from years spent in a collar. Did the killer remove it?"

"He was a freeman, a member of the Trill-Mercers. Freed last year to be exact. He stayed and was paid to protect his kin on the top floor."

"He must have earned it well," said Emlyn.

She looked at the man's hands, then around the room. "No weapons." She turned one of his hands and studied it front and back. "He has not held a weapon in his life, or at least, never did any hard labor. Nor are there any calluses or abrasions on his knuckles. Protection is too strong a word."

Colmane stared at the back of Emlyn's head as she continued to inspect the body.

"Miss Emlyn, do you ever think of freedom? Tell me honestly."

She did not know what was more shocking, the question, or being addressed by an honorary title. It made her miss a beat.

"My . . . collar has no key."

"Heard that one before. I wonder if the Merri-Grews said the same thing before the Isle of Bel massacre."

Emlyn held back the disgust at the comparison, as if she could ever do such a thing.

He went to the other side of the room to look out the window situated next to the doors of a balcony as Emlyn rose, spotting something on the ledge. "Scuff marks on the rail, from boots. The killer definitely exited through this window."

She took a peek below. There were two limestone walls, at least thirty yards from each other. They were connected to the pleasure palace all the way to a nondescript, plain five-story building on the other side. It made an elongated, enclosed courtyard. Below the window, Trill-Mercer gilla bathed in a man-made clear pond. They sang a sad song. Its lament of loss wafted up the walls and through the windows.

O'brother can you hear us sing?
Can you hear the birds in the trees
or the rustling of the leaves
Can you hear the crack of thunder?
O'brother does sound travel, does it ring?
In the ground laid to sleep.
Sleep well o'brother sleep well.
Rest well, rest well o'brother."

Some of the other gilla counseled each other in the middle of the courtyard where many chairs and tables were located. Hands upon their heads, they sobbed, adding to the sorrowful song. The older ones, most without collars, prepared meat and vegetables near the other house. As they cut, they held themselves glumly. Next to them were others vigorously washing clothing in a large metal basin, using the act as a type of meditation to cope with the recent loss.

All the men and women were bred to be ideal beauties. Most telling was how content they seemed to be despite the murder of one of their own. Such an insular folk with a strange belief that they were being punished by some God and had to earn their freedom. She doubted any of them knew what their ancestors did to deserve such a fate.

"Think any of them might have seen the killer?" Asked Emlyn. He did not respond. "Colmane?"

"What did you say?" He turned his head in her direction.

"Did anyone see the killer?"

"No . . . whoever it was, they were wearing a mask and a hooded cape."

She gave him a queer look. "Is that not a bit odd?"

"Not at all. Many do not want to show their identity in a place like this where they could be easily recognizable. A married man for instance, whose wife disapproves of places like this, would not like word getting back to her."

"So no one paid enough attention to determine gender?"

Colmane shrugged. "No, not specifically. He or she did not speak, only passing notes. But the killer was tall, around six foot by accounts, and you would have to have quite a bit of strength to do all this."

He walked to the body and peered into the terrified eyes of the dead man. Colmane reached into his own pockets and brought out two fennis. He closed the eyes and placed them on the freeman's lids.

"I was working on a theory that the killer's intended victims were gilla that have failed in one way or another. I think the killer views freemen as failed gilla. Perhaps he thinks of their freedom as some sort of punishment instead of an ultimate reward for rendered service."

"It seems likely that Thacia was the target," said Emlyn assuredly.

He crossed his arms. "I considered it, but I've had no chance to converse with the girl yet. She was too upset to question properly last night."

Colmane went to a panel on the left side of the room and grasped a pearl doorknob. "She's in the room next door. Return to a respectful mode."

"Of course, Master."

He turned the handle, opening the door to an equally large bedroom.

A well-proportioned woman wearing only a red silk robe, embroidered with white flowers, sat in the middle of an almost blindingly white fluffy bed. She startled at the sound of the creaking door, jumped off the bed, and quickly went to the window, ready to jump out onto the ledge below.

Her body trembled, obviously afraid of being next. She calmed herself down as Colmane stepped into the room behind Emlyn.

"I'd rather not see your pretty little bottom flattened on the ground, so restrain yourself from jumping out that window if you please."

"Master Colmane!" she exclaimed, her fear taken away. The girl immediately got to her knees, then prostrated herself on the floor.

"No need for that. Get up."

As she rose, her face showed grateful relief, until noticing Emlyn's weapons. The sight of a martial in one of the bedrooms made her tense up.

She narrowed her eyes, looking from Emlyn to Colmane with noticeable anger, but he slapped her across the cheek, making her fall back on the bed. Her robes sprawled about like falling feathers.

The split second it took for Colmane to turn from a caring and understanding master to hard and vicious surprised Emlyn. She felt a little sorry for the girl despite how martials were typically viewed by the likes of pleasure gilla; stuffy, arrogant, chaste statues with no passion were the sum of the slurs.

"I do not care about your tradition when hosting her kind! I do not care if you fear her or resent her. She is my associate for today, and you will treat her as a superior, for she has the right to chastise you. Are we clear?"

Thacia's cheeks reddened, contrasting with her platinum-blonde hair. "Yes, Master." Her voice wavered and dried from Colmane's sudden fury. She swallowed before sitting upright, making sure not to meet his eyes.

Her voice was controlled with just a twist of sultry, exactly as she was taught. "How may I serve you, Master?"

Colmane crossed his arms. "Last night you went into hysterics upon seeing the body. Were you two close? Speak freely, gilla."

She looked up at him. "May I pour myself some water?"

"You may."

Thacia stood, still holding her cheek and kept herself steady, then headed to a white nightstand with a clear glass pitcher and a simple glass cup on top. With a trembling hand, she took her time pouring the water and then drank it like a quick shot of whiskey. She poured again, then turned slowly to face them, but she did not look up. Instead she stared into the cup, letting the ripples remind her of some memory, and whatever that memory was, it seemed to calm her.

She gathered herself up, managing to find a return to a persona she seemed more comfortable in. It anchored her. She raised her head to look between the two, much more confident in overall deportment.

"I have seven brothers and sisters. You would think that would be a bit alienating. No, we were close, and Fionn . . . well . . . he was the best eldest brother one could have, simple as that. He—"

She stopped, clearly not used to talking like this about herself to a master, but Colmane did not make any motion for her to cease. He was letting her go on.

"He helped us. Comforted us. Talked us through . . . every moment of disobedience. Made us understand, not with a heavy hand but with love. We celebrated his freedom." She looked to the ground. "That he would still be here watching over us." She choked up again.

"Walk me through the previous evening."

Colmane prevented her from slipping too far into those memories. She lifted the cup to her lips and drank again.

"My shift was over, so I was taking a nap in the courtyard."

He raised an eyebrow, questioning the act.

"I'd had enough of hearing my siblings service customers in the other rooms. Certain spots in the courtyard can be very peaceful at night when everyone's asleep." She continued, "Well, Rory came to fetch me, saying a customer was paying a lot of money for my services. He said the customer was waiting with Fionn in my room."

"Did he mention anything about this customer?" asked Colmane.

"Rory didn't speak to . . . whoever the brosthun was. He only mentioned a heavy black cloak and a filigree face mask, a full mask, with an eagle's beak." She said this making a pantomime of a cape and mask.

"Why was the killer after you?" asked Emlyn.

Thacia stared at her wide-eyed. The hair on the back of her neck stood as fear crept into her face. This was something she had not considered. Her finger pressed to her lips as she retreated into remembrance, turning the cogs in her mind. Colmane took a cigarette case from a pouch on his belt and lit one.

"I-I've no idea! Do you really think this . . . person was after me?"

Emlyn crossed her arms. "He was going to pay for you. Have you ever failed a client? Perhaps disobeyed someone in a more public manner?"

Anger creased Thacia's forehead. "How dare you ask me that!"

"Give her an answer!" Colmane's commanding voice boomed through the room like thunder.

Thacia sat hard on the bed, making her body bounce a little on the fluffy mattress. She twisted to face them, offended, but clearly afraid of Colmane. She held sternness in her voice. "No! I'm a good girl!" She grabbed her collar with both hands. "My collar has no lock!"

Emlyn bowed her head. "My apologies. I didn't mean to insinuate that you were a bad gilla."

Thacia opened her mouth to say something, but snapped her jaw shut. She looked Emlyn up and down, studying her form. Her face relaxed with the motion, releasing the anger. She turned her head down and stared at her lap, lost in thought once again. "No. There was plenty of time to do me harm. It was just Rory and I who came into the room, and Rory is a small thing who weighs no more than a feather."

"Master."

He looked at Emlyn. "Yes?"

"Maybe the killer was indeed after Fionn. He came here after Thacia's shift. There is little reason for a Trill-Mercer to leave their palace, free or not, unless they are leased. Perhaps he was looking for the best opportunity to strike and found it."

Colmane rubbed his chin. He understood what Emlyn was saying but felt he had to say it out loud, let it soak a little. "That is a possibility. Freemen do not advertise their status, so it would be easier to discern such a thing in a place like this where everyone working here is obviously related. And if they wear no collar, then you can be fairly certain they were freed."

Thacia looked between them. "You're saying that this . . . monster is targeting freemen?"

He looked down at her, narrowing his eyes. "That is not your concern. Return yourself to a respectful mode of speech."

Frightened, she lowered her eyes. "Yes, Master."

Emlyn paid no mind to Thacia. "Master, we should check the ground outside the window."

He finished the cigarette and put what was left in Thacia's cupped hands. "Agreed."

They were in no hurry as they walked back down the marble steps. Thacia trailed a few paces behind them. As they went by the last white marble banister, past the Venus Áine, Emlyn noticed a large open door.

The warmth of the room emanated into the stark high opulence of the open foyer. She could spot at least four blonde-headed children and one light-brown-haired child. Emlyn suspected there were more she could not see in the library of floor-to-ceiling bookcases. They were paying close attention to a distinguished-looking woman in her forties reading what seemed to be an engaging story. The older blonde woman looked very happy in what she was doing, with creases appearing around her mouth from a genuine smile. Emlyn listened closer at the last few words and knew it was an old shootist story.

The woman snapped the book shut and declared the class ended for the day. In the next instance a total of eight children stampeded out into the foyer. The three stopped to let the children pass by. The kids slowed down after realizing a master was near. They avoided Colmane but stared at Emlyn in curiosity as they went by. Thacia waved to them happily and talked to one of the older girls who was very concerned about Thacia's emotional health. She responded by giving the girl a well-squeezed hug and reassured her that she was indeed okay.

Emlyn realized something as the kids left through the back door into the courtyard. She swung her head toward Thacia.

"Those children, they're collared. Do they know they're gilla?"

Thacia looked a little bewildered at the question. "Of course! It would do no good for our purposes to tell them they're free. To hide them from the realities of the world, that would be cruel."

Emlyn scowled and looked her up and down with disgust.

Thacia crossed her arms, furrowing her eyebrows. "Did it do you any good?"

Emlyn turned and faced her fully, almost nose to nose. This . . . pleasure gilla had no right to question martial methodology.

"Obviously," said Emlyn.

Colmane interrupted them with his room-filling voice. "Enough! Come along, Emlyn!"

She looked into Thacia's eyes a few seconds longer, daggers trying to penetrate a wall. Emlyn turned to follow him out.

Thacia went up to the doorway, looking after them. At the same time, she was watching the grave men and a druidi priest coming from the opposite direction. The blonde-haired man running the counter joined her at her side. "What did you learn?"

"More than I wanted to hear," she said, sounding downtrodden at the sight of the grave men.

* * * * *

Colmane looked up at the window the killer used to escape, the same one Emlyn looked out of earlier. He shielded his eyes from the bright sun. He had been waiting until daylight to take a look but did not see as much as he was hoping for.

"He must have dropped down each ledge. I'm certain the killer was a man, and he would have had to be at least six-foot-five to—"

"Master, I found something."

He looked from the window to Emlyn, who was thigh-deep in the large bathing pool. Her skirt was floating around her on the surface, and her sleeves were soaked from searching the rocky bottom.

Behind Colmane stood a large group of Trill-Mercers, their golden hair glistening in the sunlight, only broken up by a few darker shades. They looked rather angry at having a martial in their pool. Of course, they would say nothing against it with him there.

He'd already questioned all of them but did not get anything more than Inspector Nary was able to extract. But when they mentioned hearing a large splash, then seeing a large figure climb out of the pool and over the wall, Emlyn hitched up her skirt and marched into the water. After thirty minutes, he was beginning to lose patience, but finally Emlyn found *something*. The Trill-Mercers leaned in as their annoyance was replaced with curiosity. She held a small round silver object that looked like a half kint.

"What did you find?"

"An ownership tag. Not a Trill-Mercer." She made her way to the edge of the pool and passed it to Colmane.

"His, you think?"

"Likely so, Master."

After leaving the courtyard, he flipped the tag. "Sissa Delvia. Property of house Barrentine." He closed his fingers around it. "A high gilla, or at least bloodlined! Sissa can be a male name. Do you think this is our man?"

"Hard to say, Master. Delvia is no name I know of, but gilla records could show something."

"That is the easy part. I will have to question the Barrentines. If high patricians don't want to talk, then they don't have to. And you"—he pointed at Emlyn—"will have to question their martials."

She didn't show it, but the prospect of another outing from the insula thrilled her.

He turned the coin over a few more times before placing it in his vest pocket. Then he held out a hand to shake.

Emlyn stared at the hand, uncertain of what to do about it, but as odd as it seemed, if a master wanted to shake hands, then it was best to shake. She tentatively reached out and shook. She had no idea why a catcher would bother to touch her in such a friendly manner when he had refused to take back his handkerchief earlier, it made no sense.

"Thank you, Miss Gwen. I will come by once I have found the name. Soon, if the gilla is high in your or Thacia's way."

The label of high gilla was attributed to anyone born and raised in servitude. Mass breeding or breeding pens were outlawed long ago to keep the number of gilla down, but breeding two individuals was not unlawful. You just had to pay for the license and record changes, which were relatively cheap for people of means.

"Farewell, Master."

After shaking his hand, she watched him disappear around a far corner. She kept staring at that corner perplexed. His dichotomy of treatment, his moments of being in control of everything, cool as running water, then bursting into violent fury, made her curious about the man. She never had to deal with catchers. Were they all like this? She wondered if it was some sort of test. Perhaps he was only curious since he claimed to have never really interacted with a martial except in passing.

She walked back to the insula, avoiding the sun as much as she could by staying in the shade of the tall buildings. It took her longer than she would have liked, but for some reason she did not feel bad about it. She loved being out.

In sight of the insula gates where the servants enter, she let out a sigh in a longing goodbye to the outside world.

CHAPTER TEN
-ENEDDIA-

Emlyn could swear that the walls were closing in. A feeling that had been a constant companion for years. Each day they moved closer and closer, but now they felt especially near. The walls pounded like a sledgehammer on thin metal, sending reverberations through her skull. The table felt rough under her hands despite the smooth polish, and the hard wood of the chair seemed to ignore its useless cushion. And she looked everywhere except at her grandmother.

"Can we just take a minute or two?"

Cali sat on the opposite side of the table and leaned over. Her long snowy hair coiled on its surface. The lines around her eyes moved up in reaction, a smile that Emlyn knew all too well. A familiar blanket of warmth, but Emlyn was determined not to fall for that this time.

"You're doing well, but I need you to finish. Are you having trouble with this one? Is that why you want to stop?"

"I don't want to stop. I just need a break." She leaned back and rubbed her eyes.

Cali reached over the table and tapped one card. "Finish these first, *then* we can talk about a break."

Emlyn put her hands in her lap and looked down at the five expert-level personae cards spaced evenly out before her. All except the last had a painted image of a man in common positions and modes of dress, in color, with clear details.

She tapped the first one. "He's rich."

Cali took the card and turned it facedown. "He's a farm worker."

Emlyn shook her head, disagreeing. "He's dressed down for labor, but his clothes are tailor made. His posture is not bent from years of hard work. He might have the money to hire field hands or buy gilla, but his expression tells me he enjoys it. I would take him for being an honest man."

Cali grinned. "Very good!" She flipped it back over. "Now for the next one."

Emlyn violently wiped her hand across the cards, sending them flying off the side of the table.

"That was uncalled for," said Cali as that smile turned to concern.

"Why am I doing this? Is there some point to it?" yelled Emlyn.

"You need to read people at a glance—"

Emlyn threw her arms to the side and stood up. "But why? I'm fourteen and have no future in business!"

Cali's expression returned to warmth with only slight annoyance to her voice. "We are making you ready for the world, for whatever might happen. If you think these lessons are boring, then fine, they are as fun as you're willing to make them."

"Yet Sylvia is receiving a different education."

"Sylvia is the heir to the Chronister fortune and must learn their family business."

"What are the Gwens then? Some type of ambax? Bodyguards? I know we are not cousins! Not directly! Is that why you and my parents are armed and around Mr. and Mrs. Chronister all the time?"

Cali leaned back in her chair and looked up at Emlyn, straight in the eyes. "If I told you that we're trusted ambaxes who have served the Chronister house for many generations, would that satisfy you?"

Emlyn breathed deep to calm herself. What she just did was disrespectful to her elder, one she liked. If Stella was here, she would have received the beating of a lifetime, but she was not, only kind but stern Grandmother Cali who did not deserve her ire.

She bent to pick up the cards, then sat back down. Cali leaned over the table, snatched the cards away, and put them back in their box so fast that Emlyn had little chance to respond. Instead she only managed a perplexed look.

"You can have your break. I need to go speak with your father," Cali said, letting her annoyance show in full with a twinge of anger. Emlyn could not help it and thought it was directed toward her.

"Am I . . . in trouble?"

"No, this is not your fault. It's his."

Emlyn's heart dropped. Her papa was a strong man, but she had not intended to get him in trouble with Cali. It was the rotten cherry on top of a stale cake.

* * * * *

This was not the courtyard garden, but a small walled-off area with grandiose plants taking up most of the space. A straight path went through the middle to an iron gate.

Emlyn sat on a concrete bench next to the path with her back against the wall of the house. Beside her was the kitchen entrance, where a few of the paid servants came in to work. Ms. Cord had commented on her gloom and gave her a sugar dough pastry hoping it would cheer her up. But the pastry sat untouched by her side.

She stared out of the gate, watching people pass by. It was like looking through a barred portal to another world.

She kicked the grass in frustration, overturning the turf.

A low voice sounded through the wall to her left. A sultry female voice. "Hey, Emlyn."

Surprised, Emlyn scootched to the other side of the bench and put her head close to the brick for a better listen. "Yes, who are you? How do you know my name?"

"I know a lot about you. Go to the gate, and I'll introduce myself."

She did so, heart pounding and laced with curiosity, but when the stranger came into view twirling an open umbrella against a slender shoulder, Emlyn backed up a few steps.

"Do you remember me?"

"You're . . . Eneddia. Sylvia's aunt. You hurt me when I was a kid. You . . . said I was a gilla."

Ened closed her umbrella and hooked it over the inner part of her elbow.

"Yes, yes I did. I am truly sorry for that. I . . . had trouble managing my anger back then. Can you forgive me?" Ened reached a hand through the bars. "Can we shake on it? No hard feelings?"

Emlyn stared at the hand for a moment before moving forward cautiously and giving it a gentle shake.

"There. Friends again. Back then it was purely a misunderstanding on my part." She got closer to the bars for a better look. "I say, one friend to another, you seem very confined. Are you not happy here?"

Looking side to side at the walls, Emlyn bit her lip. She wanted to spill all of her frustrations over . . . everything. Most of the time she would confide in Sylvia, but this was not something her friend, the homebody, the one who got anything she wanted, could understand. She needed an adult to understand, though, and everything about Ened screamed understanding. She looked inviting; her eyes were truly caring. Emlyn remembered her as very plain, but now she seemed to be doing very well for herself. Her outfit was that of a wealthy woman going about town. A white heavily laced dress with a sunhat that sported gigantic pink flowers framed by brown feathers pinned to a purple ribbon.

"Ah, it's true," said Ened. She put a finger to her chin in thought, then snapped her fingers. "I have it!"

"Have what?" asked Emlyn, unsure.

"When was the last time you had flavored ice?"

Emlyn blinked rapidly.

"You never had flavored ice before? What kind of place is this?"

"I'm . . . um . . . not allowed many sweets."

"I bet Sylvia gets all the sweets she can manage and then some."

Emlyn's nose twitched as she tried to hide her annoyance by looking down. She was being spoken to like a child, not the soon-to-be fifteen-year-old she was, but it didn't seem to anger her this time, and perhaps that was because so few people ever treated her like this. Kind and understanding of her frustrations.

"It's not fair, is it? She gets so much more than you. She does not get beaten, rarely scolded . . . How about I take you out for ice? You can pick any flavor you like."

"I . . . don't think I should," she said, looking around wearily.

"You can trust me. I'm Chronister blood, after all. Think of it as a little vacation. I'll have you back here before supper, all right?"

Stepping outside the gate, with more than a little trepidation, Emlyn looked about the city street at the throngs of people tending their own business and paying no attention to them. Something told her this was not right, that she should turn back, but as she looked back at the insula, it worked its foreboding darkness upon her. She would have spit on it, if an insula could feel one way or the other about such an act.

As they walked out of sight from the insula, the cacophony made her heart beat in a pleasant rhythm. She sighed, breathing out all the anxiety and pent-up tension. Happier than she had been in a long time, she could not help but smile and share all that she viewed as unfair.

Emlyn talked about her odd education, the marksmanship, knife fighting, and assessing threats. How the only things they taught both her and Sylvia were basic education in mathematics and literature.

"It's just all a cumber!"

"Uh-huh."

"I mean, I enjoy shooting the revolver . . . a lot!"

"Right."

"I think I'd enjoy learning knife techniques just as much if it wasn't Stella teaching it."

"Yeah."

They sat next to each other on a bench resting on a swath of green grass in the middle of one of the main city roads. Trees dotted this strip of land, and people were everywhere. Behind them, on the other side of the road, a grand wedding was soon to commence. Emlyn kept glancing back at the group, curious about how it would be conducted. She wondered why exactly they were waiting to go inside the temple.

She put the little wooden spoon in the finished orange ice cup and looked to her side at Ened. "I'm sorry, my life must be boring to you."

"No, no, I respect your family and how they do things," said Ened. "I should say that I've grown to have *great* respect for your family's legacy."

"Our legacy? You mean the, um, ambax thing is true?"

"Yes . . . ambax, that's a way to say it. You've been ambaxes for the Chronisters for many generations now. You didn't know about this?"

"No. That's . . . well. Why is it hidden from me if that's the answer?"

Ened shrugged. "It's just the way they do things."

"But . . . why? I don't get it." Emlyn huffed. "It's just unfair leaving me in the dark. They won't even let me go anywhere unless it's the country estate, and when we go there, I'm watched constantly. Well, except when Sylvia convinced me to sneak out with her to the festival last year. I got beaten well for that one."

This got Ened's attention. "Sylvia convinced you to sneak out?"

"Well, I wanted to go, so I went. But Sylvia never gets beaten. We actually had a lot of fun! I wish we could go this year!"

"I thought you didn't like Sylvia?"

"No, no! I love Sylvia! She's my best friend!"

"But you said it was unfair."

Emlyn sighed and twiddled her thumbs. "Well, yeah, I'm a little jealous, but . . . she never treats me unfairly. Not really. She even sneaks me treats when she can. It's just our parents, you know?"

"I most certainly do."

They sat in silence. Emlyn fidgeted by lacing and unlacing her fingers on her lap. "I think I should head back."

"Tell me, Emlyn, does your father or mother ever leave the insula without you?"

Emlyn thought for a moment. "Stella goes with Mrs. Chronister to balls pretty often or to see friends."

"Outside of the city?"

"No, Papa does sometimes with Mr. Chronister."

"Oh? What reason would they leave the city?"

"Umm . . . handling the country estate. Business stuff, I think . . . I, um . . . should be getting back." Looking over at Ened, a feeling of unease overcame her.

Ened's disposition melted into fiery desperation, sending alarm bells ringing in Emlyn's head.

At the same time, they spotted two peacekeepers pointing at them.

Ened stood up and grabbed Emlyn's forearm, making Emlyn drop the cup to the ground. The sultry voice turned cold and menacing. "Come with me."

But she pulled against her. "No! Lemme go!"

Emlyn punched at her but missed by a hair's breadth. People started to notice the commotion.

Ened dodged another punch. From the other side, Emlyn spotted Stella flanked by two peacers. Stella's eyes bored into her, making a frightened shiver run through Emlyn's bones. She wrenched her arm away from Ened with such force that she almost fell face first on the rocky path running through the green swath, but she caught herself in time and dashed as fast as she could to the temple.

The bride stood on the right with her entourage behind her patiently waiting to be let in. The door was open, and dots of light burned inside, they were waiting to be admitted. The bride was not hard to pick out: a short veil hung from a gold crown, with colorful sprouting flowers, matching the long airy dress that fanned out behind her on the stone walkway. On the left of the entrance was the groom, wearing a military uniform of a gray long jacket with three stripes at the end of each sleeve. Polished black boots matched his belt, and his moustache was long and brown, coming to a point an inch below his chin. Behind him stood a vigilant, mean-looking gilla with a nasty scar running down the side of his face.

The unyielding loving gaze between the two broke when Emlyn shot past them, up the middle, barely touching the steps leading to the entrance. Even though the mean-looking gilla reached to grab her, she dodged, shooting through the doors. They would not dare follow.

Standing a few feet past the threshold, it occurred to Emlyn that she might be committing sacrilege and became slightly distraught over the thought. There were no seats, and luckily the priests at the other end had their backs turned. She dashed behind one of the columns lining the inside of the temple and then forced herself to calm down.

She looked out from behind the pillar; it was very dim except around the altar located in the middle. A dozen bright lanterns were spread out in a semicircle. Flowers hung from the rafters, and rose petals littered the dirt floor. Ritual incense wafted up from the head of Dé Brigantia, mother of all, represented by a gigantic statue sitting at the apex basked in sunlight from above. An altar stood before the Goddess's gleaming surface. Sitting beside the all-mother was a sacred oak. Its branches went twisting up through the opening in the roof. In front of the oak was a much smaller statue the size of a regular person holding two bowls before her. Emlyn recognized this as the all-mother's aspect Dé Áine.

"Yes, she is beautiful."

The gruff, sweet voice almost made Emlyn jump out of her skin and prepare to run.

"It's okay. I'm not going to hurt you."

She turned swiftly to see an old man in long white robes. His gray hair was waist-length, and his beard was just as long. The man sat on a bench connected to the entirety of the perimeter walls, something she did not notice before with the light being so dim. His legs spread wide due to his girth as he leaned forward, putting an elbow on his knee. He stroked his beard. Emlyn noted his kind eyes as they contemplated her.

"What's troubling you, child?"

"Nothing! And I'm not a child!"

He leaned back. "My apologizes, young lady. May I at least have the pleasure of your name?"

She bowed in the same manner as her father: fist placed on the chest, legs together, then bent at the waist. "Emlyn Gwen."

The man's eyes shot with recognition. "Ahhh, one of the families who fought with Lucanis."

"You know?"

"It is common knowledge."

He looked at her, almost appraising, as if she was a gilla. It made her uncomfortable, but she felt immobilized. Frozen like one of Medusa's statues. The man nodded, having come up with some sort of decision in his own mind.

"I am Graccus, a wandering priest between the temples of Dé Brigantia."

Her shoulders slumped down. It was apparent that, at least for the moment, he would not reveal her.

"Why are you sitting in the dark?"

He started stroking his beard again. "It is my duty to lead the new couple. After the ceremonies here end, I'll lead them over to the public statue of the mother Goddess and her consort. I'm sitting here because I find the temple ceremony a lovely tradition."

"Oh."

A procession of priests and priestesses came through a plain door at the back of the temple. Each held an instrument: tambourines, drums, pipes, and strings. They lined up in the middle of the aisle, then were instructed to split into two groups. Each group went to opposite sides close to the pillars. Two other priests closed the entrance doors, and then the players started to test their instruments.

"Why are you here, young lady? Are you running away from something?"

"No, I . . . need time, time away from that insula. Time away from everyone."

"Then indulge this wanderer; I've never had the chance to speak to someone like you. Come, sit, and I will explain the ceremony as it happens."

She walked slowly to the hard stone bench and sat. "You said someone like me?"

"Someone with a famous name, of course."

The music came together in a flowery upbeat melody. The high priestess appeared from the plain door in the back of the building and walked to the front as the entrance doors were opened again.

"So I'm not in trouble?"

"Did any of the other priests see you?"

"No."

"Then relax, I'll not reveal you."

She looked at him, surprised and grateful. "Thank you."

Graccus leaned toward her as the priestess turned back from the entrance and approached the altar, with the couple following a few feet behind.

"The high priestess is the human representative of the Goddess; the couple must wait for her to lead them into this sacred space."

The couple made it to a circle burned into the wooden floorboards and stepped within it as their entourages came up from behind throwing a rainstorm of petals. The priestess also stepped inside, put on her best smile, and began speaking in an older language unknown to Emlyn.

"Oh, it's so beautiful," said Emlyn, wide-eyed.

"As it should be."

"I hope I can have a ceremony like this someday, but how would I find a husband when I'm not allowed beyond the gates? It's not fair. None of it's fair. They tell me to shoot and fight, to be perfect, that I'll be like my parents. Well, I don't want to be like my parents, I don't want to be an ambax; I don't even want to be in the insula, yet I'm good and stuck!"

"What do you want?"

She huffed. "Ugh, I don't know. To walk past the gates with no one throwing a fit over it. That would be a good start."

The tambourines, drums, and all but one of the strings ceased, then a young priestess started to sing in that unfamiliar language. It was slow but uplifting, and Emlyn could sense that it had to be about love. The couple moved around the altar to stand in front of Dé Áine. The bride put her hand in one bowl.

"She's putting her hand in dirt. It represents the womb of the earth."

The groom put his hand in the other bowl. After a moment he brought his hand out, and it was drenched in water. He held something betwixt his fingers. Emlyn narrowed her eyes.

"He holds a seed and water, along with earth, it makes the seed grow."

"Oh, I see. All this represents sex," said Emlyn sheepishly.

He chuckled. "That is a good guess. That's the start of it, but this part is more about promoting the fertility of the two."

She smiled at him. "That's still sex."

A small rectangular blue rug was placed before the couple. They knelt at opposite ends, knees falling on the edge of the rug as the priestess came to stand in front of the Dé Áine statue. The bride held out the hand covered in dirt, palm up. The groom placed the seed in the dirt, and his wet hand grasped the hand of his soon-to-be wife on top and held it there; they looked sweetly into each other's eyes.

The high priestess had a little trouble bending down, for her age was advanced, but after a moment she managed it. Her face said that it did not bother her, but her body told a different story. She draped a white-and-red ribbon across the joined hands and began to wrap, over and over, around and around. Not too tightly, but just enough, stopping at the wrists.

"Now they are joined in the eyes of Dé Brigantia."

The music picked up again, and the couple stepped back into the circle for a moment to accept the adulation before slowly making their way to the door. Their friends and family parted for them, and rose petals rained once more.

"I will be leading them to the public statues in a moment. There the ribbon will be unwrapped. They'll wash their hands and then formally accept the ribbon from the Gods as a sign of their approval. Do you pray to the Gods?"

She was so entranced by the ceremony that it took her a moment to realize that he had asked her a question. She spat out, "No, they do nothing for me. I still get beaten and treated unfairly no matter how much I pray. They don't listen."

Graccus looked at her and smiled warmly. "Miss Gwen, let me give you some advice. I believe it will help."

He stroked his long beard. Sitting this close, she could see how unkempt it was, how it held all the smells of the road. Emlyn imagined herself as a wandering priestess, long, wild hair down to her waist, wearing dusty white robes, performing ceremonies in remote forests. Most importantly she would be able to go wherever she pleased. Maybe then the Gods would listen. The man's stare and one raised eyebrow arching up in her direction snapped the daydream away.

"Listen to me carefully."

She nodded.

"Think of the Gods as the sum of the planet we walk on. They are the birds in the sky singing for our enjoyment. The beauty of the beetle crawling over your foot before you stomp it to death. The child's cry after birth while the mother closes her eyes for the final time. Is it perfect? Is it fair? No. As the Gods know, we should learn too; there is no beauty in perfection. Perfection, fairness, these things do not strengthen us. Do not make us ready for what lies ahead. If we had everything the way we wanted with no hurt or pain, then there would be no story to ourselves. Only lethargy would remain. Are you familiar with that word, *lethargy*?"

Emlyn nodded.

"Good! Then I will charge you with a geissi; that is a type of task or prohibition. Do you understand?"

Emlyn nodded cautiously.

"I want you to go home after this and read about the God Under the Hill."

"That's the God of servants and gilla."

"Yes." He nodded. "I think you will find him very interesting since you're being pushed to become an . . . ambax was it? Yes, the spirit Gilla was a kind of trickster, you see, but found enlightenment in the service of Dé Brigantia and Dé Ard."

She swallowed and looked at the dirt floor, unsure if she wanted to do that or not. He sure seemed like a nice man, and his advice was a gift in a way. Plus, she would feel awful if she did not follow through on his request.

"Let me see your hand."

She did, and he turned it, looking at her palm. His eyes darted about, reading the lines. By now the newlyweds were outside along with their entourages and priestly players still strumming and banging their instruments, waiting on this interesting druidi.

"What do you see?" asked Emlyn.

"You have two paths: one an unbroken spear shaft, the other a winding river."

His other palm came to rest on top, and when he moved it away, she stared at a polished piece of amber. The light from the lanterns glittered on its surface. She stared at him confused.

"These were used in the old days to heal; let it heal your mind. Let it bring you back to the Gods. And remember that the will of the Gods is not for us to perceive." He stood up. "Ah! These aching bones! It's time for me to lead the procession. Come, follow behind me."

She did what he asked. Upon reaching the door, Graccus motioned for her to stop as he kept walking down the steps and in front of the procession, who all seemed relieved to see him.

She could see her father with Stella and Mr. Chronister standing on the other side of the group, waiting. Graccus motioned at them. And Stella started walking toward him, but Briar stopped her, shaking his head, resulting in her ferocity bubbling to the surface. Andreas touched her bicep, and she backed down. Looking about, Emlyn saw no sign of Eneddia.

Graccus spoke with her father only a short time, then he looked up the steps and spotted her poking her head out from around the door. She froze. But Briar's face beamed lovingly, and when she was sure she was not in any trouble, Emlyn stepped out from the door. The wandering priest nodded, and her father made his way up the steps after giving a nod to the mean-looking gilla with the nasty scar.

The procession proceeded down the street.

Briar wrapped his arms around her. "I'm so thankful she did not get too far with you and that you were just startled seeing your mother coming at you in her usual way."

"How did you know?"

He put his large hand under her chin and moved it back and forth, checking for blemishes. Finding none, he placed his hands on her shoulders and looked seriously into her eyes. Those eyes never scared her like they did with others.

"What did she say to you?"

"Only listened to me, that's all. Wanted to know about my life."

He almost shook her. His grip hardened. "Did she tell you anything?"

"Only confirmed that we are ambaxes! The thought crossed my mind before, but I didn't believe it then."

Briar loosened his grip, put his palm on the side of her cheek, and kissed her forehead. She looked up at him curiously.

"Papa, how did you know Ened led me away?"

"Ms. Cord saw you talking with her through the gate. She immediately informed us."

He placed his hand between her shoulder blades. "Let's head back."

For once, she was glad about that. Glad that she was seen and found. Glad to be heading back, but as she spotted the familiar gates, her heart sank to its very depths. It was back through the bars, into the cage, never to leave again.

CHAPTER ELEVEN

"I'd acknowledge the Skaldane thunder God if he would send just one bolt of lightning to start this piece of shit! Push it!"

Emlyn was sitting in the driver's seat of the Vitru Frig. She flipped a switch and pressed down a discreet black button. There was no response from the engine. Again she tried, but nothing came of it. She shook her head no, and Colmane growled in frustration, banging his fist against the motor.

He unhooked the extra battery, which had turned out to be a dud, and placed it in the grass next to the dirt road. He slammed the side-opening hood down, making the auto rock back and forth.

They were an hour outside of Londinium, two hours on foot, and another forty-five minutes to go before reaching the Barrentine estate. The terrain was for horses and carriages, not autos. To say it was a bumpy ride was an understatement. The cushy seats had made it tolerable, but just barely. This part of the country constituted nothing but hills, and the constant up and down drained engine batteries fast. Colmane found himself unlucky with the spare.

He hung his vest on the hood and leaned against it with a lit cigarette in hand. He pulled the brim of his newly purchased white hat down further, attempting to protect himself from the sun. Emlyn hunched down with her back against the auto, doing her best to stay within its shadow. Again she thanked the Gods for the practicality of her wardrobe and color choice: a simple cream blouse and brown skirt.

"You know the problem with Gods?" he said, oozing with spite. "They never answer. Useless when you actually need them."

"I wouldn't say that, Master.

He looked over at her and spoke with a dismissive air. "Oh? Tell me, why would any God listen to a gilla?"

Emlyn shrugged. "We bow the lowest."

Colmane paused, surprised, then laughed uproariously. "Good to know that you have a sense of humor. It's said that martials are unburdened by it."

This time she laughed. Emlyn could easily understand why someone would think that with their constant even demeanors.

He reached into his back pocket, took out a white handkerchief, and dabbed the sweat away from his forehead. "There are no Gods, just us. I heard you martials go through something called a breaking? I was told it's especially grueling."

"Yes, it was." Emlyn looked off into the distance where the emerald hills met the sky, enjoying the flight of birds against the blue.

"What God did you pray to for it to end?"

"I prayed to many Gods, Master."

He raised an eyebrow. "Did they answer?"

"I suppose, in a way. It did come to an end."

He bellowed out a laugh. "Not much of an endorsement for the Gods, but I have a feeling you were not simply praying for that."

"Forgive me, Master, but it's forbidden to speak to outsiders about the details of a breaking."

Colmane huffed and crossed his arms. "Convenient. I guess you would wiggle your way out of telling me even if I was a high patrician." He scratched his cheek. "Eh, I can't blame you for that really." He sank to the ground and crossed his ankles. "Want to hear a story? It could make the time go by faster."

"If you wish to share, then I will listen."

He grinned, showing his teeth. "A perfect response."

Colmane told a story that Emlyn wished she had declined to hear. He was up in this area some years ago hunting two runaways. He found them in a wooded area. A male gilla was using a hammer and chisel in an attempt to remove a female gilla's collar. Upon realizing there was nowhere else to run, the male attempted to bring the chisel down into the female's flesh, killing her. But Colmane yanked the girl from the log just in time. The chisel's only damage was a nicked ear. Afterward the man got to his knees and begged for him and his wife to be let go. The notion that he called the girl his wife somewhat amused Colmane at the time, and he still found it funny enough to chuckle at remembering it. Once their mistress came to claim her property, she gave the girl to Colmane in payment for his services. She was the only gilla he owned and, by his account, was docile.

Pitiless. A man who sees me as nothing more than a temporary tool to get to the position he most desires. That would explain why he treats me as he does with me being an extension of my mistress. She could not help but feel glum over the thought. He had been confusing, but she hoped that he was different, and she supposed that in certain ways, he was.

He moved his hat down over his face, signaling sleep. If he was actually asleep or just did not want to talk further, she did not know.

The silence of the next twenty minutes went on far longer than it had the right to. She brought her braid forward, hating the way it rubbed against the auto when she moved her head. She stared at it for a moment, then undid the braid with fury. But she had no idea why the feeling overcame her. Certainly it had been building up since Stella made her do it. She put her head back against the auto, relaxed, and wished there was a tree nearby, plenty of bushes, tall grass, something that could produce enough shade. That was when she spotted a glint coming over the horizon of a far hill.

"Master."

He moved his hat back to the top of his head and looked at her. She nodded down the direction they came from. Colmane saw the glint too and stood up to get a better look.

"Horse and cart coming this way."

It took another ten minutes for the wagon to reach them. A man wearing an almost comically large straw hat, that seemed downright practical for this heat, drove the cart. He wore brown boots that were worn down and dirty from years of work. A leather satchel crossed over his chest and shoulder. Underneath rested a sweat-stained blue shirt. The sleeves were rolled up to the elbows. The shirt was unbuttoned down to mid-chest, showing fine curly blonde hair. Around his neck was a large red handkerchief that he used to wipe sweat away, and under that was a steel collar.

He stopped the horse in front of them. "Whoa, whoa there!"

The horse settled, a good strong red Kymry trotter. There were a few back on the Chronister estate, and while she had learned to ride, she had never developed a love for them, but she did admire their strength of spirit.

He glanced at the auto, then addressed them properly, but in a northern Gael accent. "Master. Ma'am. Auto on stutter, eh? Do ya happen to be headed for me master's estate?"

"If your owners are the Barrentines, then yes," said Colmane.

The gilla nodded. "Yes, Master. Come on up. Yer martial can sit back there." He pointed. "Got some nice soft straw there for ya to lay on, ma'am."

Colmane climbed up in the front and sat next to the driver. Emlyn went to the back and pulled herself up to sit in the surprisingly sweet-smelling straw. She let her legs dangle out the back.

"Do you have your papers?" asked Colmane.

"Oh, aye." He held the reins in one hand, reached into his satchel, and brought out a folded sheet of paper as Emlyn made a study of two deer dashing into the grove of trees far in the distance. She lay back in the cart, contenting herself with the blue sky and the occasional flock of birds. The lack of cushions and bumpy road could not dent the sights and smells of the paradise laid out around her.

* * * * *

Emlyn was standing up in the back and spotted a large Roman-style villa on top of a soft sloping hill. Before them was a dirty stone wall in front of a grove of old trees surrounding the hill. The most striking features were numerous sharpened long stakes poking out of the ground next to the gate. On the ends of these stakes were bleached skulls. Half of them were missing their jaws, others were wired on.

She decided to look at anything else but that macabre sight. Far in the distance were extensive grazing fields and then a large forest. She knew that on the other side of the forest was the capital of the old Iceni tribe, the city of Venta. In ancient days it acted as a border town for the Roman territory before Lucanis united the isle.

Four martials seemed to appear out of nowhere. They opened the gate and lifted their guns from their holsters, causing the driver to rear up the horse.

The driver leaned toward Colmane. "Don't worry, Master. They don't recognize ya is all. Jus' don't make any sudden movements."

The driver whipped the reins, making the horses walk slowly forward. He stopped the wagon a few feet in front of the gate. The oldest of the martials, with a shock of white hair and a long bushy moustache, approached. He had a hard face with a few scars running down under the side of his jaw to the middle of the neck. Probably a good fight against some predator. Nonetheless, the scars made his square face look all the harder and uncompromising.

"I am sorry, Master, but we are expecting no visitors today. Please state your business."

"Of course." Colmane reached inside his vest and showed a round badge with the initials G.A. and his name underneath, all surrounded by an engraving of linked chains. "Erasmus Colmane from gilla affairs. I'm here to investigate a discrepancy in the Barrentine files about one of your bloodlined gilla."

The old martial looked rather surprised. "Who? Affairs said that everything was in order last year. Did something happen?"

"That is none of your concern, gilla," Colmane said with a sneer.

The martial backed up a few paces. "Of course, Master. I mean no offense. Might I inquire who that is standing in the back?"

Colmane looked behind. "Oh yes, this is Emlyn Gwen. Owing to a favor, she is on loan to me for protection." It made sense. The countryside could be dangerous for lone travelers, and this area was known far and wide in Kymbri for banditry. Emlyn hopped out of the back and stood before the martials.

"Well met, sister martial. I am patriarch Goss Dunmor." He held his fist against his chest and bowed. She returned the gesture.

"Well met."

Colmane watched this with studious fascination.

The driver spoke up. "Goss, their auto is on stutter up the road a ways, broken down. Big yellow thing, can't miss 'er."

"Cobb!" yelled Goss without taking his eyes away from his study of Emlyn.

A very young martial ran up to him, probably not far out from his breaking.

"Run up to the house and alert the master. Then find Mr. Lofen and accompany him to the auto."

The young man bowed and ran off.

The martials stood on each side of the wagon and led them into the estate, straight up a brick road that became more elaborate in its design as they neared the house. A sprawling two-story facade greeted them. Roman columns ran all the way across the front, holding up a relief of carved figures involved with farm work. Above that was a porch with a solid marble railing. Emlyn assumed this villa had been around since the Romans. If not, then it was a superb recreation.

A large round fountain stood proudly in front of the house acting as the center of the hill. In the middle of the fountain stood a statue of a wolf. Its stone teeth lacerated the neck of another wolf with many wounds present in its matted fur. This was a symbol for the war of two wolves fought between the Britonnic-Kymry forces of Lucanis and the remnants of the Roman empire led by Pilontis. It was excellently crafted if not a bit gruesome. It brought to mind the statue that sat in front of the Chronister ancestral estate, but it featured the Chronister achievements during that war, such as being first into Londinium. The only gruesome thing about it was the severed marble head of General Tirisius lying on the pedestal.

They wound around the brick road circling the statue.

Next to the house stood a white garage with four arched portals. On the other side, the brick led down the hill to a pristine barn. Connected to that was a fence where a few horses lazily grazed. A fancy white stable sat on the opposite side of that fence, and behind the stable were a number of well-maintained buildings where people, probably ranch hands and gilla, mingled about.

Emlyn, walking behind Goss, could hear cows and chickens in the distance. Looking out to a far hill beyond the barn, there was a horde of cattle being led by a few drovers. This was one of the primary sources of income for the Barrentines.

"Sir, this is a beautiful estate."

"Ah, thank you kindly, Miss Gwen. The hilltop is always a sight, but call me Goss if it do ya."

"It will if you don't mind referring to me as Emlyn."

Goss smiled. "Ae, Emlyn. I assume the Chronister estate to be grander."

"It is grand, in a different way. I have not seen it in many years. My mistress prefers the insula."

"How anyone could prefer a city with such terrible air and foul-mannered people is far beyond my understanding," said Goss.

Something was off about him; something was missing. A flittering look in the corners of his eyes seemed to signal to her about longing. She could not put her finger on why this was and why it made her uneasy.

The main door opened and out walked the master of the house, dressed down in brown trousers and a hastily tucked-in white shirt. The mistress strode out after him in an ankle-length light green silk gown. The neckline plunged to her belly button, which was decorated with flowing blue symbols swirling out from the navel and covering the entire belly. Her name was Muire Barrentine, and she held a babe only a few months old covered in the same swirling pattern.

Emlyn remembered that the family of this mistress were of far northern origin. Further north than Alba. For a few years after birth, they see a child as still attached to the womb.

Most places in the far north still held the classic image of barbarians in the eyes of many Kymbrians. Emlyn was not one to buy into stereotypes wholesale. It was only strange behaviors and rituals that made people uncomfortable, and this particular belief of decorating the child with a temporary woad meant that complications arose after birth. That the mother hoped to protect the babe with some form of supposed magic. Emlyn believed in the Gods but also believed that the Gods no longer gave out those graces. Still, it was an unnerving sight. She looked up at Colmane; his mouth twitched.

After the mistress came her martial, as tall and as old as Emlyn and at least seven months pregnant. She was being helped out to the porch by an older gilla.

Then followed a few family members, a patrician man, his equally fine but much younger wife, and a son who had taken his first few steps into manhood not all that long ago. He looked nothing like the woman, but at least the appearance of these people explained the glut of martials on the property.

The Barrentine babe would have its own martial in time, if everything went well. The kids would be raised together at another property to lessen the risk of finding out the ruse, as most retired martials were sent to help run an estate such as this one, like her grandmother Cali and a few others from the extended family.

Colmane jumped down from the wagon.

"Mr. Colmane."

"Hadrian Barrentine?"

They shook hands, but the master of the house was perplexed.

"We always welcome agents, but I must confess, I'm confused. I would like to know what this is all about and why we were not alerted to your arrival well in advance."

"This is a small problem," responded Colmane. "If there was a phone line installed, then this could have been handled without a trip. Besides, your yearly inspection is almost due. Best to get it over and done."

The wife scowled. "I knew we should have had a line installed."

"That would cost a fortune," said Hadrian.

"We've more than a fortune to—"

He eyed her, and she threw her hands up.

"Okay, okay." She smiled warmly at Colmane.

He took his hat off, put it to his chest for decorum's sake, and smiled back.

"Please, come inside. We have tea on," she said with the sweetest expression.

With hat in hand, he gestured to his side at Emlyn. "This gilla here is on loan to me. If you don't have any objections, I would have her conduct the inspection of your gilla quarters. She is certified."

This was not an odd thing; the Barrentines probably expected it. They did raise some questioning looks when they noticed she was a martial. Hadrian was about to say something, but his wife touched his arm, cutting him off.

The mistress gave a mischievous smile. "Of course! Roff!"

One of the martials who followed the wagon perked up and stood straight, ready for instruction. Emlyn noticed Hadrian's lip twitch.

"Get her watered and answer any questions she might have."

Roff came up to Emlyn, grinning like he had just won a prize. She returned the grin and bowed. He was a few years younger than Emlyn, perhaps nineteen. He had a bright face, strong jaw, high cheekbones, and brown eyes that matched his long pulled-back hair. She smiled at him pleased at what she saw, and he returned the gesture. He then glanced at the younger-looking woman near the entrance to the house. Emlyn assumed that he belonged to her. But it was Mistress Muire who was truly in charge here and could order another of her family's martials around to an extent.

Emlyn turned to follow him, but Colmane grabbed her forearm before she could go any further. "Remember what we talked about."

She nodded.

* * * * *

Emlyn looked right and then to the left at the long single-floor building that housed the martials. She found it quite luxurious, very spacious and comfortable despite the walls being made from stone. It was far more inviting on the inside. Estates were where martials usually went to retire when they became too old to perform their duty or their owner died before they did. If there was one thing that high gilla had over low gilla, it was a greater sense of security when it came to getting old. Though she assumed that not being able to pick your partner and knowing that your children would all be Gilla did not seem like an exactly equal tradeoff for most.

"Does it meet standards? I hope so, feels like home now."

She looked down at the small notebook in her hand. Then she took out a pen from the spine and made a check at the end of the last sentence on the list, detailing how clean and well-maintained the facade needed to be. Above that line were a dozen other instructions with checks, notes, and numbers on standard and non-standard items. There were six bedrooms, each one only accessible from the outside. Retired martials could be liberal with non-standard items that would usually be forbidden to most other gilla, except on certain days, such as alcohol, tobacco, and various trinkets. Though she was absolutely sure that these martials were allowed such things, it was only proper to present the list to the owner of the property to double-check. Personally she did not care if any of the Dunmor martials had an entire pub hidden in their closets.

"Yes, it checks the marks."

She looked back toward the barracks, where the low gilla slept alongside the transient ranch hands. She couldn't imagine that any free man would be happy with a sleeping arrangement like that. Permanent ranch hands received their own one-room house. The foreman got a house with two bedrooms and was allowed a family.

"Roff, how long have you been here? You seem like you're more of the city than the country."

He gave a grin that did nothing to hide a sad twinge. "A little over six months now. Mistress Derreli insisted that we come and support her sister as soon as the complications with the baby came to light."

"I see. I do hope that you are able to make it home soon."

Roff shrugged. "I like being near my family, and it is more exciting out here with the patrols we go on. But I do miss the balls the mistress went to. And the food—Derreli was venturous with her meals. Mistress Muire, not so much."

"Can I ask you something?"

He suddenly looked a bit frightened. "Ah, of course."

"Those heads outside, what are they about?"

His body loosened and he sighed. "Oh, that. Our bandit problem has become worse over the last few months. They are there as a warning."

"I see," she said.

Roff gazed at her. She gave him a charming smile, causing him to clear his throat with a cough.

"That's it then. Everything looks to be in fine shape." She returned the small notebook to her pocket.

"I guess we should go back to the house."

Halfway up the hill, they were stopped by Goss marching toward them looking very foreboding.

"Grandfather, is everything okay?"

He stopped in front of them but looked to Emlyn. "Yes. Emlyn, Master Colmane will be dining with the family tonight."

She was glad to hear it. It would give her more time. "Very well."

"May I ask if you've been trained to ride a horse?"

Emlyn shrugged. "I know the basics."

"Good! Epona and Rian need to be taken out. Think you could help us with that?"

She nodded. "I'd be honored."

"Roff, saddle the two along with my favorite mare!"

"Yes, Grandfather." Roff placed his fist on his chest and bowed before walking away toward the stables.

Goss bellowed out a laugh after his grandson was out of earshot. "The boy fancies you."

"I know," she said with another wry smirk.

* * * * *

Twelve minutes on the trail, they had traversed a few hills but could still see the villa back on the horizon. Despite the beautiful scenery, the constant smell of cow dung kept her nose wrinkled for the entire ride. It didn't seem to bother Goss or Roff, who were used to such smells. Night had begun to descend fast upon the forest stretched out before them. Emlyn was last in line, and she kept wondering why they were heading this far out.

They trotted down the path into the forest. The growing shadows of the trees engulfed them as if they had entered a portal to another world.

The thickness of the wood seemed insurmountable as they turned the corner on the narrow trail. The gold, red, and purple hues of sunset could still be seen through the breaks in the canopy. The crickets sang out into the twilight, and a few birds still chirped a song or two. Alongside the trail ran a stream. Its whirling water made a rhythm that soothed and could probably lull one to sleep like in the old fae stories.

Emlyn retreated into thought and continued to wonder why they were this far from the estate if bandits were such a problem in the area. Goss was hiding something. Colmane had told her of the Barrentine patriarch Cerisus, who was killed by bandits a year ago. He was burned alive along with his martial. It reminded her of her father and Andreas getting shot during an ambush laid by brigands.

If these bandit mobs could take out a martial, then why is Goss not being weary now? thought Emlyn.

Roff slowed his mount to ride next to her. "Emlyn, I hope this is not presumptuous of me, but Colmane said you were on loan. How does a martial get loaned out to a pleb?"

His tone did not sound disrespectful, and it was a fair question.

"Mistress Chronister owed him a favor."

"Ah." He chewed on his lip, considering something as he continued to ride next to her.

"This might seem like an odd thing to ask, but has your mistress bred you yet?"

Emlyn raised an eyebrow. "No, why?"

Roff remained silent for a moment, then made sure his voice was not more than a whisper. "There's talk that I am to be bred."

"You sound scared of this prospect."

"No, no, it's . . . it's an unknown."

Emlyn adjusted her position on the leather saddle, and what came out sounded bland and rehearsed. "Breeding is a service to your owner.

It is part of your duty to produce children. It is nothing to worry over or be afraid of." She could not believe she had just said that. Her own anxiety over the notion made her dread it, and Roff was in the same boat. What right did she have to lecture him?

Goss laughed. "I could not have put it better myself! Don't let the boy worry you! Nothing stops him from fretting!"

Red crept up into Roff's cheeks, and he looked away, embarrassed.

"Emlyn, humor an old man and come ride beside me!"

She spurred her horse to a trot, then relaxed as she came up beside him.

Goss shook his head. "The poor boy, he's awkward around women."

"No I'm not!"

"Some men have it worse around women," she said.

"True, but when talking about the sexual act, he fumbles and stumbles. Brigante bless him, he's trying. Even when Sissa was still here, he couldn't bring himself to relieve his frustrations."

"Grandfather!"

"Sissa, that's the girl Colmane is here to question."

Goss had a look of surprise. "Question? The girl is dead, eight months hence! Was that not in the records?"

Emlyn furrowed her brow. "No, only that she was owned by the Barrentines."

He rubbed his chin while looking down at the pommel of the saddle. "That passes strange, strange indeed."

"What did she die from?"

"Accident. There's a gully near the house to carry runoff stormwater. She fell into it and smashed her head against a rock," he said nonchalantly.

"Oh, I'm sorry."

"You can say that to her father when we get back. The low gilla you rode in with."

"I will."

Emlyn's eyes darted to the side. The noises of the forest lessened, and an odd feeling wafted into the air. Goss too looked suspiciously about after hearing a few limbs crack. Emlyn glanced back at Roff, who was doing the same, watching the tree line with his hand resting on the butt of his revolver. He spotted her looking at him and nodded seriously.

The horses reared as two men jumped out from behind the trees and onto the narrow road, brandishing poorly maintained revolvers.

"What's the meaning of this?" yelled Goss in irritation as his startled horse turned in a circle.

One of the men, disheveled and dirty with long ratty hair, stepped forward. "How does it look, old gilla?"

"Do you know who we are?" asked Roff.

"I know you as a pansy-eating calf! Now hand over yer guns an' knives, an' we'll treat ya fair! If you don't comply, then find a bullet right in yer head from the rifle of a deadshot. Shoot ya right between the eyes he will, ex-forty-second rifleman. Ya understand me?"

Goss leaned forward against the horn of the saddle, placing his forearm across it. Emlyn knew his fingers were inching toward the handle of his revolver.

"And what do you have planned for us?"

"Sell ya! Won't get much for an old man like you, but the other two will fetch a fair price!" he said, almost drooling at the mouth.

"This land is owned by the Barrentines. You are trespassing and threatening not only two Dunmor martials but also a Gwen. Are you sure you want to take that chance?" asked Roff evenly.

The two men laughed. "Yer outgunned!"

That was when Goss, for a split second, glanced at Emlyn. She cross-drew her revolver and fanned the hammer four times, hitting the two in the shoulder. Two shots rang out from elsewhere. One bullet hit a tree next to Emlyn as two other men fell from overhanging limbs forty yards away. Her horse only reacted by shifting its backend to the side.

Goss had his revolver trained on the two men, who were now holding their bleeding shoulders. "Throw those pieces of cac pistols into that creek."

He motioned the barrel toward the creek running beside the trail. They scowled at him, but they obeyed and tossed the guns in. The water splashed.

"What, are ya goin' to kill us?"

"You intended to kill a martial owned by the Barrentines. That is as good as trying to kill a Barrentine. So yes . . . I could, but I've not decided."

He cocked the hammer. Their eyes went wide, and their knees hit the dirt trail in record time. They begged and pleaded for their lives.

Goss gently uncocked the hammer. "Here I thought they were getting bold, but they're all jibs and gobbs. Roff! Get off your horse and tie their hands!"

He looked back. Roff had his gun in his hand, but with his other hand he held tight to his thigh. Blood gushed out from between his fingers. Goss turned the horse and galloped to his side. He jumped off quickly.

"I'm fine, Grandfather. It's just a graze."

"I'll be the judge of that, boy. Lift your hand away."

He did so reluctantly. Goss peered into the wound, then stuck a finger in.

"May Dagda club you to death, old man!" yelled Roff through the searing pain.

Goss snickered and slapped Roff's thigh, making him wince in torment once again. "Thata boy! You'll be fine. It's deep, but no cleaved artery."

He turned, reached into his saddle pouch, and brought out a tin case. He opened it and took out gauze, then wrapped his grandson's leg tightly.

"Now get down. Have them strip, and tie their hands. The mistress will decide what to do with them."

Roff obeyed as Emlyn kept her gun trained on the men. While their shoulders were bandaged, they stared at her, and she knew they were waiting for an opportunity to escape. Their hopes were dashed, though, when Roff tied them together and had them sit down.

Goss came up to her and patted the horse's flanks. Emlyn lowered herself to the ground.

"A great mare, is she not? We get them used to gunfire early in their life."

She looked at him, and annoyance came into her eyes. "You used me. You knew these men would be here, somewhere, waiting."

"We exist to be used, Miss Gwen. There is a bandit problem in this part of the country. Our cattle get stolen quite often, along with a gilla or a free man here and there. Taken into these woods and sold in Venta on the other side. And when you have a Gwen around, then you had better make use of them while you can. So I thank you for your assistance in apprehending a few of these pathetic brosthuns."

She turned, still not happy about it, and walked to the two shot down from the tree. Goss followed her. The closer one still moved and moaned when Goss pressed his foot down on the bullet wound located in the middle of the man's gut.

"Looks like he might have a few broken ribs too." He unsheathed his knife. "Have you killed before in that city of yours?"

". . . Once."

He gestured to the other one further down. "Then go handle the other."

"Do they have to die?" she said with some anger.

Goss gave her a long hard stare of annoyance before spitting to the side.

"This one is gut shot. He would not make it back, nor would I take him if we had the means. I have no intention of letting these

cumberwhirls use up more of our resources. The other over there"—he
pointed again at the man further down—"is bleeding profusely from the
side of his cheek. It would be a mercy to put him down. Even if he did
survive, I doubt he would speak properly again."

As she approached, no other sound came through this man besides
the gurgle of blood being processed through his gullet. He writhed in
pain back and forth in his attempts to scream. Most of his cheek was
missing and she could see bits of broken jaw poking through. He noticed
her shadow and turned to look with fury and hatred in his eyes. The
man was unafraid of what was coming, so maybe his bandit friend was
right about him being a military rifleman. It did not matter. His rusted
rifle and hawk eyes stood no match against a martial.

"Think of him as an injured horse!" yelled Goss.

The sniper was holding the upper side of his neck, where the bullet
exited, trying his best to stop its flow. He gurgled something at her, a
curse perhaps. Emlyn brought up the barrel of her gun and pointed it at
his face. The man's eyes did not change as she pulled the trigger. The
woods reverberated, and she could hear critters dashing away in the
darkness. Her first deliberate kill.

She felt a pat on her shoulder. "Come on, eagle eye, time to head
back."

Emlyn said nothing. She barely hazarded a blink. Her eyes only
faced forward, not one glance spared for the dead men who were tied
over the horses. The other two walked naked behind them with their
ropes tied to the saddles. Roff was the only one riding. Emlyn and Goss
walked the horses by their reins. It was a long procession through the
grazing fields. As the sun finally went down beyond the hills, a deep
darkness fell with it and hung about like dense fog. No one said a word.
Well, Emlyn and Roff said nothing. Goss whistled a tune as if there was
nothing amiss. It came across as eerie, and Emlyn would not have been
surprised if the black dog ran toward them from the shadows with
blazing fiery eyes.

When they came near the barracks and ranch houses, the workers and Gilla filed out to watch them pass. As soon as they realized what was happening, they followed behind them as they made their way up the slope to the main house. Together the Gilla and hands taunted and jeered at the two naked bandits. They spouted curses and spit, making one bandit try to hide his head between his outstretched arms. A few were able to rain down some punches, and an old woman hit the other across the back with her cane before Goss shooed them away. It was quite the fanfare.

Some insisted on their murder as appropriate recompense. A man ran up and yelled something about his young son being sold to those Mithran pig-bulls, but once again Goss, being more vigilant this time, stopped him from causing harm to the captives.

By the time they stopped on the brick road in front of the main house, the mistress had heard the hooves and the shouting crowd. She stormed out, wearing her dining gown. The master followed along with the pregnant martial lumbering behind. Colmane came last.

"By the Dé! What is going on here?" demanded the mistress.

Roff carefully lowered himself from the horse and undid the ropes that connected the naked bandits to the saddle.

Goss handed the reins of his horse to a young man. "Boy, put the horses in the corral and the dead men in the barn. Tomorrow we'll use their heads as examples on the corners of the property." The crowd cheered at that.

He turned to the mistress and gave his explanation. "We caught these men in the woods. They threatened to take our weapons and sell us. When we refused, the imbeciles attempted murder."

"Hang them!" yelled more than a few followers.

Roff had the brigands stand before the steps leading up to the house.

The mistress scowled and stared at them with nothing but cold menace. "You . . . you steal my cattle! You take the free workers and gilla alike with no care for their status! Despicable, contentious wrecks!"

She spat in each of their faces. One tried to curse but only got half a word out before Roff pushed him to the ground, making the man bust his nose on the edge of the step. Roff then violently pulled the man's disgusting hair back, forcing the bandit to his knees. The blood poured from his nostrils. Goss hit the inside of the other bandit's knees, making him kneel as well.

"You have the audacity to try to kill my martials?"

The bandits grinned, not bothered at all by her anger. Seeing this, the mistress relaxed her shoulders and allowed a disconcerting smile to spread across her face.

"I know what to do with you. There is an old law. Not many remember it, but it allows the target of an attempted murder to reduce their attacker . . . to gillahood. An attack on my martials is the same as an attack on me! And I will invoke that law!"

The smugness of the bandits evaporated. "You can't! We're free!"

The other spoke. "We're at least supposed ta get the three choices!"

Her smile grew broader. "You men are lucky. I happen to have an agent from gilla affairs here tonight. Mr. Colmane, make my new gilla see that they have no recourse."

He looked at each of them with more than a little glee. "Gentlemen, the law is on the books, and martials are considered extensions to their masters in this law. You have no option in this."

"Mr. Colmane, can you stay the night and write up the papers on these dregs?"

"Absolutely, Mrs. Barrentine."

She turned to look back at the bandits, the same glee dancing in her eyes. "Goss, throw them in an unclean stall and chain them. Tomorrow you can make them docile. Perhaps after their fellows see their friends as cowed gilla, they will deign to raid elsewhere."

"Yes, Mistress." He too looked gleeful at the prospect.

Mistress Muire turned to the house and rubbed her eyes. "Why couldn't one bandit be a female? Too many males work this estate. It's creating a displeasing air about the place."

Colmane spoke. "Perhaps you could sell the bandits in the city for a female or two."

"I suppose I will have to, as much as I hate those fetid streets."

The crowd started to disperse, following Goss to the stables, but Emlyn stayed behind and so too did Colmane. They stepped away from the porch. He lit up a cigarette; its light was like a beacon in the darkness.

"Emlyn, were you part of that mess?"

"Yes."

"Any trouble?"

She shook her head. "Not for you, Master."

Colmane took a long look at her, then blew the smoke out.

"They would not tell me much. Danced around the subject for a while and eventually said that the gilla was stolen by bandits. They needed more practice with the lie. Were you able to find anything?"

"Sissa is dead."

Colmane looked down. "I thought so." He then took another drag.

"Fell into a gully about eight months back, bashed her head on a rock . . . Goss was genuinely surprised that this was not in the file."

"Damn it all!" He threw the last bit of the cigarette to the ground and smashed it underfoot. "The immediate family is hiding something. I'll try to dig around some more, but you keep on those martials. We need to know why the killer had her tag. So connect the dots."

* * * * *

The fire roared and the laughter sounded throughout the dark hills. It was late, and a few stars finally poked through the foggy night. Six martials, along with a mixture of twenty low gilla and free workers, sat around the fire made between the worker houses. They all stared at Goss in awe.

Goss threw out his arms. "So there we were, staring the bandits down! Then Emlyn Gwen—yes, the same Gwen family who fought with Lucanis during the war of two wolves!" He pointed to Emlyn, leaning against the barracks, a fair way outside of the story circle.

She crossed her arms but looked far from amused.

"She gripped her revolver, and fast as a flash, she whipped it around, fanning the hammer four times!"

He made the motion with his hands fanning an imaginary gun. "The two sharp-shooters were killed instantly! The other two wounded in their gun arms!"

"You didn't kill one, Goss?" asked a young worker.

He laughed. "I barely had time to draw my revolver before it was over!"

Many looked at each other in surprise; a few turned their awe toward Emlyn. It seemed that Goss was considered an excellent shot in their eyes. She was not thrilled about the story. He was more interested in weaving a good tale than revealing exact details.

Emlyn nodded at those looking her way, and attention was placed back on Goss as he continued the story.

"Why did she kill only two?"

"Simple, my lad, the mistress needed a few alive to show what would happen to other bandits when they're caught! As for your other concern, Emlyn knew, as all martials know, an unseen man with a rifle is more dangerous than a known man with a revolver."

Enough was enough, she turned and walked into the darkness. She looked to the ground and thought upon what Sissa's father said earlier that night when she managed to corner him. He talked about Sissa being a bright girl, but that she got into too much mischief upon gaining her bloodlined status. She pressed him on what he meant by that. Sissa snuck food apparently. The girl gambled with new workers, often putting the use of her body on the line as if it were she who owned it. Sissa was caught numerous times trying to hoard the worker wages she won, naively saying, "One day I will hand so much money to the mistress that she will have no choice but to free me." She was often forced to give the money back to the workers. This was not old Rome where you could, perhaps, buy your freedom. Probably the most important detail he revealed was that the wound was on the back of her head, not the front.

Emlyn squinted her eyes and scrunched up her nose. She considered that the girl could have twisted when she fell, or got knocked in the back of the head by the killer. How could a gilla tag from way out in the country end up at the bottom of a pool within a big city pleasure palace?

She ended her musings by running her hand through her hair and putting her attention to the music of the crickets. She didn't want to get lost wondering about these things right now. She put her destination in the forefront of her mind. What would she say to him? What was she supposed to do? Emlyn only knew that she wanted to do this; she had to know before the inevitable with Maield.

Before she reached the door, Emlyn decided to put faith in the Gods and made a silent prayer to Áine. The door was already open, and for a moment she thought maybe someone was here that shouldn't be, but then a man coughed and she knew it as Roff. She gently pushed, making the door squeak open.

Startled, he went from sitting on the edge of his bed to his feet. While presenting the bandits to the mistress of the house, he had hidden his pain, but now with the light from the fireplace illuminating everything, the agony of the wound was clearly plastered on his face.

"Emlyn!" he said while holding his wounded leg wrapped in fresh bandages. "What're you doing here?" he asked a bit irritably.

She considered backing out, but stood fast. "I want to be with you."

"What?" He stared at her, confused.

Wanting to roll her eyes, she only said, "You know what."

They gazed at each other for what seemed like an eternity as the firelight danced and the shadows swirled about their faces, while the crickets sang tunes in unison. Then she started to methodically undo the buttons of her cream blouse. His eyes followed her nimble fingers, and he licked his lips. Her fingers undid the last button, and she let her blouse fall. She reached to undo the hooks of her brassiere.

"Y-you're allowed to do this?"

She stopped and looked at him. "There is no rule that forbids me."

His rasped, "Good."

The pain of the wound did not seem to impede his focus as he walked carefully to her. He stood two inches taller. He looked down at her with parted lips and reached around, lightly brushing her breasts. With little effort, he undid the hooks, then let the brassiere fall.

He looked at them as if he was uncertain, but only for a moment, then cupped one breast, passing his thumb over the rosy nipple. She moaned, and it seemed to goad him on, telling him that what he was doing was right and should continue.

They met each other's lips in a frenzy. He started undoing her gun belt. Then in that instant something came into his mind, and he pulled back and looked deeply into her eyes.

"I have to tell you . . . I-I only know what to do with men. Master Hadrian, he . . . since I arrived, he uses me almost exclusively. I don't . . . I never . . ."

She hushed him. "I know. I figured it out when you were showing me around your room."

"That obvious?" He smirked.

"Just your reactions from the gifts he's given you."

During her inspection, he was delighted to show her his room, but he became oddly quiet when she asked about a dozen trinkets sitting on his shelf. When he admitted, under his breath, that Master Hadrian gave him the pieces, she knew what was going on. She found the parallels between them unmistakable, as if the Gods meant this to happen.

"Our owners have their appetites, and so do we. Let us enjoy each other for as long as we can."

"Your mistress—"

He did not have time to get his question out. Emlyn had no intention of discussing the games she played with Sylvia. This right here was what she wanted in this moment, and she could wait no longer. She put her lips to his, and he began to taste her. The strong, calloused fingers attempted to slide her gun belt over her hips. She shimmied once, allowing it to clank to the floor, and her brown skirt went with it.

As his hand slid from her shoulder blade to the curve of her back, his muscles tensed. He pressed himself tightly against her. She could feel him hard against her abdomen and wanted nothing more than to free it from its confines. She attempted to do so, but as she succeeded in undoing the two buttons on his trousers, he grasped her biceps and looked deeply into her eyes again, but said nothing, only showed a type of feral lust.

He whirled around and pushed her hard onto the bed. On her hands and knees. It was unexpected, so she attempted to turn to face him, but he would not allow it because his fingers snaked their way into her hair and pulled. She gasped, then moaned in unfamiliar pleasure as he entered her.

It started slowly, with him getting a feel for her and the rhythm, but as she bucked back, his thrusts started to pound against her harder and harder, his animalistic instincts taking over once again.

She braced her arms against the headboard and grunted along with him for each thrust. The release of it all made her scream, but he placed his palm over her mouth, making her hold still as he kept the rhythm. Then five of the largest thrusts slammed into her. He slowed, and she could feel her heart rate again, boom-boom-boom, like she had run an obstacle course. Roff removed his palm.

The entire world was in a spin, and she had to close her eyes and shudder. He must have felt it ripple through her body, because he gave one last good thrust. She breathed out, slowly, and in that breath she almost felt free. There might be no rule against it, but the mistress would not be happy if she found out. She resolved to never let that happen. She would keep it as a secret.

A wet kiss fell onto the back of her neck. She smiled and used her fingers to try to control her disheveled hair. Suddenly she could feel his breath as he whispered to her.

"We are animals, are we not?"

She almost giggled. Legally they were, but she understood what he meant. "Yes, yes we are."

Roff huffed and pulled out of her. They both flopped down onto the sheets, and despite its rough spin, it felt like silk. They looked at each other, her on her stomach, him lying on his back. Smiling in satisfaction. Then he began to laugh.

She raised an eyebrow but did not lose her grin. "Why do you laugh?"

Roff put his hands behind his head and looked wistfully at the ceiling. "Oh, Mistress Muire, she wanted this to happen. Such a clever woman." She started playing with his chest hair as he continued, "She does not like that Master Hadrian conducts intercourse on a martial property owned by her family. I think she is hoping that you will talk about her, and me, to your mistress. Have me bred with you and out of her husband's clutches."

Breeding martials just to produce more candidates for martialhood was not unheard of. It was usually done if there was a lack of martials for a soon-to-be-born high patrician. But it didn't come cheap.

He looked at her. "She doesn't love him, you know; I think he feels much the same. She had to marry him for decorum's sake. She was with child when Master Cerisus was killed, so it's the younger brother's duty, if he is not already married, to step up and marry his brother's widow."

"That is an odd custom," said Emlyn. He nodded in agreement.

It was not long before the adrenaline subsided, and the pain came back to him in full force. The wound was bleeding through the wrap.

She found the needle and thread that was used to sew up the wound, cleaned it, and knelt before him as he sat on the bed with feet planted firmly on the floor. Emlyn redid the stitching; five in total, with as much care as she could manage. To Roff's credit he barely made a peep. She washed up and sat on the bed beside him. He put an arm around her, and she leaned in.

They stayed there listening to the crackling fire, taking in the scent of embers mixed with their sweat. Outside at the campfire, someone began playing the citarra in a slow rhythm before a pipe of some kind joined in. The sounds drawn out from the pipe were long and sorrowful. A deep male voice followed suit, with a lonely and menacing wobble in his gruff cadence.

"Accord, Accord! Intruder, enemy, spy!
He of the horde!
Betrayer of kind!
Killed by Themis sword!
Decimated by lies!
Accord, Accord! Not one of mine!"

Roff rubbed his forehead. "Ugh, that's unsettling!"

She laughed. "Your grandfather knows how to set the mood."

He chuckled. "Probably doing it to annoy me."

"I think he's trying to scare those bandits," said Emlyn.

"Or killing two birds with one stone."

Emlyn giggled. "If that's the case, then the stone missed."

He kissed her slowly, lovingly. She loved the feel of his lips, rough but sweet. She broke away from it. Her face fell into sorrow.

"Emlyn, what's wrong?"

"Roff, I have to tell you something. I would not feel right if I left without you knowing, not after this."

He looked over at her, surprised and a bit confused. "Whatever could it be?"

"I . . . undid my braid on the way here."

It took a moment before realization flooded him. "What? You're bound to someone?"

"Yes." She looked down with more than a little guilt.

He put his hands on his head. "We've angered the Gods. Aw cac! They will make us pay for this!" He calmed himself down and swallowed. "Why would you do this?"

"What I said to you out there, about breeding . . . it wasn't me. I'm scared, immensely scared. He seems like a good enough man, but I didn't want . . . it's too fast." She sighed and looked to the ceiling. "If I had a choice, you would be someone I choose . . . but I don't have any choices."

He stood up and carefully went to the mantel above the fireplace where the trinkets rested and took out a cigarette and match that were hiding behind one of them. He lit it with shaking hands.

"I would say that you have just made a pretty big choice here. You chose sacrilege."

"Roff, I—"

His voice became deeper and slightly menacing. "Please go."

* * * * *

The next morning Colmane noticed a change in her disposition, but he said nothing. Not even on the drive back to Londinium did he seek to question her about the dark cloud that had fallen over her.

The problem with the auto was that there was a short-circuit within the start button mechanism created when hooking up the spare battery in the wrong position. Colmane had blushed at his mistake even though it was a common one.

Colmane admitted that he was not able to discern anything other than a strong feeling that, somehow, the Barrentines were involved. She of course told him what Sissa's father had told her, and she was glad for the distraction.

"But if the killer did hit the girl on the head and threw her in the ravine, then why was he on the estate?" she asked.

"I don't know. Every ranch hand and gilla has been accounted for in the last year. Perhaps he passed himself off as a transient? Could be that the Barrentines knew about it and are trying to cover it up due to the stink it would cause."

He finished his cigarette and handed the butt to her. She looked at it and was reminded of Roff's anger from last night. She had not seen him and did not check up on him; it did not seem like the right thing to do. He made it clear that he did not want to see her for fear that the Gods would curse him further. Still her heart and mind seemed to have dropped out and tangled. The bright day, the breeze created from the moving auto, the birds flying above, and the never-ending emerald hills had no effect on her mood. She flicked the butt out the side of the auto, then proceeded to braid her hair while thinking of the two dead men whose heads now decorated the gate.

Chapter Twelve

Lanterns giving out soft light lined the path. The full moon gave everything an eerie glow, punctuated by the light of fireworks exploding above the city. The loud booms and cracks released sparks that flowed outward like streamers. In the distance was a constant bright light from an alcove where everyone in the insula except the patricians gathered to celebrate the nation of Kymbri in its fourteen hundred and sixty-third year. No one worked on this day. Instead they did their best to commit to revelry in its fullest—drinking and debauchery, along with various other entertainments.

Emlyn kept her distance from Maield as they walked onto the rock path leading into the garden. Her fingers nervously laced and unlaced behind her. She had an inkling of what he planned to do. They had spent a long day wandering the busy streets of Londinium trailing their owners. It was challenging, keeping an eye them while obeying the order to get to know Maield. What could one say to someone who would, most likely, become your breeding partner? But lo and behold they fell easily into conversation. There was barely a moment when one or the other was not talking. She actually liked him. He was a constant gentleman who seemed to revel in that self-notion, and she found it charming in an old-fashioned way.

The blue and green from the fireworks reflected in her eyes. She wondered if he had been broken in the same way. Did he end up kneeling and kissing the feet of his master? Thankful for a kind touch along with the respite from the constant pain and mind-numbing boredom? Was his mother just as terrible, his father perhaps? All subjects to discuss later. He had to be just as sore about such events as she.

Maield broke the silence. "I assume this is where you trained?"

Emlyn looked at him and then in the direction of the shed. She wasn't expecting that. ". . . Yes." It came out in almost a hiss.

Suddenly she was thinking about those months of horror.

Emlyn became aware of his gaze, not the gaze of someone evaluating her as a gilla but of interest and attraction.

"I assume it was an unpleasant experience?"

She placed her full attention back on him. Her eyes turned from sorrow to amusement. "Was what you experienced pleasant?"

He looked down and smiled, then eyed her. "Not too different from yours I think. Only different in the way of men and women."

Emlyn nodded in understanding. It was a sore subject for him, and now he knew it was the same for her. There was another long moment of awkward silence between them.

Low and curious, she asked, "Let us say that we are bred. What is your plan if we have a child?" She was almost afraid of the thought with all that entailed.

"I hope that is something we would both work upon. I would like us to be partners, not only when it comes to the training of our offspring."

She smiled wryly. "More than just getting along? Are you talking about falling in love?"

"Yes, or as close as we can get."

This made her chuckle. "You're an odd duck."

"I know we are not supposed to be too close, but that was from a time when martials being killed was not uncommon. They had to easily attach themselves to another partner. Do you not think it could work out differently in this day and age?"

That didn't seem true. She remembered the death of her own father, and the gruesome burning death of the Barrentine martial, Batt. Both had been killed by brigands.

"You certainly seem confident that our owners will wed."

Maield stopped on the spot; Emlyn did the same. He turned to face her and grasped her hand. She allowed it and could not help but blush slightly as he did so.

"My confidence lies with my master. However, I am not viewing our interaction as an outcrop of our owner's union."

He brought her hand up to his lips and kissed the back. Emlyn's blush deepened, and she found herself stepping closer. He was two inches taller than her, so she had to look up into his eyes.

"That is unusual for a martial," she said.

He smiled knowingly, seemingly pleased at her positive response to the concept. "It is, but I see that the thought does not bother you. In truth I think you have become excited by the idea of being in love with me."

Emlyn's blush became a deep rose, and she tried to hide it by focusing her eyes downward, but his fingers found their way under her chin. He lifted her chin so that she could peer back into those brilliant hazel eyes speckled with hazy blue. He furrowed his brow and worked his jaw back and forth.

"I was eleven when they broke me. They took me to the small walled garden, and my ankle was locked in an iron shackle. Chained to a post, I was naked and freezing, beaten daily, and with that came the mind games, until I broke. It was such a relief when I submitted to a caring touch."

She was taken aback. More talk of such a painful subject, but it showed he was committed. Even though it brought the mood down, it did not die. "Yes, mine was similar, except I was fifteen and it involved a shack."

"Fifteen! Why do you think they waited so long?" asked Maield, surprised. It was indeed a very odd thing. Male and female martials are generally broken between the ages of ten and twelve. Sometimes thirteen on occasion.

"My guess is they wanted to make sure my mistress and I were close enough, but honestly I never thought much about it. It's in the past now."

Maield put a hand delicately on her shoulder.

"If that is what it takes to make a martial as fiercely loyal as you, then you, and your parents, should be commended!" He smirked. "Let us quit all this breaking talk. Tell me, did you enjoy yourself today?"

She shrugged. "Somewhat."

His eyebrow raised. "Somewhat?"

"Well, I did not get to see anything because my companion was being too distracting."

"Oh, hah!" he said, clearly amused by her jest.

He gently traced her jaw with a finger like a feather falling against her skin. She craned her neck and kissed him hard. A flood filled her mind. None of the cascading emotions were easy to sort out, which only made her more frustrated and wanting. She pulled back.

He looked down at her with a loving smile. There was no ceremony here, no deference, no walls, no worries. Not now at least. It was simple, and that was rare in her world. She wanted more of it.

She could feel his hot breath on her cheek. Her eyes fluttered. This was the opposite of Roff, who was so animalistic. Maield was gentle, enjoying the leadup. Even though Emlyn sensed the tactic, it was something she knew she wanted. Her entire body was tempting her mind to keep going.

"C-can we?"

With his hand on her left shoulder, he trailed ever so slowly with the nail of his index finger up to her neck. She had never been touched like that by a man before. There were no tender caresses with Roff, only savage lust. Not that it was a bad thing per se. It was beyond pleasant, only . . . different. Then there was Sylvia. She had fun when Sylvia's desire was upon her, with her *games*, but her mistress's touch was different in a way that was hard to explain. Perhaps it was the difference between masculine and feminine; she could not say. One thing was for certain: she was damn curious to find out what more Maield could do. She found him pleasant, optimistic, and handsome with narly a fault. It felt right to her, very right. And he wanted to change how martials did things, how they were supposed to feel about one another, how they would treat their children. It all looked bright, and she admonished herself for her previous fear over this, a fear born from how her own parents interacted. Rude and disinterested in each other.

Maield smirked and twirled a few strands of loose hair trailing down from Emlyn's forehead between his fingers. "Can we . . . what?"

"You know." She found her breathing growing heavy and came close to losing all of her air when his hand reached around the small of her back, drawing her body next to his.

"You've never done this before?" he asked.

There was no reason to tell him about Roff. He didn't need to know.

"No." Her eyes were pleading as if she thought he would respond in the negative and call his pursuit off. She hoped not; right now all she wanted was for him to be inside her, and she could feel his rod throbbing, begging to be let out of its confines.

"I must admit, I'm rather surprised. Your mistress never allowed it as a treat?"

She shook her head.

"Did you ever ask for it?"

It took her a moment to respond as she looked down at his trousers. "No."

"Then ask me."

Emlyn bit her lip and glanced as his loins. He nodded

She did not wait. She glided to her knees and did not fumble even once as her nimble fingers undid the buttons of his trousers. Then gave him release.

* * * * *

Sylvia vigorously waved her silk fan. The extra air finally gave her some relief from the heat since the newly installed ceiling fan was on stutter. As a result, all the windows were wide open, and the loud booms and cracks from the fireworks could be heard clearly, exploding over the city.

Luxury indeed, she thought irritably.

She looked over at her mother sitting on the couch opposite her with a game of Brigands between them. Camilla had taken a break from playing and conversing. Instead she was breathing heavily under all those extravagant purple layers. She had her own silk fan trying to cool herself down. Everyone put on their best and brightest colors for this day, or there was the option of traditional, or costumes representing past heroes. In fact, costumes were what the royals involved in politics and representatives did at night during their annual ball. If Sylvia had involved herself in politics, that is where she would have gone. She would have hated it, even if they had working ceiling fans installed.

Sylvia was dressed practically but not cheaply in a cuff-sleeved eggshell blouse with heavy embroidery down the front. Tightly wrapped around her sleeve was an armband of the Kymbrian flag and emblem—a field of white with two swirling golden wolves fighting each other a golden lily. Most wore this armband, including her mother and Lucius. Her light blue skirt was the latest style, pinched at the waist with no flouncers underneath, going all the way to her ankles. The length showed off her intricately carved brown leather heels. Her mother hated it, of course, and expected her to wear something just as insanely elaborate as herself. Sylvia had refused, and that started a heated argument. Her side of it was that Lucius did not appreciate extravagance for its own sake and she agreed with him on that sentiment, while Camilla recounted the virtues of clearly showing your status in life. It was the first fight they had in a long while. Their anger lessened as the day wore on. How could it not, spending all day outside within the splendor of the citywide festival?

There was a parade marching through the streets in the late morning hours. It started with fluet and aulos players dancing and swirling, letting their skirts and wild dirty hair flare out around them as they blew on their ancient wind instruments. Their naked torsos and chests were decorated with temporary woad designs of various animals that represented different kinds of ancient land spirits. They were followed by belled frame drum players jumping side to side in rhythm. Then there came the Alban northern Gaels beating their drums and bellowing on their Caledonian pipes. Along with three long-necked carnyx with their bulbous pigs' heads giving out a high deafening cry that chilled the bones. They were followed by a procession of wandering druidi priests. Some carried oak branches, others threw oak leaves into the crowd as blessings. Behind them was a large litter. On top sat marble statues of the mother Goddess and her consort. People in the crowd constantly scrambled up to kiss their feet. The Teyrn came next, riding in a deep red auto with Kymbrian flags waving in the back. Flanked by the royal guard in their shining breast plates and blue-plumed steel helmets with their rifles nestled in their arms. The Teyrn was very old, covered in liver spots, but he still looked proud with his chin up and his hands resting on top of his ornate cane. Behind the auto walked the members of the Aeludai Cened made up of thirty high patricians followed by the hundred or so of the regular Cened. Lastly was the military with the new mechanized brigada in front. Sylvia's eyes went wide. She had a military contract, but she was just a cog in the wheel of invention and rarely ventured out to see them work. Four gigantic armored autos lumbered along with huge tractor-like wheels. The entire crowd started shouting, "Light of Kymbri!"

After the parade, they made their way past jugglers, mimers, and dancers to Deru park. Before entering, they turned down a rhyming challenge. The man immediately apologized upon realizing that they were high patricians.

The park was ready for a ceremony. The head priestess upon a dais anointed the Teyrn with an oak branch laden with leaves and water. He was unable to kneel before the statue of Brigantia, so he was allowed to sit in a simple wooden chair. He leaned forward and kissed her feet, humbling himself. The crowd roared with approval.

After stopping for a moment to meet a member of the Aeludai Cened, one Marcus Corret, they went on to Iria park, where a brilliant play was held about the war of the two wolves. Sylvia was delighted that Alma Minceed narrated the entire play. "And so, as it has come to pass, no part of the isle was ever conquered again!" The applause was deafening.

Another play followed, dealing with the Seaxones and Frisii trying to invade Gallia. They were pushed back. Kymbri, Gallia, and Erie reciprocated, thoroughly decimating their armies and creating the nation of Gaelland. Kymbri had no interest in ruling it, but many Erie settlers went there due to a famine back home, and now barely anyone in Gaelland could disclaim Erie heritage. That was when Sylvia looked back at the three martials. Emlyn and Maield sat close in lively conversation. Emlyn laughed at something he said, and Sylvia felt her face going red. She swallowed hard, turned back around, and for the rest of the day she could think of little else.

"Darling, are you well?"

Sylvia snapped out of her remembrance. "Oh, yes. My mind was far away."

Lucius was still leaning his forearms on the banister of an open window looking out over the garden.

Camilla looked at her from head to toe and back up again. "Is the heat affecting you?"

"I said I'm fine!"

"You've no reason to speak to me in such a way. I am only concerned."

"I'm . . . sorry, Mother. So you enjoyed the Skaldane incursion play?" The worry on her mother's face did not leave.

"Yes, and I cannot believe that you were not paying attention. It was wonderful. Marvelous. If they put it in the Royal Theater, I will take you. Drag you kicking and screaming if I have to."

"I will gladly go with you. I was . . . distracted today."

"Over what? Surely not work. On the one day where it comes close to sacrilege to do so."

Sylvia looked down at her lap. "I cannot say."

"Sylvia, you have always been a strange one. But lately your strangeness has overrun the cup. You should be happy. You have found a good man here." She nodded toward Lucius.

Camilla suddenly started coughing and immediately produced a handkerchief and put it to her mouth, expecting phlegm, but found nothing within the whiteness of the cloth except drops of spittle. Sylvia sat across from her mother, now looking at her with concern.

"Mother?"

"I'm fine, darling, for true, I'm fine. It will pass."

Sylvia was not so certain. She remembered her brother Cassius and his hard, straining cough being of like sound and consistency. A prelude to horrific spasms and bleeding from the orifices, along with a host of blood-oozing rashes. Emlyn's brother, Thom, died soon after of the same illness. It was lucky that the rest of the family did not contract the disease. It had been an especially terrible sickness that ran through the city that year, and it knew no difference between rich and poor. They called it the red sickness due to the rashes and bleeding.

"Do stop looking at me in such a way, dear. It's just a cold."

Lucius handed her a glass of water. Camilla gracefully took it but was unable to hide the shaking in her hands. She smiled at him gratefully.

"Such a fine gentleman. Thank you, Lucius." She leaned back and took a moment to relax from the fit.

"So, tell me, when are you marrying my daughter?"

"Mother!"

"I have the right to know, do I not?"

Sylvia grumbled, "Do you have to be so impertinent?"

Her mother stretched her arms across the back of the peach couch, along its golden frame. She chuckled. "She speaks of being impertinent! Who snuck out of the insula to go to some poor man's festival, hmm? And never apologized for it might I add! Who boarded up half of the rooms? Who was it that bought a former low patrician from a gilla block only for entertainment? And she wants to call me impertinent!"

Lucius waved a hand dismissively. "I believe an impertinent comment here and there adds a bit of spice. I know I'm not offended by the question in the least."

"A man after my own heart!" proclaimed Camilla.

"But to answer your question, Mrs. Chronister . . ." He paused. "Marriage is entirely up to Sylvia."

Sylvia smiled. "You see, Mother? Some men indeed move with the times."

Camilla harrumphed. "The girl should choose the suitor, but it is up to the parents to determine if said man is good enough or not."

"It is not performed that way anymore." Sylvia smirked as she took a sip of wine and placed the glass back on the center table.

"Listen here, prissy miss, there is an elegance in tradition missing in today's youth, and you're telling me to let it all go in the way of snow melt? As long as I am alive, I will keep that tradition and many others, thank you very much!"

Camilla might have been loud, but she did not sound truly upset. Not that her mother was ever the type to lose decorum.

Lucius turned around and went back to the window. "It is a good sign that our martials are becoming so well appraised of each other."

Sylvia stood up quickly and went to stand beside him.

"Where?" she asked in dire curiosity.

He pointed and raised a curious eyebrow. "Over there behind the bushes."

She looked where his finger directed. The bushes were moving, and she spotted two bodies behind it . . . two naked bodies.

Sylvia flushed with anger, contrasting with her elegant, puffy-sleeved blouse. She caught herself and forced her emotions down, but it was not quick enough to escape Lucius's notice.

"My apologies. I had no notion that you restricted your martial in such matters. Don't punish her too hard; it is only natural."

She put a hand on her forehead, closed her eyes, and tried to force the image out of her mind.

"Yes, yes, of course," she agreed.

Camilla started coughing again, this time with much greater force. Sylvia rushed to her with Lucius close behind. She put her arm around her mother as the last cough came out. Camilla spat into the handkerchief and drew it away from her. Soiling the stark white of the cloth was a stain of bright red.

*****

Emlyn and Maield laid back on the cool grass, panting so hard that they had trouble finding the words to speak. Their bodies glistened with sweat and seemed to reflect the moonlight and the myriad colors from the luminous fireworks. She let out a light giggle, making him look over at her with a contented smile. "You enjoyed that one, hm?"

Emlyn closed her eyes, shutting out the stars in the sky and basking in the afterglow as the waves of pleasure subsided. "Oh yes."

"Good, but I find it hard to believe that you've never done this before. It certainly seemed as if you knew what you were up to. Tell me that an explanation exists."

She frowned and looked at him. "I . . ." She did not want to reveal that she was with Roff only a few days ago; Maield would most certainly see her as a liar. She wondered if Sylvia's games could truly be called intercourse. Surely not. She decided to trust him with this information. After all, it was likely that being partners would be certain. Deep down she hoped it was. It no longer seemed like such a bad thing.

"My mistress uses me . . . from time to time."

He did not look surprised. "Does she use you in that way often? Does she use anyone else?"

"From time to time." She repeated. She had no intention of giving him any further details though. Emlyn could see that he was waiting for more information.

Music from a citarra breezed into their ears. Maield produced a flicker of disappointment, then sat up and reached for his pile of clothes, bringing out his belt pouch. He produced two rectangular pieces of cloth. He handed one to Emlyn.

Maield wiped down the back of his neck while Emlyn cleaned underneath her breasts and down her body. He could not help but watch as she rubbed herself down like she was taking a bath. They both would certainly need one after this.

"Would you like to join the rest of them?" asked Emlyn.

"Yes. We could use a drink. This took the water right out of me." She laughed.

"They should have any drink that you desire," she said, smirking.

He grinned mischievously, "What I desire? Now that is something I do not get to hear often." He turned to her, reached out his hand, and stroked a strand of her hair between his fingers. "What if I desire another kind of drink?"

Swift as a whip, he positioned his head between her legs, making her laugh, but she sank into satisfaction as his tongue swiped at a particularly sensitive nib.

When they were too exhausted to continue, they found themselves without anything to clean up with. So they shrugged and did not bother since their owners gave them leave for the rest of the night. There was no worry about decorum this late in the evening.

They followed the sounds of the citarra, cymbals, and drums down to the western alcove: a semicircular concave built into the wall. It was close to twenty feet long, and within were two doors, one on the right and one on the left. One led down to the kitchen and the other led to a storage room, which was open, revealing barrels unstacked and tapped.

The alcove also contained every servant and gilla in the house. Well, almost, Mira seemed to be missing. They all were standing around leaning on empty barrels, stools, or sitting on the stone floor. A few had instruments in their hands. Others were playing dice games or standing around drinking out of metal cups. Even her mother was there in the corner smoking, paying attention to nothing but the lit end of her cigarette. It was her mother who spotted them first.

Stella threw the cigarette on the ground, stomped on it, and glared at their sweat-covered bodies, messy hair, and disheveled clothes. Anger grew on her face and became red fire. Stella had the old mentality: martials should never have sex until bred, when it was certain that their owners were joined. As preposterous as that notion was, with all the examples through history, it did not matter to Stella. Her mother said nothing because the rest of the gilla and servants interrupted. They knew what happened and cheered them for it.

"Lil Emlyn finally got herself a fine rodding, eh?" yelled Donnon, a greasy young man who serviced and drove the autos. He extended his arm, and in his hand was a tambourine the color of his dirty-blonde hair. He shook the instrument, producing a light chaotic sound. Emlyn could not help but smile.

Ms. Cord sat upon an old, well-worn chair next to the door that led down into the kitchen. She held an old battered frame drum and peered at Emlyn with a knowing grin. She then started beating the drum lightly with the tipper.

A young and fair male bloodlined gilla named Bramble Roi, who helped the gardener and his assistant as well as performed odd jobs for Ms. Cord, banged his hand on a wash basin turned upside down. As he banged, he kept in time with the cook. Then Strawberry, sitting on a barrel, started strumming a few chords on the citarra. Emlyn had no idea where she had learned to play the instrument and marked it as an instance of the girl revealing another one of her remarkable skills. The tempo started to pick up. Soon the steward, gardener Fagan, his assistant Olier, Cord, and the other two housemaid gilla, Willow, named for her thick straight hair, and Lemon, named for her sour face, all burst out in chorus.

> "Hey there lil soldier
> Will you stand up for me?
> For my hunger is grateful, let's not be wasteful!
> I'll get down on my knees!
> Let me top that little drop!
> I'll fulfill yer every need!
> In the middle of the day, out in the rain!
> How my heart will dance with glee!
> So stand up for me lil soldier!
> I will give you all me strength!
> Through Áine's cord, you'll never be bored
> of head, waddle, or length!"

Everyone, including Emlyn and Maield, burst out laughing. Everyone except Stella, who just looked at the ground scowling.

"C'mere, have a drink. Relax fer once!" said Miss Cord. Everybody, already drunk to the gills, echoed the sentiment.

They began to swill back numerous concoctions. Primarily mil milis, a type of sweet liquor mixed with a hearty beer. Emlyn and Maield learned that they missed Mira's branding earlier that day and how the stubborn girl refused to join in and could currently be found sulking near the Dé Brigantia statue. But Emlyn did not really care. Dealing with whatever ill Mira perceived was unconcerning, and forcing the girl to the alcove would only ruin the night.

Olier with drunken agility jumped on top of a barrel and took a moment to balance himself before slowly standing straight. He put a hand over his chest and lifted his chin. He had everyone's attention by this point, waiting to see if he would fall.

"My fellow countrymen! Over fourteen hundred years ago, we defeated the Roman remnant! Drove those olive-smelling swine into the sea!"

A few of the free men raised their mugs in a salute to his words.

Olier continued, "Kymbri is the shining light of the world! They all look to us to provide the future! All except the Mithrans, who are blind to their own backward bull-worshiping ways and think they're better and more . . . enlightened than us. I fer one look forward to the coming war. I relish the thought of glory against those olive lovers, fer they are Rome returned to claim what they see as theirs. So let us drink our fill tonight and make ready our bodies to fight the bull tomorrow!"

As one in the morning rolled around, the exuberance wound down to relaxation. The fireworks had stopped but the smell of sulfur subtly wafted in the air. Strawberry strummed a low, sad song about a man who went to find his kidnapped wife only to find her dead. After discerning how she ended up there, he went to avenge her. Instead, a steady fall into madness became his fate. The free men listened intently to this song while smoking thoughtfully on their pipes, and even Stella joined in on a few verses. Donnon, Cord, and Maield were gathered in a circle engaged in debate as Bramble listened, fascinated to learn further of martials. Emlyn sat on a box that Maield was leaning against, content to just listen. Donnon had interrupted a conversation about the prevalence of gilla versus servants in Kymbri.

"I'm gonna have just as much as them, don't you doubt it. I will be the master of a grand house. I'll rise above them, you'll see!" said Donnon.

Ms. Cord shook her head in a knowing way and clucked her tongue. "They're yer betters for a reason, but yer a young lad, so I'll forgive ya that. Jus' don't go bad-mouthing the mistresses of the house. Or I'll spank yer arse with me spoon I will, and care none if you be master, servant, gilla, or a damn sea captain!"

Donnon had a sudden fearful look, and gulped, because he knew the cook never made idle threats and cared nothing for status when it came to discipline. There was a rumor that when lady Sylvia was a child, she misbehaved in the kitchen and received a spanking she never forgot. Only Emlyn could say if it was true. It was, but she had no intention of confirming such a thing.

Picking up where he left off before Donnon interrupted, Maield continued, "Who knows if any gilla will be around in a generation or two?" They looked at him. "Technology is moving fast and taking over industry. It is making manual labor obsolete. Take this insula for example. Fifty years ago, I bet this entire house was open and taken care of by a whole platoon of gilla, with few free servants."

Emlyn looked at him curiously. "Maield, this has nothing to do with money or technology. The mistress is very focused on her work and does not want to be spending so much time dealing with all manner of servants and gilla."

Maield just nodded, taking in the information.

"Indoor plumbing, electric lights, washers, freezers are wonderful things. So easy to use that even a master can do it!" interjected Bramble. Seeing the look on Maield's face sent fear shooting through the boy.

"Gilla used to be better trained too," he said with ice dripping from his voice.

Bramble looked down at his lap, embarrassed and shivering like he was suddenly cold on such a hot night.

Maield continued, "We used to take in any poor sod begging gillary in exchange for food. Now we are more selective due to rising costs, and so most gilla within the city now come from criminal stock with stilted choices."

A stilted choice was where there were two choices presented to a criminal instead of three. Usually it was the exile option that was taken out. Reason being the constantly changing trade routes, lack of scheduled ships, and no room on said ships.

He continued, "Yes, things seem better on the surface right now, but homelessness is at its highest. There are very few unskilled jobs and no option for those in dire straits. Workhouses would rather work people to death than lose profits. We are changing too fast."

"Did fae fiddle yer mind, boy? Ya need more opportunity to see outside yer walls! They're plenty of jobs for those that try, or do you say that the rise of the equites middle class dun't count? An' *they* want to be as their betters, that means keeping gilla, or servants. I know if I decided to heave meself out of this place, I'd be able to cook in any household! Perhaps what it really be is that ya believe yer own position will disappear. 'Cause martials are indeed fadin' away."

Before Maield could respond, the assistant gardener Olier suddenly came up from behind with a drunken Strawberry on his back. Her arms were wrapped around his neck, hanging like a cap draped over his shoulders.

"We got that war coming! That'll give people somethin' to do!" exclaimed Olier.

Strawberry kissed his shoulder, obviously far too drunk to even attempt to strum the strings anymore. "Are you joining the rank and file, Master?"

He kissed her on the lips. "You bet I am, you sweet gilla. Gonna kick those bull lovers all the way back over the Rhine."

She giggled as they ran off to do who knows what for however many hours.

Maield pointed to the two and asked Emlyn more than anyone else. "I hope your people do not act like that outside of this celebratory day."

Miss Cord answered after taking one long draw from her pipe. "How do your people act on a day such as this?"

"With a degree of decorum," Maield responded, standing a little straighter.

Cord looked him up and down before turning her gaze to Emlyn. "Emlyn girl, I think I disapprove of yer new fellow. Too uptight, thinks he's better than all us."

Maield harrumphed. "Your disapproval means nothing to—" He did not finish, for he was shocked at Ms. Cord's speed. Suddenly she stood uncomfortably close, staring up at him with ferocity.

"Ya don't scare me, boy! For someone who talks of decorum, you have precious little yerself, for ya forget that yer a gilla talking to a free woman. And if ya were of this house, I'd give ya the beating of a lifetime I would!"

He looked down, seeming to find a measure of humbleness. "Yes, yes, of course. Please forgive me, ma'am."

She looked him up and down again. "Suppose that'll do." She turned and gestured at Bramble. "Come, ya need to pay fer speaking out of line."

Bramble went dead white and croaked out the words, "Y-yes, ma'am," and got up to follow her. Ms. Cord said nothing as she went through the door leading down to the kitchen.

Maield looked at Emlyn and smirked; she was in a bit of shock at the situation. "Your cook is quite something all right, just like you said."

Emlyn blinked, then stifled a giggle.

No more than an hour later, many had retired to their beds. A few had passed out in the alcove. Olier had Strawberry bent over a box that Emlyn was passed out next to. Her head rested against the wood of the container, out cold to the world and unaware of the rodding going on above. Stella watched from the corner and waited for the servant to stop screwing the maid before going to Emlyn and rousing her so she would be ready to serve in the morning.

* * * * *

Mira had remained within the garden, hidden in resentment of the party and all the people involved in it. Besides, the garden was brilliant under the moonlight, and she did not want it ruined by some nasty, drunken servant trying to take advantage of her.

She had dazzled in the beguiling colors and monstrous explosions of the fireworks. It made her heart pump pleasantly faster.

As soon as the display ended, the walls seemed to loom in like dark foreboding barricades. She sank deep into her current reality and likened the spectacle to being a bird in a cage who had seen freedom bursting in brilliance upon the wall of the black sky. She sat in the grass and stared up, trying to recreate the incredible cacophony of color in her mind.

A light hot breeze was gathering, rustling the trees under a night sky full of stars. It brought a smile to her. She could not remember smiling in such a way, *In what, two years? Since Anton perhaps?*

She gingerly rested her head in the grass, looking up at the expanse in hope of forgetting the invisible bars and the throbbing pain from the brand on her shoulder. She knew she would be punished later for sleeping in the garden, but that no longer mattered. She rubbed her hand against the bandage on her shoulder one last time before losing herself to sleep.

She was jolted awake by hands heaving her up and pushing her against the tree trunk. She winced as her shoulder burst into terrible pain. She was able to clear her eyes and see that it was the martial of Lucius. Was he back for seconds?

He looked like he was about to rip her head off. Fear raced up and down her spine, and she found herself locked in place by her mounting terror.

Wadded up cloth was shoved in her mouth, and he placed a longer strip over her lips and around her head to keep it in. He easily lifted her up and over his massive shoulder. She wanted to scream, or at least kick, but what good would that do when she was just a lowly gilla and he a martial? She hoped that this was just some vivid dream. A familiar nightmare filled with a multitude of horrible things, but this had pain, actual pain.

He opened the door to an old decrepit shed that produced a smell not unlike old sweat. There was nothing in the shed but cracked dirt and a rusted metal stake standing straight up in the middle with a rusted chain attached to a loop at the top.

He walked to the back of the shed, then grabbed her by the waist and brought her down from his shoulder, flinging her to the ground. Mira's head hit the dirt hard, causing a cloud of old sawdust to waft up. The gag somehow managed to fall off. She coughed and tried opening her eyes, but her vision was rattled and dizzy. She wanted to throw up.

Before she could recover, Maield had her by the throat and lifted her to her feet. She tried to say something, but a sputter was all that came out. He forced her to stumble back against the wooden boards, making her squeak out a breath.

"Just get it over with. You want to get a bigger piece of me, go ahead, just don't hurt me anymore," she sobbed through the gurgle of words.

He leaned into her and traced a finger down the side of her face to the neck, where he suddenly grasped her. That meaty paw easily wrapped around her slender neck above the collar.

Maield's thumb slid from under her chin to the tender middle area of her throat and kept rubbing there. There was barely any pressure. Just enough to let her know the location of his finger and what he could do. Like an alpha wolf with its jaws around the throat of a younger pack member to show superiority. She wished he would get it over with, the anticipation of death seemed far worse than the act.

"No, little morsel, I do not want you. I can have any gilla girl in my master's arsenal. I want something much more intriguing." He paused to let his words sink in. His thumb sank into her neck.

She squeaked again from the pressure.

"I need you to confirm some gossip for me. Watch your mistress and her martial. Whenever they are together, I want you to be close. Look at how they interact, and if anything stands out, tell me."

He let go of her throat. Her knees hit the hard, compacted dirt, and she started sobbing.

"Do you understand me?"

She looked up at him with pleading eyes. Of course, she could not look for long, so she put her head down. "Y-yes."

"Then kiss my boots, trup."

She moved to his boots; the act of doing so seemed to take forever. His boots were covered in dirt and other unspeakable sludge gathered from the street. She wrinkled her nose in disgust; her entire body tensed, causing hesitation.

"I expect these kisses to come about sometime this century."

Mira leaned forward and pressed her lips to the grime-covered boot. She lifted her head quickly and kissed the other as fast as she could just to get it over with.

"That was lovely." He bent down and lifted her chin. He held it cupped tight between his fingers, but her eyes still looked downward. "Look at me."

She obeyed, looked in those dead eyes, and shivered. "You will be checking in with me each week, and I expect progress within the month. If you do not bring me something meaningful, then it will be a simple thing to drag you to a quiet place, just like this one, and slash your throat! And you know what? No one would care."

She burst into tears. Maield pushed her over and left her there, a miserable wretch. The image of her returning to the homeland, to cheering crowds who would hail her coming as a bright new day for their country, faded. An image she could no longer grasp hold of because it no longer seemed real. Only this was real: the fear and the anguish. Who was she kidding? There was no escape, only ruin. To bring *their* ruin was the only path forward.

"You-you're trying to bring down this house?"

Maield was getting ready to close the door, but he stopped and looked back at her, startled by her words. "Perhaps."

She started laughing, low at first, then quickly turning maniacal as she got back to her knees.

"What is wrong with you?" Annoyance and confusion mixed in his face. He approached her cautiously, ready to bash her into the ground if one wrong move was made.

"Why didn't you start with that? I want to see them brought to their knees. I want to see you light the fires."

CHAPTER THIRTEEN

-THE BREAKING-

The room was decorated for the sensibilities of a teenager, yet it still had some of the trappings of a child's playspace. A dozen dolls were arranged, alone and dusty, on the top of a storage trunk at the end of the bed. On the ready table under the window, where Emlyn had climbed out to save a kitten many years ago, a large blue elephant and white lamb with black beaded eyes sat prettily on their stuffed haunches.

The one thing that did not seem to belong in this room was an old doll's house standing in the corner, carved by hand from oak wood. It was an item gifted to Sylvia from her parents on her sixth birthday. A family heirloom that was of significant importance to her great-grandmother Davinia. It stood as an almost perfect recreation of the Chronister insula, but her reaction to it was unexpected and upsetting to her parents when the sight of the old thing scared her to the point of tears. The smell of age emanated from it. The floors seemed to take on the grain of the real thing, and much of the tiny furniture was true to life, an exact copy. There was a sinister purpose to it; at least that was what her deep mind always told her. It made Sylvia think that whoever carved it was trying to perform some black magic upon her family. She worked herself into such a hysteria over it that it produced a plethora of nightmares for many years.

In the end, she accepted the thing out of obligation, and so it sat making indentations on the hardwood floors, gathering dust until her governess had the mind to clean it, or sent a gilla to do it. As it was, she ignored the wretched thing, so it never moved from that spot and had always remained an old, musty darkness in the corner of her otherwise bright room.

A few days ago Sylvia celebrated her fifteenth birthday, and as she sat on the side of her bed combing Emlyn's hair, all she wanted, the only thing she wished for, was to admit her love and go to the seashore with Tabby by her side. She brushed the long chestnut hair, never increasing or decreasing the speed of the strokes. The horsehair bristles combed down to the ends, where it curled near the middle of Emlyn's back. She sighed in silent contemplative delight and basked in the sight of the luxurious brown strands each time they fell back down to rest upon the broad shoulders.

For the entire year, she tried to come up with a way to tell her. A hundred different ways at least, but each solution was discarded. She wanted to say it, blurt it out, to shout, sing, to even whisper her love would be grand, but she didn't . . . Instead she narrowed her eyes and tried to focus on the hair.

Wouldn't it be something? Maybe I can think of a way to tell her . . . She swallowed and stopped that train of thought. Instead she looked down at Emlyn from above and became transfixed on her slight movements. Her breathing, making the chest gently move up and down. How it made her proportioned muscles move subtly, and that beautiful nose. Then the best thing: the brown amber of her eyes. Sylvia's heart pumped faster, and she felt a familiar heat building, slowly spreading out bit by bit. She adjusted her legs and almost missed hearing Emlyn ask what the problem was. She had ceased brushing her hair.

"Hello! Anyone home? Is Sylvie in there?" teased Emlyn.

Sylvia started brushing again. "Sorry."

"Are you thinking about Valance?"

That boy they met at the festival last year? That was an odd thing to bring up. If anything it had seemed that Emlyn had a heart for him, not herself, despite all the letters.

During the festival, she had noticed that his interest was solely focused on Tabby. However, a few months later he started sending letters about his interest in Sylvia on an almost weekly basis. She always balled up the letters and threw them in the trash.

"No, I am not thinking about him in the least."

"Sure you're not! I've plucked a few of his letters out of the bin! I know what's going on! You love him and you're embarrassed to admit it!" Emlyn laughed.

Emlyn must think that the letters were being responded to. For someone being trained to spot small details about people, Tabby sure seemed to have a glaze over her eyes when it came to Sylvia. Yes, her friend could see so many things, but not how much she loved her.

Sylvia smirked and decided to tease back. She used the flat side of the brush to hit her lightly atop the head.

"Ow!"

"I don't respond to those letters, and *if* I remember correctly, he had a heart for you, not me."

"But, I thought—"

"You think too little of yourself, Tabby."

"Why does he send you letters then?" Emlyn asked curiously.

"Well, I am going to be the mistress of this house one day, so I think he's being pushed to do so."

Emlyn thought about that for a moment and looked over and up at her. "Do you think we'll see him again? Perhaps at the shore?" She had an air of hopefulness in her voice.

Sylvia certainly hoped not. "He is . . . not your type, Tabby. You can do better."

A sigh vibrated through Emlyn; Sylvia could feel it through her legs. She didn't like saying such a thing, but Emlyn would listen.

Besides, she only met him once and that was a year ago. Not only that, the letters made it clear that Valance had no further interest in Emlyn, and she did not want to tell that to Tabby.

She needed to get her out of this place. Besides a few outings to the family estate and a few wonderful weeks at her great-uncle's peach and apple orchard, they had been cooped up in the insula for most of their lives. Neither of them were allowed out without strict supervision. Now, after all this time, her parents agreed—both sets of parents finally agreed. They would be able to go to a popular coastal spot for patricians. Without that strict supervision they hated so much.

Emlyn was in a teasing mood about overpowering and outshooting all the boys they knew. They knew very few boys; most of those were family members. Emlyn exclaimed that she would never marry a man who could not best or equal her at target shooting.

Sylvia could only think of embracing her, feeling her lips next to hers. So she teased back like she did care about such things, and it went on like that until bedtime. They said goodnight to each other, and as Emlyn flipped the light switch, she glanced at those warm fields of amber. The switch gave out a metallic click. The room was pitch black, and she listened to her own heightened breath. She found sleep difficult to grasp. Her mind was a whirl and couldn't find rest no matter how hard she tried. No girl was supposed to feel this way about another girl. It seemed to be coming from her stomach: a queasy feeling followed by a rush of barely conceived emotions. She would need to tell her about it soon, and hope for the best and prepare for the worst.

The comfort of a bed would not come for many hours for Emlyn. She was assigned reading material each day and had to accomplish what was given to her. Today she had put it off for far too long and did not relish the thought of being punished for not finishing. Also what she did not finish today would be added on top of tomorrow's assignments. Punishment in itself.

She was bored to say the least. To stave off dreariness, she had decided that this was as good a time as any to do as the druidic priest said. Not just to fulfill the geissi but to hopefully gain some insight from this God of servants and the traditional namesake of those in forced servitude.

Gilla was once the guardian of the seven doors beyond the bridge of twilight. Clad in gleaming armor, he stood proud and unwavering. He would open the door to whatever fate a spirit was bound to, and he did his job diligently. Until one day when he was stunned to find a woman with fiery red hair crossing his bridge. She was the most beautiful woman he had ever seen. Her name was Rianod, and her voice was as warm as a summer breeze, and her eyes were like golden honey.

He bade her to stay and talk for a while. She did so. In life she was the favored priestess of Brigantia. Rianod was to enter the second door and be reborn as an important person. It was the Goddess's gift to her. But he kept her there for a very long time. When she walked toward the door, he bade her to stay.

Three refusals passed her lips. But he would not take no for an answer. He chained her to him, ankle to belt. Brigantia was not happy. She turned Rianod into a gigantic black dog with fur as dark as shadow and with eyes of a red moon. He ran and was chased through hill and dale.

After countless years, she caught him but refused to lay her jaws upon his neck. Following him in the mortal realm, she had fallen in love and said that she would stay with him. Brigantia and her consort appeared, displeased by both of their transgressions. Gilla prostrated himself before the Goddess and flattered the Goddess on her beauty before begging to serve her.

Brigantia decreed that as punishment, Gilla would serve her while chained at the ankle. In his gratitude, he kissed her feet. Rianod was cursed with the form she wore and placed as the guardian to the seven doors for a thousand years.

Emlyn's mind filled in the blanks, and the story became sort of brutal. Rianod lost everything in the end: her place in the second door, her form, her love, and possibly her virtue. She then kept performing the duties the Goddess tasked to her. Emlyn felt nothing but tragedy.

Of course, the story was trying to tell her to take pride and comfort in service to your betters, to humble yourself and know your place, follow the rules. At least it was not a boring tale. Unlike the eastern etiquette book she was supposed to be reading instead of this one. *Now that's a book full of inane, senseless things!* she thought.

She pushed *Of Gods* to the side of the table, put the etiquette book before her again, and once again found the verbiage unnecessarily long. It droned on and on to the point of becoming a foreign language.

She blurted out in frustration, "Cac!" and grinned at hearing herself cuss; it certainly felt like the right thing to do. She looked down at the pages of the book again. The words began to blend and became one big blur. Why was she learning this stuff? She had been steeped in etiquette since, well, since she could remember. It seemed redundant when she could be reading one of the more militant philosophy books from the east. She always enjoyed reading those. She rubbed her eyes in an attempt to rid the dreariness. She reached into her pocket and thumbed the polished piece of amber, hoping that it would somehow help keep her awake.

She rose to her feet and fought her fatigue with each step as she made her way to a tall bookcase standing proudly against the wall. It was not so high that she couldn't reach the top shelf. Emlyn was five-foot-eight by last measurement and would continue to grow according to her last doctor's visit. She reached up and pulled a book down. "Give me a good adventure any day, even better if it's based on a bit of history."

She glided her hand over the engraved leather cover before opening it up and taking in the smell of the pages mixed with the heady scent of leather. It brought back all the memories she had of reading this book throughout her life. She closed it and studied the cover. The name was

The Pistoleros from Tolido in a fancy script. Below that it read: "A Collection of Tales About Those Brave Shootists." And beneath those words was an embossed design of a six-shot revolver even though they used caps back in those days. Emlyn thought about how proficient she had become with the weapon herself. She wished she could shoot one now and feel that thrill of hitting a target dead center instead of being cooped up in a dusty old room studying boring books of no merit.

She thought about the adventures within these pages. None of the characters had a home to call their own, and this never seemed to bother them. They were free to roam the country helping those in need, freeing towns of smugglers and pirate scum, and settling disputes between ancient families . . . after they saved a damsel or two, of course. They loved life and lived it to its full measure, and here she was stuck behind four walls and a small attic window tasked to read the most boring book imaginable!

Moonlight shone into the round stained-glass window, high up near the steepled ceiling. She smiled, but the pleasure seemed to leave her as clouds came to obfuscate the sky outside. Her smile faded. She reached up and put the book back in its place, then situated herself back into the chair, hunched her shoulders, and started to read the etiquette book again. She wondered for the ten-thousandth time in her life when all her questions would have an answer or if she would go mad first.

A few minutes went by just staring at the pages when she heard a knock on the door. She did not move from that spot, just stared. A second knock made her jump out of her seat and dash to it. She started to open the door when it was violently pushed in. She jumped back, but not fast enough. Her wrist was grabbed by a familiar hand.

"Papa? What're you doing? That hurts!"

The door opened all the way, revealing Stella. Emlyn looked back and forth at their impassive faces. Their eyes were cold and demanding.

"Am I being punished? I'm studying. I'll be done by midnight."

Grandmother Cali's face appeared in the doorway. The lines at the edges of her mouth crinkled up, following her warm smile. "Tonight all those questions, those frustrations, the secrets you tried to uncover over the years will be revealed."

Her face lit up in exuberance. Papa let go of her wrist. Stella's and Papa's faces still looked dire, but Cali's warmth made her move forward to follow. She wondered what was wrong with Papa. She expected this of Stella, but not from him. She yearned for answers, though, and so did not question it. As they walked, Cali handed her a cup of liquid and bade her to drink. She did and found the taste to be surprisingly sweet.

It was a calm night, and everything in the courtyard was bathed in the eerie glow of a full moon. The garden was devoid of insects making their nightly melodies. Even the sounds of the city beyond the walls seemed nonexistent. The only thing that gave evidence that this was all real was a breeze that gave a feeling of oddness coasting on a late July chill.

Sylvia's cries sliced through the silence. The night seemed to give the sobbing an echo that bounced off the walls of the insula. Emlyn was still at the arches, and she could see Sylvia standing before Mr. and Mrs. Chronister in the garden.

"Why is she out here? Why is she crying?"

Her family said nothing. Briar just grasped her bicep and thrust her forward. Cali did not follow, instead she stood back at the arches. Cali undid the top two buttons of her white blouse and flicked out a steel collar along with its attached tag.

"Papa? What's happening?"

"Silence!"

He was so stern. Emlyn obeyed and swallowed the lump in her throat. She was led out onto the walkway and told to stand between Sylvia and a newly erected pole that was hammered deep into the earth that very morning. She had wondered what it was for. She asked about it and received no answers, but she still wondered and got the idea that whatever it was for, it had something to do with what was happening now. She found herself fearing it, knowing that whatever it could be, it was one thing for sure: a pillar of malice.

Her parents stood side by side a few yards away in a very formal stance. Perfectly straight with arms going down to closed fists. Emlyn looked beside her at Sylvia, still wearing her nightgown, the top of which was wet with tears.

"T-they, they told me . . ." Sylvia sobbed.

That was when Emlyn noticed the red mark on her cheek. Sylvia had been slapped, hard. Her concern grew into anger, which built up to a rapid boil.

"Sylvie! What—"

Andreas stepped up to Emlyn; she looked up at him with contempt. Before she could say anything, he slapped her. Not with his palm but with the back of his hand. She fell to the ground like a stone thrown from a building.

"Tabby!"

Andreas stopped his daughter from bending down to comfort her friend. After a few seconds, Emlyn started to peel herself off the ground.

"Keep standing there, understand? And you, stay on your knees!"

Emlyn found it hard to sort her thoughts, not knowing what she could say at that moment with her mind too rattled to think. What was there to do but get up to her knees while trying to put those thoughts back in order?

Andreas went to the Gwens. "Let us start."

Stella and Briar bowed with fists on their chest.

Briar took Emlyn by the upper arm, forced her to her feet, and led her stumbling to the shed. He threw her against its frame. Her back hit the old gray wood with a loud thump. Her brain seemed to find its path again.

"Papa! Why're you doing this?"

She looked between her father and her mother. Emlyn could barely find the words. She was so confused wondering if this was really happening. It didn't feel like it, but it was. By the Gods, it was happening to her! Remembering Cali flicking the collar out, a lightbulb blazed to life in her mind, then busted.

"No . . ."

Briar's booming voice resounded through the air.

"Take the gown off!"

"What? No!" Her confusion and fear made her back press against the shed wall as if she would dissipate through the wood.

"It is not yours! It never was! All of your clothing, everything you thought you owned belongs to the Chronisters!"

"No, Papa. Don't do this." She pleaded hoarsely.

"Take it off or we'll rip it from you!" Briar's voice held disappointment at her disobedience.

Emlyn's waterworks started again as she slowly began to remove the gown, but it was not fast enough for Stella. Emlyn didn't notice her coming with a face full of annoyance and impatience. The gown was ripped away from her body. She tried to hold on to it, but it was wrenched from her grasp. She was naked, and the night breeze, or the fear, or both raised goosebumps up and down her body. She did her best to cover her nakedness with an arm across her chest and a hand over her crotch.

As Emlyn's gown was ripped away, Sylvia came back to herself. She ran to her, but Andreas grabbed his daughter by the collar of her nightgown. She looked up at her father, pleading. "Don't let them do that to Tabby! Why won't you stop them? Please, Daddy!"

Emlyn fell to her knees shivering like a cornered rabbit. "W-why're you doing this?"

"Because you are a gilla, a servus, an asel!" exclaimed Briar.

She looked at him, disbelieving, then furrowed her brow in anger. "No! I'm not! I am not!"

Stella grabbed her hair, lifting her to her feet as Emlyn let out a scream and tried her best to fight, but to no avail.

"Oh yes you are! You might not admit it tonight, but you'll know, and you will accept it!"

Briar interrupted. "What your mother means to say is that it's in your blood. That is why you will accept your new role as Sylvia's martial."

Emlyn's eyes went wide after hearing this. "No . . . No!"

Stella's famous impatience got the best of her. "Enough!"

She led Emlyn by her hair to the post. She screamed and jerked the entire way.

Emlyn was held against the wooden pillar as Briar took her hands and tied them securely on the other side. She could not move with how tight the rope was. Testing it resulted in a grating pain against her wrists. Her bare back was exposed to the Chronisters while Briar and Stella stood in front of her, making sure that she stayed still.

"Papa, this is not right! You can't . . . ." She took a moment to swallow, trying to ease up her tightening throat before continuing. "I'm not a gilla. I can't be! Sylvia and I, we're friends!"

Briar grabbed her jaw hard, forcing her eyes to look into his. "You are not equal to Sylvia. You are not even equal to a servant! Sylvia is your mistress, and that is all she will be to you. Your mistress! Just like Camilla is your mother's mistress and Andreas is my master!"

Briar and Stella unbuttoned the top of their high shirt collars to expose the steel bands around their necks. They flicked their tags out.

Emlyn let out a wail that sounded more like the squeak of a dying mouse. She understood now that everything had been a lie. The pieces fell into place. That time in Ened's garden. How she had always been treated compared to Sylvia. She felt sanity slide away as realization took a firm hold. The cords snapped, and only a few strands held together. She struggled to hold on, but she grasped what was left and held it tight.

"Daddy! Make them stop!" Sylvia grabbed her father's right sleeve, pulling the fabric down and coming close to ripping it. His annoyance showed on his face, but she continued to plead while staring up into increasingly angry eyes.

"Please! They're hurting her!" With his left hand he grabbed her wrist and shoved her arm away. With his right hand, he shoved a coiled whip at her chest.

"Not I . . . but you will."

She looked at the nine-tailed whip as if it was alien to her, some artifact whose purpose was unknown. She looked back up at him and choked out, "She's my best friend. I love her!"

Camilla spoke up with a tone that made all this seem like just another day, like some routine, deftly practiced. "She's a gilla, darling. From the very day she was born she was a gilla, and since then she has been your gilla, even though you did not know it at the time. Now you must enlighten Emlyn of her station in life."

Andreas shoved the whip into Sylvia's hands, making her grasp it. "But Daddy!"

He furrowed his brow. "Don't *but* me, child! She is your gilla! Do as I've taught you with the others!"

Sylvia was suddenly aware that when he had taught her to use a whip a few months ago, it was not to maintain discipline but to get her ready for this. She stood in horror. They had lied to her ever since she could speak. She had difficulty swallowing.

"Th-that's Tabby! I can't hurt Tabby! She's my best friend!" She almost broke down then and there.

Camilla chimed in again. "Sylvia. My best friend was Stella, and look at us now, happy in our roles. You and Emlyn will feel the same way in a few years. That's the way of things."

An edge of rebellious contempt came bubbling back up. "What if I don't want that?"

Andreas had enough. His impatience was evident in every movement, eager to get this over and done with. "You will want exactly that, because that is what is expected of you!"

However, Camilla kept a cool but stern tongue. "Nothing is going to change the fact that she's a gilla, dear. If you don't whip her, then someone else will, and I can promise you that it will be much worse for her."

Tears started to come, but she did not betray even a sniffle. She turned to Emlyn, not wanting to look at her. Instead she kept her head down, looking at the leather-braided handle of the whip, contemplating its woven pattern. She tried to grope for some meaning to all this but found that her mind was a whirlwind sweeping up every thought and emotion, leaving piles of refuse in its wake.

A gilla walked through the garden entrance, swishing down the stone path. The sheer skirt and top flowed with the movements in rhythm with the low breeze. From a distance this gilla looked female, and the gilla was indeed feminine as anyone could be, until the flat chest and slight bulge in the crotch became apparent as he got closer. He carried a folding chair under one arm and carted something behind him: a standing record musicura. One of the many inventions that the Chronisters invested in a generation ago. He looked happy, humming a tune. He went past Emlyn and Sylvia as if he had not noticed them.

Camilla exclaimed in a jovial tone as he got close, "There you are, Bootsie! Just in time!"

Bootsie was a common sight around the house. He had been there for over five years now, but after Kittie left, he spent most of his time serving Andreas and Camilla directly. He unfolded the chair, making sure to set it firmly on the ground, then smoothed the seat just before Camilla lowered herself to the canvas fabric. She proffered her cane to him. He took it gracefully, setting it up against the musicura. He then opened the top of the musicura, folding it out like wings. He brought out a teacup and small pitcher, laying it on one of the winged doors. He then poured, not spilling a drop, and handed it to Camilla. Next he brought out, from a door in the lower half of the contraption, a small glass and a fine wooden ice bucket. He placed them on the opposite wing from the tea and dropped two ice cubes in the glass, making a very audible, refreshing clink. Then he brought out an amber bottle with no logo which could only be Andreas's favorite spiced rye. He poured the liquor in the glass and handed it to him.

Camilla sighed, contented. "Start the music! It'll mask the screams a bit. Oh, and Bootsie?"

He stood at attention. "Yes, Mistress?"

She looked up at him and smiled. "You've been such a good boy, and it's not every day that one gets to see the first night of a martial breaking. Would you like to watch?"

His face lit up. "Oh yes! Thank you, Mistress!"

He cranked the box's handle, lighting up the many buttons running along the extended piece jutting forward from the upper middle of the box. He pressed one of the buttons, the box clicked, and a few seconds later an operatic voice blared out:

"I found you at the dock in down market
Where you signed your life away to the sea,
and dear I fear I'll miss you when your coffin returns.
For I loved you as the reaper.
Oh, when can I find you in the sleepy reeds?"

The whiskey, and the smooth sultry voice of Assalie Mhyron, helped to calm Andreas's nerves. Probably a calculated move by Camilla with her uncanny ability to predict behavior. He noticed that his daughter was refusing to look at Emlyn and gently pushed her forward.

"Go on. Look at her."

She did so, wiping the tears from her eyes before looking back at him.

"We will not leave here until you whip her!"

Each step seemed to take an age. Sylvia stopped within the perfect distance and became horrified when Emlyn's head perked up in alarm upon hearing her steps. What looked back at her was the most horrific and sad face she had ever seen. The hurt in Emlyn's eyes made her want to break into a million pieces.

"Sylvie. Please! We're friends!" Emlyn choked back a sob. "We have so much fun, just you and I! Don't you remember? Don't you care?"

Of course she remembered. She wanted nothing more than to throw the whip in her father's face, cover Emlyn, and cry right along with her. Then where would they be? Nothing good would come if she refused; perhaps much worse would befall Emlyn. There was no other way. No place to go. She was in the correct position, so she slowly raised her arm.

Emlyn watched Sylvia raise the whip ever so slowly. Her mouth fell open. She was confused. Then a streak of betrayal hit, bounding into anger. It was all driven away in an instant as the whip came down with a loud crack. Emlyn screamed out as the pain rippled through her body.

Andreas kept yelling, "Again! Again!" Immediately followed by more white-hot flashes of pain.

Time seemed to ebb away. Emlyn had no idea how many lashes she had taken. She just wanted it to be over. The blood trickled down her back, and oddly enough it cooled the skin.

Finally Andreas told Sylvia to stop.

As they released her wrists from the bindings, she came to, and a wave of pain hit as she tried to flex. Screaming and moaning was the recourse, but only a squeak managed to escape. Her eyes cleared, and as she looked around, the world seemed to be made up of blurry shadows, dark menacing figures standing all around her.

Her arms were pulled, being dragged away, and as her vision cleared, a view of Sylvia then came into focus. She wanted to hate her for treating her like an object, to condemn her so-called friend, but she found herself unable to hate Sylvia, who was on the ground, sobbing into her hands. She only felt sorry for her. It was the last feeling she had before unconsciousness came.

She was awoken when her head bumped the ground, but everything was still black. There was a click behind her. As Emlyn's eyes adjusted, she could see soft light between the boards. She was in the shed! She panicked, adrenaline kicking in. The pain seemed to go away, and she tried frantically to reach the door but never made it. Her body wrenched, then her face struck the dirt hard. The new pain made her grimace. Something around one of her ankles kept her from going any further.

She reached down and felt the cold manacle locked securely around the left ankle and then felt the chain connected to it. She followed the chain's length to a steel spike, feeling down to where it entered the soft dirt. She tried with all her might to get the spike out of the ground. She tried and tried but eventually gave up. Emlyn sat down to catch her breath. *Yes! I can knock the boards out!* she thought and rushed over to the other side of the shed, but she fell flat on her face again. Shoving the pain aside, she tried reaching out to the boards, but she was only barely able to touch them with her fingertips. Quick as Mercury, she got up and rushed to another side, only to experience the exact same predicament except that the boards were further away.

That was it . . . all she could muster. Emlyn crawled back to the middle, found a large pile of straw, and collapsed. She breathed out in exhaustion, then sleep quickly washed over her.

* * * * *

A quivering eyelid lifted, and soon the other eyelid followed. Shafts of light illuminated the surroundings. She got up on one elbow, wincing in pain as she stretched her back and took stock of the shed. There were the old wooden planks, the straw beneath her, but not much else other than what she had noticed last night.

The floor was dirt, and there were no rocks. It was too fine to pack and make it into something hard to throw, but too coarse to properly blind someone. She lifted the chain a bit, her eyes trailing it to the lock attached to the loop on top of the stake.

Her face lit up with an idea. She hurried to the stake and started spitting around where it entered the earth, but soon stopped when her mouth became dry. She tried to pull the stake out, but it was not enough. She thought for a moment and then realized an alternative. She proceeded to squat over the stake and pissed on it—a long hard piss. She turned, grasped it, and pulled with everything she had. Eventually it gave. She fell back hard, sideways on the dirt, knocking the breath out of her and almost screamed in pain due to her back hitting the ground, but she held a hand over her mouth to keep from doing so.

When the pain subsided, she sat up and felt proud of such an accomplishment, she took the stake in hand, ignoring the smell of urine. Her eyes focused on it, and she realized that she did not want to kill anyone.

I could knock them out. Papa told me how to do that, but if Papa opens the door . . . what would happen if I managed it? I'm not going to be a gilla! I'm not a gilla! Any escape scenario was ridiculous, she knew this, but Emlyn put the thoughts out of mind and just hoped Papa would not open that door. Any adult besides Papa.

"Help me!" she croaked. Surprised by the weakness of her voice, she gathered herself and put more force behind it. It wasn't easy; it was like spitting dust.

"Let me out!" She went to the door and banged on it, yelling for them to let her go. She could get close enough to peer out between the slats and spotted two figures sitting a few feet away. She watched their lips move and knew what they were saying.

Outside the shed in a wooden folding chair sat Camilla, dressed exquisitely like always, reading the morning newspaper. Emlyn's noise did not bother her one bit. She folded the edge of the newspaper down so she could look at her husband.

"Nothing interesting in today's paper?" asked Andreas.

"Nothing of note, dear." She folded the paper and handed it to him.

Andreas sat in his own folding chair only a half a yard away from his wife. Between his legs was Bootsie, still wearing the long sheer skirt and blouse. It must have pleased Camilla to see him that way in the guise of a new obedient gilla girl. She did this all the time to Bootsie, who never seemed to mind it. Emlyn had asked him one time why he was okay with such things. He was honest and said that it had its element of fun, and it was much better than getting beat up in the streets for how he moved and talked. From what she heard among the gossip of gilla and servants of the house, Bootsie had declared himself a gilla in front of Mrs. Chronister right after one of those beatings, and she accepted his declaration. Now, Emlyn hated him. He knew too that it was all a lie, and he just stood back and watched! She continued doing her best to scream for help.

Mr. Chronister rolled up the newspaper and bopped Bootsie lightly on top of the head, signaling for him to stop. Camilla snapped her fingers, and Bootsie rose to his feet and went to grab a pitcher sitting on the wing of the musicura. Bootsie then poured the black steaming liquid into a coffee cup being held out in Camilla's hand.

Emlyn let out another wail and started beating the boards with the stake.

Andreas had his coffee cup held out too, but the wailing made him roll his eyes, and he motioned for Bootsie to stop. The gilla knelt in the grass next to the musicura.

Mr. Chronister came to the door, and Emlyn got ready by standing to the side. She lifted the stake, but the door did not open. She could hear voices just beyond but could not make any of it out since they were speaking too low. She could tell, though, that Andreas was talking to her papa. Emlyn peered out front between the boards again.

Her father had his back turned to the door. Because of that she could not make out everything that Mr. Chronister said. But she caught wind of her intelligence being mentioned. The rest was just too low to make hide nor hair of.

Finally they started to speak up. "After her experience last night, I can tell you that her mind has not caught up yet."

Andreas put a hand on Briar's shoulder. "You would know, old friend."

"Yes, Master. How is little Sylvia?"

"Sequestered herself in her room, refusing to come out unless we declare, in writing, that we've set Emlyn free," Andreas said with more than a little amusement.

"She's a feisty one. I wonder how long it will take for her to realize that you have the master key."

"Soon I hope." Andreas put his hands in his pockets and shrugged. "Well, I suppose it is my turn at the game board."

Her papa really did call him master. She was glad to hear that Sylvia didn't cave to them at least. Then her ears caught the sound of a key being pushed into the lock, so she backed to the side of the door again and lifted the stake above her head, intending to knock him out. She brought it down, but a hand caught the iron. Andreas knew exactly where she was, and Emlyn did not think about the possibility of Mr. Chronister having any sort of ability to defend himself. He wretched the stake from her hands, and with the other he pushed her hard to the ground.

"Gilla are not permitted to strike their masters!"

She sniffed and got to one knee. "I'm not a gilla!"

He backhanded her, and she found herself staring at the dirt once again. He grabbed her hair and lifted up, causing her to grunt in pain.

"You call me the same thing a gilla calls every man! You say: *Master!*"

"No! never!"

He backhanded her again, sending her sprawling down. This time blood was trickling from her lower lip. He turned her on to her back and put a hand on her neck. She grabbed that hand, but to her disappointment, it did not budge. She attributed it to weakness from having no food or water in at least twenty-four hours.

"You might be thinking that someone will help you, or of escape. Let me be clear, we have been performing this process on your ancestors for over a thousand years. You were fated to be a martial, a gilla since you came out of Stella's womb, and interfering with the making of a martial is considered a great sacrilege. There are also grave legal consequences for doing so. So no, you have no one on your side, no one to come to your rescue. You will come to find that only two choices exist: give in completely and proudly join the duty that has bound all of your kin, or starve yourself to death. But it is good that you're putting up a fight against the inevitable. It means that you'll be a wonderful protector for my daughter."

Andreas kept holding on to her neck as she felt the chain connected to the manacle being moved. Out of her periphery she managed to see Papa drive a five-foot-long stake into the ground with a sledgehammer. It was much longer than the last, and she knew it would be impossible to move. The moan she let out was like a small, wounded animal that suddenly realized it was surrounded by predators. She started to cry through each raspy breath.

Andreas let go of her and left her alone, slamming the door like a jail cell. Hours went by with Emlyn lying where she was dropped, sobbing until the well went dry. The insula had always felt like a cage, and now it had only gotten smaller.

Chapter Fourteen

-Almost Nothing-

Her eyes had trouble opening in their lethargy, and it took great effort to force herself awake. She had no idea if it was the same day, the next day, or perhaps many days had passed. One thing she did know was that she was thirsty. She did her best to cry out for water, but either she imagined it or her throat could not produce a sound loud enough to be heard by anything other than her own mind. No one came.

Emlyn lifted her eyelids once again, it was a different time of day, but it was light outside. She heard a bird singing. It had a lovely voice, making her smile, but as wakefulness took over, she realized that it was not a bird she was hearing but a woman whistling. She clawed at the dirt, moving herself slowly, attempting to see the woman who shared her shed, but as she turned, the door was shutting along with the echoing click of the lock. The bowl sitting beside the door caught her eye. She looked at its wooden sides disbelieving that it was real, but it was . . . she could swear it was. She mustered enough strength to crawl toward it, but the chain attached to the manacle on her ankle reached full length. She pulled the chain taut and reached her arm out and could touch it with her fingertips, bumping it just a little and making some water spill out. She froze and put her tongue over the top of her lip as if it would help with her concentration to steady her hands. *Slow and steady*, she told herself over and over again.

Emlyn strained, feeling like she was about to rip her body in two. Soon enough her fingertips were able to maneuver the bowl closer to where her hands could grasp the pitted sides. She collapsed on her belly. Slowly she brought the bowl closer and closer, walking her fingers over its surface until she could fully grasp it. The water felt so good against her lips and slightly sweet.

* * * * *

It was the next day. She knew this because she used the water bowl from the previous day to make a deep mark within the dirt. The second count came when the door was cracked open again, and a hand reached through, leaving another bowl of water. Then it tossed a half-eaten piece of bread onto the dirt near her. The hunger made her scramble for it. She was ravenous, not minding any of the dirt on the bread. She had to get to it before the ants. It was like this day in and day out: a scrap of food thrown her way and a water bowl sitting at the door. She tried a few times to piss on the stake again when she had enough water in her to do so, but to no avail. It was buried too deep in the ground. They would come in to collect the bowls and noticed the cuts in the ground, which they erased. Time started to stretch and bend again as the feedings became irregular.

Between feeding times, the only way she could get her mind off the hunger and weariness was watching the ants make their little hills next to her. They were trying to remake their territory after she ruined their home either on purpose or by accident while sleeping. She watched the ants, fascinated, and soon enough she started to imagine rebellions, betrayals, and conquests between the ant kingdoms. Little ant soldiers climbing up ant hills to fight their little ant wars. She came up with little plays of their little lives, and when an ant died in the story by the godlike rule of her thumb, well, she needed more sustenance than what little she was given.

230

* * * * *

Searing pain woke her. The immediate sense that came was the smell: a scent of charcoal and tanned leather burning over a flame. She gargled a scream but found that there was cloth pressed tightly in her mouth between her teeth and around her head. Lying on her side, she could not move. Her arms were outstretched above her and under someone's knees. Her wrists were tied. With what, she did not know, and something was putting pressure below her waist. A knee pressed down just above her own knees, a knee that was attached to her father. He was peering down at her with an impassive look on his face. She wanted to touch her thigh. She wanted to touch that area so badly to rub the pain away.

Hundreds of sharp stings dug into the burning as if someone was rubbing a beehive against it. A flood of tears soaked the cloth gag, as her muffled scream was heard by all in the shed. She looked down toward where her mother held her ankles. Her calves were bound, and a man she did not know was on her upper thigh, holding a small metal cylinder that fit perfectly in his hand. At its end was a very nasty tiny bundle of needles. The unknown man looked into her eyes and smiled. A smile meant for comfort, but Emlyn saw right through it . . . It was sinister. She heard someone else sobbing and looked further away. In the corner stood Sylvia, and it looked as if she was about to collapse, but Mr. Chronister steadied her with his hand on hers. From her hand protruded a long iron, hot at the end, showcasing a glowing eight-spoked cart wheel. Emlyn was branded, she knew that at least. Many gilla on the property had possessed such a mark, but usually on the back shoulder. Tears were flowing down Sylvia's face.

Sylvia was forced to do this! Emlyn thought, but she also thought that her so-called friend did not protest enough. Sylvia was going along with it, and now it was Sylvia, with her parents' encouragement, who marked her flesh. She endured the rest of the markings being buried into her thigh. Sweating and hurting, she lost track of time. Not that she had been any good at keeping time lately.

She was able to turn her head enough to see that the full Chronister house brand was now upon her thigh, oozing and weeping blood and red ink. The strange man quickly applied a salve before he wrapped it with a padded cloth. She tried to lash out, furious at everything and everyone, and with what was happening to her. They held her tightly, but it didn't stop her from trying until the realization that she now bore a gilla mark sank in. It was all true, she was never actually free, no fluke, no accident. She was a gilla living a lie to produce some sort of result she could not see. A brand could be hidden, but it would always be there to remind her with scar tissue.

"No, no, this is not me, I can't be this! It can't be what this was all leading up to!" she murmured.

She thought back to all the fighting skills she learned. It could not help her now, but it was taught to her for a reason. She had thought it was just for protection.

She thought of Kittie and how they played patrician and servant. Hadn't she always been the servant in that game and Kittie the patrician? They played it almost every other day, and when Emlyn was bored of it, Kittie would convince her to play anyway. Now Emlyn knew that it was no game. She started to hyperventilate and felt pressure release from her body. She could feel her blood pump through her veins. The shed started to spin, and her world faded into the void.

* * * * *

An ant crawled on its little mound of dirt, as a conqueror would when taking a new land for himself and his kind. She snatched him up with her fingertips, quickly putting the squirming legatus in her mouth. She turned on her back as her new brand throbbed dully in the movement. Luckily the maddening itch in that area left her a long while ago. Hasn't it been a while?

After her branding, she was left with her hands tied together. Its long tail was tied to another stake six feet away. She was stretched out between the two. This prevented her from scratching the area, which would ruin the bandage, hence keeping infection away. Every so often, one of the butlers or maids would enter and roughly pour water in her mouth. Or the tattooist would come in, reapply the salve, and check for any sign of infection.

Now she was untied and had no interest in doing further damage to herself. In fact, she did everything she could to ignore it, but the dull ache was there, pulsing and hot, taking her away from her time watching ant theater.

*****

It was sometime around dusk. She could tell by the pink light coming from the slits between the boards. The sweet sound of a few crickets helped her to relax and leave her mind for a bit. She imagined her feet in the grass while watching those crickets hop around rich green fields, the fields she remembered from the Chronister estate. Her toes splayed out and curled downward, clinging to the turf as if she would not have another chance.

In the back of her mind, she knew that dusk brought pain. It meant that at any moment the creaky shed door would open and Mr. Chronister, her father, or her mother would come in and start lashing her back. Through the red-hot heat, she would cry out to her parents for comfort, but she knew that no comfort would ever come her way. Their impassive faces spoke their indifference to her suffering. Who did she have? Who cared? Sylvia cared. Even though she went along with everything, she cared.

The door creaked open, and Emlyn crawled as far away from that door as the chain would allow. Mr. Chronister was at the threshold, his imposing figure looming in like an overwhelming shadow. He marched in toward her as Emlyn tried to move further away even though she knew she could not. She tried to fight, but her muscles were so weak. Her punches had no effect whatsoever as they fell lightly on his chest; he ignored it like the buzzing of insects. He grabbed her branded leg and stretched the limb out. She just laid down, looking away, already exhausted.

Andreas bellowed, "Sylvia!"

Emlyn could not help but to lift her head and look through the darkening doorway. Sylvia passed through the threshold, each step as timid as a dog who had been scolded one too many times. As soon as she entered, her nose wrinkled. Emlyn thought about how pungent the smell in the shed must be. Then she realized that it must be coming from herself since she had not had a bath since being thrown in here, whenever that was. Perhaps it was also coming from the cac and piss swimming around in a bucket sitting a few feet out from the corner.

"Come here," said Andreas.

Sylvia walked in unsure, cautious, and tense to the bone, and for each step she took, he unwound Emlyn's bandage. By the time she managed to get there, he only had to unwrap one more time to reveal the brand. He did so excruciatingly slow, making Sylvia tense even more.

Emlyn had no idea what was going on, only that it was different. She could at least count how many times she had been whipped. Was that going to change now, causing her to lose track again? She looked at Sylvia and stared right into her.

"Sylvia, do not look at the gilla." He unwrapped the last few inches, and as Sylvia's head turned downward, he revealed the brand. In neatly burned flesh and red ink was the full Chronister house crest: gilly flowers around a cart wheel, a dead wolf on top, and an eagle above. She backed away to the door, keeping her eyes on the brand, but she bumped into Mrs. Chronister, who kept her from leaving. Camilla placed her hands on her daughter's shoulders and looked over at Emlyn.

"Your brand healed well. It's very pretty." Camilla's calm voice was jarring, and it made Emlyn shiver.

Sylvia looked down and started to cry, but Emlyn noticed that Mr. and Mrs. Chronister were looking her way, expecting some sort of response.

No, I will not say it. I will not thank them for putting me through all this pain. I will not call her mistress or acknowledge myself a gilla, no. As inevitable as it was, and she knew in the back of her mind that she would have no choice in the matter, she would hold out, oh yes, to her last breath if she could help it.

The Chronisters realized that a response would not be forthcoming, so Camilla ushered Sylvia out and shut the door behind them. When it latched, it seemed to ring about in Emlyn's ears and she knew what was coming next. There was no whip or leather belt, just the back of his hand hitting her cheek, same as the first night, except with more force behind it. She found herself sprawled on the dirt floor, rocking back and forth with her hands over her lips. She could taste the blood filling her mouth. The pain occupied her mind so much that she barely heard him say, "Bad girl! You should thank the mistress when she compliments you!" She did not fully register this, neither did she hear the click and lock of the door as he left.

* * * * *

When she awoke again, a man who very much looked like the definition of a doctor knelt over her, taking notes in a little leather journal. He noticed her wakefulness and motioned for her to sit up. She obeyed, and he changed positions to look into her blank face. He did not touch her. Instead he held a silver pen up and told her to follow it with her eyes. She was apparently successful since he mumbled something about her motor functions being good and then wrote the results in his journal. He then put the pen on her swollen, bruised cheek, making her wince as he moved her head to the side.

"Please, help me," she croaked.

He wrote again in the journal and closed it with an angry smack, making her slide herself back in fear. He did not seem to notice this action and left without another word. She was given the sweet water again soon after.

She had never felt more like an animal, like she did not matter, but the worst came later that day when Mr. Chronister came in with Sylvia before him. She was holding the whip and raised it like a viper ready to strike. Emlyn moved as far away as she could manage, covering her head, curling up her body for protection. Sylvia lowered the whip, looking very guilty for raising it in the first place. Mr. Chronister went to Emlyn and tied her wrists first. Then he stretched her out between the two stakes, belly against the ground. He tied a cloth around her head between her teeth. Then as he backed away, he commanded, "Sylvia! Do it now!"

And she did.

Emlyn received many beatings in her life, but this was worse. It was deeper than anything she'd felt yet. It cut in more ways than the physical and she kept asking herself why over and over like a slip of a music disk. Like so many times before, everything faded to black.

* * * * *

Time was mutable, and no longer seemed important in the grand scheme of things. The beatings and humiliations became erratic, and what was up and what was down seemed less important to her than holding on to her will. She turned to the Gods and prayed to Dé Brigantia and Dé Ard and every single one of their myriad aspects. She prayed to the great sun and moon. Then turned to the ancient Greek Gods, Minerva and Helios, as the light ebbed and flowed from between the old wood boards. She prayed to the witch Goddess, Hekate, to work some magic on the locks. She would bow low to the mountains the ants had made in hopes of seeing the God Under the Hill. She did not see him, but she still made little sacrifices of little ant bodies. She prayed to the high Gods and pauper Gods alike, even to the Mithran bull killer. No answers came and no signs were given. Her conclusion was that the Gods did not care . . . This was tradition, after all. *Why would the Gods interfere with tradition, when they themselves are supporters of it? Only the Gods can do what they want.*

Emlyn thought she was crying but the pitter-patter of the rain hitting the wooden roof woke her again to this world. Not that her dreams were much better. They were full of horrors where everyone she knew became monsters. A drop splattered on her cheek. The roof was not very successful at keeping out the rain, for a puddle had formed beside her head. She lethargically moved, stuck her tongue into the puddle, and began lapping up the water. It was bitter from all the filth.

How long had she been there? Months? Perhaps years? Emlyn had no clue. It only felt like a long time, and the air was getting cold. By now the ants had lost all of their entertainment value, and she resigned herself as just another hill for them to conquer. It did not matter now. She could not tell the difference between dusk and dawn anymore. It was all the same. Nothing had any meaning, no one would save her, and no one would care for her. There would be no soft hugs, not even the caress of empathy, only pain, hatred, and indifference. She only wanted to get out of this shed, but she was so weak, and she knew that the only way out seemed more appealing as her mind kept sliding ever so slightly out of her grip. She needed out, Gods, she desperately wanted out. No, she could not bring herself to starve to death, could not bring herself to use her long ragged fingernails on her wrists. There was only one way. In that instant, she succumbed to the reality of the situation, and it seemed that she still had strength enough to cry a few drops.

Mr. Chronister entered the shed. He stretched Emlyn out between the spikes; no words were spoken, no screams, just numb acceptance. She complied with any which way that Andreas wanted to move her. He only spoke once to tell Sylvia to enter. Sylvia did not sob this time. Besides their feet stepping on the wet ground, Emlyn heard nothing. The whip touched her back in a snap, making Emlyn grit her teeth. She could tell it was Sylvia. She had whipped her more than three times now, and Emlyn could sense the difference between her strikes and everyone else's. It was lighter, reluctant, with longer pauses between each flick of the wrist. Emlyn let it all go as her eyes became fountains. She was done, she could not take this anymore.

One kind word, please! Just stop! Please stop! She did not say those words out loud. So she tried again.

She raised her voice the best she could. "Please! Please stop . . . Mistress!"

It did stop. The Gods could not make it stop, but that one word made everything cease. He untied her as she sobbed. She was left there alone, curled up in the stinking straw that had been her bed for who knows how long, left thinking of what she had just done. She sealed her fate, but what else was there? Where could a gilla run to?

I'm a gilla, just a gilla. She was tired of fighting the inevitable. There was no door, only a long pit, and she let herself fall completely into the dark, no longer clinging to the edge by her fingertips. She let herself fall and fall into that unknown blackness, and as she fell she wished for that kindness. Just one kind touch, even a smile would do.

Mr. Chronister came in alone the next day with the whip, and Emlyn performed a semblance of a ritual that all new gilla of the house performed when first meeting the master or mistress. It was one she had seen more than a few times. As soon as he stepped in, she got to her hands and knees and crawled, less than elegantly, to his boots. She planted a kiss on each one in supplication before crawling backward a few feet and leaning back on her heels while keeping her head lowered. She could see his boots turn and walk out, and then she heard that old familiar click that would haunt her dreams for years to come.

* * * * *

She tried her best to count the days, but lost track after a week due to her erratic sleep pattern and the odd times they brought her food. Whenever the door started to open, she would be on her knees, head down. They would stand in front of her without a word, bend down to put a bowl of water on the ground, and then drop a morsel. Usually it was a roll filled with some kind of meat or vegetable curd. She would not touch it until they were gone, whoever it was. Then she would scarf it down, ants and all.

One day was memorable: she received a full meal. It was shoved between the crack of the door. It was roasted lamb, steamed potatoes, and string beans. Ravaging the meal so fast, she left no trace that it had ever existed.

* * * * *

Emlyn woke and immediately could tell that she was being carried over a shoulder, but she could not see anything. A blindfold, yes, a blindfold, had been put over her eyes and tied at the back of her head. She started to panic, but whoever had her held on tight.

The next thing Emlyn knew she was being thrown into water. She imagined that she reached the bottom of that dark pit. The blindfold slipped off. She came to the surface sputtering, splashing everywhere. Then she desperately looked around her and realized this was the washroom for the gilla of the house. Besides the bathtub, the mirror, and the wash counter, it was stark white and large enough to feel small within it. She did not know what to do. Who put her there? A noise came from the hall, and she looked at the doorway that had no door attached. Her eyes were wide, and she tensed, anticipating pain for being off of her chain, out of the shed, and no longer in the ants' playground. All of whom probably died when she was thrown in here, or were currently swimming to safety.

A cart pushed past the doorway. Her fingers clutched the sides of the tub as her long nails bent against the ceramic. The cart pusher came into view. It was Bootsie, dressed in the knee-length grayish-blue female maid livery typically worn by free servants. Camilla enjoyed seeing him dressed in such a way. He did look like a woman in it, except for the flat chest of course.

He saw her moving back in the tub, looking for an exit. "Oh no, hon, I'm not going to hurt you," he said in his light voice as he lifted a scrubbing brush and soap. "I'm just going to help you out with that stink you have going on, all right?"

She did not move and kept a hard grip on the tub. He approached her with caution, trying to soothe her as one would soothe a skittish mare.

His calming melodic voice sang out, and it almost had its intended effect. "Shhh, it's okay, you're safe. I always help Mistress with her bath, but master told me just to leave what you need next to the tub."

He slowly put down the brush and soap in arm's length of the tub, keeping his eye on her the entire time, but when he looked into her eyes, he saw something. Emlyn knew that whatever it was, it scared him to the core, for he visibly shivered. He backed away and briskly walked the cart out without looking back or saying a word.

She scrubbed herself clean and washed her hair with hard soap, making the bath filthy as the grime flowed off of her. She finished washing her hair, and had just started to relax when a hand suddenly grabbed her near the scalp and pulled her up and over the tub onto the floor. She landed on the white tile with a wet smack.

"You're wasting your owner's time, girl! Dry yourself! Clip those nails, and hurry!"

Stella kicked her in the thigh, making her scramble to the counter where a towel, brush, and clippers were waiting. She attempted to dry and comb her very damp hair when Stella took the brush from her hand and threw it to the floor. With shaking hands Emlyn clipped her nails. The moment the last clipping fell off, Stella grabbed her by the hair again and started to pull, making her bend over and follow inelegantly along out of the washroom and down the hall.

Stella let go for a moment, tied Emlyn's hands behind her back, and then continued to pull her by the hair. They entered a room that Emlyn could not discern from her field of view. Stella changed positions, making Emlyn stand up straight while she was still being controlled by her mother's hand curling tighter.

She realized why Stella had tied her hands when she got a good look at the room. Empty metal folding chairs took up most of the area. Bootsie and one other gilla were just finishing setting them up. Bootsie stared for a moment before returning to his work. She then looked in the direction the chairs were facing, and there in the front of the room was a black marble column with two gold piers as a base: a whipping post.

She fought the binding and tried with all her might to move away and against her mother, but Papa came up from behind to help restrain her. They walked her over to the post. It was a long walk that seemed like a march of death.

"No! No, please! I'm a gilla! I know I'm a gilla now!"

Briar held her against the marble as Stella unbound her wrists and then re-bound them on the other side. The marble was so cold but not as unpleasant as the whip; in fact, she assumed the cold would probably make it worse. Her knees buckled.

"Stand, or I'll whip you myself," warned Briar.

She obeyed.

Briar and Stella walked off to the side of the room and stood next to each other, leaving their crying daughter on the column.

She had no sense of time in the shed, but here she could count every second, and every second was a nightmare.

Eventually a door opened, and she could hear people coming in. Metal chairs grated as the watchers took their seats. She so desperately wanted to take a look but knew she was not supposed to, and in this position it was very difficult for her to side eye. Those in the seats seemed to be talking about her; they had lost some bets to Andreas on when she would break. There were also comments about her body, specific parts too. They speculated about how big and strong the offspring would be if she were bred with one of their martials. She never felt more like some prized horse. Was she not truly equivalent to one now?

The crowd hushed as Emlyn heard light footsteps coming near her. Someone stood up from a chair.

Andreas's voice bellowed out, "Friends, family, distant cousins!" A few chuckled at that. "May I present to you, my daughter, Sylvia Chronister!" Applause broke out. Emlyn could tell he was now talking to Sylvia, but loud enough for the crowd to hear. "This gilla has not had a kind word or a kind touch. That is only for you to give. Will you do so?"

He handed her something that Emlyn could not discern, but it became clear when Sylvia unfurled it. She knew the sound well at this point: it was a whip. Emlyn started to sweat, anticipating the pain, but instead she felt a hand in her hair. Not the hard, controlling hand of Stella, but smaller, soothing. She still tensed up though. Then Sylvia spoke, and it sounded like the most beautiful voice in the world next to her ear, and it was only meant for her.

"It's okay, Tabby. You're safe."

As she said this, Emlyn could feel caresses on her upper back. A shiver rippled throughout her entire body, as if a pleasurable chill suddenly hit her in the warm night air. Sylvia's hand was back on her head again, and it started to stroke her hair, downward toward her neck.

"You have been very good, my . . ." There was a waver in her voice mixed with regret. "My girl, my protector, my gilla." Sylvia put her forehead against Emlyn's back.

The room was deathly silent.

Sylvia sniffed. "You are mine. You belong to no one else but me. You serve me and all my areas of influence. And no one will hurt you ever again."

Emlyn couldn't help herself; the tears came without notification. They seemed to flood her entire face in a never-ending hot torrent. The relief she felt was unbearable, no more pain, she was telling the truth and she could not take these gentle caresses any longer. The stroking and words felt so good, but at the same time worse than any biting sting of a whip.

She hit the bottom of that deep dark pit with a smack that reverberated throughout her body. She leaned into every touch, and now what little was left of who she was melted away, replaced with something else she could not quantify, an almost nothingness. She fell to the ground like a heavy sack.

Stella unbound Emlyn's wrists, and as soon as Emlyn was free, she turned around and clung to Sylvia's right leg as best she could with the long dress in the way. Soon she made her way to Sylvia's bare feet, covering them with her lips.

Sylvia was afraid to look down at first, afraid of what she might see, but she had to ask the questions that were expected of her. She steeled herself and looked. Emlyn was staring right back with obvious want and need. Sylvia gulped. She reached her palm down, and Emlyn rose to put her cheek to it, kissing the palm before returning to the caress. Sylvia wanted to cry but she could not. That was not what was expected of her right now.

Her father handed her an opened steel collar. She took it and held it before her. There were no keys to this collar. It would not be removed until Emlyn had her own child and played the game that their parents had just won. Then it would be placed back at an appropriate time. If this was done at the proper age, then the collar would allow room for growth, but this one would fit perfectly. She looked at the attached tag; it had Emlyn's name engraved on it, and it said that she belonged to Sylvia. Then she turned it and read the back: it was Emlyn's nickname. She wondered if Stella had a nickname as well. She knew others did, but

Stella did not look the type. She shook her head free of the wandering thoughts and went on with the ritual.

"Kneel before me." Her voice wobbled, unused to commanding Emlyn.

Emlyn looked at the collar a moment before doing what she was told. She got into position.

"What are you to me?"

Emlyn sobbed as she gave the answer. "A gilla. Your gilla!"

"What am I to you?"

"My mistress."

"I give you your blood name. Present your neck to me, Emlyn Gwen." Sylvia held the collar under one side while keeping the other side up. Her hands trembled.

Stella gathered Emlyn's hair, holding it up and behind her like reins. Emlyn put her neck above the bottom side of the collar. Then Sylvia closed it, and it snapped. She swore she could feel Emlyn shiver through the floorboards.

Emlyn started kissing Sylvia's hand excessively. She moved it away and placed her hand on Emlyn's head, petting her, smoothing back that damp chestnut hair as everyone started clapping. It was a sound like some distant static on speakers. Dark fae shouting in delight. But there was only her and Emlyn right now, and Emlyn was no longer the girl she knew, the girl she loved. As she looked into her eyes, she could only see the cold. Her inner fire was frozen over, dark and dreadful.

"Thank you for coming to see the result of this breaking! Another chain has been forged in this age-old tradition! It is my pleasure to inform you that Emlyn lasted three months, a feat only bested by Feryn, the great-grandson of Oghan Gwen!" declared Andreas.

Another voice spoke up. "Go ahead and rub it in why don't you!"

Everyone in the room except Sylvia and Emlyn laughed.

"Yes, yes. Let us all retire to my study where we can discuss how you will pay me for losing the bet, Ellis!"

Another round of laughter erupted in the room.

Sylvia knew what was expected of her next. She closed her eyes and took in as much air as she could. She breathed out and looked down. Emlyn had her eyes closed, rubbing her cheek against the palm. A palm that was wet with her friend's tears.

I was told that this would last for a while. That it's best just to let her rub up against you like a cat until it passes, but it still seemed odd when I first heard it. It seems odd now. Sylvia smiled half-heartedly and told herself that she was glad to give her friend—no, her martial—a little comfort after an ordeal that she could only scarcely imagine.

She bent down to get eye level with her, but Emlyn quickly bowed her forehead to the floor and trembled. Sylvia could hear the visitors start to leave.

"No, Emlyn." She lifted Emlyn's chin from the ground. "You did not do anything wrong. You can look me in the eyes. After all, you are . . . my martial."

For what seemed like a long moment, they stared at each other. Sylvia saw very little behind the amber.

Then Emlyn responded in a whisper, "Thank you, Mistress." She kissed Sylvia's hand.

* * * * *

Sylvia was heading to her bedroom. She stopped every twenty yards to quizzically look over her right shoulder at Emlyn, who heeled at a constant five paces behind her. Her father said that it would be best to let her follow and sleep in the same room for the first night.

Something was boiling in her mind. She knew it would be easy to make love to Emlyn if she desired it, but it would be nothing but a mistress using a gilla. No matter how Sylvia herself felt, it would never be anything more than that in Emlyn's mind, and now there was the further complication that a mistress should not use a martial in such a way. For some reason it was considered unseemly, unrefined, and desperate.

When she stepped inside her bedroom, Sylvia stood aside from the doorway.

"Emlyn. Bed." She pointed to the far side of the room. Emlyn could see that the dolls were no longer on the storage trunk. The stuffed animals were gone. Where Sylvia was pointing was where the creepy dollhouse once stood. Now it was replaced with a mat, a pillow, and a thin blanket, all of which were a stark white. Emlyn went to her knees on the mat and watched as Sylvia paced the room lost in thought.

The new mistress ran past the last three months in her memory. At the beginning, she was forced to review the history of the Chronisters and Gwens. She learned exactly how the facts were hidden from her and Emlyn until the time was right. She reviewed every little detail when it came to martials and even went to the estates of other high patricians. She found out that Valance was indeed interested in Emlyn, but the next day after the festival he and his best friend went through the breaking.

As she did her series of visits, she talked to the new martials. All of their breaking traditions were a little different than the next. She also visited different trainers in the city to learn about gilla. Much of it she already knew, but breakings usually happened between ages ten and thirteen when education on gilla in general were usually conducted. The most interesting trainer was Hornbow. She was pleased to find that Kittie was still there, free in fact, and his paramour. She found Hornbow himself to be like a magician on stage. She was delighted and charmed by him to say the least.

As light as things could be during these visits, returning home always brought a dark cloud over her head. There was something she noticed, something she had that the other patrician kids did not: those deep-seated feelings for their martial that went well beyond friendship. She blamed this on her parents, then on Kymbrian society in general. She knew she could forgive her parents in time, but she still had this giant ball of disgust within her.

"Mistress?"

Sylvia came back to the here and now. She looked at Emlyn waiting there patiently like a gilla should.

"Oh, Tabby. I'm so sorry." She cringed . . . You were not supposed to say sorry to gilla.

She looked the new gilla up and down, thinking that Emlyn was so beautiful naked, kneeling there so prettily. Sylvia bit her lip as she shivered. She could use her. Could she not? By all the Gods she wanted release, and Emlyn was there, wanting to be touched. Her eyes begged for it. She removed her clothes and placed them folded on top of the trunk. She went to Emlyn and knelt so they would be face-to-face. She outstretched her arms to the sides and motioned for Emlyn to come to her. Emlyn blinked and then moved into the embrace and laid her head against Sylvia's clavicle. She finally had her in her arms like this; she had waited so long to hold her so.

Sylvia let out a moan that was half pleasure and half agonized rage. Her face scrunched up as she killed her need for release, letting her rational mind take control again. She pushed Emlyn away holding her shoulders, keeping her at arm's length. She looked into her eyes, still seeing the coldness but also bewilderment.

"This is not right. This is not what I want."

Emlyn's confusion was tinted with a hint of fear.

"No, you have done nothing wrong." She kissed Emlyn on the forehead, then hugged her. Sylvia laid her head against her shoulder. "It has been so hard for you." She sobbed, "I'm so sorry."

She lifted her head and looked into Emlyn's blank eyes. "You have to be tired. Lay down and sleep. Okay?"

"Yes, Mistress."

Sylvia looked down, furrowing her brow, and took a deep breath. When she looked back up, Emlyn had covered her body with the blanket and her eyes were closed, head resting on the pillow.

She reached out her hand. Her fingers curled around the chestnut hair. They trailed down to where the slight wave started at the ends and then lifted, taking in how each strand fell and landed back in its place. Emlyn let out a whimper while trying to get closer to the warmth of the hand.

Over the last three months, Sylvia had snuck out to the shed many times. She never spoke above a whisper in fear of being discovered. Even so, Emlyn did not seem to hear. She whispered about all that was hidden inside, how she truly felt. How she hoped Emlyn would come out the other side of this just fine and not be like those other martials. Possessing eyes that could cut glass, and deadened as if the light had been snuffed out. For hours she had lain next to that shed just talking. Now, in her room she lay down again facing her, and even though she could see her face, it still felt like the shed walls were between them. They were just invisible now, and somehow that seemed so much worse.

She reached over and ran her fingers across Emlyn's cheek, wondering if the Emlyn she knew was still in there. She would have given anything to see the eyes of that girl again.

"I will just have to be clever and find you again, love. I will figure out how to have you back in one form or another, Tabby."

But in the back of her mind, she feared that they would never relate in the same way again.

* * * * *

Emlyn opened her eyes. A face loomed in front of hers. Fear jumped up into her throat. "Papa!"

She scrambled away, her naked body hitting hard on the gigantic stone bench before her back hit the glass wall. With no option to go any further, she looked at her surroundings.

"T-The conservatory? How did I get here?"

Her father did not look like the same man that coldly tormented her over the last three months. The lines on his forehead spoke of concern and his eyes were kind. It made her think of a light switch being flicked. He moved his hand out in a calming motion, but he did not touch her. "I'm not going to hurt you, blood."

She scrunched up, pulling her legs close to her body. Her hands clutched her knees. "You have!" she said, almost hysterical.

Briar put his elbows on his knees and laced his fingers. His face contorted, concentrating on what he wanted to say next.

He let out a long sigh. "I was a few days shy of my twelfth birthday when I was thrown in that shed. I lasted a little over a month. It's . . . easier at that age."

Emlyn loosened a bit of her tension upon hearing this. She had an inkling that her parents might have gone through a trial, but she had not given it any deep thought.

"You didn't refuse what was done to me! Not one bit!"

He rubbed his chin. "Would you die for Sylvia?"

She blinked, not expecting the question. "Yes. I would have died for her when . . . we were friends." He flexed his fingers before lacing them again. "And now, my blood?"

Looking to the side, biting her lip, she responded, "Yes."

"Will you kneel before her when she commands you to?"

She looked down, trying to hide her reddening cheeks behind her knees. Her voice came out in a low whisper. "Yes."

"Good . . . that is very good." He took a moment to breathe out a long sigh. "My father did this to me, and when you are bred and produce offspring, then you will do this to them. You will not enjoy it, but every generation of Gwen must. It must be so that we can give a Chronister the protection that is expected. We must be completely devoted to that duty."

She did not like the thought, but it was true. It would happen. She would be bred with a martial that her mistress chose, and she would have no say in the matter. She disliked the thought of putting her theoretical children through this, but it was the last statement that made her heart sink, and it opened a path of empathy toward her father.

He talked with her for what seemed like an age. He revealed that this was a tradition and that no Gwen was an exception to it. It was cruel, but by the end of the talk, Emlyn could not pretend she didn't feel like she belonged to an exclusive group. A group with rituals and history that went back many hundreds of years. She wanted to know more. Even though they were just gilla, the breaking itself rammed that home, they were still special. It allowed her to grasp at a meaning to all the pain she went through, a purpose.

The thought of the girl she was before the shed was gone. It was now replaced by Emlyn the martial, whose purpose was to protect her mistress, Sylvia.

Briar nodded and, looking satisfied, stood up and held out his hand. He was holding something. "Take it."

She timidly reached out her hand, and he released the object, letting it fall into her palm. "The wandering druidi gave that to you, did he not?"

Emlyn looked down at the smooth polished amber twinkling on her palm. "Yes, he did."

"Then it's something your mother will not dare to confiscate. Ill indeed to steal away a druidi gift. Come, everyone's waiting for us."

"Everyone?" She stood and followed but did not take his hand. She still felt sensitive, and a part of her wanted to be with Sylvia right now, kissing her feet. The thought of Sylvia made her shiver; she didn't know how to feel about that.

"Your blood is in the garden."

Emlyn had no idea what he meant by that.

Out in the garden there stood twenty-three people. Most of them she recognized as family members, and she could not help but notice that they all wore collars like hers. She instinctively touched her own collar and keenly felt its weight.

They all kept their impassive eyes on her as they approached a small stage with an altar. On top sat a knife with an onyx handle with a silver vine-and-leaf pattern, the one she practiced with so many times. Beside it was a revolver sporting the same motif. Most of her family were staring at her, and in her nakedness, she felt suddenly vulnerable and self-conscious. She had to keep reminding herself that this was nothing more than some ritual prepared for her and what she had become.

The crowd parted, creating a path that allowed them to walk to the stage. When they climbed the five steps to the platform, Briar turned to face his daughter. He snapped his fingers and pointed down.

"Kneel."

She did so without hesitation. Briar grasped her hands, holding them out in front of her, palms up.

"I'll hold on to your stone." He whispered and pocketed the amber.

She kept her palms up as he turned her head down to look at her shadow being cast by the braziers on both sides of the platform. She could see her father go away, and another shadow darkened her vision.

Blood was brushed onto her palm. When she looked up, blood was flicked on her face by Stella's boney fingers. Emlyn did not know exactly what it meant at the time, but she had a notion of the meaning dancing around her mind. Perhaps it meant that she would now spill her own blood in protecting her mistress? Maybe the blood of others as well? That was not far from the truth of it.

A prayer to the Dé and the God Under the Hill was performed. The cadence of the prayer was of a droning, practiced repetition in numerous old languages flowing into each other with no measure of stumbling. She smelled the blood on her face and had the sense that it was moon blood mixed in with some animal or another.

As the prayer went on, a drum started to beat in five-second intervals. Emlyn thought of Sylvia, her mind winding down to the very core of how she felt toward her former friend, now mistress. It was made certain that they became close friends as the years since their birth went by. It worked without a hitch, and the two never grew tired of each other.

She now recalled all the times their parents had manipulated them. They loved them of course, in their own ways, but manipulated them nonetheless. Poking and prodding them to do kind things for each other. Always the right thing that was needed at the right time to make them even closer. A tightrope was successfully walked. It could have all come crashing down, but it didn't. Not after a thousand years of careful crafting. The road and its dangers were known, and they were now victims of that tradition.

What choice did they have in this masquerade designed to cover up who they truly were, only to have the masks ripped away at the hour of midnight? Who she was seemed a lie. Closely guarded and constructed with matchsticks, designed to be torn down at a moment's notice. One push off a cliff.

Emlyn the martial gilla was what really existed. Not Emlyn the prisoner, not Emlyn the explorer, not Emlyn the best friend, and definitely not Emlyn the free woman. She was and always had been a gilla, her true self. Another knot in a long, proud tradition. Sylvia was what mattered, not herself. She was nothing compared to her. But there was still a tradition that they shared, and that tradition ruled them, setting a course for their future, a prosperous future where everyone knew their place.

The ritual ended, and the extended family cheered. All of it was noise in the background of Emlyn's mind. She stayed in her position even as the musical instruments were brought out and the cascade of singing started to flow. Then when she was whisked off of her feet, the world seemed to spin before her until she was face-to-face with her grandmother, who was still spry after all these years even with the bum leg. She dressed her so quickly that Emlyn barely felt the fabric come to rest on her body before it was done. She looked down at the black, flowing ankle-length dress. It was much plainer than what she had been used to, but that did not seem to matter anymore.

"Thank you, Grandmother."

The older woman, who even in her old age had a good inch in height over Emlyn, smiled, wrinkling that old face into something warm and nostalgic like a hearth being the heart of a home. Her grandmother had always been that hearth.

"Welcome to the family, Emlyn, my blood." She placed her hands on Emlyn's forehead, smearing the blood up toward her hairline and using those cracked fingers to smooth it back into the strands.

Hands wrapped around her waist, spinning her around to face her father. He took her hands, and she could feel the blood covering his palms. Then he grabbed her wrists and put her hands on his cheeks, smearing the blood downward. "I'm so proud of you, Emlyn, my blood."

Again, she was grabbed by the waist and was facing a tall, handsome cousin not much older than herself. He laced his hands with hers and twirled her around and around in time with the music. She began to smile, slowly but surely, it felt like such a long time since she had done so. The handsome cousin said the words that would become the tagline whenever she remembered that night: "Welcome, blood."

It went on like this, every family member sharing the blood and the words for a long time. So much so that Emlyn had lost track of the number. By the end of the dance and the sharing of the blood, she continued moving her feet in time with the music laughing like a lunatic. They all laughed right along with her.

When the blood dance was over, the music changed. She kept dancing right along with the four-beat time of the drums and the fast, plucking rhythms of the strings. She opened her mouth and added her voice to the chorus of her family.

They told stories of their history, to make her understand this long proud tradition, and she listened eagerly. By the end she found her need for touch gone. She was ready to take her place, to accept her role. She would dive into it with gusto.

Chapter Fifteen

A thud sounded through the side door, carrying through into the kitchen.

"That would be the paper," said an older gray-haired gentleman known as Phelps, who was a part-time butler. Part-time because there was little need for the position with half of the insula not in use and very few staff members to worry about, and even fewer visitors now due to Madam Camilla's illness. Plus, Emlyn and Stella performed similar duties, so Phelps sat in the kitchen helping Ms. Cord prepare breakfast. At least he liked to think he was helping. In truth, he only diced a few chives and was enjoying a few beers for the better part of an hour.

"Then make yerself useful an' get it. I'm elbow-deep in these guts!" Sure enough Ms. Cord was standing before a utility sink, her arms deep within, cleaning a sheep's intestine to use later for dinner. Blood was clearly smeared above her elbows, and he was glad he did not have that job. Not that Ms. Cord would trust him in cleaning it properly. His eyes were drawn to her rear, and she seemed to sense this. "Go on, ya lazy cumber! You'll get yours later!"

Phelps smiled and sighed. Like a sloth on its best day, he stood up and walked to the door. When he opened it, he could hear the paper being brushed to the side, so he reached down and around, grasped it, and brought it in.

The next hour passed by in relative silence as Ms. Cord finished preparing breakfast. The smell turned from the reek of the intestines to sweet and savory pork. Phelps kept sipping his beer while reading the paper as the *shike-shike* of a peeling knife being used on potatoes echoed out from Mira sitting cross-legged in the corner of the kitchen.

Breakfast was placed on silver trays, then set upon the kitchen table. Mira looked into Cord's face, pleading.

"No, ya can't, too soon. 'Sides, Emlyn will take it before ya even get there."

Phelps stood, folding the paper as he did so. "You don't want her staring you down, eh pretty gilla? Not pleasant. I'll handle it; she doesn't scare me, not one bit!"

Mira gazed at the floor with a sad look on her face. "As you say, Master."

"Ya see there? Getting better with her words! An' I *almost* believe she wants to do it!" exclaimed Cord. "Phelps, the mistress is in the conservatory."

He placed the paper on the tray, lifted it by its handles, and then promptly went up the plain wooden stairs ending in a platform. From there the stairs continued in three different directions. He took the left way, reaching a small inconspicuous door. On the other side was an elegant hall done up in reds and bordered with gold. He wondered if it was actual gold. He took another left, rounded the corner, and then he almost ran right into Emlyn.

"By the Gods, you scared the fire out of me!"

Emlyn bowed. "My apologies, Master."

He looked her in the eye a moment and trembled. "Yes, well, here!" He shoved the tray into Emlyn's hands, abruptly turned, and walked as fast as he could back down the hall.

Emlyn inspected the tray: coffee in a porcelain cup, one boiled egg atop its server, two thick slices of ham, and salted potato chunks with chives on top. The appropriate utensils and the paper bookended the tray.

The door to the conservatory creaked open and in came Emlyn. She set the tray down on a rolling table in the corner, succeeding in avoiding any sound.

Sylvia looked small within the room with nothing but the morning light to illuminate her. She sat on a red-cushioned, white-iron chair. All around her were floor-to-ceiling windows, serving as the walls that held up a stippled glass roof, covered, on the outside, by canvas. She held a smile, enjoying the rays of the morning sun streaming in as if an ancient God was sending his blessings down upon her. The silk robes she wore looked like they were made of light, yet there was a sadness to this scene. Her smile was troubled, and her posture was tense. Like a ship entering stormy weather.

"Mistress, your breakfast is ready. Would you like to eat now?"

She felt . . . all right, glad to get her mind off her mother lying sick in a bed upstairs. Had to be a morning thing, always her most relaxing part of the day when her mind was not accosted by these terrible things. "Of course, bring it over here. I do not feel like leaving this chair right now."

Emlyn smiled and nodded, then went to the other side of the room to fetch the rolling table. Sylvia could tell that Emlyn wanted to ask about Camilla but did not want to trouble her, and that was just fine. The more her thoughts could drift away from the woman spending her last days on earth dying in that forsaken bed upstairs, the better.

A collared dove flew past the window. Sylvia noted how the light filtered through the wings. There were many of them out there pecking about in the garden, but she did not mind it. She enjoyed their gracefulness even though others viewed them as little better than pigeons. What did pigeons or doves ever do to deserve such disdain?

The rolling cart appeared beside her. As she looked at the food, her stomach growled. She did not realize how hungry she was. She expected to just leave it there and let it get cold before giving it to Emlyn. But looking at the perfection on the plate, her stomach seemed to remember her refusal to eat dinner last night and changed its mind.

The last thing left on the plate was one piece of the thick-cut ham. Sylvia stabbed it with the fork and lifted it out for Emlyn to take. "Here."

Emlyn grasped the handle of the fork, lightly brushing Sylvia's fingers. She ate the last piece as her mistress rustled the paper before opening it.

Gossip was something Sylvia avoided; she likened it to the ramblings of bored children. You just say, "Oh, how terrible, dear," then move on with whatever business you were in the midst of. Concerning yourself with gossip could have adverse effects on your relationships, especially if the wrong person got wind of it. So it was best to not concern yourself at all and ignore it as best you could. She had been aware of all the gossip surrounding her family for years, but the contents of this article had nothing to do with her or her family personally. Instead, it concerned a bet that was made with Lucius almost two months ago.

Sylvia's troubled face fell in disbelief as her eyes scanned each line. Her mind went through a number of appropriate expletives, but her mouth only hung open and nothing more.

"Mistress?"

Sylvia folded and handed the paper to Emlyn. "Page two, first article."

Emlyn opened it, found the place, and began to recite.

"On October fifth, theater patrons and professionals alike mourned the loss of one of their own. Alma Minceed, aged twenty-three, died in her home from an accidental fall on the stairs. Found by her husband, he was promptly brought in by peacekeepers for questioning. The inspector for the case and the Minceed family were unavailable for comment at the time as the investigation remains ongoing. Alma had no known relatives, but she will be missed by the community at large for her acting talents and her charitable fundraisers. A vigil will be held at the Oak Theater tonight, open for anyone who wishes to attend." There was nothing in the short article about Alma's freewoman status.

"I'm sorry. I know you enjoyed that play," said Emlyn. She folded the paper and put it back on the tray.

Sylvia did not mind, since she was uninterested in reading anything more. The thought of what she might have to do made her sick, and she wished that it did not.

"No, I did not think much of it to be honest, but Alma was worth the price of admission. When did Lucius say he was arriving?"

"At noon."

Sylvia nodded. "Look in on my mother, then lay out a tea dress for me on the bed."

"The cream-and-peach one?"

"Hm, oh yes, that one sounds nice." Sylvia seemed to be halfway to somewhere else now.

Emlyn dipped to curtsey before leaving with a worried look.

* * * * *

A cool breeze blew through the garden, a chill respite from the intolerable heat. But despite the pleasant breeze, she felt the frustration of growing discomfort. *I should call this off; I have more pressing things to worry about. He would surely understand that. I know what he wants. Despite neither of us winning the bet, he thinks that it is beyond time to—*

Her thoughts came to a full stop as she heard a loud thump.

The sound led her over to the conservatory. The doves flurried their wings and flew away from her presence. Her eyes followed them as they flew up and away, out of the garden. She searched for the source of the sound. One of the window panels had an imprint of dust in a vague shape of a bird. Looking to the ground, there, lying on the loose dirt was one of the collared doves, dead. It had hit the window so hard that it busted its head wide open and more than just blood was oozing out.

She bent down and gently picked up the bird, being careful to keep it away from her dress. She had no problem with letting the poor thing's blood run like bright red veins across her fingers to spill to the ground in tiny droplets.

"Mistress?" Emlyn's voice startled her.

"Oh! Yes, Tabby?" Sylvia turned and saw the horrified look on Emlyn's face, eyeing the bloody bird she held. "He . . . hit the window."

Her imagination had no problem conjuring up how she must look, like a mad woman. Maybe Emlyn thought she was . . . well, not in her best state, and how could she blame her for that? She would have done the same if their positions were switched. Emlyn's face grew concerned.

With care, Emlyn reached her hands out. For a moment Sylvia thought she was going to be embraced, then remembered the dead bird.

"I see, let me handle it," said Emlyn in a most calming tone, like soothing a skittish horse.

Sylvia blinked a few times as she realized what she was doing and handed the bird to Emlyn, who then smoothly laid the poor thing on the ground. After Emlyn stood up, she reached into her skirt pocket and brought out the handkerchief made of fine cloth that Colmane had left with her. Then she spat on it a few times, took Sylvia's hands, and began washing them, getting most of the blood off. Sylvia watched the top of Emlyn's head with some fascination as she let her palms be cleaned.

"Tabby, I—" But she could not find any words.

Emlyn finished and put the bloody handkerchief back into her pocket.

"You have too much weighing on you. Try to relax. Try to have fun while Master Donsill is here."

She nodded. "Yes, I will try."

I will try. I will try for you, Sylvia thought.

Emlyn inspected Sylvia's hands, the back, the palms and under the nails. "He is waiting in the front foyer. I will bring him here if you're ready."

Sylvia nodded her assent.

Emlyn walked back into the house with the dead bird in hand as Sylvia kept her eyes on her. Her cheeks flushed, realizing that she would not be able to keep the promise she made to herself when she and Emlyn were fifteen right after the breaking. She had to do this for Emlyn's sake and for her family's sake. Marry Lucius and have his children. Emlyn would always be there even if she did not resemble the girl she once knew in anything but looks and name. She would be here, be happy with Maield, and that was what counted. Sylvia willed her mind to get through this, and when marriage came and Emlyn was bred, then it would be fine . . . it would all be fine. She just needed to hold on and not let Emlyn, or even the thought of Camilla on her deathbed, distract her from what must be done tonight. She needed to be able to get through it.

* * * * *

The birds were singing, and the smell of perennials soared on the light breeze. It was a beautiful day, at least it should have been. The incident with the dove quickly left her mind. Conversing with Lucius was better than Sylvia expected. She was quite surprised at how skillful he was at keeping her mind away from her mother's illness. Last time they had too many distractions that kept them from conversing properly, but now it was only the two of them sitting on a bench under the grove of trees in the garden. Their full attention was on each other, speaking about politics while being served tea and pastries by their martials, who kept stealing loving glances at one another. The two martials were commanded to switch the person they served, which provided a bit of laughter as the martials pretended to be clumsy: drop trays, break porcelain cups, and serve too much of this or that. This was hilarious for her and Lucius, so used to their martials being an example of perfection. When the martials were told to go take a break, so they went and made love under the statue of the Dé Brigantia. Though not so far away from their owners to not be noticed. Sylvia forced her misgivings about it down

Lucius talked about his military experience since that came easy to his mind. He refrained from telling anything bloody, since such violence held no interest to her. She tried to help him understand some of the eccentric inventors that she backed. Their hopes, dreams and how it all worked together to bring in new ideas and revenue.

With everything going on, the realm of electricity was something she spent less and less time deal in. She could not keep her mind on such things with her mother in bed upstairs, coughing and spitting up blood. She shivered thinking about it.

Eventually Lucius put the matter of Alma Minceed out on the table. "It seems that we have both lost the bet."

"Indeed, it seems so. The poor girl. Have you thought about going to the vigil tonight?"

Lucius held a pipe. He lit it and took a few puffs, blowing out smoke rings. "I've never spoken a word to her, and I would feel greatly awkward. Did you have a mind to go?"

"No . . . and much for the same reason," said Sylvia with solemn cadence. She held her glass to the darkening sky. "To Alma Minceed! May her killers be found so she may find peace across the last lonely bridge before the door!"

He looked at her, amused, questioning, "You believe she was pushed?"

"For true. What young person falls down the stairs in a well-built, well-lit house in the middle of the day?"

"Do you always imagine such terrible scenarios?"

"Do you not look at all the possible outcomes?" asked Sylvia.

"I'll only say that it is a possibility, but it is also just as likely that she lost her footing or twisted her ankle."

"Yet the peacekeepers took him in for questioning." She smirked.

"Suspicious, yes. However, it is no reason to make it true in your mind."

Sylvia's head felt like it was taking a slow swim in a murky pond. By now it was six o'clock. She'd had two glasses of wine, or perhaps it was three. She should have been concerned if her levity was any indication. Maybe a headache was coming on. That would have been no surprise, but she felt fine otherwise. Better than fine, she was stupendous.

Lucius looked at the ground and seemed genuinely sad over the unexpected death that figured so prominently in their bet. "I know I did not win, but that is no reason to hold ourselves back. Do you not think in similar fashion?"

Sylvia looked down at her empty wineglass. What is happening here? She felt . . . perfect for once and incredibly turned on. Why? Lucius had never made her feel this way before now. Only Emlyn made her feel like this, so what was happening to her? The wine was sweeter than usual. Did it mask the potency? The possibility that she could have drunk four glasses occurred to her.

So what if she was drunk? This was expected of her. She wanted to push those old feelings for Emlyn aside and develop some sort of genuine lust for a man, to keep with the traditions. Be attracted to men, get married, have children, run a household as it had been done for hundreds of years and a hundred more if she would just agree to be with him and make not only her mother proud but to make her ancestors proud as well.

Keep the line going, and no one will ever have to know who you really are. Make my mother proud, make my ancestors look kindly upon me, make Emlyn . . . happy, she thought.

* * * * *

The door to a guest bedroom decorated in cream with white trim swung open, slamming against the wall. In came Sylvia pressed tight within Lucius's arms. She let him walk her backward into the room and to the bed. He pushed her, and she landed on top of the fluffy sheets with a bounce. He stood at the side of the bed and began unbuttoning his blue silk vest, never taking his eyes away from hers. His sharp moustache twisted upward, following his grin.

Sylvia started undoing the flat pearl buttons on the upper part of her dress, but with less confidence, verging on uncertainty. He gave her the time she needed.

Emlyn walked in with Maield following close behind and stood at opposite ends of the room.

The supports rattled, making the long swirled wooden posts shake. Lucius left enough room between them to satisfy her finger's curiosity upon his chest and stomach. She wondered at how a leisurely man could keep such good care of his body. She hoped the swirling motions she made upon his chest hair would make her feel something toward him.

He moved his hand tenderly across her face, then pressed his lips to hers. He leaned her back on the bed and slid a hand glacially down her body, feeling every shiver and goosebump. His fingers crept like a spider below her undergarments and across her pubic mound.

Sylvia groaned as he worked his fingers inside her. His lips planted kisses down her throat, over her clavicle, and gently down the slope of a breast. He swirled his tongue around the areola and performed playful bites. She had to close her eyes, and when she did, an enjoyment could be reached, but every time her eyes sprang open to a new heavier bite, she saw him and her arousal ebbed. Seeming to sense this, he put his head between her thighs, and it was not long before her breath became heavy in response. The reality of who was doing it could be easily dispatched.

It was not long before Lucius grew bored with this act and promptly lifted himself up and over her again. She could smell him: a scent of musk and sandalwood, reminding Sylvia of her father. She grimaced. He put his hand over her eyes, then thrust into her. She kept her eyes closed and did her best to work the imagination. She tried thinking of the times when she had Emlyn bury a hand inside her. The ecstasy started to build, but it was not enough. When he took his hand away, all she could see was him. She started to feel a little more pain with each and every thrust, yet she went on trying to force her body to react to this man.

Her eyes ran away from him to Emlyn. She hoped that the sight of her might do it, might dispel her body's negativity toward Lucius, but she noticed something that seemed greatly concerning despite it being proper and, she supposed, right. Emlyn had her attention focused entirely on Maield. In that moment, she imagined Emlyn with the other martial. And in her mind's eye she had seen that the two truly liked each other. No—something more than just merely like. She had seen Emlyn's happiness in that gaze and knew that she had never and would never look at her like that. That kind of love was lost to her. Any possibility was shattered and swept away during the breaking. But Sylvia wanted it, more than anything she wanted to feel it. A tide of anger rose.

"Nooo," she said, sounding weak.

Lucius increased his thrusting.

Sylvia grimaced as if she had bit down on a lemon. "No. No!" She thrust her arm up at him, but he did not stop. "Get off me! Stop!" she yelled.

As she tried to squirm out of his grasp, she hit him across the eyebrow with her elbow by mistake, and he started bleeding. Everything seemed to stop; she didn't move and neither did he. No noise of evening insects came from the garden and no songs from the birds. Even her heartbeat seemed to have no rhythm.

His eyes went from surprise to malice. In the next second, it felt as if her left cheek exploded with fire. Memories splashed before her eyes, and for a moment she could swear that Lucius's image was replaced with her father's.

Sylvia missed hearing the boots of the martials scrape against the hardwood floor. She missed hearing the click of their guns, but when she opened her eyes again, she could see Emlyn standing up with the barrel of her revolver pointed at Lucius's back. Her finger was firm on the trigger. She turned her head to see that Maield had his own revolver pointed right at Emlyn's head.

The room was still. They were all statues made of tension. Finally, after what seemed like hours instead of a minute, Lucius breathed out, long and slow. He looked over at the revolver, then peered into Emlyn's face, and he seemed remorseful. "For what it's worth, I am sorry." It was obvious that he was not apologizing for the situation but for something else.

Lucius carefully lifted himself off the bed. Maield and Emlyn lowered their guns but kept them in hand as Lucius put his white dress shirt on and adjusted its collar. As he buttoned his pants, Sylvia seemed to gather her wits about her.

"Lucius, I'm sorry, I just—"

He interrupted. "I know perfectly well the reason why."

Sylvia was shocked. "What?"

"I'll only say that when you look at me, you're as dry as a poorly prepared bird."

Her anger leaped. "How dare you speak to me that way! Get out of my house!"

"I will be out your door in good time." He finished buttoning his vest, slicked back his hair, and tweaked his moustache before motioning for Maield to follow him. At the door, Lucius stopped and looked back at Sylvia. "We will meet again under different circumstances."

Sylvia's voice became low with a menacing growl. "Leave."

Maield tried giving Emlyn one last glance, but she refused to return the look, instead turning her head in a menacing sneer.

* * * * *

The sky was a void. No stars shone and no clouds could be seen. A small kerosene lamp spread its light over the wooden bench, the same bench that Sylvia and Lucius shared earlier in the day. She sat on the end, supporting her elbow on the black iron armrest.

She thought she could, she really did—she tried . . . failed, miserably, and the consequences would depend entirely on what Lucius said to the other high patricians. That she only likes women; nothing really wrong with that ultimately. As long as she married a man and produced a child, but then there was the mockery. Her family's business was so carefully built during her grandfather's time when they had nothing, except an old name. Now possibly all laid to ruin because Lucius knew, she was sure of it, he knew that she loved Emlyn. No one would want to work with her after hearing that. The laughingstock of patrician society. Falling to lust with one's own martial.

She felt it all coming down like beautiful drops of failed hope soaking into the earth, absorbed, never to be seen again. She wondered what she did to displease the Gods. Did it matter?

What God would punish you simply because you love? she thought. *It would be everyone else who will judge, and they will.* Her reputation would be the price. Not only a recluse but obsessed with her martial.

"Mistress."

How she hated being called that by her of all people. She missed hearing Emlyn call her Sylvie so many years ago now.

"Mistress?"

Sylvia looked over her shoulder and forced a smile. "Emlyn, please. Come sit with me."

There was plenty of space on the bench, but instead she sat at Sylvia's feet, beside her legs. Sylvia gave out a low, frustrated sigh. She looked down at the top of Emlyn's head and found herself reaching out to stroke her hair. Emlyn craned her head back slightly. More memories came, and the tears threatened to bare themselves.

"I'm sorry, Tabby. I know you liked Maield."

For a moment, Emlyn did not respond. Then she laid her head against Sylvia's thigh. "It's okay, Mistress. There will be other suitors, other martials. I just wish I could know why."

"I . . . wish I knew. We . . . did not click I suppose," said Sylvia, barely able to get it out.

Emlyn sniffed, and Sylvia knew she was crying. Quickly, she returned to stroking Emlyn's hair, trying to keep her own tears from forcing a response. Both of them crying over this just would not do.

Minutes passed with no words between them. The occasional ding of autos on the streets contrasted with the consistent melody of the crickets. All was still and foreboding.

"Mistress?"

"Yes, Tabby?"

Emlyn did not respond.

"You may speak."

Emlyn rubbed her eyes, getting rid of the last of the tears. "Is reconciliation possible?"

She thought about it. It could be possible, but to do so, crawling back like a supplicant after all of this, would be beyond humiliating.

"No, I do not believe so. Let us talk about something else for a while, okay?"

"What would you like to talk about?" Emlyn began slowly undoing her braid.

Sylvia thought for a moment. "Oh, I know!"

It had been a few weeks since Emlyn first went investigating with Colmane. She had been so worried about her mother and about the relationship with Lucius, she had forgotten to ask what happened. It was never in Emlyn's mindful wheelhouse to volunteer information like that unless it involved Sylvia.

"The case. Tell me how the investigation is shaping up."

"There's not much to tell, Mistress."

"You know how much I like mysteries."

Emlyn nodded and recited her story. About Colmane's lateness, the ride to the Barrentine estate. Meeting the martials there. Being manipulated into taking down some bandits. That part really surprised Sylvia, and she felt sorry for Emlyn for having to endure it. But it was the new information about the Barrentines that kept bouncing around in her mind.

"The Barrentines, you know, I had talked to them before not more than seven months ago at the Heretes House charity auction."

"I remember," said Emlyn.

"You did not hear what Muire Barrentine said to me."

Emlyn moved her head and looked up at her curiously.

"Well, it boils down to this. Her family has little wealth left to them, but her husband on the other hand . . ." She looked down into Emlyn's eyes and continued stroking her hair. "Well, I'll just say that he was wealthy enough. I found it odd that he had died not more than a month prior. While she dressed in black, she seemed rather jubilant. She admitted to me that they buried him and his martial fast with no viewing of the body. Which I guess explains why I did not hear about it. I think they did this because inheritance is not bestowed until the funeral rites are over."

Emlyn's eyes went wide.

"Tabby, what is wrong?"

There had been two more murders since the estate visit, and both of the victims were gilla, high-priced ones at that. The populations of gilla and freemen were in terror, and immense public pressure was being placed on Colmane and inspector Nary to solve this case quickly. Those patricians who paid a good amount of coin for their properties were afraid of losing their investment in one thrust of a knife. Even the papers had joined in the panic, calling the murderer "The West End Gilla Slasher." This caused a few vigilante groups to be riled up, and when they began patrolling the streets, riots broke out. When they started harassing not only gilla but free people, the peacekeepers stepped in to disperse the angry mob, a mob who thought the killer might graduate to dispatching children. These groups were usually started by freemen who were probably alone and afraid. Likely trying to gather protection around them.

"Thank you, Mistress," said Emlyn.

"Did . . . that help?"

"I think so. I have a hunch. I hope it's only a flight of fancy."

Sylvia once again started twirling her fingers around the strands of Emlyn's hair. Emlyn almost purred and put her head back on her mistress's thigh, and soon enough she began kissing that area. Sylvia smiled and enjoyed the feeling for a moment before stiffening her fingers and roughly holding the strands. Of course Emlyn knew that she was not in trouble; it was part of this little game. Sylvia's heat had quickly come upon her, and her cares started to melt away one by one. She brought Emlyn's head back and put her lips to hers as if some ravenous hunger had overtaken her.

Out in the darkness there was a click and a low flash. Neither of the women saw it due to their eyes being closed, but Sylvia thought she heard the click and decided that it must be some animal scampering about. All thoughts about it left her mind as she focused on Emlyn's eager lips.

* * * * *

A small, calloused hand removed a loosened grimy brick and put the portable box camera in the recess as far back as she could manage. She had to be careful for the camera was worth more than herself eight times over. Maield had taken pleasure in telling her that.

The brick was placed back where it belonged with some effort. Mira looked to the left, then to the right, hoping she was not seen. She felt like a creeper, as if this was not her sneaking around. It didn't feel like her, and as far as she knew it could be a dream.

It's this or a slit throat, she thought. When Maield told her what he expected the mistress and the martial to be guilty of, she did not get it.

He frustratingly clued her in. Still, she had no idea how this was supposed to bring the house down.

A chill ran down her spine like some cruel touch of death's cold finger. Mira looked about at the deserted street that would normally be busy and loud throughout the day. Now it was dead silent, and that silence scared her the more she waited. Someone had to be watching.

Pull yourself together. This'll work out. If you freak, it'll all be over.

She checked the brick once more, making sure it was perfectly inconspicuous. Then jostled it once again before sprinting back to the servants' entrance of the insula.

Chapter Sixteen

It was Colmane's idea to come to the Royal Theater, twelve blocks away from the insula. Emlyn did not enjoy the walk one bit. But it was okay since Colmane's habitual tardiness allowed her to drink some water and gain a much-needed nap in the lobby. Needed because she often stayed up all night with Sylvia and watched her slowly unravel bit by bit while feeling helpless over what to do about it.

Colmane had spent this last month searching various costume shops and theaters around the city. He learned that the mask the perpetrator wore was not cheap and had to have been of such fine quality it must have come from the most gilded theater around. At least he hoped the Royal Theater would reveal some clue no matter how small since the public were howling for results. And thus they found themselves within a small costume room.

The smell of moth balls and oils permeated the air, not foul, but sharp, as if the nose was stuck inside a vinegar bottle. The moth balls and oils were used to keep the costumes in good condition. They pretended to ignore the smell as they stood and looked about the rather small room packed to the brim. The clothing was broken up into ten sections, with decades and epochs labeled above, giving a sense of order to a room threatening to burst in fabric-laden chaos.

Colmane started thumbing his way through the clothing, beginning with a section labeled "War of the Two Wolves." Emlyn watched his back and took note of his body language. His entire focus was before him and nowhere else. She then, out of the corner of her eye, spotted a section labeled for the time of the Tolido shootists. She found herself drawn to it, remembering the old stories she used to read.

As she pushed through each set of clothing, her fascination grew, though she was pretty sure these outfits were exaggerations at best. It was the names that grabbed her, forced her eyelids to go wide with wonder, a sense of long-buried excitement bubbling to the surface. She had wanted to be like them. Live the life of a wandering gun for hire. But that was not her fate, and who knew how much truth there was in those stories.

She heard keys jingle, then a key tipping into the lock and then a murmur of disbelief. The door cracked open. She grasped the onyx handle of her revolver, and a second later it was leaving its holster. In one smooth motion the barrel whipped around and pointed at the forehead of a balding man who had poked his head through the crack of the door. His shock was almost comical.

The door flung open as he tried to put his hands up but managed to trip as he tried moving backward, smacking against the door frame. Before the man could blink twice, Emlyn came upon him. She grabbed his collar with her free hand and pressed the barrel hard against his gut just under his bandaged arm. With her thumb she threw back the hammer. By the look of frightened understanding in his eyes, she could tell he heard the click and could sense that he understood what the consequences would be if he tried anything funny.

"Y-you're a martial! How-how did you get in here? It was locked! Did he send you?"

Colmane came up behind Emlyn and looked over her shoulder.

"Sent us? Whom do you mean?"

The barrel of the gun backed away from the man's gut. He breathed a slight sigh of relief even though she still had her revolver pointed at him and could shoot him dead at any moment from the hip. Colmane stepped in and brought out the affairs badge that he kept hidden in the inner pocket of his vest. He held it up for the man to inspect.

"Speak to me!"

"Oh Gods!" He drew the words out. Then he broke down. "Please! Don't take me away, I didn't mean to! He-he forced me! Look at my arm!"

He lifted his bandaged arm as much as his pain tolerance would allow.

"See?" His desperation came through with every motion.

"Answer my question now, or I will take you to affairs and torture the information out of you!" said Colmane with a menacing growl in his voice.

"Tall . . . a tall man! Formal like, like a bloodlined gilla!"

"So he was a gilla?" Colmane said to himself. But the man took it as a question.

"I think so! I mean, he reminded me of one!" The man looked over at Emlyn, who still had the revolver trained on him. "He was like you, with the same eyes!"

Colmane took the man's attention back. "Tell me a story."

The man looked at him for a moment, not comprehending, then it dawned on him. "Well, um, it's my duty to look after the costumes!" The man took time to gather himself before continuing.

* * * * *

His father had been bloodlined. He was born a gilla to the owner of this theater, and after forty-five years he had been called to his master's office and told that he would be free in a few months once the paperwork was filed. His aches and pains did not go unnoticed, and his master had been fond of him since his youth. He did not know how to feel about his coming freedom, but the master said that he could do the same job, except now he would get paid and have a gilla assistant.

He wanted to whistle a song as he got closer to the costume shop. He pursed his lips, but then he noticed. Something was off. The door handle, yes, that was it. There were numerous scratches—deep scratches.

Someone tried to pick the lock! He unhooked the keys from his belt and held them firm in his hand.

He peered at the door and did not notice the footsteps running up from behind him until it was too late.

He was pushed with violent force, face first against the door. Pain shot through his cheek, and the immense pressure being placed on his upper back made him imagine being crushed by a boulder against a mountain.

A strained, gruff voice that sounded like the cadence of someone who smoked and drank too much spoke next to his ear. "Hand me the keys."

"N-no! Brigand!" he yelled.

The gruff man sent a giant fist into the gilla's kidneys. As his body dropped down to the side, the stranger's hand tried to pry the keys from the man's balled-up fingers. The gilla threw his arm forward and down, wrenching his fist away from the gruff man.

The stranger growled with anger, then began driving blows back and forth at the kidneys over and over again. The man screamed in pain, and that was when the stranger shoved him to the ground.

"Stop screaming. Give me the keys."

It was difficult, but he managed to croak a word out from his throat. "No."

Kicks rained into his stomach, making him curl up. The stranger grabbed his hand, the one holding the keys, and straightened his arm out. "If you do not give me the keys, I will break your arm."

The stranger gave him a moment to release his grip. When he did not, he found the stranger to be good to his word. He felt a bone in his arm crack and the searing sharp pain that came with it. He screamed again and found that he was unable to keep hold of the keys. The stranger had them now.

He heard the lock turn and the door open, and what could only have been a few seconds later, the stranger was standing over him once more. The gilla managed to turn his head, and staring back at him were the most cold, dreadful hazel eyes that he had ever seen. He felt a chill creep over him as he recognized that the man was among the well-wishers after the latest performance. The stranger had walked up to him, praising the accuracy of the costumes and wondering if he could see the rest in the back. However, this man was no master. Yes, a freeman, and if a freeman was not employed with the theater, then they were not allowed behind the curtain.

The stranger gave a ghastly grin, showing yellow teeth and grayish gums. "You are a good boy. Consider yourself lucky." With that the stranger left.

* * * * *

"What tipped you to him being a gilla?" asked Emlyn.

The man thought for a moment. "Well, it was the way he carried himself. The way he talked, you see?"

She nodded.

He untucked his shirt from his trousers and lifted, showing bandages around his entire midsection. He let his shirt fall back down when he was sure the two had a good look.

"I still refused, by the Gods I refused! I kept to my duty."

Admiration danced along Emlyn's face.

"So this happened the very night of the murder at the blonde palace. Hmm . . . was there anything else? When he talked to you after the play? Anything that could aid our investigation?" asked Colmane.

The man thought for a moment. "No. Not that I can recall, Master. He just asked about the gilla here. I suppose that was a bit curious."

"Yes. Tell me, have any of your gilla failed in their duties in some way?"

He thought about this. "Well, they're nowhere near to my level, but they're all good girls and boys from what I can see. They try at least."

"All right, I've one more question for you if my associate here has none to offer: Did he take a silver filigree mask?"

The man took no time whatsoever to respond. "Why yes, one of the few we use for masked ball scenes or to spray a little pig's blood on it for our terror productions. It's quite the striking mask. I was sad to see him run out with it. If you find it, my master would be prepared to offer some reward."

"He ran?" asked Emlyn.

"Of course! I screamed bloody murder! They did not get here in time though." A realization fell upon the man's face. "Did-did something happen? Is that why you're here? Oh Gods! Was my mask involved in . . ." The man could barely get the word out. "The murders?"

Colmane's lips curled downward. "That is none of your concern."

"Of-of course, Master." He lowered his head.

Colmane jerked his head toward the door in a gesture for Emlyn to follow him out. She holstered her revolver and followed but stopped in front of the gilla for a moment and smiled at him. "He was right, you are a good boy."

The man was left in his costume shop, shocked that a martial would praise him in such a way.

Outside the room, Colmane stifled a laugh. "That was a nice thing to say."

"He might have lost the keys, Master, but he was willing to give his life to protect his owner's property. It is to be admired."

"Admired . . . It would have been a waste if he died for it. He's worth more than every single outfit in that room. To even consider throwing his life away to protect such frivolity . . . Well, his master does not know true value when he has it."

"Pardon, Master, but I would think that he does indeed know his value, or else he would not have been freed and given position."

Colmane waved his hand in dismissal. "That's stoic thinking. If he knew, then he would not entertain the idea. Anyway it is a tiring subject. What do you think? Do you really believe the killer is a martial?"

"I, hmm, I really don't want to believe that. It seems impossible. After all, we are not capable of this."

"Not capable? Are you not educated on how to kill people?"

"Yes."

"Then how are your kind not capable?"

"The notion to kill when it does not involve protecting our owners or their property is ludicrous."

The edge of Colmane's lip curled up. "You killed in the name of another on the Barrentine estate, or did you forget that?"

"No, Master, I certainly did not. I shot those men for my own protection and dispatched the other two out of pity."

"Hm, is that how you see it?"

She stared into his eyes seriously. He faltered slightly, losing that infuriating smirk. "Master, I do not justify it. Have you ever participated in a gun fight?"

He shook his head.

"If you had, then you would know that there is no time to think about who will live or die, you react and nothing else." She gulped and looked quickly to the floor. "Please, excuse my impertinence."

"Point well taken." He brought out a cigarette case from his pocket and put one between his lips. She lit the match for him. He started walking.

She swished the match and flicked it down. "I have a theory of my own, Master. I didn't want to believe it, but after hearing what that man said, it has become more real. But I am afraid of what we might have to do."

"Tell me when we're outside."

By this time, they were out in the lobby. A lobby full of monied people waiting for the next show. It was so full that Colmane had to nudge himself between them and apologized every time he brushed up against somebody. Emlyn did the same just with more deference. She became aware of how very few of these high patricians had martials, and she thought back on what Cord said to Maield about martials becoming less and less needed.

She noticed something that was very out of place in this crowd of flawless, gilded patricians. A boy no older than twelve in doctored clothing that squarely belonged in the Stints instead of the Royal Theater. Oddly, he was wearing a brown scarf wrapped tightly around his neck. Emlyn's eyes widened, the boy was pickpocketing and doing so deftly until he was noticed by the only other martial who tried to swat at him. But the boy easily dodged backward, giving the martial a toothy grin. He bumped into Colmane's leg. His grin faltered at the feel of a large hand upon his neck. The boy looked up into Colmane's annoyed face.

"Go apply your trade elsewhere, boy."

Colmane pushed the boy violently toward the door. He looked back at both of them in wonderment as he stumbled out and disappeared out of sight.

* * * * *

"This is a bad idea. Do you know what would happen to me if the peacers catch us? Not even my standing with affairs would save me. The black priestesses would *howl* for my head!"

Emlyn dressed in a simple black skirt and a black shirt. It amused Colmane that they tailored it to fit her perfectly. "Privilege at its finest! It seems that gilla have it better than the poor in this day and age. I have no earthly idea why they would want to run away!" he said to her when they met at the insula a few hours after parting outside the theater.

She had rolled up the sleeves of her dark gray jacket to the elbows and had old gray, well used, work gloves protecting her hands. On her belt was a small hammer and a chisel poking out of a yellowish leather pouch. She shrugged. "Like I said, I have a good hunch."

Colmane leaned against the dusty stone of the catacomb entrance and looked at her in disbelief. He too was in black and had a fresh pair of work gloves hooked to a belt loop. "A hunch. You want to do this on a hunch?"

"There has been no headway for weeks. So, Master, would you prefer to sit at your desk twiddling your thumbs while being berated by the public and your superiors for a while longer? Or do you want to solve this once and for all?"

Saying something like that would get a gilla punished. Colmane, however, gawked before stifling a laugh. "Very good, Emlyn, very good. Your point is once again *well* taken. Let's take a risk."

Colmane patted his vest pocket. "I entertained your . . . hunch and did some research that should prove quite useful. That is, if we see what you expect to see."

Colmane put his hand on the cold black iron of the gate and opened it slowly so that the creaks from the rusty hinges would not be loud enough to hear from a distance. Inside the gate were steep stairs leading down into a foreboding blackness. Emlyn gulped. Colmane brought out a small lantern and flipped a metal button on its base. A white light in the lantern pulsed on and flickered before settling. He nodded at her, and they both walked down the steps, placing each foot carefully upon the polished stone to mask the clicking of their boots. The loudest sound turned out to be their heartbeats filling their ears with a rapid *thump-thump-thump.*

They did not speak along the way; an echo would bounce off the walls and send priestesses running after them. Beating up a priestess would be a terrible idea, entailing a rebuke not only from the druidi arbiters but from the Gods as well.

The electric light from the lantern revealed arched doorways as they stepped down into a long hall. There were fourteen arches in all and seven on each side. At the end of the hall, the passageway split off to the right and left. They went on, looking at the plaques above the portals, trying not to pay much more attention to anything else. There was a constant feeling that someone or something was coming up from behind them. This caused Emlyn to constantly look back, but there was nothing. She brought out the amber stone given to her by a wandering druidi many years ago and kissed its polished surface. They came to the end of the hall, and where it split, there were other plaques with various numbers.

Emlyn strained to hear any sound that did not come from them. No drip of water, not even the scurrying of rats. This area of the catacombs was as clean as the Teyrn's palace, but it possessed an unsettling coldness that was still, as if a thousand eyes of a thousand ghostly faces were upon them, waiting to breathe once again. Emlyn wanted to get out of there as soon as possible. This was no place for the living.

The plaque at the end of the second hall pointed right, and the other pointed left. They went right, down another long hallway with the same open archways. Finally they stopped in front of one, and Colmane raised his lantern.

He whispered, "There . . . That's the number."

Emlyn looked up at the numbers eleven nineteen above the archway and followed Colmane into the crypt. She cast her eyes around the room and noted thirty plots built into the walls with large slabs covering access to them. On the back wall were even larger tombs with decorated slabs, full of carvings varying from Gods to animals all dancing to the light; this was where they headed. Colmane briefly made a circular motion with the lantern. The light danced upon the brass that spelled the names of the occupants.

"There's the dusty brosthun." The lantern revealed the name of one Cerisus Barrentine, and then below that was the name of his martial, Batt Dunmor. Emlyn reached into the leather pouch next to the buckle of her belt and brought out a vial full of red liquid.

"What are you doing?" asked Colmane.

She held the vial closer to the lantern and peered into it. "We're performing dark work here."

"Supernatural protection? You can't be serious."

"I could be wrong about this, Master. If I am, then I would rather not suffer the wrath of the three. I bought this from a Morri woman. It should work."

"Why do you believe that bunk? If the Gods exist, then the last person they would be concerned with is a gilla."

By this time she had opened the vial and tipped it so that the blood would come out. It had to be blood, since Morri women used it in their spells, or parlor tricks as Colmane would say. Emlyn was having a difficult time getting the blood out since it was mixed with some sort of thickening agent.

"Gods do not affect tradition. Besides, as I've said, we are the ones who bow the lowest."

"Yes, yes, it's a nice sentiment. Too bad it's all bunk. Dé Ard doesn't control the sky, Dé Brigantia is not the mother of the land, and her aspect Morri do not control fate or dark forces of any kind. The natural forces can be explained through science. There's no dark magic working against you when something bad happens."

Emlyn ignored him as a large drop of blood came out of the vial onto her finger. She spread the blood in a circle upon her forehead and put a line through it. Colmane shook his head. She walked a few steps toward him. He quickly put both of his palms up, stopping her from coming closer. "No, no, skip me. If it was only tradition, fine, but you really believe this offers protection."

"But, Master—"

"If it concerns you so much, then I'll just keep a lookout while you pry it open," he said, annoyed and just a little too loud.

She corked the vial. "Thank you for understanding, Master." Emlyn smiled and continued, "You rarely treat me as a gilla at all."

Instantly she knew that those were the wrong words. She was more surprised at herself than the content; she was never that sloppy. Even when being pushy or talking back, it was always polite and laden with advice. How could she have allowed herself to mimic his nonchalant demeanor? But it really was not about that at all. It was about questioning him, his job, and how he treats those who are considered little more than animals. Of course, he expected a gilla to be a gilla at all times, no matter how he personally treated them. Suggesting they were equal in the slightest was something only a new low gilla would do.

His eyes seethed with ire, and he kept his teeth clenched so he would not shout. "How I treat you is none of your concern. I may find the functions of a martial fascinating, but that does not make you any less a gilla in my eyes. Do you understand me?"

It was like Emlyn had looked upon a Gorgon, stunned, then turned to stone. As soon as the last word came out of his mouth, her knees unfroze and hit the ground. She put her head to the floor with her arms outstretched before her. "I apologize, Master! Forgive me, Master!"

He took a moment and just watched her in this pose. After a minute she wondered why he was not speaking, then it occurred to her, he was admiring her figure in that position. She felt a wave of unease, and for the first time, she wondered if Colmane had plans to use her in a sexual manner. Sylvia would not like that and would charge him a hefty fine and cost him his job since he did not have permission to do such a thing. He would be ruined. So no he wouldn't, he wasn't stupid. But she knew that he was imagining it.

He sighed in exasperation. "That's good enough. Get up and go to work before you forget yourself again, gilla."

"Yes, Master!" She slid back to her knees in a well-practiced manner, then got back on her feet. In one swift motion she grabbed the hammer and chisel from her belt and went up to the slab. She poised the chisel at the thin crack between the granite and the polished stone wall.

Colmane went to the archway and leaned against its frame. If he saw someone coming, they would have enough warning. As the hammer hit the chisel, he could not help but flinch.

Emlyn wondered if the sound reminded him of the two gilla he told her about outside of the Barrentine estate. Did he feel bad at all about such things? She sighed, knowing he indeed held no remorse or uncertainly about it.

She tried to work as quickly as possible because the noise it made could fill an amphitheater. As she got to the middle, the slab started to slide off, and she tried to hold onto it but was surprised by its weight. She realized it had been opened before.

"Master!"

He looked over at her and noticed that she was having a hard time keeping the slab from falling, hence breaking the carved pattern on the front. He rushed over and got hold of the other end. They lowered the five-foot hunk of marble carefully and placed it on the ground with minimal sound.

They stood back up, breathed in, and then experienced the wretched smell of a burnt body. Colmane reached into his pocket and brought out a handkerchief, using it to cover his mouth and nose.

Emlyn put her hand above the square recess of the tomb and peered into the pitch-black hole. Colmane lifted the lantern, giving light to the entirety of the plot. For a moment, Emlyn thought she had seen the face of the dead brigands. Their eyes spoke of dread but investigated hers with no fear. But the image was gone in an instant. She blinked and shook her head. She had hoped beyond anything that her hunch was wrong, but this proved her right.

Masters were typically buried with their martial so they could protect them on the bridge, beyond the bridge, and into whatever afterlife they were bound, but one of them was missing, there should be two. The master had been shot and then burned along with his martial. The smell told her it was true, but then where had the remains of the other gone? Colmane and Emlyn took a long look at each other before she reached in and quickly dragged out the body. It fell to the floor with a thud and they cringed from the sound of flaking paper. Emlyn undid the ropes holding the sheet in place around the body. She folded back the cloth, revealing the completely burnt corpse beneath.

"Gods, the smell!" exclaimed Colmane.

The first thing Emlyn noted was how tall this person was. She put her gloved hand on the head and moved it around.

"Master Cerisus. His height was five-seven, and he should have a bullet wound in the head."

"Correct," said Colmane.

"So this should be the martial."

"Should be?"

"Yes, Master. The martial was burned alive. Whoever this is, he's at least two inches shorter than Batt, according to the records you provided, six-three, and he should be much broader in the shoulders."

"Surely the fire would burn a person's girth away."

She noticed something else, got closer, and put her hands upon the corpse's hips. Then she slid a finger between the legs.

"What're you doing?"

"This . . . is not a man but a rather large woman."

"What? How did they miss something like that?" said Colmane in surprise.

"The family coveted his money, and the quicker they were able to put Master Barrentine and his martial into the ground, the quicker they received inheritance. It's easy to overlook, to miss."

"So . . . let me get this right: we have someone else's body, probably one of the bandits who burned inside the carriage, and so the body of both the master and the martial are missing?"

"Yes, Master. That seems to be the right of it."

"Cerisus was a frail man and would never be able to move bodies. So it was a martial, but I did not expect the killer to be a dead martial," said Colmane.

Emlyn sat down and put her forehead against her knee. The concept of a martial being able to do something like this was unreal, and the facts did not level with her psyche. She had hoped she was wrong, but there it was, right in front of her.

"They lied! They lied to me!" He started pacing back and forth in the crypt with his hand on his chin. "The one thing I don't get," said Colmane as he took out a cigarette and lit it, "Is what exactly the family was hiding from me."

He took the cigarette out of his mouth, blew the smoke out, and with the same hand pointed at Emlyn, who looked up at him questioningly. "The way I see it, there are two possibilities. One, Muire had her husband killed. Two, she was covering for Batt . . . or, by the Dane's Hel let's add a third one, she's guilty of both."

"Forgive me, Master, but I think you're getting ahead of yourself."

He took a drag, stared at her, and then blew out the smoke. "You're right. I've a gilla to catch first."

CHAPTER SEVENTEEN

The boardwalk was as still as the stinking sewage water below. They were above the Benelok that fed into the Tamisis river: the main river running through Londinium out into the Kymbri sea. The silence was only interrupted by the occasional howling of a dog and the squeaking of rats darting across the path. This was the Stints: the poorest area in the entire city and notorious for its violent crime. So Emlyn was paying close attention to the surroundings, but she did not ask Colmane why they were there. He put her in her place back in the catacombs, and she did not feel comfortable in pushing familiarity. Besides, she had a lot on her mind, and not just with the foreboding surroundings.

Everything about this investigation told her that Batt was responsible for the murders, but she found it difficult to wrap her mind around the fact that a martial would kill indiscriminately. She had to take him down. It would be a duty to the city to do so, and the thought had a bit of a poetic ring to it.

Emlyn kept an eye on every dark nook and cranny for possible assailants. She noted more than a few outlines in the shadows watching as they passed.

"Do you think they will come at us?" asked Colmane.

Emlyn was not surprised he knew. He'd been side-eyeing her and following where she focused her gaze. "No, Master. They know they've been spotted."

"Good . . . because we are going right through them."

Colmane turned, and Emlyn moved along with him. As they went by, she could see the faces following them, and now that they were closer it became apparent that not all of them were cutthroats or thieves but looked more downtrodden and hungry. When they turned a corner, she was facing a little community created by the urban homeless. This took her by surprise, for she had never considered something like this existing in the city. Oh, she knew there were homeless, of course, but this was a step beyond her imagining.

Colmane was not fazed. He moved forward and stood in the middle of this small village of forty or so skeletal figures as the reality of this place kept Emlyn glued to the spot. These people seemed barely alive. They clutched half-dead babes at their breasts, cooked rats on makeshift spits, and slept in rotten wood crates. Every bit of clothing had holes, and through those holes could be seen red, burning rashes. No smiles were present. They all seemed to be what she imagined as draugrs from Skaldane legend, shambling about with no purpose other than to find sustenance.

He stood amidst them, standing straight, hands on hips, with an eye of contempt. "I seek an audience with Ollivander!"

They waited for some time. To Emlyn it seemed like they were being ignored.

"I seek an audience with Ollivander!" he said with more gusto.

A few minutes later a small voice called out, "You the ones seeking the boss?"

"Finicus! Is that you?" Colmane yelled, unsure of the smaller shadowy figure emerging from an alleyway.

A boy strode out from the shadows, carrying himself in complete confidence with his back straight and his thumbs hooked in his belt loops.

He headed toward them. The boy wore a loose Alban knit cap with a short bill, turned askew. His slender shoulders filled a strained and stained shirt; it was hard to tell its original color. His yellow plaid pants were in similar shape and much too short for his frame, with patches poorly sewed on. The most surprising thing about him, though, was the tight steel collar around his throat. It must have been on him for a few years, because he was too big for it, and it threatened to choke him if he grew any more. No tag was attached. It was most likely yanked off long ago. Emlyn wondered about the boy and why, with Colmane being a catcher and all, had he not apprehended him?

"Yes, sir, sure is! Trusty ole Finicus at yer service!" he mocked as he bowed. The boy looked up, and she recognized him: the pickpocket from the theater. The out-of-season scarf he had worn concealed his collar.

Finicus took a moment to consider her. "Wow, a martial! Traveling in grand style, Mr. Colmane! Grand style!"

"Clamp your jaw, Finicus. I am in no mood to listen to your jab. Lead me to Ollivander," demanded Colmane.

"Okay, okay, just being light is all, you curmudgeon," grumbled the boy. "This way." Finicus motioned for them to follow.

Emlyn wondered about their relationship. Colmane was wolfish when it came to his job from what she had seen and heard, so why was this boy allowed to be free?

They followed through labyrinthine alleyways that seemed to only grow darker and more confusing. The blackness successfully blocked the sight of grime but did nothing for the smell, which went from merely annoying to dead fish and bad meat being slowly cooked over a fire. They had turned so many times in the dark that the four directions became topsy-turvy. This confusion must work for the boy and whoever else used the alleys, helping to keep them safe from gillars, orphanages, conscriptors, workhouse thugs, and gangs.

They turned yet another corner, and a light could be seen at the very end of a long, narrow alleyway with buildings on the sides looming upward like gigantic stone monoliths. They passed numerous other alleys leading between the buildings with little faces, speckled and dirty, looking out from the shadows. As they got closer to the light, many of the children stepped out of the alleys to watch with curious eyes. All of them had hard faces and, if you only looked at those faces, there was not much of a difference between them and an adult.

An older kid, taller than the rest, stepped into their path. This steadfast boy had a cold, dullard look with round beady eyes and an overbite that made one front tooth stick out further than the rest. His speech had the sound of a hiss of air running through a broken flute, and Emlyn assumed that he had more problems with his mouth than his overbite.

"Why you bring 'em here?"

Finicus shrugged. "They want ta see Ollie." He hooked a thumb back over his shoulder. "He's been here before and is a friend to us. The other is a martial gilla." The surrounding children were in awe upon hearing those words and edged closer. The taller boy stood his ground, placing himself into a power stance to block the path.

"Come on, Duck!" said Finicus. Duck must be the name the slow boy went by.

"Nuh-uh, no way will she bring weapons ta see Ollie."

Finicus went up on his toes but still could not get face-to-face with this boy called Duck. That did not matter to Finicus though. He poked a spear-like finger into Duck's chest.

"Are ya forgetting that I've been a member way longer than you? Where's Ollie? He wouldn't stand for this!"

Duck made no move. "Yer not special, Fini. Everybody got ta follow the rules."

Finicus rolled his eyes, threw his arms out to the side in frustration, and then turned to look at Colmane and Emlyn, sizing them up.

"No offense, my friends, but ya need to give up whatever weapons ya got." As he said this, he looked to Emlyn.

"No, these are important to my station. They are one of a kind."

"Them's the breaks. You can trust me to look after your irreplaceable valuables," said Finicus with an eager smile.

"No," responded Emlyn, crossing her arms.

"Emlyn, give him your weapons," said Colmane impatiently.

Emlyn balled up her fists, then released the tension. She slowly drew out her revolver and, one by one, took the six rounds out and placed them in her skirt pocket. Then she took out her knife and handed them over, butt and handle first.

"You better keep them safe. They're worth more than your life."

Finicus was immediately surprised at their weight. He took a minute to stare in awe at the weapons, almost drooling on the inlaid silver vine pattern curling up from the butt of the onyx pearl reinforced handle. He stuck them both in his belt in a similar fashion as she had, minus the holsters.

"That hammer and chisel too, if ya please."

"Is that considered a weapon as well?" asked Colmane.

"Of course! Besides, Ollie needs some form of payment."

"Payment! I could just take you on a trip to gilla affairs, you little swindler!"

Finicus tsked. "That might work on me personally, Mr. Colmane, ya got me by the balls." Many of the kids snickered at the word. "But not when you're seeing Ollie, and Ollie will not stand for it, nor will he agree to any request ya might have without payment. Just think of it as a donation to the orphanage. And it's such a small donation." Finicus rubbed his index finger and thumb together in a universal sign for payment.

"Emlyn." That was as good as an assent coming from Colmane, so Emlyn took the hammer and chisel and held them out. Finicus made a kind of clicking sound with his mouth, and another boy at around eight years old stepped up and timidly took the items from her hands, then hurried back within the growing crowd of children.

Duck moved out of the way, allowing them to walk in. The narrow alley ended, opening up to a wide area in a T shape. Numerous barrels and crates against the far wall were arranged to resemble a patio. On the right side of this open space was the entrance to one alley, and the same was on the left, yet another dark alley. It was obvious that none of the children lived in this spot, but it served its purpose for acting as a sort of hideout for the day. It must have been one of the many places they rotated to. The constant moving made them hard to find. This space was lit by an ornate black iron lamppost casting a sickly yellow glow upon the occupants of the patio.

Finicus walked them up to stand before a long-haired blonde boy sitting cross-legged on an old barrel. He was hunched over with his elbows on his knees, reading a cheap fenni novel. He could only be Ollivander. He was flanked by half a dozen rough-looking older boys with hard faces that had seen better days. Emlyn and Colmane stood a few yards before him. The other children filed up next to the walls, making a resemblance to a royal court.

Ollivander laughed, and his voice echoed gruff and quick with a hint of a crack from oncoming puberty. "Ah! He fell for it! Balloons! He bared his ass as they looked through their spy-eyes!"

The boys around him feigned laughter. It was apparent that they had no idea what he was talking about. Finicus coughed, but Ollivander shushed him while still looking down at the short book made with the cheapest of paper. They waited for an uncomfortable minute until Ollivander shut the book and handed it to the boy next to him.

The area was completely silent even with the few dozen children standing by. The silence was interrupted by Ollivander clapping his hands twice before throwing his arms forward and out. He was missing his right eye, and even being a few yards away, Emlyn could tell by the abrasions on his neck that he had worn a collar for many years.

"Fini! I've not seen you for a week! I thought you abandoned us . . . or maybe the catchers got you." Ollie looked at Colmane wearily as he said this.

"Oh!" Finicus suddenly plunged his fist deep into his left pocket and stuck his tongue out, but he found nothing but a hole at the end with two of his fingers poking all the way through. He looked down at it, disbelieving what he saw, then quickly patted all his other pockets. His eyes were wide, and Emlyn noticed him becoming just a little fearful.

"What are those items in your belt?" asked Ollie. "They look like they'd fetch more than a few kints!"

"Th-the dagger and gun of this martial." He cocked his head toward Emlyn.

Ollivander sighed, and like a snail moving after a lethargic rest, he lifted himself up and off the barrel. The sound his mud-caked boots made on the cracked bricks was audible to every ear in the alley. Even Emlyn and Colmane found themselves holding their breath.

The two boys were roughly the same height, but Emlyn could tell through Ollivander's face and stubble that he was a few years older. They were face-to-face, but he did not look at Fini. He just nodded as if he were having a conversation with himself. Then in a great burst of movement his hand rose and fell toward Finicus's face. Finicus flinched and closed his eyes, like a steel shutter ready for the impact, but quickly realized he felt nothing. He opened one eye and looked at the palm a few inches away from his face. That palm then playfully patted him on the cheek twice and retreated to Ollivander's side. The child leader had an amused smile on his face.

"You have a week to pay triple tribute." His smile turned to a deadly serious frown. "And if you do not, then you will have more than the Morri to worry about. Am I understood?"

"Heh, clear as glass, boss!" said Finicus nervously.

Ollivander turned to Colmane and Emlyn. "I know you, Erasmus Colmane, but I did not think you would be able to afford a martial."

"She belongs to the Chronisters. Her name is Emlyn."

Ollie raised an eyebrow. "What do you want here?"

"I need you to keep an eye on a few properties. See if anyone suspicious is lurking around. If you see anyone, anyone at all, then report it to me." Colmane, as he said this, reached into the pocket located inside his vest, brought out a folded piece of paper, and then held it out for the boy to take. Ollivander snatched the paper from his fingers and unfolded it. His eyes quickly scanned the document.

"I'm glad to know that you can read," said Colmane with surprising menace for someone attempting to curry favor. The boy ignored him.

"Duinn Street, that's easy enough, but Hillock, Valcum, and Iceni are rich neighborhoods. My boys would have suspicions cast on them." He folded the paper and put it in his pocket. "And how about the payment for time and risk?"

The kid who'd approached Emlyn so timidly acted the same when approaching Ollivander, and he put the hammer and chisel in his hands. Ollivander gripped the two items as if he was holding on for dear life.

"No . . . not enough for what you ask. Nice hammer though. Perhaps if you were asking us for the slip. This is not worth risking my boys. Five half kints. Of course, further donations help to support these children." He nodded. "Yes, that will suffice, I think."

Emlyn knew how explosive Colmane could be, but when the knuckles came sharply down upon Ollivander's cheek, it looked like the world went askew for the boy as he fell flat on the ground. She imagined that Ollie expected no lasting harm to come to him within this little kingdom, so she was surprised to see the boy turn to look up at Colmane as if it had all been no big deal. She suspected that he experienced numerous fights with heavy hitters. Ollie spit out the blood gathering in his mouth while looking up at Colmane, who was screaming at him.

"You're nothing more than an urchin running a little puppet show! I should march you straight down to affairs! I'm sure I could find records on you! Then I'll put you, *all of you*, exactly where you belong!"

Colmane's throat found itself next to the edge of a rusty blade. The kitchen knife was being held by one of the older boys who had come up from behind. Colmane moved his eyes about and noticed many of the children had brought out makeshift weapons. He looked over at Emlyn.

She had her hands up and was rather amused at the reactions from the these kids.

Ollivander pushed up off the ground and steadied himself on his feet as if this was barely an inconvenience. He brushed a hand down his sleeve, dislodging some dirt. "I don't take kindly to threats, Mr. Colmane. You think too little of us low people. Teach him a lesson."

"You dare threaten the next dalarwain of gilla affairs!" All but a few of the children started walking toward him, intent on doing him harm.

"Wait!" They all turned their heads to Emlyn.

"Are you finally going to do something about this?" asked Colmane.

"Yes, Master. I am." Emlyn slowly brought a hand down, letting the children be sure of every movement she made, and reached into the hidden pocket on her skirt, then brought out eight full kints.

"No," said Colmane menacingly.

"I am supposed to protect you, Master. That does not mean the only option is violence."

One of the boys snatched the coins from her hand and promptly brought them to Ollivander, who then held each one up for his inspection.

"You are a wise gilla." He put the kints in his pocket. "I'll send Fini to inform you . . . *if* we find anything."

Ollivander did not take his eyes away from Emlyn. She thought that, despite Colmane's anger, the kid was more weary about what she could do. It made sense. It was likely Ollivander heard a few stories about martials throughout his life. A catcher would seem small-time and less dangerous in comparison. He beckoned Finicus over and put an arm around him, pulling him close as they turned their backs. Emlyn strained to hear but could not make out what was being said.

Ollivander patted him on the shoulder and pushed him away. Finicus strode to Emlyn and did his best, with minimum fumbling, to mimic the smoothness that she demonstrated when handing over her weapons, but it still looked clumsy. She put them back in their holsters.

The children were getting louder and started chanting, "Leave! Leave! Leave!" and crowded near them, only leaving one avenue open for an exit.

"You've no more business here! Leave! Go! Shoo off!" Ollivander waved his arms about. The blade was removed from its place against Colmane's throat. The boy holding the knife pushed him back, and Colmane let it be known that he did not take kindly to this.

"How dare you!"

He was about to step forward to intimidate the boy but stopped as all the kids in this makeshift shanty court closed in and continued the chanting, "Leave! Leave! Leave!"

Emlyn and Colmane briskly turned and headed down the open alley. Each breath taken by Colmane seethed with bitterness; each motion of his body boiled with anger.

Once they were far out of sight, he let it all pour out onto Emlyn.

"Are you a martial?"

"I . . . don't understand—"

Colmane interrupted, "You're barely a gilla! You can't even perform your duty! Why did you let that child humiliate me? You're supposed to be protecting me! Not let a blade fall by my throat!"

Emlyn was astonished. She didn't react with violence because she knew that her mistress would be appalled if she did so. And Emlyn was sure that somehow, somewhere deep down, she would tarnish herself if she killed or even hurt one hair on those children's heads. Besides, she did not believe these children would go so far as to leave one nick on Colmane no matter what he did to them. It was an act. Just intimidation.

"Master, they're children," she pleaded.

"Then they have you fooled! They might look like innocent children in your eyes, but their minds grew up long ago, and they would as soon knife you in the back than let you get away with your purse!"

She doubted that, because they took no more than what Emlyn offered. Then again, Colmane had many interactions with them, unlike herself, who had never even heard of a gang of orphans before. It had no bearing on protecting her mistress, so why would she? No matter how she tried to justify Colmane's feelings on the matter, it just did not sit right with her.

"You need to realize that this is a cruel world. You do not sit above it! What do you think would happen if you were suddenly just a low gilla? Do you think you'd be sitting pretty behind a mistress in a palace like the one you live in? No, you wouldn't! No one would be afraid of your eyes, for you would be on equal footing with the lowest of dregs! You would be without your precious privileges!"

Emlyn did not respond because she was still stuck in her state of astonishment.

"Is that why martials never run away? Unless their mind snaps such as the cac we hunt now? Because of privileged ignorance?"

Emlyn thought about how well Stella would get along with Colmane. "I am sorry, Master. I am what I am."

His body seemed to relax at those words, and what came out of his mouth was much calmer but still stern. "So it would seem. If tonight has proven anything to me, it's that you're not what I thought you were."

No more words were said between them as they walked. A long measure of awkwardness grew to fill the void. She followed him and his electric lantern: going right, going left, then another left, then another right.

Colmane stopped and looked around him. The bluish light from his lantern lit up a tall brick wall before them, and a few rats squeaked and darted to the corner shadows at the base. He turned to her, and with the light, she had a good view of his face. His eyes were looking for an exit.

"I'm utterly turned," he said, annoyed.

"Ollie said you'd lose your way, but it looked like you two needed cooler heads before seeing me again."

Colmane turned and raised his lantern, flooding Finicus in blue. The boy had to shield his eyes for a moment.

"Gods, tryin' to blind me or somethin'? Ya want out of this maze or what?"

Colmane lowered the lantern and nodded cautiously. Finicus beckoned for them to follow.

Emlyn and Colmane made sure to follow close behind. Just in case the boy was planning to pull some juvenile prank and leave, making them even more disoriented and turned around.

It did not take long to find the way back out of that dead-end alley: straight for twenty yards, then a right for five, and a left for two. Voila! They were back on a main street eerily absent of people.

It was uncomfortable to be the only ones on a street that teemed with life during the day. It was now dreadfully dead during late hours as if all those happy people were flushed into the Tamisis to make way for ghosts and dark creatures.

Colmane checked his pocket watch. "Past three. Bluebell Avenue I believe."

Finicus put his hands in his pockets and shrugged. "Yes, sir, best place to pick a few pig-haves."

Colmane placed his watch back in his pocket. "Good. Emlyn?"

"Yes, Master?"

"I'll contact you when you're needed, understood?"

"Understood, Master."

He walked off rather hurriedly down the street to the heavily lighted crossway.

"Sure is a pleasant man, isn't he?"

Emlyn nodded before looking down at Finicus. "Thank you for leading us out."

"My pleasure! I've never seen a martial up close, much less held their weapons. Where ya off to now?"

"My mistress's home is on the other end of this street."

"You live in an insula? On this street?" he asked with disbelief. Bluebell avenue was known as a place where the wealthiest high patricians made their home.

Emlyn smirked. "Of course."

"That must be nice. Always wondered what the inside of one of those places looked like," he said.

"It's nothing to complain about."

"Oh I am sure. Well . . . I guess I should go," he said, showing disappointment as he turned to leave.

She put her hands on her hips and asked, "Would you like to see?"

* * * * *

The handle of the kitchen door jiggled before clicking, then opened with a barely perceptible creak.

"Everyone is still asleep, so keep noise to a minimum," whispered Emlyn.

"What you mean is that I'm a runaway so keep quiet. Be like a ghost."

Emlyn almost laughed. "Yes, you have it exactly."

A shrill voice came from further in the kitchen. "A runaway?"

Mira came into view. Her hair was disheveled from sleep, but she was still wearing the sheer blouse and skirt. Finicus's face lit up when he saw her.

"I'm going to tell the Mistress!"

Emlyn crossed her arms. "You can. Go ahead, but do you think that's a wise move, girl?"

Mira stood for a moment just looking at her. Emlyn could see that she was trying to work something out in her mind. A jumble of ungreased gears grinding together. Emlyn narrowed her eyes, and that put fear into Mira, who promptly dashed to and through the doorway leading to the stairs. She cursed Mira's sudden obsession with following the rules.

Finicus's eyes followed Mira as she ran out. "Are *you* sure that was the right move?"

"Don't worry about her."

"Hey, if this'll create trouble, then I'll go," he said, concerned.

"How badly do you want to see this place?"

"Umm, badly?"

"Then you will just have to take that chance."

Finicus looked as if he was about to run but then unclenched his hands and relaxed as he saw the smirk spread across Emlyn's face. "Oh, ha-ha, very funny."

Then she said seriously, "I promise, nothing adverse will happen to you."

* * * * *

They spent most of their time in the garden since she wanted to avoid anyone who might be up early. Finicus walked around the statues, marveling at the workmanship. He was not afraid to touch the statues representing the Gods. He asked about their construction. She had to be honest, she didn't know much about how they were made. She only knew they were created two generations ago by a renowned sculptor called Lars Beadre. Finicus had inquired no further on the matter, though it was easy to tell that he was interested in learning more about the subject.

"I need something to do when I'm old and out of this collar, and well, it seems interesting. Like you're chipping away the ugliness to reveal something beautiful, ya know?"

She did not expect those words to come out of the mouth of someone so young. Of course, what Colmane said about these kids growing up fast had a ring of truth. Finicus meant what he said. It was in his eyes, and the eyes never lie.

It was time to go. Cord would be up soon, and it was a terrible time to get punished. She led him back down the kitchen stairs and was about to pass the threshold when a familiar voice in its singsong cadence struck her ears. "There you are, Emlyn! Come on in and bring the young man with you."

Emlyn did as instructed. Finicus jumped behind her. He peered around her to see who had spoken and looked for an exit.

Sylvia had her chair turned from the kitchen table toward them. Her knees were crossed, but the posture was relaxed. A white silk robe clung to her body and flowed down, reaching the floor, tied in the middle with a thick silk ribbon. Her long black hair was down and disheveled, but the bags under her eyes were most telling, she had not had any sleep that night. This had become a common occurrence lately with Camilla's failing health. Emlyn would stay up to provide whatever her mistress needed, mostly comfort and a shoulder to cry on. Emlyn was only happy to provide and didn't mind her own lack of sleep.

Ms. Cord sat across from Sylvia in a plain woolen nightgown, her graying red hair done up in a plait. At her feet knelt Mira, who looked none too pleased about being in that position.

Sylvia rose and walked a few steps toward them. "So that is the runaway boy hiding behind your skirt?"

Emlyn turned and looked down at Finicus. His body tensed, ready for an attempt to dash out the door.

"Ah, ma'am, yer scaring the poor thing!" Cord brushed Mira to the side and made her way to a rounded ice box in the far corner.

"I am not," declared Sylvia. She bent down to get eye level with him. "I see you are looking for an exit. You have nothing to fear from me. I am not in the habit of harming children. Do you like milk? I've some here."

Finicus considered Sylvia for a moment, then relaxed and stepped away from Emlyn. "I'll take it, if ya put a drib in one of those coffee cups."

Ms. Cord laughed and motioned to Mira. "Pour a coffee for the lad."

Mira scowled but got to her feet, grasped the handle of the carafe sitting on the table, and started pouring.

He puffed up his chest, putting confidence back in his stride as he walked to the table and sat.

"This isn't right! He's a runaway!" yelled Mira in desperation.

"Well, isn't this a surprise. An' you were doing so well, girlie," said Ms. Cord. She pointed to the small pantry that was still acting as Mira's bedroom. "Go an' stay there till I tell ya somethin' else!"

Finicus kept a close eye on Mira as she sulked to the pantry.

After she carefully shut the door, Ms. Cord continued pouring the coffee in his cup.

He looked up at her and nodded. "Thank you."

"Of course, lad." Cord filled Sylvia's cup, then went and hoisted herself up on the preparation table in the middle of the room. Ms. Cord never had more than two chairs, one for herself and the other for a guest. Her explanation was that servants should not spend much time in the kitchen and gilla should sit on the floor. She produced a cigarette pack from the side pocket of her gown, pulled one out and lit it as Sylvia plopped down onto the free chair.

Finicus looked suspiciously at Sylvia over the rim of his mug.

"Emlyn, why did you bring this boy here?"

Emlyn went and stood behind and to the right of her mistress. "He helped Master Colmane and I."

"Did he now? Well, young man, you are to be commended."

He put down his mug but only gazed to his lap, looking rather sheepish. "That mean you'll treat me well?"

Sylvia was confused. "Please, explain your meaning." She leaned back and crossed her arms.

"Got me in yer house, a gilla that costs ya nothing."

Sylvia put an elbow on the table and leaned in. "Is that what you want? To be placed as a gilla in my house, is that why you wanted to come here? I can have a much more comfortable collar made for you."

His hand shot up to the steel band sitting tight around his neck like he had forgotten it was there. Everything about him became a cornered rabbit ready to jump up and run out. Sylvia reflected seriousness, being obvious that she would indeed accept him into the house if he wanted it.

"N-No. I don't," he said, almost panicking.

"All right. Okay. Then let us start with introductions; I am Sylvia Chronister, and that is my cook, Ms. Cord. I believe you know Emlyn."

He spied the cook, who had not moved, then put his full attention back on Sylvia. His shoulders fell, and he was able to gather his composure before reaching out his hand. "The name's Finicus, Fini to my friends!"

Sylvia stared at the boy's hand for a moment, dirty nails with grime covering his palm, but she reached out and shook anyway.

"Pleased to meetcha, umm . . ."

"Miss Chronister will do." She relaxed too, leaning back into the chair.

Finicus took a long sip, staring at her the whole while as he finished his cup.

"You must be hungry."

"No, Miss Chronister, don't let me be a bother."

"It is not a bother." Sylvia snapped her fingers. "Emlyn, help Ms. Cord prepare breakfast for our guest."

"Thank you," whispered Finicus under his breath.

"Think nothing of it."

Bacon was removed with tongs from the greased frying pan and placed on a big plate with three strips of fried fish. The savory smell permeated the kitchen. Finicus stared at the plate before him like he had never seen such a thing and began shoveling it all down his throat as if someone would try to take it from him before finishing.

"I think if anyone came near that plate, he'd bite their hand off!" Cord laughed.

Sylvia watched him. The joy on his face made her smile. She waited until most of the food was packed away, then continued, "So how did a runaway gilla end up on the streets?"

He stared at her a moment like he was considering what to say.

"Well . . . Mama was a gilla, Papa was a gilla. Their owners decided to let me be born, sold Papa off before that could happen, sold Mama a few years after that. I was six I think. Ran away soon after."

"Oh, dearie, that's quite a long time to be by yer lonesome," said Ms. Cord.

"Quite a long time to not be caught," said Sylvia.

Finicus bit into the last piece of bacon, then scooped up the last of the fried fish with a two-pronged fork and took it in with one big bite. He responded with the fish still in his mouth. "Mr. Colmane caught me a few years ago, shouda never have pickpocketed a catcher. Instead of turnin' me in, he had the bright idea to use me to catch other runaways, an' he never fails to threaten me over it, if I'm not consistent helping him." He finished off the bacon.

"I must admit, he did not strike me in such a way," said Sylvia. "He came across as a serious man who appreciates a good gilla. Not a man who would stoop to such low means."

"Ae, he's all those things, gets his job done at least, an' I s'pose that's what counts, but he can turn on ya in an instant." He snapped his fingers, then pointed at Emlyn. "I s'pose yer gilla can tell ya all 'bout that."

Sylvia looked questionably up at Emlyn, who only nodded.

Finicus continued, "He can be a right brosthun sometimes, may the black dog take him." He gulped the rest of his second coffee down and placed it carefully on the coaster. He stood up. "Thank ya for the hospitality, ma'am. I better go."

"Are you sure you do not want to be a part of my household? Three hot meals a day, good clothes, a room, a bed, perhaps even an education."

Finicus sat back down, lifted a finger and ringed it around the inside of his collar, relieving the stress of its tightness. "I'd be a gilla, or are ya offerin' me freedom?"

"I am not going to guarantee anything like freedom. You are bloodlined, after all. There would be a legal fight with your previous owners, but I'll not rule it out of the realm of possibility one day."

He appeared to think about it. "I'll have to disagree with you. I'm no gilla. That is not a life for me. Yes, ya might treat me well, have a warm room an' all that you say, but I'd not be free, I'd be stuck behind walls. So despite the risks, I mean to remain free . . . on my terms. No offense to ya, ma'am."

"There's no freedom in starvation, lad," said Ms. Cord.

Sylvia continued, "You could get stabbed. Placed back with your owners, put in a workhouse. I hear those places are quite terrible. Is that the risk you mention? If you find yourself in any of those scenarios, would you regret not taking what I have offered you?"

Finicus, now on his feet, smiled ruefully and shrugged. "Thank ya again for the hospitality, but I must be going."

Sylvia smiled back, trying to hide her worry. "Very well then. I wish you well, Fini. Emlyn, make sure he arrives safely at any destination he desires."

* * * * *

The beginning stages of morning light were ascending. The streets stirred with a few people headed to work appearing like half-awake apparitions on the sidewalk. Servants of all stripes jogged past the side gate to get to their destinations on time. Mixed in with them were gilla running early errands for their owners. Emlyn and her charge had just stepped down onto the short concrete servants' walkway stretching from the kitchen entrance to the six-foot black iron gate. They made their way straight down the path. Finicus had a clean red scarf wrapped around his neck and a bag tossed over his shoulder full of fresh and dried foods, enough for him to repay his debt to Ollivander. He stopped, causing Emlyn to whirl around.

"What's wrong? Did you change your mind?"

"Miss Gwen, can I ask ya a personal question?"

"Ask away."

"Is it true that martials have no key to their collars?" Finicus said, genuinely curious.

"No reason to deny it. Yes."

"That's looney!" The anger in his voice was unmistakable.

"A martial is a gilla for life," she said, raising her eyebrow.

"Sure, legally, but that's not what I'm sayin'. I've known gilla; none—and I mean none—truly like it. Oh, sure, they can play Ms. or Mr. Perfect 'Master, can I do this for ya?' 'Fancy a drink, Mistress?' But that's just trying to make the best of a bad situation. It puts a bit of power in their hands, get it? You don't, ya talk like it's the only thing ya ever wanted. So why? Didn't ya ever want to be somethin' else?"

This came out of the boy's mouth in a torrent, and Emlyn, for the life of her, could not understand his interest in this. The boy certainly was perceptive. She supposed he had to be to survive this long on his own. Finicus had confusion, anger, and more than a bit of fear packed into that tiny face. Emlyn wanted to respond with her belief of what she did being a matter of duty to a timeless and proud tradition. But the thought of what she wanted to be hung in the air, and so she took a moment to consider. She had dreamed of being like the famed Tolido shootists who operated on the Iberian peninsula over forty years ago. It was a silly fantasy, kids' stuff, akin to a gilla saying they would be king one day . . . But was she not an expert with the revolver? Was she not something just as legendary with more history behind it?

"No," she responded.

A look of shock and disbelief overtook his previous emotions. "I . . . don't believe you."

"Be quiet," she interrupted, her head perked up, looking toward the gate. An odd sound.

Everything seemed still, like walking through the woods while being stalked by a predator. Emlyn concentrated, trying to hear any little out-of-place sound. She heard light steps in rapid succession. Whoever this happened to be was trying to remain as quiet as possible. This told Emlyn to move and intercept—now.

She did so in sudden fury. Emlyn cleared the short walkway with two dashing steps to the tall iron gate. She grabbed the cold bars and thrust it open and out. Then held the bars tight as a body thumped against it and fell backward, yelling, "Cac!"

She looked through the bars and saw a man in a dark robe sprawled out on the ground, holding his bleeding nose while rocking back and forth. For a moment she thought perhaps he was just one of the early morning commuters.

"Emlyn!" yelled Finicus at the top of his lungs.

Emlyn turned back to the walkway and saw a man in a similar dark robe climbing the steps to the kitchen door. She reached for her revolver and suddenly found a knife stuck in her shoulder, thrown from the shadows, a great big bloody knife!

The man had his hand on the doorknob. In desperation she pulled the knife from her shoulder and growled. A trail of blood followed the blade as she lifted her arm and forced the pain to the back of her head, then threw.

The robed man had the knob all the way turned when the knife settled deep into his throat, splattering blood all over the four square windows. He gurgled as if he was trying to speak, then fell into the door, making it fly open. As he hit the ground with a splat, a scream sounded from inside the kitchen.

Big burly biceps wrapped around Emlyn's arms and torso, then squeezed, keeping her from reaching either of her weapons. It was the man she had hit with the gate. She could feel his blood trailing down the back of her neck.

"Don't bother struggling, you've nowhere to go."

Another man walked out from the bushes and stood before her. He was the one who must have thrown the knife. He was smaller than the other two and had his hood up, obscuring his face. She spit in it. Emlyn found a knife pressing against her jugular. He was quick. His voice sounded strained and just a bit hoarse. "You're going to regret that."

Though he was trying his best to hide it, she could tell that he had a slight accent. It reminded her of some eastern accents, but she could not say which one.

"You'll regret stepping foot on Chronister property!"

The man smiled crookedly. "If a veneti ever beat me, then that would be the day I deserve death. Where is she?"

Veneti meant the same thing as gilla. It gave his origin away. It was a term popular on the eastern mainland. This man had to be Zarmatian.

"Who are you talking about?"

The lines of his forehead worked, calculating exactly what he should say to her. He had information that he was unwilling to share. Maybe he would do so later, when Emlyn could get him to the ground. She ran through scenarios of just how to achieve that goal.

"The girl! We followed her here! We know she resides in this house!"

Emlyn knew then that they were not here for her mistress, or brigands looking to ransack the place.

"Mira? The kitchen gilla?" Emlyn responded, confused by the reason these three would be looking for her. Perhaps the girl wronged them somehow when she was a patrician.

Glee glinted in his eye. "Yes, that's the name she hides under, curse her blood!" He thought for a moment as he moved the blade further up her throat. "So she's a gilla now. That makes things easier . . . I'll make a deal with you. Hand her over to me, and I promise to not harm you or anyone else in this wretched place."

"If I do not?"

He licked his lips. "Then you will die. I have the advantage, do I not? Besides, she's just a worthless gilla, why not give her up?"

"I don't know, gilla are very expensive in today's market."

"Don't get saucy with me! But if it's coin you want, then I have it."

A sound came from the door, and without taking his eyes away from Emlyn, the man drew his pistol from beneath the darkness of the robe. He threw his arm back and pointed the barrel at Sylvia and Ms. Cord's shocked faces.

A second was all it took. A slight glance back to see who he would be shooting at; it was enough for Emlyn. With her legs, she pushed against the ground, sending as much force as she could back against the man holding her. He bent back, allowing her to draw up her legs and kick the smaller man with both feet. The force sent her and the bigger man stumbling backward as the smaller one pulled the trigger as he fell. The bullet missed Sylvia and Cord by a few yards. He fell on his side, grazing his head against the first concrete step. The gun hit the ground with a clack. He howled in pain as Emlyn struggled against the larger man. It took some doing, but she was able to get enough upper body distance between them to allow her to fling her head back against his broken nose. Chunks of bone cracked into the nasal cavity. He let go of her. Figuring the bigger man did not have much fight left in him, she leapt as soon as her feet hit the ground, landing on the smaller man like a hawk on a mouse.

The stranger found the long side of a martial's knife digging into his throat, and to show how serious she was, Emlyn let some blood flow out from where the blade met flesh.

"You threatened my mistress. You will die for that," she growled, her eyes burning with red-hot anger. "But first, I need to know—"

"You'll hear nothing more from me, veneti! And don't think that I'm the last!"

Before she could do anything else, a crunch could be heard coming from between the man's back teeth. He grinned, then began to sputter and cough as white foam bubbled up from his mouth then down his cheeks. Emlyn cursed to herself, knowing that at some point the man had managed to put a cyanide tablet in his mouth, a little thing that slowly dissolved, eventually killing the person, but sped up when bitten into.

Emlyn gritted her teeth and removed her knife from his throat, then took a moment to watch the irrigation of blood trickle around his neck. She looked to her mistress, whose eyes were wide with shock, staring at the dead man at Emlyn's feet. Sylvia trembled. This was the first time she had seen somebody die. Sure she watched Cassius die in his bed, but this kind of death was new and, judging by her face, terrifying.

"Mistress."

She blinked, then looked at Emlyn with an unbelieving stare.

"Ms. Cord, could you please take the mistress inside? I will be with you shortly."

Cord seemed shocked, but for her that was on the surface, it was just the suddenness of it all. Cord grabbed Sylvia's wrist and dragged her inside. "Come on, Miss Sylvia, a lil rye will do ya right."

It was then that Emlyn noticed Finicus was nowhere to be seen. Probably ran off when he got the chance.

She checked the man's robe for hidden pockets, finding a folded sheet of paper straight off. She unfolded it and found the addresses of every relative, marked out, as well as the addresses of the country estate and the insula, which was circled. Emlyn knew that the extended family were okay or else there would have been some word about it by now. No, these men caught wind that she was with the Chronisters at the insula, but somehow missed the fact that Mira, or whatever her name had been, was now a gilla. It made sense since the records for such things tended to be tightly held onto by affairs. She continued to search the man's pockets and found nothing else of importance.

She turned to the bigger man. He was lying where he fell, not breathing. She had hoped he could answer her questions, but the bone shards must have gone too deep. Emlyn searched him as well before checking the man at the door, once again finding nothing else of relevance.

She took a moment to sit on the steps and took a long hard look at the dead man with the knife protruding from his neck and shivered. The pain in her shoulder became acute. The adrenaline was wearing off. By this time there were many onlookers staring through the gate in amazement. She didn't care. Removing her blouse was difficult, but she managed. Then she removed her knife and cut a strip from the dead man's robes and wrapped the temporary bandages around her shoulder and chest.

By the time she marched back through the kitchen, Sylvia seemed to have recovered from the shock over a glass of aged rye.

Ms. Cord looked up at Emlyn. "I've called the peacers."

Emlyn nodded in response, knowing that someone would be here anyway due to the gunshot. Next was the small pantry.

The handle was almost ripped out, making a sitting Mira move back against the shelves of provisions in fear. "I'm sorry! I'm so sorry!"

"Who are you?"

"W-what, m-ma'am?"

"Your name is not Mira!"

Sylvia came up from behind. "What are you talking about, Tabby?"

"Those men, they were looking for her. Why would three men risk their lives for a low patrician? When I let it be known that she's a kitchen gilla, they still wanted her. We need to know why before more of them show up."

She handed her the list. "The entire family could be at risk."

Sylvia unfolded the paper. She gasped. "Dé Brigantia have mercy!"

"Peacers outside, their guns are drawn," said Cord from around the corner.

Emlyn slammed the pantry door shut and locked it.

It took an hour for the peacers and one sleepy reporter to get the full story, move the bodies, and wrap Emlyn's shoulder properly. Luckily the wound was not deep and missed anything vital.

Sylvia had decided to stay inside, not able to look at the dead men before becoming sick. By the time Emlyn locked the door behind her, she was swaying from fatigue. She felt worn out, that gravity was working against her.

Sylvia noticed and sighed. "It's over. You should get some rest."

"I'm sorry, Mistress, but we're far from finished."

"Oh! Mira." Her face fell while saying the name, not relishing the thought of what might have to be done.

Sylvia never took to the belief of torturing gilla. Even her mother hated it, except in the case of the breaking. If a gilla was holding back information, then she preferred playing a mind game; it got the same results with less pain.

Emlyn came close to ripping the pantry door from its hinges, ignoring the pain it produced, now the adrenaline was back. It made Mira scream and bury herself in the corner. Emlyn reached down to grab her by the collar, but she flailed her arms. Emlyn caught her wrists, then slapped her, making Mira stop long enough for her to be pulled to her feet.

"What is this?" she pleaded.

"You have a lot to answer for, girl!"

Mira immediately grabbed Emlyn's forearm, trying to wrench away from the unforgiving grasp. It made no difference. Emlyn was much bigger and much stronger than she.

Ahead of them was Sylvia, leading the way with a ring of keys dangling from her hand. She was not happy and looked supremely anxious.

Mira could sense that something unpleasant was happening and it was going to be happening to her. She struggled, only stopping the fight after Emlyn slapped her a few more times. The mistress grabbed ahold of a bookshelf next to the wall. She pulled, and it started to move, making a scraping noise against the wood floor. Behind was a secret door. She opened that one too and flicked on a light on the other side. They headed down a long flight of rickety wooden stairs that squeaked with each step.

Mira started to panic and tried to wiggle away from Emlyn again upon seeing a dusty old marble whipping post sitting erect upon the wooden floor. As they came within a few feet of the pillar, she started to plead, "No, no, please!" She managed to free herself from Emlyn's grasp by falling to her knees and continuing to beg. "Please, what do you want from me? I'll do anything! I-I'll behave, just . . . please don't whip me!"

This did not move Emlyn, but knowing her mistress's disposition toward the act of torture, she allowed Mira a chance. "Who are you?"

Mira looked down and found herself croaking it out. "A gilla, a gilla named Mira."

Normally this admission would be a good thing, but in this situation, it was not the looked-for response.

"That is not what I am asking of you! Who were you *before* you were made a gilla?"

Mira blinked a few times. "Mira Sauden!"

Emlyn yanked her up by the hair, now long enough to properly grab hold of. Mira gave out a wail, then Emlyn led her to the far side of the basement to hooks protruding out from the stone wall. Each hook supported a few sinister-looking handheld instruments.

Emlyn released the hair and put a hand around the back of Mira's neck, then picked up a nine-tailed whip and blew on it, dislodging the built-up dust. She made sure Mira could see it nice and close.

"You're not a stupid girl. You know exactly what I mean, and you know what will happen if you do not tell us what we want to know!"

She cried but managed to say something between all the blubbering. "I-I don't know—"

"So you're going to feign amnesia? Perhaps you were bumped in the head? I'll do just that if you don't tell me what we want to know!" Emlyn turned her around.

Ms. Cord sat on the steps from where they came, facing them. "Poor thing, has to be done though. Maybe it will get the haughtiness out of her. Would be bout time!"

Mistress Sylvia was standing as far as she possibly could from the familiar pillar, and to be honest, Emlyn had her own apprehensions about approaching the dreaded thing.

Mira was shoved against the coldness of the marble pillar. The dust coated her blouse and skirt. Her tears came like a pitcher turned over, while Emlyn fastened her hands around the post with a sturdy rope. Next Mira found the sheer blouse covering her upper body being cut then ripped away, leaving her with just the long skirt. She felt the whip being draped down her back. She shivered and squeaked out her fear.

"Please no . . . don't."

A bit of the girl's accent appeared, but Emlyn took it as slurred speech and brought her arm back, ready to strike. Emlyn knew how to do this, but she never had the opportunity to practice on a real live body. Yes, it might be a learning experience, but she could not find joy in this like some others did. All she saw was a gilla, like herself, tied to this monstrosity in the same way she had been, and for a moment she found herself in Sylvia's shoes all those years ago.

"Devana!" She cleared her throat. "Devana Ilyina Mousf Mizamir! Please . . . stop!

Sylvia's eyes went wide, and she came forward. "What? Say that again!"

Mira swallowed. "Devana!"

"The last name? Tell me, girl!"

"Mizamir!"

Sylvia got close to her. She did not quite believe what she was hearing. "Are you related to the Mizamir royals?"

"Yes . . . yes, Mistress!"

"Cac! Surely ya don't believe that!" said Cord suspiciously. "Beat her. She'll sing the truth to ya."

"I'm telling the truth, Mistress! I'm . . . I was Zareen Devana Ilyina Mousf Mizamir!"

Mira felt the rope around her wrists being untied. She sighed with relief.

"You believe her, Mistress?" asked Emlyn.

"Yes, well, I think I do. What would she have to gain by lying about such a thing?"

"Sylvia, she's a little gobb who will tell ya anythin' ta get out of a lil pain! Trust me, she still thinks herself above any gilla, even above you," exclaimed Ms. Cord.

"Has it not occurred to you, Ms. Cord, that the reason she thinks she's above me is because the girl *was* royalty?"

Cord was not having any of that. "Let's say it's true, then ya must take her to the closest peacer!" She paused for a moment, looking down before raising her head again. "Let's say she is who she says she is, then think about yer reputation. You'd be a hero, an make the Zar republic fast friends with us."

Sylvia tapped a finger on her chin, thinking about this. It would help counter the rumors about her that Lucius already let loose among the patricians. In fact, it would blow them out of the water. Everyone would conveniently forget. But . . . "I'd be condemning her to death. It has been over two years since the Mizamir were overthrown. She would have been fifteen at the time, with little knowledge of the atrocities her father committed. Why should she be blamed for that?"

"Because she still believes her place is on that throne she does. Believe me, I'm with her every day, I know! She schemes and hates."

Mira knew better than to speak up in defense. She sat on her knees at the foot of the pillar with her head down but listening.

"Mistress, if I remember correctly, the entire family were executed, including the daughter," Emlyn interjected.

Mira looked between Sylvia and Emlyn.

Emlyn continued, "One of the men outside had an accent. I suppose it could have been Zarmatian. Also, I doubt that three assassins, bounty hunters, or whatever they were, would be hunting her if she was not important in some way."

Sylvia was lost in thought. No one interrupted her in this, but Mira grew uneasy.

"Please, Mistress! I don't want to die!" wept Mira as she leaned forward and put her forehead to the floor, then reached out for Sylvia's closest boot and began planting kisses all over it.

"Stop that foolishness!" Sylvia was stern in voice, but not as stern as her mother could be—she was never able to conjure up that kind of steel. But Mira still backed away and shook with fear.

"Emlyn, bring me a chair, and a drink, and pour one for yourself and Ms. Cord, okay? Oh, bring a drink for Mira as well. She's going to need it."

Emlyn went back up the stairs while Sylvia looked down at the top of Mira's trembling head. It took all of two minutes for Emlyn to return with a wooden folding chair and a tray of four tonic waters in tall glasses. She bent to let Cord, still sitting on the steps, take a glass, then did the same for Mira, who quickly grabbed it and gulped half of it down. With one hand, Emlyn unfolded and put the chair down right behind Sylvia.

As Sylvia sat, she never took her eyes away from Mira. She settled herself and spread her hands over her lap.

"Okay . . . tell me, Mira, how did you end up coming all the way from Zarmatia to Kymbri?"

Mira took another sip, then stared into the bubbles. Seeing them pop reminded her of the gunfire.

Chapter Eighteen

-The Zareen-

Devana was named after an ancient Goddess of the hunt, though she never developed strong feelings about the divinities one way or the other. She remembered when she asked the priest, "If the Gods are so powerful, then why would they concern themselves with mere mortals?"

The priest had stood open-mouthed before an avalanche of words were hurled her way, none of which had any luck in sticking to her mind. Still, she followed the weekly rites diligently because that was what a good zareen was supposed to do.

She was born the sixth in line to her father's throne, the Zarcon, Belzir Ankfur Allix Mizamir. She was the baby, with five older brothers, whom she loved dearly. She possessed no aspirations for the throne. Women were never allowed to rule by themselves unless matters became desperate, and she was absolutely fine with that. Her desires were simple: find a husband, marry, have children, then find servants, and veneti who kept themselves well hidden. In fact, Father had a husband in mind for her already, and she found him charmingly handsome. She knew this because what occupied her hand was the first picture she had seen of the man, a lean fellow in a military uniform covered in medals upon one breast. His hair was slicked back, shaved on the sides, blonde, or a light brunette, she couldn't tell. She placed the tip of one finger on the picture and traced the contours of his square jaw.

She placed the photo back into the box sitting on her lap and brought out a folded letter. She opened it and read it for what had to have been the hundredth time.

My dear Devana, my little bee. These last few years of fighting have been long, too long to be without the presence of your happy face. The faces that have surrounded me for so many years were dour, but a turn in the war has occurred—we are winning. I will not bore you with the details, for I know how you loathe such talk. My daughter, please come see. I would celebrate the coming victory with you by my side. Arrangements have been made, and the one who bears this message will convey the details. Before you depart, give my respects at your mother's tomb—All my love, your father.

It had been three years since she had seen her father. To keep her safe from the uprising, he had her and her mother sequestered in a small house, far into the country. Her mother caught a sickness and died a year later.

The train car bounced, waking Kreshova, Devana's third cousin, closest confidant and royal companion. Royal companions in Zarmatia could only be of royal blood, and cousins with no claim tended to fill it. She looked at Kresh sitting across the aisle, a young woman only a few years older than her with the same wheat-colored hair as herself. Kresh yawned, wiggled back into the seat and into a deep slumber.

She folded the letter and put it back in the box between her future husband's photo and her mother's diamond hairpin sitting on top of several other letters sent by her father and brothers throughout the years. Devana placed the lid back on, then slid it under the seat in front of her.

Besides the low rhythmic grating underneath the train, this private passenger car was as luxurious as one would expect for the zareen. The walls were a luscious, deep red, with chair rail molding and solid stained-pine picture-frame molds beneath. Gold filigree outlined the windows, in the corraí style of faraway Kymbri—golden gusts of air, spiraling and blowing golden leaves around the dark woodland outside. In contrast, the light of the moon produced an eerie glow upon the icy snow-packed dunes. The forest beyond was black, creating lunatic patterns between swaying branches. She imagined how scary it would have been if it was not all flowing briskly by her. How terrifying it would be to walk amidst those trees.

Devana leaned back in the soft chair, and sleep fell upon her like a blanket, bringing happy dreams of the days to come.

* * * * *

The metallic screech wrenched through her, sending her crashing into the back of the seat. Confusion muddled her mind, until she heard gunshots ring out like Erie banshees. She stood, shot through with fear.

"Kresh! Kresh!"

"I'm here. I'm here. Shhhh." Kreshova hugged and soothed her. "We have to be quiet."

"I heard—"

"Yes. Shhh."

She looked into Kreshova's eyes and blinked, not sure if she was still dreaming or not. "What's going on?"

"I'm not sure. I'll look outside. See if I can get some answers."

"No! Don't leave me!" She tightened her grip on the sleeve of Kresh's long lilac coat, but found her hands being brushed away.

"Don't worry, I'll be right back."

Kresh walked to the front of the car, opened the door, and carefully peered out before disappearing to the side.

The cold air crept in as Devana stood shivering in the middle of the aisle. Her eyes were glued to the door, and the harder she stared, the more it seemed to bend and distort.

Rapid machine gunfire rang out across the open valley. She jumped and felt a scream coming up her throat, so she placed a palm over her mouth to keep it in.

Her attention was driven to the window as instant fire from rifle barrels lit up the night. The constant popping echoed in her mind, and as she heard screams, tears started to pour out of her eyes, yet she did not cry out or sob. She crouched and put her hands over her ears in an effort to keep it all out.

"Zareen Devana!"

A familiar voice. She looked up. "Anton!"

The young man at the door was no more than nineteen with brown hair usually slicked back, now disheveled from exertion. His uniform was covered in snow as if he had been rolling in it. He breathed heavily and his eyes were half crazed. This scared her a bit when he marched toward her and grabbed her bicep with a tight grip. "Zareen! We have to go!"

She spotted blood on his sleeve and felt sick.

"Zareen, move!"

"Yes, I-I need to get something."

He let go of her.

She immediately went to the floor and saw no box under the seat. Her heart beat frantically as she scanned and spotted it a few rows down. As soon as she grasped it, Anton wrapped a heavy coat around her and was pulling her away.

The cold air hit her skin like stinging bees. She pulled the man's coat tighter around her small frame. Anton helped her down. Her feet plunged in the snow, and at first she did not think it was that deep until they walked a few yards away from the tracks.

She sank down two feet and fell face first into the snow. It was cold, so cold. He lifted her and helped her up a short but sharp incline.

The gunfire started again, and people yelled and screamed—for what, she had no idea. But as the sounds got closer, she turned to look and spotted three rebels in civilian clothes with red scarves tied around their arms, pushing a soldier ahead of them. They violently shoved him against the train car, and she barely had time to turn around before the rebels unloaded their weapons into his body, making blood spray against the car like thrown paint.

"Don't look, Zareen." Anton turned her around. "Hurry, they'll see our tracks and come for us."

They headed into the black woods. The trees looked like sinister shadow figures with elongated limbs that threatened to reach out for her, grab her and never let her go until she was squeezed to death. Then the darkness was once again lit by gunfire. The bullets embedded themselves in the trees around her, and she would have fallen to the snow again if it wasn't for Anton lifting her up in his arms. But as he did so, she dropped the box, its contents spilling out onto the forest floor.

"No, no! My box!"

"Leave it!" yelled Anton. He was able to run while carrying her over his shoulder. Deeper into the woods they went, letting the dark swallow them up. Leaving their past behind.

* * * * *

"We found a stream and walked within it to a small town where we found shelter in a barn. But we were woken by the sound of the rebels, so we escaped back into the woods. Later I had learned that they passed Kreshova off as me and shot her." She took a moment to control herself. The memory was obviously painful. "They knew of my escape though."

Mira took another sip of water. Sylvia leaned forward, showing further interest.

"For months we ran, never staying in one place for too long before someone showed up to assassinate us. Eventually, after what seemed like months, we reached the house of a sympathizer in Gaelland."

She took another sip and sighed before continuing. "Our benefactor taught me your language and how to hide my accent. With a lot of work, and goodwill, I was planted into Kymbri patrician society."

* * * * *

Their closeness grew during their journey. Anton hated her at first, he was from a poor family and she, well, a zareen. She thought he was lower than her, little better than a servant. Devana did not appreciate his skills in keeping her alive, not one bit. But after so much time together, they warmed to each other's presence. He viewed her as a little sister, and he became like a brother.

The door burst open, breaking the wood around the knob. Kymbri soldiers in their grays and blues rushed in, guns drawn. Devana, now Mira Sauden, turned from her drawing desk, startled. Anton, now her cousin Ducas Sauden, was sitting on a high-backed wicker chair next to the window, reading a book. He shot to his feet.

"Put your hands up!"

Anton did so. "What is this about?" he demanded.

A higher-ranking officer came in from behind his men. He wore a military-issue Alban bonnet that sat upon his head. He seemed unconcerned that he was coming into a low patrician house unannounced. His face was severe and looked unfamiliar with the concept of smiling.

"Where are you hiding Marius Venti?"

"Who are you talking about?"

One of the soldiers bashed Anton in the stomach with the butt of his gun. Anton did not fall, but he did hunch over in excruciating pain.

"You know who I mean. There are more than a dozen witnesses who declared that he ran into your domus! So where are you hiding him?"

"Sir, I am telling you the truth," said Anton with so much difficulty that his accent slipped. Mira's eyes widened, and the slip did not go unnoticed by the stern leader.

"Where're you from?"

Anton stood up straight. "Up near Hindre."

"You don't sound like anyone from Hindre that I know."

"Do all people from Hindre sound alike?"

The man got close to him and made a study of Anton, from the feet and stopping at his deep brown sunken eyes. He turned to look at his men. "Search the domus!"

He looked between Mira and Anton; he did not lessen that stern visage that verged on anger. "I'm Captain Géar, and you will remain where you are until this search is concluded."

A clothed female gilla rushed into the room, holding a glass of water. He turned, and she kneeled before him, then proffered the glass. It balanced with nary a wobble on her palm. He took it, and she smoothly moved into the corner and became inconspicuous. She obviously belonged to him, for he looked at her with great fondness.

"I noticed that you have no gilla. Isn't that odd for a patrician?"

"We're just not comfortable having gilla around us. We prefer servants."

"Sure, sure. You two look nothing alike. Are you sure you're related?"

Mira felt cold, he did his research before he entered. The reason he stated had to be a ruse. He handed the glass back to the girl, and she dashed back out of the room. Right after, one of the soldiers rushed in and whispered in the captain's ear. The captain shot Anton a hard glance. "Bring everyone here, now."

Mira felt a chill run down her spine. She turned to Anton, who was pouring sweat, and his eyes were darting all over the place. His panic sat on the surface, and Géar had to have noticed.

Anton lunged at the captain, knocking him over. He grabbed Mira by the wrist and pulled her out of the room and into the hall. He sprinted to the front door. Somehow she managed to stay beside him. The narrow hall echoed with a pop, and Anton's frontal lobe burst out of the confines of his skull, showering her with brains and blood. He bowled over, what was left of his head smacked against the hardwood floor. She screamed, her back hit the wall, and she kept screaming as she slid down.

"Quiet, woman!"

She looked up at the soldiers. One held Anton's folded Zarmatian uniform. She had no idea he had kept it.

"W-why?"

"Your neighbors were suspicious, and his papers did not add up, but I never thought he would be a Zarmatian soldier." He grabbed her hair, making sure he had a clear target for his spit. "Traitor! Trying to hide your lover? A spy?"

"No!"

He thrust her to the floor. "I should execute you as well, but I'll not deny the public their satisfaction!"

* * * * *

"I thought they caught you in bed with him?"

"A lie."

Sylvia rubbed her chin. "Please continue."

"After shaving my hair and letting the populace spit in my face, they had me make the Kymbrian choice. Prison seemed an easy way to have me disposed of, so I thought I'd have a better chance to survive as a gilla. That I would be hard to find, and . . ."

"Go on."

Mira gulped. "Find a means of escape."

"Do not fret, many seek escape at first. You're not the first to think of it." Sylvia leaned back and drummed her fingers on her chin while looking down.

"Mistress? Are you going to kill me?"

Sylvia stopped drumming and moved her head up to look at Mira with an unsettling blank stare.

She stood up, folded the chair, then held it out for Emlyn to take. She began pacing the room. "This is too much." Her voice quivered. "I have too much on my plate right now. Deciding on if an enemy zareen should die or not. Too much."

Mira became intensely nervous. "Please, Mistress. Don't turn me in to the state! I'll be shot!"

Ms. Cord spoke up quite fiercely. "Yer a gilla, they'd not give ya that dignity, they'd hang ya pretty head!"

"Mistress."

Sylvia took her gaze away from Mira and placed it on Emlyn.

"You should keep her."

"Explain," asked Sylvia.

Emlyn crouched near Mira, who looked at her, anticipating something horrible. "She has potential."

Ms. Cord gave a short laugh in disbelief.

"It seems that Ms. Cord does not agree with you," said Sylvia.

"Mistress." She said this in a tone that could make anyone pay attention. "At the auction, there was only one who bid against your will—Hornbow."

This made Sylvia stare at her in surprise. "Hornbow was looking to add her to his stable? So he had seen something."

She considered this a little too long for Mira. A shiver ran across her body, and she felt compelled to respond, "Pleeease. Keep me. I'll be the best gilla you've ever had!"

Cord laughed again.

"I am not turning you in," said Sylvia.

Shock spread across Mira's face, quickly replaced with jubilance. She lunged forward, grabbed Sylvia's closest boot and kissed its leather over and over again.

"Thank you, thank you, thank you, Mistress!"

Sylvia moved her boot away from Mira's grasp. "Enough of that!"

Cord had stood up in contemptuous surprise, but she said nothing. It would be overstepping her bounds.

Mira's eyes looked up to Sylvia. "You will . . . keep me?"

* * * * *

"No, please! I'll do anything, I'll be a good girl!" Mira whined.

"We've heard that one before!" said a less than happy Ms. Cord.

Mira tripped after being shoved into a guest room and fell on top of a bed, a fluffy, insanely soft bed. It had been over a year since she had been atop one, and the feeling stole her breath.

The door shut. She ran to it and turned the handle, finding it locked, then beat on the door while begging to stay and serve the house. But her pleading fell on deaf ears, and her throat soon became hoarse.

She gathered herself, planted down on the floor, and seethed. She was so uncertain of herself and her place that it was maddening. Her mistress did say that she would not turn her in, to the senate or to the crown, so there was that. That did not mean the mistress could not change her mind, of course. She was just a gilla, after all, and breaking your word to a gilla meant nothing. It would be no loss of honor for the free. She put a hand on her forehead in frustration.

"Stop thinking of yourself as a gilla! You're not! You're royalty, and obviously that still means something!"

She got up and went to the window, opened the green silk curtains, and saw, just beyond the glass, iron bars, and beyond that an alleyway. A sigh escaped as she backed away and sank down on the bed with a huff. She would just have to wait and see.

* * * * *

"Emlyn, go and get some sleep. You're barely standing. You can tell me how it went with Colmane later."

Emlyn was drowsy and on the verge of dozing on her feet. The shoulder wound was throbbing. She performed an awkward curtsey. "Thank you, Mistress." And left the room almost dragging her feet along the way. As she placed each foot on the steps leading up from the kitchen, it almost sounded like a hammer doing its work.

"Ma'am, would you like my opinion?"

"I have always valued your opinion," said Sylvia, standing across from Ms. Cord at the prep table.

Cord put her hands on the table and looked at her seriously. "Ya *must* turn her in. That's the right thing ta do."

Sylvia waved off Cord's worry. "I understand your concern, but I'm not going to be responsible for a girl's death, especially not one of royal blood. I don't even know if I should keep her as a gilla. It's like making a high patrician a gilla. It's wrong."

"No, ya don't understand. She's the enemy, from a regime that hated our guts. She can grovel an' beg at yer feet all day long, but she's the enemy and must be taken care of. Knowing what I know now makes me glad that I did what I did to her. An' you don't know, they might take her prisoner instead, an' keep her fer any number of reasons."

"Doubtful, Ms. Cord. Doubtful when we are trying to make strides with the Zarmatian republic."

Ms. Cord sighed. "Well, I said my piece."

"Yes you did," said Sylvia with coldness in her voice.

Ms. Cord leaned back, arms crossed, considering her, then turned and started striding to the stairs. "Sleep. Perhaps you'll do the right thing after ya get ya some rest."

Sylvia looked down at the worn woodgrain of the prep table. Her mind was awash with this added pressure. First her mother, then Lucius, now she had a zareen as a kitchen gilla, and it was hard to believe that part. Though she was sure the girl was telling the truth, it seemed like the start of some steamy play, but inverted and distorted through stained glass.

She would get some sleep, but not quite yet. Instead she poured wine into a cup and found herself walking the garden. Down the path was the statue of the Dé Morri, the otherworld aspects of the great Goddess. People from Kymbri, Erie, and many in the northern mainland only believed in two Gods, but both had many aspects that could be prayed to if something specific was needed. The statue was small, depicting three women in long flowing gowns back-to-back. The three in one representing past, present, and future, among other more dubious functions that she had no intention of speaking in fear of grave repercussions.

Her knees hit the ground before them, she placed the wine beside her, then called their names. "Agroná, Arawn, and Dread Des of the veil, please hear me, I've three favors to ask."

She reached under her night dress and pulled out a small dagger with a golden hilt, she had been concealing it within a garter. She took a lock of her black hair and cut it, lamenting at the sound. She put the blade in her palm and cut across her lines, wincing as blood sprang up and ran to the edges, trying to escape between her fingers. She put the hair in her palm, then poked a few fingers into the wine. She flicked the droplets on the wound and squeezed.

Sylvia bit her lip, trying to close out the pain, then reached up and spread the gruesome mixture upon their stone feet. "Please, women of the mire, of battle, and golden fields. Do not let Lucius spread what he knows about me. Let me work all this out and prove them wrong. Grant me insight into what should be done with the zareen. I will follow whatever you advise . . . and, if it is not too much to ask." She gulped. "Grant my mother safe and painless passage over the bridge."

She sat back and waited, just in case they would show an immediate sign. She sighed. Why should she expect a sign? She leaned forward and put her head to the ground in supplication, then proceeded to plead the same thing repeatedly, bringing herself to tears.

CHAPTER NINETEEN

Slender fingers stroked over Emlyn's bare shoulder and down her arm. She shivered with the delicate touch.

"That was lovely. Thank you," Sylvia said, purring into Emlyn's ear.

They sat naked in front of each other, relaxing upon a large bed with disheveled royal blue sheets gathered around them. This room was located on the top floor and her favorite to spend time in. This was a room that held no bad memories for her, hence why there was not much beyond the bed itself, the wardrobe, dressing table, vanity, and a silver-edged mirror. True minimalist with brief flashes of opulence.

One wall was nothing but gilded windows that came up into a point, barely encroaching on the rounded ceiling. They provided a wondrous view of the western half of the city if you looked past some of the taller buildings. Below was a view of the entire garden bathed in morning light.

"You're welcome, Mistress."

Sylvia placed a hand on Emlyn's cheek. She stared at her with wondering eyes edged with a sad tension. When her thumb caressed the edge of her lips, Emlyn kissed it sweetly. This made her mistress giggle, and for a moment she glimpsed her as a young lady again, before all this tragedy.

Sylvia glanced at the knife wound. It was an inch long, healed quickly with the druidi ointments, but it still shone red and angry. She pointed. "Does it still hurt?"

Emlyn smiled ruefully. "Sore, but not distracting, Mistress."

A slight smirk curled in the corner of Sylvia's mouth but faded quickly to a frown. She looked at her foot hanging off the bed and curled her toes.

"I'm sorry, Tabby."

"Whatever for, Mistress? Was I not completely pleasing?"

Sylvia tapped a finger to her own lips. She seemed to be deep into her thoughts. "No, no, you were magnificent like always. I'm just sorry for the stress I've put on you . . . especially now."

"Stress? Mistress, I am more than happy to carry some of your burden. I would carry its full extent if I could."

Sylvia patted Emlyn's thigh tenderly. "Thank you, my sweet girl."

She leaned in and pecked her on the lips. "I'm famished. Would you be so kind to fetch breakfast for us?"

Emlyn closed the door gently behind her. She had her clothes back on, a simple blue skirt and white blouse with a bit of trailing lace on the sleeves ending at the elbows. Of course, her black gun belt was buckled around her hips and a wide brown leather belt was buckled tight around her upper waist. She had a wide satisfied grin, but as she turned, there was Stella in restrained fury. Emlyn dropped the joy she held and furrowed her brow in preemptive defiance.

"Once again you decided to ignore my advice," Stella said with a disgusted scowl.

"I always appreciate your advice, but it does not mean that I have to follow it. That's why it's called advice and not an order."

"Insolent child!"

"I am only obedient to my mistress, and with her I am never insolent. You raised me to be that way, to respect and obey my owner, and that is what I'm doing."

Stella clenched her fists and started to raise them.

"Go ahead, Stella. Hitting me will not change your mistress's condition. You would be hitting another martial, and if we truly fight, then that would be a disruption and unfair to our owners."

Stella unclenched, but her ferocious eyes did not abate. She turned on her heels and walked away like a chastised soldier who did not think she should have been chastised.

The footsteps faded down the hallway. Emlyn let loose her breath. She'd had no idea she was even holding it. She did feel sorry for Stella, who was more on edge than usual, and for good reason, but she did not feel sorry for what was said. It had to be said and she was glad to move the pot away from the burner.

Emlyn walked down the familiar well-worn kitchen steps, lost in her thoughts. She felt mixed up. She was happy to have pleased her mistress; after all, she existed to please. But there was something else, that sadness behind the Mistress's eyes. It could have been only the fact that Camilla was dying, but it felt directed towards her. There seemed no reason to it.

She was jolted out of reverie upon reaching the bottom of the stairs. Finicus sat at the table with Ms. Cord. He looked almost unchanged from when she had seen him last. A white plate was before him with numerous crumbs from toast and bacon scattered across it.

"Emlyn!"

It was apparent that Finicus was untouchable as far as affairs was concerned. Walking around with your collar in full sight with no tag was a quick trip to the cages and then resale if no one claimed you. And Finicus seemed the cock of the walk. He almost jumped to his feet, then stopped in his tracks. Remembering his manners, he picked up a crumpled napkin from the table and quickly wiped his lips before throwing the napkin down onto his plate.

"What ya did to those guys the other day was great!" He was so excited that he was almost bouncing up and down as if some great force propelled him. There was a fair bit of talk about what happened at the Chronister insula a week ago. Plenty of witnesses, and so it eventually showed up in the paper, page three, article two. Her name was actually mentioned. The mistress had cut it out and framed it herself. She had to remind Emlyn to be proud of the article. Few martials got a chance in this day and age to protect their owners from a real threat. Sylvia was making light of the situation which was how she was dealing with the incident, but Emlyn could not see it that way. She could only think of the blood, the three dead men, and her own dire fear that she would fail to protect her mistress, there was no closing your eyes to that.

Ms. Cord leaned on the table. "Fini here has come calling for you."

Emlyn placed her hands on her hips. She quite liked the kid. Due to the numerous adventure stories she read as a child, she had a fondness for the sardonic miscreants that often populated their pages. Fini did not exactly fit the bill, but he was very close.

"Is that so?" she asked.

"Uh, yeah. Mr. Colmane needs to see you immediately! I'm to take you to him!"

She crossed her arms and raised an eyebrow in a question. "So he's finally found something. What did he discover?"

Finicus shrugged and smirked, a seeming trademark of the boy. "I've been told ta not divulge a thing until ya get there."

"I have to serve and eat breakfast with the mistress first, then we'll head out."

"No, he has to see ya right away."

"I'm sorry, you'll just have to wait."

Finicus sighed heavily in exasperation.

Ms. Cord stood. "I'll take the tray ta her. She made the investigation part your duty so go on with ya."

As soon as Emlyn stepped outside the iron service gate, she noticed two men who thought they were being inconspicuous as they tried to blend in with everyone else. Light colors in Kymbrian styles, it was *too*

Kymbrian—that was their first mistake. Second was that when they tried to hide the fact that they were looking at her and Finicus, they turned their heads away quickly.

Finicus led her back down the same twisting alleyways from a week ago. Even in the daylight, it was labyrinthine and hard for her to keep up with the direction they were headed or where they were exactly. The smell was not as bad at first, since they were not in the Stints and luckily no one followed.

Finicus spoke the entire time, gesturing as if he were in a play, talking on and on about Emlyn's fight with the assassins. "You were so fast, they didn't stand a chance." He tried to mimic her kick. She remembered it being a closer contest, but then again, the papers did embellish the incident.

"Why did you run away?"

He looked at her as if she should know the answer. "I'm not waiting for the peacers, and not sticking around to answer questions. I would have been taken in. I can get away with things as long as I'm not anywhere too long. 'Course Colmane gets me out of jams, but it's soooo inconvenient. I told him it would be better if he removed my collar, but he says ya catch more flies this way."

Emlyn nodded, understandable if not a bit distasteful. It wasn't long before she spotted Colmane resting with his back against the wall. He had a beef sandwich in hand, and as they approached, he pretended not to notice them. They stopped a few feet away, and he kept eating until the sandwich was gone and licked the juices from his fingers. He wiped his hands with a napkin, scrunched it up, and tossed it to the ground.

"You're late, Finicus."

"Hey, don't blame me! I had ta wait for her!"

She looked down at him in mock betrayal. He smirked back.

Colmane looked at Emlyn with an unconcerned expression, but there was a hint of amused wonderment. "Well then, that can't be helped. Emlyn, come here." Colmane pointed at the spot right before him, and she obeyed. He whispered so that Finicus could not hear, "Are the rumors about your mistress true?"

"Rumors, Master?"

"Don't play dumb. About her preferring the fairer sex, namely you. That she cannot stomach to bed anyone else."

Emlyn considered for a moment. "They're just rumors, Master."

Gilla catchers knew traditions as well as anyone, and all of them knew that a patrician should not use their martial in such a way. These rumors were supremely vile, an attempt from a vengeful man to ruin her mistress. Of course, they were only rumors for now, no hard evidence, but she hoped her mistress would find another suitor soon and quell this vile gossip once and for all. Emlyn had a sneaking suspicion in her mind that the reason Lucius was rejected had been because of her. Sylvia never had a man, maybe all their so-called games ruined her to the prospect?

"For your sake I hope you're right. By the way, congratulations on the article. I suppose you do know your business after all."

Deeply gratified that he no longer seemed angry or annoyed at her, she bowed. "Thank you, Master."

He gave a slight nod. "Let's get on with this. Look across the street."

Across the street were several dilapidated buildings. Most had painted signs proclaiming structural instability: Condemned. There was no doubt about their state. Many had broken supports, cracked columns, fallen balconies, mold and wood siding devastated by rot. Any plaster showing on the outside had numerous holes created from stress fractures or mischief. The reprobates had a good time, for every inch was covered in graffiti ranging from gang turf insignias to squirting cocks and other such lewd acts.

These houses sat on Duinn Street, a true blight upon the city, and Emlyn wondered why they had not been torn down yet.

"See the one on the end?"

"Yes, Master."

"That property is owned by the Barrentines. I thought it would take a few weeks, but those little rats really came through for me."

This was one of the four streets Colmane kept a watch over through the gang of orphans. Apparently he expected them to not follow through, but they were true to their word. Now the orphans could have another day of freedom in their imaginary fiefdom.

"Finicus said they spotted a rather large man fitting the description, coming in and out of that house every night. Most of the local stay clear because they think it's haunted. What do you think?"

"I think that is the best lead we've had."

"Thata girl. Let's confirm it."

He smiled playfully, and she returned the expression. Colmane was not going to let anyone else have the glory, especially Inspector Nary, who now seemed miles behind them in the investigation. He turned to Finicus and put some half kints in the boy's hands. "Keep a watch out."

Finicus thumped his fist over his heart like a soldier. "Ae torix!"

They kept low, walking across the street, only getting a few stares from people who decided it was none of their business before going on their way. The house had shuttered windows with broken slats. The porch was thick with cobwebs. Weeds grew unburdened by human interference. It was the very definition of seedy. No one would want to go near it for fear of ghosts or fae folk . . . or a ceiling crashing down upon them. One of the cracked columns holding up the deck above was missing huge chunks from its length, which made them both a bit leery as they approached the steps.

Emlyn made sure to keep her voice low. "Master, why would a family such as the Barrentines sit on this property? Why have they not done a thing with it?"

"Hm, from what I gather, they are trying to wrench all the properties on this block away from whoever currently owns them. I cannot guess their reasoning. Maybe to build one of those department shops."

As they crept up the steps, Colmane drew out his gun from the inside of his vest. This was the first time she had seen it. Emlyn noted it as a stub-barrel Molen-Jir revolver. A small thing that could get the job done at close range and made a huge noise, which she expected was typically all he would need to scare whoever he pursued into submission. Even her revolver had a few Molen-Jir parts, namely the reliable trigger. She had to admire Colmane's taste in firearms. She too drew her revolver from its holster, wincing from the dull ache of the wound created by that damn knife.

He nodded toward the door for Emlyn to approach first. His prowess to defend from an aggressor should not go underestimated, since some runaways do try to fight their way to freedom. But this was something Emlyn was trained for. If any trouble presented itself, then she was the one best equipped to handle it with force.

She approached the door, trying not to make a sound, but the rotten wood still echoed too loudly. This man was a martial, and if he was worth his salt, then he would have heard it.

She leaned her back against the doorframe and quickly counted the extra rounds on her belt, then opened the cylinder to check if it was fully loaded. Emlyn knew that it was, but it made her feel more secure. She flicked the revolver, setting the cylinder back in its place. She placed a hand on the door and lightly pushed in. Indeed it was unlocked, and it looked as if the locking mechanism had busted long ago. She pushed a little harder, and the door squeaked open, making her cringe from the waft of deterioration inside. It stopped as it thumped against something. Emlyn doubted it was a person; it did not sound like it at least.

She crept through the opening, holding on to the door. She grasped its edge and flung herself, skirt whirling the dust into a cloud, she slid around to face the back of the door, gun pointed at nothing but a pile of rubbish with a fair number of flies buzzing about. She motioned for Colmane to enter.

"By the great Gods," Colmane exclaimed despite being a nonbeliever. He pinched his nostrils for a moment before remembering that he had a handkerchief. He held it firmly over his nose.

The place looked even more disheveled on the inside. Cobwebs crossed almost every open space. Luxurious chairs were piled on top of each other in the main room like a rickety monument. The stuffing within the cushions was pulled and now housed rat nests. Bones were scattered all about. Emlyn thought they might be human bones.

On top of this heap of broken furniture were two tiny statues of Dé Brigantia and the Dé Ard representing no aspect of themselves that would approve of this ghastly display. Both looked dower in the light streaming from the hole in the ceiling. The musty smell mixed with feces overwhelmed Colmane's handkerchief. Emlyn was shocked. Maybe the culprit didn't think so, but it was at the pinnacle of sacrilege.

She looked down and noticed that their footprints could be seen clearly patterned in dust. No other footprints could be determined, telling her that this killer never came in or out the front door.

"This place is only two stories. You take the lower level, I'll take the upper level."

"Master, I must insist we stick together and that you keep to my back."

"I cannot take the chance of him pushing by us."

Emlyn knew not to deny him any further and just nodded in agreement.

"Here, take this." He tossed her a cylinder, about four inches in length. "It's a charge for the lantern. It'll give out some light on its own. Hold it at the bottom where the button is so it won't burn you, and make sure to conserve its energy. It runs out of power quickly."

Colmane crept up the main stairs behind the ghastly monument and beyond Emlyn's sight. She huffed.

Does he not realize how dangerous it is to go against a martial? Of course not, he's never fought one, or seen one fight, and probably does not believe in the stories either. If he did, he would realize that the two of us do not hold the upper hand right now.

Two halls were located on the first floor. One was completely dilapidated with the ceiling above now piled high on the floor, making the hall impossible to maneuver through. Emlyn went to the right hall, the end of which led out through an archway into a bright garden. She knocked webs down as she went, doing her best to keep her focus and not grow annoyed. The long hallway greeted her with two portals to the left; one had a closed door, the other door was wide open.

Cautious, all senses on high alert, with a heart beating like giant pounding drums in her ears, Emlyn dashed to check the open room. She stood in front of the doorway, legs apart, feet planted firmly, and revolver pointed into the dark. She breathed out slowly, without taking her eyes away from the darkness. Slowly she reached into the hidden pocket of her skirt and brought out the charge. After clicking the button, the electric light ebbed and pulsed before settling. She held it up, and the dark retreated. Barely.

The room was empty—well, almost empty. The walls still had peeling paint stripping itself down the side. A small pile of trash rested in one corner next to another open doorway, but not quite open. It had copious amounts of debris on the other side. Mold covered the wooden floors, then there was the dead body in the far corner. Emlyn walked across the middle of the room, the wood below her feet felt soggy and bent in response to her weight.

The dead body was that of a man who looked to be somewhere in his thirties. Flies buzzed and maggots squirmed around a gigantic gash leading from his belly to his chest that looked far too skilled to have been created by a novice knife-fighter. She squatted down for a closer look. His eyes were gone. The killer could have taken them, or perhaps an animal made a snack of them when passing by. With so many rats running around this place, she guessed they were the culprits.

His clothing has been mended by hand more than a few times, thought Emlyn. *My guess is that he was looking for a place to sleep. However, the Morri deemed him unlucky.* The sentiment seemed appropriate.

A shot rang out and a scream, in Colmane's voice. She stood up and strained her neck to hear the surroundings better. Three more shots in rapid succession by two different revolvers.

She ran out of the room, hearing four more shots along the way. As soon as she got back to the area with the monument, she darted up the stairs.

The second floor had little in the way of walls, just the wooden beams outlining the rooms which were above the one she had been in. Huge chunks of plaster and pieces of wallpaper still lined the bottom as if someone decided to do some hasty demolition with a sledgehammer.

There was Colmane, close to the floor, doing his best to hide behind one of the thin beams. Beyond the room, there was the garden or courtyard of this old domus.

Colmane finished reloading his gun, leaned out and began unloading the chamber, shooting out into the courtyard at a figure standing in the open upon a high walkway that snaked around the perimeter. She noticed the blood pumping out of Colmane's shoulder. Emlyn jumped the ruined plaster wall while angling herself between the beams. She kept an eye on the figure, and though he was far away, she could sense his hesitation. His gun went from pointing at Colmane down to his side. The surprise did not last long, he raised the revolver again. The killer knew now that he was dealing with another martial. He shot, hitting the beam, sending splinters by her face. Luckily none of them took to digging into flesh.

"What're you doing?" asked Colmane.

"You forget that you're trying to outshoot a martial who has a superior gun and superior ability to use it! Not only that, but you're also left-handed, and you've been shot in that shoulder, affecting your aim!"

She shot at the figure, barely missing but close enough to make him take cover. "Master, you need to get out of the killing zone!"

He stared at her a moment as she fired again. "Okay, let's go."

"Go ahead of me."

Colmane made his way out of the room, keeping low as Emlyn stayed and kept her revolver trained on the figure. As the man poked his head out, she would shoot, sending him darting back down. Soon, the killer got tired of this and began shooting wildly. All the shots went wide, allowing her to back out slowly.

She found Colmane with his coat lying across his lap, sitting against the wall near the stairs. His shirt on the left side was pulled down from his shoulder, exposing the wound. He pressed his handkerchief against it, doing his best to staunch the blood flow. It was not all that bad. He was not taking any issue with it or overreacting. Just perfectly calm, which was a good sign.

Emlyn smirked. "I see you're handling that well, Master."

"Two years in the Teyrn's army as a medic will get you accustomed to blood."

Emlyn nodded. "Forgive me, but from here on out, it would be best if you leave this up to me. I can track him faster—"

He cut her off. "If a wounded man was not tagging along? Nonsense. Besides, he's headed nowhere."

He smiled ruefully, reached into his bag, and brought out a pouch. "Take a look." He tossed it to her.

She undid the drawstring. Inside were about a dozen and a half silver circular tags etched with names. Many of them were covered in dried blood.

"I found them among a makeshift shrine. I destroyed it and took the pouch, right before he began firing. That is when he hit me in the shoulder. As shiny as the day they were inscribed, yes? Since you found the Sissa tag, I had wondered if he carried them around like gruesome trophies. I think those tags are important to him. He's not going to give up the proof of his . . . *work* so easily."

She tied it back up and tossed it to him. "Okay, please take this and find the nearest peacekeeper."

Colmane did not seem very pleased with her response. "That is not going to happen."

She wanted to lay into him about being prideful, but of course that would be a very bad thing for a gilla to do. "Master, you can have the acknowledgment for taking him down. I am a gilla, after all."

"You don't get it, do you? I am just as responsible for you as you are for me. Your mistress said as much underneath all her fancy talk; she would ruin me if I let any harm come to you. Besides, what kind of man would I be if I let a gilla complete my job?"

She sighed in frustration. There was nothing she could do other than acquiesce.

He reached his good hand out to her. "Help me up."

She pulled him to his feet. He let his jacket fall to the floor, leaving it there, then pulled the left side of his now bloody white shirt back over his shoulder. "Lead the way."

She did, down the same hallway she started with.

"What was in there?"

"A dead body of a homeless man, cut stomach to sternum."

He did not ask more, and she did not offer. She jiggled the handle of the next room; it did not budge. Emlyn used her shoulder to ram it a bit and still nothing. Something very sturdy was keeping it in place on the other side. That was when she noticed a rancid smell wafting out from the crack beneath the door and wrinkled her nose, appalled by the disgusting unfamiliar stench.

"That's the smell of decaying flesh," Colmane explained. "No shortage of street urchins looking for safety between four walls. I think we can avoid that room."

Emlyn decided to move on. Next was the open archway to the courtyard garden. It was an idyllic but in an unruly peristyle. What would normally be neat and trim with an obsession for space was overgrown and half dead. A fountain sat in the middle, its water still running at a dribble but thick with algae. On the other side was a high plaster-and-brick wall with a covered walkway encircling the entire area.

Before they stepped out into the bright day, Emlyn unloaded her empty shells, first releasing the top break, then pushing the ejector rod down, sending the shells popping out all at once. She was glad that caps were no longer regularly used like back in her father's early days. The process took her all of eight seconds to complete, with a total of six loaded rounds.

Before she placed one more foot before her, a chill ran up her spine. She took the feeling seriously as a matter of training. Whatever it was, her eyes had probably seen, but the rest of her took another moment to register. She cast a long hard gaze about the area.

"What is it?" asked Colmane.

There it was, a fishing line laid out across the entrance. She pointed.

"Crafty son of a whore." Exclaimed Colmane.

Emlyn picked up a sturdy piece of rubble and chucked it at the line, hitting it. A walking stick with a long sharpened table leg attached at its end swung across the entrance back and forth, settling in the middle. They were both surprised by it, they imagined what would have happened if it was not seen it in time. A spike through one of their heads.

Being careful and slow as she possibly could, Emlyn poked her head out slightly. Sure enough, a bullet hit the side of the archway where her face was. Plaster sprayed into her eyes, making her retreat into the hall, blinking rapidly and rubbing vigorously to clear her vision.

"Emlyn, are you okay?"

"Yes, yes! I'm fine!"

Deciding that her eyes were in working order, she went to one knee, held her revolver ready, prayed to the God Under the Hill, and turned her body out from cover. As she hoped, the killer's shot was too high, allowing her a small window to pull the trigger. She took that moment, sending the bullet grazing the killer's left bicep. It might not have been a kill shot, but it would have to do. It was enough to make him bleed out, and possibly leave a trail.

Colmane stepped through the archway. Cautiously looking around as Emlyn stood up. She did not bother to ask him to stay put. He was seeking glory, and a gilla could not tell a free man seeking glory to stay back and take it easy, wounded or not.

The killer did not shoot, knowing that he no longer had the drop on them.

There were not many places the killer could run off to; it was a rather small domus. Unless, of course, he ran out the front door, but Colmane had that covered with his next gamble, and hopefully the crazed martial was as insane as Colmane hoped him to be.

"Batt Dunmor! Yes, we know who you are! Do you want your trophies, your insignificant pieces of trash? I have them! So come and get 'em!" He hoisted the bag full of tags into the air, making them jingle.

A roar of rage emanated from behind a marble pillar on the walkway above. A shadow figure stepped out and began shooting. They both dove for cover behind the fountain, but the man was not sticking around. As he shot and screamed obscenities at them, Batt made his way across the walkway and into the house proper.

Colmane peeked out from cover and realized that Batt was gone. "C'mon, we can't lose him!"

Colmane did not order her this time to go first. He wanted the credit for catching this man. It made Emlyn uneasy, only because it would mean a failure of duty if Colmane suddenly found himself among the dead.

She followed him up the nearest steps onto the walkway and followed a blood trail leading into the second floor of the house. The trail led under a closed door at the end. Before she could catch up, Colmane opened the door. A loud ping and a whoosh came from the darkness as she tackled him to the ground. He almost screamed as he fell on his wounded shoulder.

"What're you doing!"

His eyes followed the gesture Emlyn made with her head, toward a short spear sticking out of the back wall of the house. He let out a slow, disbelieving breath.

"Master, please let me go first from now on." She pleaded.

He realized how close he came to being skewered and took a moment to collect himself. "Very well."

Emlyn winced as she lifted herself off him. The arrowhead had grazed her hip. She could see the shallow gash through the tear of the blue skirt. One centimeter more and it would have been a real problem.

Colmane stood up and found that he had only gained a few bruises. He checked his bandage and found no problems with his wounds, other than the fact of it being there.

"Emlyn . . . Thank you. Let's not dally any longer."

She nodded in agreement and felt satisfied with his approval, but this was no time to bask in such a thing.

Emlyn walked carefully into the room, holding the charge and pointing her revolver at each corner until she was satisfied there was no danger. Colmane brought out his own light and entered.

There was an apparatus sitting in the middle of the room. It looked like a miniature scorpion siege weapon, connected with a rope going through numerous rings that were attached to the walls. The end of the rope was tied on the doorknob. The rest was just—empty, not even trash could be found lying about, but it did feel damp and musty with mold. Old wallpaper peeled off the walls, and rat droppings could be seen in the corner.

To the left was an open door, and they went to it. Besides the beams, the floor was gone. The debris rested in the hall below. Across from them were the two other rooms Colmane had explored. Since it had very little in the way of walls besides the supports and chunks of plaster clinging on for dear life, it was obvious that the killer was not hiding there.

Emlyn saw a glint and pushed Colmane back into the room. The shot rang out, and the bullet missed its target. But it sent plaster raining down on Emlyn's head. She ignored this and took a knee as she brought up her gun and pulled the trigger.

Bingo, she hit his revolver, sending it twirling to the side. It crashed into the rubble with a resounding clang.

She could hear his footsteps running back into the darkness of the room, the same room she'd found the body in. She holstered her weapon and looked behind her.

"Master?"

"I'm okay." He was standing up and had his gun ready. "You keep on saving my life. I've never owed a gilla—"

"I am doing what I've been trained to do, that's all," said Emlyn flatly.

"Nonetheless, I've never had a gilla willingly try to take a spear and a bullet for me . . . I owe you."

"I'm not something you can owe. I am property serving its function. If you feel that you owe anyone, then pay respect to my Mistress."

They made their way down through the debris. She picked up the now defunct revolver and handed it to Colmane. It was similar to Emlyn's in modification but with gold and a triskele pattern.

They followed the killer into the room with the dead body. Of course Batt was no longer there, but his blood still left its trail out the other door and to the right. Gunless and wounded, it was doubtful he had an interest in tackling them head-on, especially against another martial with a working revolver.

It was then that Emlyn heard something. A door banging, yes, that was it, but the location was confusing, seeming like it had come from below.

She turned, stepping back. As she put a bit too much weight on her heel, the floor cracked and gave way. She pushed Colmane away and in the next second started tumbling down with the plaster and rotted wood into the darkness below.

Chapter Twenty

A cloud of chalky plaster dust blew out of her mouth like steam. More seemed to stick to her throat. She turned to the side and retched and let her body try to expel it. She heaved, forcing out pasty spit, and to her surprise—blood. The fall must have banged her up pretty well. Emlyn opened her eyes and scanned herself. Nothing visibly wrong besides a few bruises and perhaps a dozen minute cuts on her arms and on the abdomen where her blouse had been ripped. None looked concerning at first glance, but they would need to be cleaned. With all the rat feces rolling around this place, it would be next to impossible to avoid infection.

"Emlyn! Are you all right?" yelled Colmane, who was looking directly down at her from what used to be the floor, now a sorry attempt at a skylight. And the light that shone through was from Colmane's fading lantern and a few sunbeams coming from two small square windows at the top of the basement walls. She turned her head. The other side of this basement was pitch black, so it was hard to tell exactly how large it was.

"Yes, Master, I'm fine!" She sat up.

"Good! I'm going to find my way down to you!"

She practically screamed up at him "No! Get out of here! Get help!" She turned over and retched once again.

With that, Colmane disappeared. She could hear his footsteps clearly and hoped he would actually listen to her and find a few peacers. Hopefully they had heard the gunfire and were already on the way.

She stood up slowly, and as she did so, the hair on the back of her neck went alert like sentinels and she knew that someone was down here with her. She scanned the basement but still could not pierce the dark. Sweat trickled down from her brow.

All was still, as if time had ceased. The dust in the sunbeams did not move; the rats and other creeping things stopped. She held her breath. Her own increased heartbeat was the only thing that rang in her ears. The dark became more menacing with its intent. He had to be here, and at any moment he would come at her.

The stillness was broken as a foot slid and a knife attached to a large hand came across the distance hurtling from the dark. It made contact, producing a nasty squish.

The state of Emlyn's body refused to let her move in time. His aim was off, and the blade missed the kidney. But it was terribly painful, so she screamed. She had no time to assess the damage, for the killer pulled the knife out and was well on his way to another strike.

She knocked his hand away, but he immediately brought it back up. She dodged in time and rocketed to her feet. He shifted right along with her, grabbed her wrist, and angled behind so that his stomach was against her back. Batt held tight. Before he could secure her, she got a hand free to grab his wrist before the point of the blade came barreling down into her chest.

Her mind came swirling back to her. The comparative muscle and grip would not last much longer. They were both martials, but he was larger, and a man, who had a stronger muscle structure. She had to come up with something quick or he would win his intent. Emlyn looked down to the floor and became elated. Batt's feet were bare and blistered. She rammed her heel into the top of his toes, making him howl with searing pain. But he did not let go, so the next best thing came to mind since he was now off balance; she pushed her body against his, sending them both careening back into a beam, breaking the wood like an axe through a log. Still there was no give in his grasp, but at least he dropped the knife.

Batt grabbed her collar and pulled in an attempt to choke her when a number of cracks and creaks echoed from the floor above and they looked up in time to see wood and plaster come at them like a hail of cannon shot.

She coughed out more plaster dust and briefly thought about how it would affect her health. She realized where she was and what she was doing. The present reinserted itself. Her eyes shot open and looked down for her gun, then she realized she must have lost it when she fell. Looking over at where she had landed, she spotted the revolver halfway under some brick. Emlyn sat up. A quick needle of pain shot up her back like lightning, forcing her to fall over again and see nothing but black.

A small moan and shuffling made her realize he was still alive. Her eyes fluttered open, and she felt for her own knife. She wondered why her hand was so slick and realized that it must be blood. But at least her knife was still there. She rolled over onto her hands and knees, grimacing from the pain, then felt another blackness pass into her mind. She willed it back. It would not overtake her, she would not allow it. She looked up and saw the killer struggling to get onto his feet.

Tightening her grip on the handle, she slowly slid the knife from its sheath. Emlyn tried to get on her feet and experienced a similar hardship. She growled at the pain. That got his attention. He turned his head in time to see her start to painfully hop to him, seeking to stick the steel into a vital organ.

Batt was bent over, holding his ribs. He turned his back, and his other hand brushed the ground and found a nice hard piece of rubble.

Emlyn would have noticed it and been able to do something under different circumstances, but as the rock came hurtling toward her, moving out of the way in time became impossible. It hit her forehead with a *thunk*; blood poured down, and she sank, knees buckling and slamming against the concrete floor. She pressed her palm against the wound and applied pressure to staunch the steady flow.

As Emlyn fought against the oncoming void of unconsciousness, she spied something that shook her to the bone. Due to the light coming through the fallen floor, she could see him better out of the one eye not affected by her blood. He was in better condition than expected. Batt's long dark hair was disheveled, of course, but not as bad as one might think. His beard was trim and, along with everything else, covered in plaster. His bloody bare feet were the only signs of what he was, a murderous, runaway gilla.

As he moved, Emlyn spotted something that gained her attention just beyond him, a skeleton in a high-back chair, almost a throne.

The skeleton, painted with colorful designs and jewelry, did nothing to hide its ghastly presence in that rotted king's chair. Its bones were lazily wired together, but every single little piece was in the correct place. Its back was held up by a board wired to the spine all the way to the grinning skull.

It took a moment for Emlyn to realize that it was not paint at all, but red, yellow, black, and brown stains from bodily fluids and fire. This must have been the missing Master. Somehow the martial survived, never got caught, and was able to steal the body of his master from the catacombs. The body that was left must have been one of the highwaymen burned in the carriage fire and everyone else had mistaken for the martial.

The killer's voice was raspy with the dust, turned hoarse like he desperately needed a glass of water. "She's done for, Master. You're safe now." He fell to his knees, leaned forward, and kissed his master's bony hand. He put his forehead where the kiss was laid.

"I'm so sorry, I'll never let it happen again. They will have to kill me first before I let them get to you." He began sobbing. "You see how I've protected you, how I made examples of lesser gilla. Haven't I atoned for my transgression?"

He paused, sucking back the spit gathered in his throat. "Do not go across the bridge, do not pet the black hound, not without me! You need a guard on your journey, for the way is treacherous and full of shades on their means of mischief. You need to forgive me so that I can follow. Please, haven't I've done enough?"

The hammer of a gun clicked, and he turned swiftly. Emlyn was barely on her feet. It had taken some effort to make her way to the gun, but she had remained quiet as a mouse as this maniac conversed with his skeletal master. A martial acting this way, it was unsettling to say the least.

She shivered. Something about this man was like looking into a distorted reflection. Emlyn blinked and shook her head. It would do no good to think about that at this moment. Speed was of utmost importance here. *Where are you, Colmane?* she wondered. She was afraid that unconsciousness would try to claim her again.

"Stay where you are!" she said weakly.

Movement did not seem to come to him. "That man, he's not your Master, is he?"

She didn't respond, instead moving closer to him.

"I thought not. He's the type who came from the streets. I know that type." He looked at the skull. "Sister martial, why are you not protecting your owner?"

"You're insane."

"Heh, you see, Master? Martials do indeed fall from their path. Yes, she is not sorry for her transgressions. I will protect you from her, until my last breath. I'll take her tag and make it my final offering to you. Perhaps then you'll see fit to accept my request."

He rubbed his lips together, then became fast as mercury, almost a flash before her weary eyes, disappearing deep into the dark area of the basement. The sound of her shot reverberated against the walls, and she had to wait as her ears came back to order.

She moved the revolver quickly, pointing at any little sound coming from that blind area of the basement. Her heart felt like it could pound its way to freedom. One false move and this could be the end.

Emlyn came to a realization. The barrel of her gun laid its sights on the skull of the dead master, and she aimed carefully. As the trigger pulled, a man yelled, "No!"

In the next instant the skull gained a gigantic hole in its temple. It teetered, then fell to the floor with a sharp crack, bursting into pieces.

A wrenching agony pierced her side as Batt's fist met the knife wound. She gasped. The white-hot pain seared into her core. They fell together, him on top, and they hit the ground, sending up a cloud of dust. He fumbled for her revolver, finally grabbing her wrist.

"You murderer!" His spit splashed on her cheek as he screamed in hoarse anguish.

She glanced down and saw that the wound from the knife was bleeding profusely. She would pass out soon.

"Look in the mirror, hypocrite!" she screamed back before headbutting him.

He loosened his grasp on her wrist, and in one swift motion she buried the gun barrel between his ribs and fired three shots, one right after the other. Then kneed him in the groin, making his balls go back up inside the cavity. He fell back, not making a sound besides his shuffling feet along with a grunt or two. His face was that of stunned silence. Batt lifted his hands from his stomach in disbelief, then fell to his knees and lay on his side against the concrete floor. His breaths became heavy and languished.

Emlyn let go of her revolver for a moment and ripped a long piece of skirt off and tied it around her waist, adding another layer to stop the flow of blood. But the wound was soaking the cloth all the way through. Still she managed to push herself off the floor and grabbed her gun along the way. Shambling over to him, she pointed the barrel at his head and cocked it back.

Seeing this, Batt forgot all pain and scrambled back to his knees in front of her, grabbed the barrel, and put it against his forehead. "Please, he's alone on the path of the Tuatha. Send me to him!"

She furrowed her brow. "Request granted, monster."

The trigger pulled, and the killer's back slammed against the cold concrete; blood splattered, then pooled out from the wound like a stream flowing over mountainous terrain.

"Cac."

She stood like a grotesque statue, staring at Dunmor's body, and wondered how it came to this. How did he fly off his tether so profoundly?

"What if I fail in my duty?" she said out loud, letting the words echo off the concrete foundation.

She felt a leech on her mind, sucking all thought away. Except for this, alone in this place, in the presence of Batt's body and his skeletal master.

Emlyn was brought out of it by someone banging loudly. She turned and saw a cellar door in the corner, not far from her initial fall. The handles of the door were wrapped in heavy chains and secured with a thick padlock. She took careful aim, trying not to sway, and then shot. The padlock broke, and with the force of the impact it fractured almost in two and fell on the steps beneath with a clunk.

She yelled, "It's safe to enter! He's dead!"

The cellar door burst inward, and peacers rushed in and cautiously surrounded her with either their revolvers or truncheons at the ready. Some seemed startled by her appearance. She assumed all the plaster dust covering her body made her look like a frightful apparition. One of them yelled for her to drop the gun. She barely paid attention. Then Colmane's voice broke through the tension.

"Don't shoot her!" He shoved past them. "Emlyn?"

He followed her gaze to the body sprawled out on the floor, soaking in its ever-increasing pool of blood.

He placed a hand on her shoulder. "Emlyn!"

She blinked a few times, then turned partially toward him. "Master Colmane, I'm sorry, I just—" She looked back at Dunmor's corpse.

Colmane did too, crossed his arms and sighed. "Did he have to die?"

She did not respond.

"Answer me."

She gulped. "He needed to die."

"It would have been preferable that he got a public hanging."

"I know. Forgive me, Master," she said in a somber tone.

"Well, nothing can be done about it now." He looked her up and down. "You look like a walking corpse. Sit down. We'll try to find something clean to wrap your wounds with. Please, tell me what happened in detail."

He made her sit on a pile of debris and listened as he wrapped another layer around her waist. Emlyn thanked the Gods it was a short tale.

"So Dunmor believed he was making up for his failure by killing gilla and freemen who failed in their duty. He should have killed himself and got it over with."

"He could not protect his master from me, so he ended himself through my hand."

"Why in the world did you give him what he wanted?"

She stared down to the floor, then over to the body being inspected by the peacers. "Professional courtesy to a brother martial."

It was a lie, but it sounded real, and she could almost believe it. In reality she did not like what stared back at her and wanted it gone. But even now the image of Batt's deranged, broken eyes staring into her own itched like a maddening rash.

"Interesting that you still respect him after all the harm he's done."

Emlyn did not respect Dunmor, but she was not going to tell Colmane the truth, not on this. How could he possibly understand?

"Listen, Emlyn, you're a gilla, and there is no forgetting that." He took her hand. "Thank you. If you were not with me, then I would have surely been killed." He kissed the top of her hand.

Her eyes went wide. That was a gesture for a lady, never given by a free person to a gilla. Then she realized something in a sudden flash of memory. She looked up at him, mouth hanging wide open.

"You followed me to the Waapole pub."

He let her hand drop and smiled wryly.

She continued, "When Mira ran, you knew exactly where she went, but you waited, placing yourself in a position where I'd notice you first. You tested me. You were already thinking that the killer was a martial, and you wanted one yourself to confirm it and bring him down. And who better than a Gwen." She held her side and winced, suddenly feeling weaker than she already was.

"I must say, that is an impressive theory." He smirked.

"Emlyn!" From the cellar entrance came Sylvia franticly lifting her green skirts and running down the steps. She had gotten through not only the reporters, who had been gathering uproariously outside and surely recognized who she was, but also through the guards, easily swayed to move aside for a high patrician. Upon spotting Emlyn, Sylvia's eyes grew with concern. She rushed over, only slowing down to spy Batt's dead body being hoisted by the peacers. When she looked back at Emlyn, her hand covered her mouth, trying to hide the shock.

"By the Gods! What happened? Look at you!" She stopped right before Emlyn, and her eyes darted over her body, spotting the wounds.

"Great mother! How could this happen twice in a week?"

"I'm lucky, Mistress."

Sylvia got on her knees, not caring about her skirt getting dirty. Looking up into Emlyn's dreary eyes, she reached and tenderly brushed

Emlyn's hair away from her face. She gasped upon seeing the nicks and cuts.

Sylvia turned her head to look up at Colmane. "Where is the doctor? Why in Helo's name have you not called for one's services?"

He crossed his arms defensively. "I have, Lady Chronister, but it seems he is running late."

"Mistress, I'll be fine."

Sylvia huffed. "Do not give me that stoic martial nonsense. You are swaying side to side. I don't even know how you're still sitting up!"

Ten minutes went by before Sylvia lost patience and left to make a call. It was not long after that the doctor showed up. No doubt when Colmane called, he neglected to mention that she was not just any gilla but a Chronister martial. Now, motivated by the prospect of fleecing her mistress, the doctor rushed over, practically ran down the stairs. By then the detectives had finished inspecting the basement and were walking up the steps. The doctor almost toppled them over.

It was quickly determined that the knife did not hit anything vital, lucky her. Every nick and cut was cleaned, everything was checked. The stab wound was sewn shut. She did not want to experience a doctor's methods again. She did not like the stitches they poked through her a week ago, and she liked it even less now. The threads going through her skin felt like some kind of weird violation. Her torso and chest were then wrapped in heavily medicated gauze. The pressure hurt at first, but the medication made it feel cool and oddly relaxing.

Peacers were milling about the domus now, and Colmane had stayed with Emlyn, sitting next to her on the rubble. They did not talk much during this time, they didn't have to. He could not say it, but she knew. Colmane respected her despite what happened a week ago. She wondered if he had ever respected a gilla before. She deserved no respect from a free person, she knew this, yet it felt so good. It felt right to gain that respect from him.

Stella, too, came down, with Sylvia behind her. The martial took stock of the surroundings before laying eyes on Emlyn.

Emlyn could not believe it; there was a flicker of shock and worry upon Stella's face. But Stella sighed and lifted her chin as she came to stand the correct distance away. The flicker of emotion for her daughter was gone, back to the Stella she knew and loathed.

Sylvia came forward and took Emlyn's hands into hers. "You look better. As well as one can be in this situation, I suppose. Still covered in plaster and whatever else, but nothing that a hot bath can't fix."

Emlyn looked up at her and smirked wryly. "One thing is for certain, Mistress: I'll have some lovely scars."

Colmane laughed, stood, wiped his hands clean from plaster dust, and performed a small bow. "Lady Chronister."

"Colmane." Sylvia acknowledged, more evenly this time than angry.

"I am sorry for putting your martial in such a dangerous situation, but I assure you she performed well, unlike anything I've seen before."

He turned to Emlyn. "Until we meet again, gilla."

She smirked at that and bowed her head. "May the Gods watch over you, Master."

He laughed at this and made his way slowly across the basement and up through the door.

Emlyn knew that they would not see each other again, and she was certain Colmane knew it too. The mistress would not trust him with her again. She stifled a sigh. Her time with Colmane allowed her to go places and experience things that would have not of been possible otherwise. And the investigation itself seemed so close to the books she once loved to read before her breaking.

Colmane intrigued her. An ambitious gilla catcher working with a gilla he quickly grew to respect, despite the naivety he claimed she possessed.

Emlyn determined right then and there that she enjoyed the investigation immensely. But then her heart sank, knowing it was back to the insula, and after this, who knew when the mistress would let her out again.

"Tabby, are you able to stand?" asked Sylvia.

With Stella's help she slowly pushed herself up off the pile of rubbish. She grimaced whenever her torso bent. Everything was fine after that until she started climbing the stairs. Her foot caught on the middle step, almost causing her to trip. Sylvia quickly took her arm and helped her the rest of the way up.

The auto waited outside. The blissful sound of the motor was like a golden chariot ready to transfer her to a comfy bed. The area around the auto was free of reporters because they were distracted by Colmane, who looked downright thrilled to be giving his account of events. Sylvia looked relieved at this fact.

Stella helped Emlyn into the back seat and settled before a few reporters made their way over. They cornered Sylvia before she could lift herself into the auto. Her face fell in disappointment. Stella stood to intervene, but the mistress waved her away and told her to stay put.

Sylvia smiled warmly at the constant questions and kept it very simple. "Yes, I loaned my property for the investigation. My martial successfully performed her duty with satisfaction." She lifted herself up into the auto and sat next to Emlyn. "Mr. Colmane possesses all other relevant details you may need."

One reporter tried to ask about the rumors, but Sylvia had already situated herself into the passenger's seat and did not answer. She nodded to Donnon the driver. The auto roared and sped off into the darkening evening. Emlyn looked back and could swear that another auto was following, hard to miss since few were on the road even in the busy hours. She alerted Stella, who nodded, acknowledging what she had seen.

The evening sky was lovely in late dusk, largely dark blue and purple with a few twinkling stars poking out from their slumber. Slumber was a pleasant notion, so Emlyn laid her head back and finally let unconsciousness take her.

CHAPTER TWENTY-ONE

It was front-page news. The article told of Colmane's superb
investigative work and his promotion that night as the new dalarwain of
gilla affairs. The page laid out how he tracked down a deadly martial
who went insane after losing his master. Emlyn's name was, for the most
part, left out of investigation itself. But they did offhandedly mention
that the case would have been more difficult to solve without the
support of a Chronister martial from the Gwen clan. She was not
bothered by this. Gilla like her rarely got glory in such a way, and if they
did, it was purely by accident.

The negative outcome of this entire affair was that martials were
more feared than ever. At least that was what the papers said. Sylvia
forbade her to run outside errands until further notice. And for a month
it felt like all those years of seclusion after the breaking, but so much
worse. There was nothing she could do about it except look out the
window and let her mind wander.

Emlyn missed her moon cycle and grew worried about pregnancy.
She had intercourse with Maield many times, and she would not have
been surprised if that resulted in a child, but it would put her mistress in
an awkward situation.

A renowned midwife was hired and rushed into the house. She
quickly made it clear that Emlyn was without a child, followed by a
relieved sigh from both Emlyn and Sylvia. The midwife attributed her
missed cycle to stress and said it might only be late. Emlyn could not

help but wonder, so she asked if she was even capable of giving birth. Did she even want to? The thought of putting her offspring through the breaking left a more bitter taste than it once had. The midwife only shrugged and said: "Can see nothin' wrong on that end."

There was no doubt, Emlyn was going stir crazy. Though she left the house only rarely in the first place, getting out, even once a month, made her breathe easier. But she took her time to recover from the wounds and work through her stress. It gave her plenty of time to revisit the books of her childhood. They were almost fresh stories since she was looking at them with what amounted to new eyes created through the crucible of the breaking. It did not help her miss the outside any less.

For over a month, Mira had been cooped up in the same room and was becoming noticeably unhinged. Emlyn could understand her feelings. It was a prison for the girl. Her mistress's mind was being pulled in so many directions that she often put aside the question of what to do about Mira. What took the most precedence was Mistress Camilla slowly and horribly dying from the red sickness. A sickness characterized by large bleeding welts all over the body and rampant fevers that deteriorated the mind. Camilla had been bedridden for over two months now, constantly falling in and out of reality, and it was only getting worse.

Emlyn carried a tray balancing a glass of water, a bowl of applesauce, and soft pork sausages. She hoped Mistress Camilla would be able to eat them, she was much too skinny and would not be long for this world if she didn't take some nutrition. The door was open a few inches, but she knocked gently before entering.

The room was dark with the only light coming from the high rectangular windows. Camilla had complained about the brightness of the electric lights, so Sylvia made sure that only natural light and candles were allowed.

Sylvia sat beside her mother's bed, holding a cold rag on her forehead.

"Mother?"

Camilla's deeply sunken right eye, rimmed with sickly purple, fluttered open as if it was lifting a great weight. "S-Sylvia?" Her voice was that of an old crone. A barbarous crow trying to escape the back of her throat.

Truth be told, she lasted much longer than Cassius and Thom, who had left the world within a month of catching the disease.

Sylvia gently moved her mother's head to look at her. "Mother, it's me. Can you eat? You need to eat."

Sylvia reached out and took the glass of water, then put the rim up against Camilla's lips. A bit of the cool liquid passed between, until she started coughing. Sylvia immediately took the glass away and put it back on the tray.

"Andreas?" She coughed. "Andreas!" Camilla seized with pain upon yelling, but her voice did not stop. "Andreas! I need you! Where are you? Andreas!"

Sylvia stroked her mother's hair, shushing her soothingly to calm her down. She did so after a little blood was coughed up on her chin and tenderly wiped away.

"I'm here, Momma, I'm here," Sylvia said gently.

Camilla looked at her again, but this time there was no recognition in her eyes. Sylvia had the applesauce ready and cut up the pork into little bites. The sausages would be a waste, but it was worth a try. As she did this, her mother kept calling out, groaning names and speaking of events.

"Daddy! Th-they're beating her!"

"Momma." She reached out with a spoonful of applesauce, but Camilla turned her head away.

"Nooo, no!"

Sylvia sighed with defeat and put the applesauce back on the tray. "Tabby, please put that on the ready table, will you?"

Emlyn did so and spotted Stella sitting at a corner desk with her head in her hands. She was sobbing.

Emlyn did not think much of Stella as her mother. Still, she had brought her into this world. Emlyn walked over and tentatively placed a hand on her shoulder.

For a moment Emlyn thought Stella was going to pat her hand and accept the comfort it offered, but in an instant it was brushed away. Why should she have expected anything different? Then this hard woman spoke.

"Sh-she's going . . . I-I can't protect her."

Emlyn froze. Dunmor's insanity flashed before her eyes. The possibility of going over the edge herself became more real. She did not think her mother would become Dunmor. She was a cuss of a woman, but strong. But here Stella was, feeling as if she was a failure and beating herself down even though there was nothing she could have done. Emlyn wondered for the hundredth time how she herself would act and still found the possibilities too disturbing. She had to force herself to move and get out of this room.

She sat heavily upon a simple wooden chair that sat right outside the door. Her leg rapidly bounced up and down. She checked her nails, then ran a hand through her hair.

The door creaked open, and Sylvia stepped out. "No, don't get up." Emlyn obeyed.

Sylvia flounced out her skirts and sat herself down on the floor across from Emlyn with her back against the wall. They looked at each other for a few moments.

"I'm sorry, Mistress."

Sylvia looked at her solemnly. "There is nothing to be sorry for. There's nothing to do besides to help her across the bridge and . . . enter the door." She choked back a sob and shook her head. "This has got to be a curse of some kind. It's the same thing our brothers died from." Her voice trembled. "The Gods do not look kindly on us, though I know not what we could have done to deserve their ire. This should not have been her time to pass. She should have had so many years yet—"

She sucked in her breath and put her head down but kept from crying.

She took a minute to recover before continuing. "I've decided."

Emlyn cocked her head, questioning.

"I'm releasing Mira."

Emlyn leaned forward, elbows on knees, fingers laced under her chin. "Forgive me, Mistress. But do you view releasing her as some type of atonement to the Gods?"

Sylvia suddenly looked up at her, surprised at Emlyn's tone, and it was the tone that drew out a response. She breathed out, "Yes."

Emlyn nodded in understanding. "Mistress, you have performed not one sacrilege to any of the Gods that I'm aware of, and I am with you most of each day."

"What about Miltin?"

Miltin, the grifter pretending to be an inventor. Sylvia sold him into gillahood a while ago. Emlyn never trusted him, not when laying eyes on the man, and she had told her mistress as much.

"I think you acted as the Gods instrument in that punishment. I think they were seeing if you truly had what it takes to play on the level of patricians."

"Patricians!" said Sylvia dismissively. "Patricians backstab and jockey for power, unwilling to contribute to this country. They only serve their vanity. They covet. By the great mother, do we ever covet *anything* of worth and hold it for ourselves? I did . . . at one time."

Emlyn looked at her askance, but when there was no answer, she didn't press.

Sylvia drew her knees up and wrapped her arms around her legs. "We, the Chronisters, fought, stole, and cheated our way back to the top of that hierarchy. And now I must shepherd that legacy without Mother and Father standing over me, and I . . . I do not think I want that. I just want my family back, damn the rest."

Emlyn got up and sat down next to her, putting an arm around her. Sylvia snuggled up to her.

"If you're being punished for being a patrician, then so is every other patrician in the realm, you know that. Yes, you make hard decisions. But you give out so much in return. Just look at how much life has changed for the better over the last eight years. You have a hand in that."

Sylvia wiped the remnants of the tears away. "Better? How can you say that it is better now than it was, when things seemed so much more simple?"

"It was never simple, Mistress."

She looked up at Emlyn's face. Most of the nicks and cuts were gone or only seen through close inspection. She could look into those eyes forever. It made her able to push everything aside and sink into those amber pools of bliss. It did not matter much if those eyes appeared deadened if she could remain within this comforting embrace. But it was only a fleeting.

She retreated, pulling herself away from Emlyn. But she longed to lean back into her arms.

Emlyn, for her part, saw none of Sylvia's longing for her. Comprehending such a thing was always hard for a martial. Something embedded in her subconscious from the breaking perhaps. Sylvia cursed the martial tradition every damn day for taking the girl she loved away.

"Come, atonement or not, I still want to release Mira." She hopped to her feet and started marching off down the hall. Emlyn caught up to her with little effort.

"Mistress, are you just going to drop her off on the side of the road?" said Emlyn in disbelief.

"I will give her everything she needs."

"The chances of her survival is low. She will always be at risk for gillahood if her brand is discovered. And she would be given back to us if some country gobb does not want her for himself."

Sylvia stopped to face Emlyn. "I've wasted enough time thinking this over. She cannot stay here. The longer she stays, the more danger we're in. But if I need to assuage your fears, do not worry, I have a plan for her. I only need another day, and I must start now, if you'll attend me."

"Of course, Mistress."

* * * * *

This room had become the world, a sad little place that held interest for only a short amount of time, mainly the first few minutes after she was tossed into it. The walls were a dull beige, the bed was the dull color of eggshell, the curtains were a dull green, and behind the iron bars protecting the windows was a dull alleyway. The rats skittering about outside were the sole highlight.

She needed something else to read. A few towers worth of books were neatly stacked in the corner. Mira was not a slow reader, that was for certain. If only she did not find rereading them as dull as the room.

She heard a cough outside the window, then cautiously moved the curtain to the side just an inch. A drunken man made his way down the alley, almost falling to one side before miraculously catching himself. He had to prop against the grimy walls to take in gigantic gulps of breath. It was the most interesting thing she had seen all week. As drunk and homeless as he obviously was, she backed away from the window as he came close. She was afraid that there was someone hanging around to kill her, and she still retained her need for mortality.

His hand fell between the bars and onto the window. It slid, making a low squeak. The sound made her shiver.

The creak of the door made her feet leave the ground. Immediately she dropped to her knees and placed her forehead on the corraí rug.

Though the mistress no longer treated her as a gilla, she found it difficult to make that switch. She had spent a month pondering her feelings about it, enough time to root out its complexities. No, she did not like being raped like she had been. It was the control. As long as she was good, she didn't have to worry about . . . everything, and it often took a lot of stress off of her mind. Stress from the fear of being a bad gilla in this insula was small potatoes compared to being a princess running for her life, living among enemies. At least she thought so.

Emlyn was right, and she could have kissed her for the defense down in the basement. She wanted to stay, be good and live simply. Her life was no longer her concern. And if anyone came for her . . . well, Emlyn could take them. She was safe here. This was the safest place she could be. She would stay.

"Get up."

Mira leaned back, sitting with her knees together, then looked up at Sylvia. Emlyn was standing in the doorway with a sad look.

"Mistress?" said Mira.

"I told you, do not call me that."

"But . . ." Her mistress seemed very angry. With rough movements, she reached around Mira's neck and stuck something within the lock of her collar. She heard it click as the key turned. Shock struck her eyes as the collar was lifted away. "Now stand up."

Mira made no movements, not even a blink, just stared wide-eyed and blankly at the rug. Suddenly her biceps were being grasped. Emlyn lifted her to her feet. Her knees were weak, and she wanted to crumple to the floor.

There was something freeing about having that hunk of metal removed. With the weight of it gone, she felt alien, like she had lost something that was too vague to hold. If she could just remember it, it would be back in her possession, but it did feel wonderful to experience the cold air against that part of her neck once more.

Emlyn practically held her up the entire way to the auto and whispered, "I'm sorry," more than once in her ear, but she paid no mind and let herself be led.

It did not hit her until they were out of the city, barreling through the clear night. They were going to abandon her.

"No, no, no. You can't."

They paid no attention.

"I don't know what to do. Where do I go?"

They did not answer.

Mira looked at the floorboards of the auto. "At one point I wanted to go home. I would have done anything . . . It was Anton who always saved me. He was responsible for my survival. Without him, I would have died in the snow. Please, please don't drop me off like an unwanted dog."

Sylvia, in the passenger seat, finally turned her head. "I am not just dropping you off."

Mira could only look confused.

"There is an old family of plebs. For many generations they have come to work for my family. They have a humble country home with a good-sized estate occupied mostly by a peach and apple orchard. I spent a few summers on their estate, and they will not betray my confidence."

Sylvia looked dreamy, as if she was experiencing a fun memory.

"They will not know that you are, in truth, a zareen, nor will they know that you were my gilla. Make sure you keep both of your brands hidden."

"What would happen if they see my brand, Mistress?"

"If they decide not to make you gilla themselves, then you will be handed over to the state, and I will suffer a significant fine and public humiliation. If you were free before becoming a gilla, then I could just abandon you and you would be legally free. Alas we have no such luck. Come up with a name before we get there."

She paused to think a moment by tapping a finger against her lips. "You were an employee of mine who went above and beyond your job description, but I no longer have use for your position, nor do you have any family or lover to fall back on. I took pity on you. And due to your wonderfully rendered service, I decided to help. Understand?"

"Yes, Mistress."

"Whatever you do, refrain from calling me that."

Sylvia turned and started searching through a leather bag resting on her lap. "I am sorry, Mira, I would have legally freed you, but that process can take a year or more, maybe longer since you're classified a traitor. I curse it."

It was difficult to free gilla coming from a criminal background, even harder if that criminal was a traitor. With Mira's situation, it could be argued in court that she had no idea she was sleeping with a soldier from the Zarconian regime. But like with anything else, that would take a good amount of time.

Sylvia turned and held out some papers for Mira to take. She did. They all had a blank line for a signature.

"These are forgeries. It is a freedman certificate. If your brand is discovered, show it and hope there is no one present who is more than passingly familiar with a paper like this."

She handed a pen to her. Mira did not write anything. It was another name, and it was all happening too fast. Everything in her life happened too fast: the train, the constant running, Anton being discovered, the auction block, all of it was *too* fast.

"Once the people who're following you realize that you are no longer with us, I will personally retrieve you, and I will work on obtaining your true freedom. Until then, stay out of trouble."

Mira bit her lip and hesitated, steeled herself, then signed a name.

The further they got from civilization, the more the auto jostled and vibrated to an uncomfortable degree. These roads were made for carts and horses, not rubber wheels and stiff springs. Nothing more was said between them as the light of the coming day turned the night sky to purple.

They had left at about three in the morning and drove through the night. It was another sleepless night for Emlyn and Sylvia. However, Mira found herself nodding off and waking up after each significant bump in the road. At one point she closed her eyes, and when she reopened them, the auto was being set in park and the sun just finished showing its face on the horizon.

She rubbed her eyes and looked about her. The fields in front of the auto were perfect, with hundreds of peach trees displayed evenly. Workers in overly large straw hats were sauntering out in the morning sun to the rows. Beside her was a domus, hardy, large, yet humble. There was a porch out front decorated with red columns. The rest was pure old Rome, suggesting that the owner had a fascination with the empirical days.

A man, dressed well in mahogany-colored knee-high boots, over pressed puff pants, and a light white coat with sleeves rolled to the elbows, stepped out from the ornate porch. His white shirt was open to just below his chest. Even though the heat wave was officially over, it was still an unseasonably warm October.

"Lady Sylvia, is that you?" he said. The motion of his chin made the gray beard, braided in an intricate Skaldane style with Grecian beadwork, bounce delightfully.

Sylvia opened the door and lowered herself down. "I am afraid so, Great-Uncle."

At a young age, Sylvia had assumed that he was closely related, only finding out later that they were related by blood only very distantly, closer in ties to her mother's side of the family. They were of plebian stock, as it was once said in the ancient days. In fact, the Cauls could trace their line to a merchant family known as Vitelius during the Pax Roma.

He took her hands and kissed them, then held them out away from her to get a good look. "Call me Mal. By the Gods, look at you! You grew to be quite a fetching young woman! Requests for your hand must be overflowing in abundance!" He let her have the use of her arms back.

She smiled, appreciating the jovial nature. "More than I am able to handle, Uncle Mal." A bit of a lie; she had not looked at any offers since Lucius. Though her refusal to reply made more people believe the rumor.

"Are you seeking our company for a while then? Perhaps to escape from all that choking fog? We have plenty of room and food for each of you, nice and fresh from the fields."

"Just for today. That is all I can spare."

He understood and turned his head down in sorrow. "Ah, yes, I am sorry about Camilla, a terrible thing for such a bright woman. I remember when she was just a little girl—"

Emlyn came around the car.

"What is . . . are you borrowing a martial?"

Emlyn turned and gave a quick bow before he recognized her.

"By Hep's beard, is that you, Emlyn?"

"Yes, Master."

"Master? Oh yes, I suppose you would be broken by now."

A look came across him as if he was having trouble reconciling little rough-and-tumble, talkative Emlyn to this tall, athletic martial who now stood before him, complete with a stoic, hard look on her face. She turned to open the side door for Mira to step out. She curtseyed. "Hello . . . sir."

"And who is this?" he said seriously.

"Miss Fanna Kursis, a servant. A very capable servant. I no longer have a position for her. The city's low in jobs for women, and she has no family to speak of. I think it would be a shame for her talents to go to waste."

"What talents do you speak of?"

"Kitchen, food service in general. She was my undercook and was looking to take Ms. Cord's place upon retirement."

He turned to Mira. "Ms. Cord, eh? Well, if you can deal with that harpy, then you might have a chance." He looked back at Sylvia. "I'll take her on your recommendation, at least on a trial basis."

"That is all I ask. Thank you, Uncle." She curtseyed and bowed slightly.

Mal patted her on the shoulder. "It is good to know that you have kept a kind heart. Come, meet my family. It has grown quite substantially since you last visited!"

Sylvia remembered him having five girls. As they approached the porch, his entire family filed out and stood in a line starting with his wife, then oldest to youngest. Most were in various stages of dress and were curious about what had their father's attention. Three of the five girls, now women, recognized her as she approached and greeted her warmly.

They quickly told tales of their adventures as children, curious to know if she remembered or not. She did. But soon she was shuffled down the line to meet the three new additions, and to her surprise, the first one was a boy of eleven. She did vaguely remember the wife, Alicia, being pregnant during her last visit all those years ago. The boy found her and Emlyn fascinating, but the other two girls were frightened by the martial. Men, women, and children keeping their distance from Emlyn was nothing new, and Sylvia always felt sorry for that.

They were given a tour of the estate before lunch and met many of the employees and a few gilla who worked closely with the family. The afternoon was left to leisure with talk of business that included Sylvia trying to explain the intricacies of electricity and investment in related proposed projects. Most of this went over Mal's head. Mal talked eloquently about logistics. She was surprised to learn that Uncle Mal had expanded into Gaelland and Gallia.

This supreme leisure was a fantastic excuse for why they were here. Of course, she was glad to be here no matter what. Memories of this place had seemed like a distant dream, dreams she had no time to indulge in as of late. It was like an island. Nothing else in the world existed except this space, this time. Nothing could touch her here.

* * * * *

Sylvia wiped the spittle from her face but kept the look of surprise. "Why would you do that?" she demanded.

It had taken Mira a good bit of time throughout the day to shake herself from the shock and malaise with how fast all this had happened. Now she felt her mind open in clarity.

"You think you're a good person for doing this, but you don't care what happened to me, what you did to me! You're doing this only to protect yourself!" She plopped herself down on the single, unremarkable bed and refused to look up at her. "Please leave."

Sylvia went to the door and stopped, placing a hand on the wooden frame. "You have every right to think that—"

Mira blurted out, "I'm not free, I have no rights, remember . . . Mistress?"

Sylvia took a deep breath. "Nonetheless, I will return, and at that time I will set you free." Sylvia left, closing the door behind her.

Mira mumbled to herself, "And then what?"

She had been given a large duffel bag full of clothing and other needed provisions, including a few new books. She spent some hours sorting her items and studying her surroundings. This room was not much bigger than the pantry, but she had a bed, a small dresser, a nightstand, and a simple window with a beautiful view of the fields. It faced where the sun rose over the cultivated hills. She had met the kitchen staff, who welcomed her but were understandably suspicious. Probably thinking that she was there to steal one of their positions. That did not matter. Whatever the owners of this place decided would be the way of it. The only thing she had to do was wait, then she could beg to be kept in her service. Or, if she was free, perhaps the mistress could set her up somewhere.

The possibilities flooded her mind, but one thing was certain: the dream of returning home and being a zareen again had faded. She had trouble holding that image, and that did not disturb her like it once had. For better or worse, this was her home for now.

Chapter Twenty-Two

The yellow ribbon circled around the palm, then down a slim pale wrist inch by inch and pulled tight after each revolution.

Painful, languorous breaths came with such gargantuan effort that after Camilla exhaled, everyone in the room felt a certain relief. For that moment, it was sensed that she felt no pain—until it started all over again.

Sylvia completed the ribbon assemblage on her arm and used her other hand to smooth back her mother's hair, hoping it offered some measure of comfort.

The doctor had said it would be tonight, told her to stay away after it happens, for once dead, the red sickness becomes more contagious. Sylvia had no intention of listening to his advice. She would however, wait a week for the showing to allow enough time for family from afar to arrive.

Fresh tears ran down her face at the thought of it, her mother lying there, stiff, in a bed of ice. Guilt laid claim to her thoughts. Her mother lasted longer than most, but it would have been better to speed over the bridge quickly to avoid a long torment.

In the corner sat Stella, who had trouble bringing herself to look at Camilla. Coming close to the death bed seemed impossible for the usually formidable martial. If her duty did not compel her to stay in the room, she would have been physically as far away as one could get. As it was, her mind accomplished that distance very well, judging by that stare, which seemed to bore into the polished wood floorboards. Nothing could bring her around.

Emlyn stood behind Sylvia, a hand on her shoulder as her mistress started another crying fit.

"I keep thinking that each breath is her last," said Sylvia between sobs.

Strawberry brought her a glass of water from the ready table. Sylvia took it and nodded to her in thanks. The girl had a dower face; it was Camilla who saved Strawberry from a terrible owner, and since then she had waited on Camilla often, always grateful for that bit of kindness. Sylvia thought that if Strawberry had the means, then freedom would be her choice. Alas she got caught picking pockets one too many times and was given a stilted choice. It would be a lucky thing if she gained a second freedom. It would be easier to argue and convince affairs to free Mira than Strawberry by a long mile.

The girl went back to the ready table and picked up a needle, black thread, and black cloth, then sat on the floor next to Bramble. They were against the wall sewing loose gowns to be worn only once at the funeral. They had finished two, with three to go, to be worn by the members of the family with the closest blood ties.

Bramble had let known his admiration of the old mistress's jovial nature. She often gave him sweets when he was younger and still learning his responsibilities. His full name was Bramble Roi, and he was the grandson of a bloodlined gilla from the Rydderch estate. He got to see his family regularly when Camilla went to visit up that way. After all this was said and done, he would have to be sent back possibly while the Rydderch clan was here. That would be just fine with Sylvia. Camilla had an interest in training gilla, but Sylvia did not.

Sitting at the open window a few feet from the head of Camilla's bed was Ms. Cord, smoking on her pipe to calm the nerves. She blew the smoke out the open window and watched it waft up into the night sky out over the garden like a swirl of grey ribbons taking flight.

A knock on the door and in came Lemon with a tray of rolled, cold towels and another pitcher of water. She placed them on the ready table, took one, and went to Camilla. With great gentleness, she dabbed the sweat off her forehead. Sylvia watched the girl's bony but smooth hand.

Lemon was bought by Camilla from a master who was simply tired of looking at her. He sought a low amount for her purchase right in the middle of Iria park. He had the girl standing atop one of the park benches as he barked and haggled her price, such a low thing to do. Camilla had outwitted the man by declaring the gilla worthless since he obviously had seen no merit in his property. And then wondered very loudly on the man's merits as a master of his house, because how could you not be able to efficiently command a gilla with all her fingers and toes. Her accusations raised a crowd, and they all were laughing at him, causing the man to shove Lemon toward her with legal papers stuffed in her hand. Then he walked hurriedly away in a sweating huff.

Sylvia looked around the room, at each and every one of them. *I have no clue what to do with them after all is said and done. They're good people, and they would be safe here, secure. Perhaps that is what mother would want*, she thought.

*****

Sylvia was unaware of how much time had passed. It seemed just a blink, but sleep must have overtaken her. She looked about the room. Emlyn was sitting against the wall next to the window. Cord packed her pipe once again. Stella was in the same position as before, head in hands, sobbing. Strawberry and Bramble were asleep, propping each other up. She did not blame them and would not punish; besides, it looked like they had finished their task with the robes.

That was when it started, the heavy, fast breathing, as if she knew the finality of air and was trying to suck the ghost back in. Any possible handhold to keep from taking the last step off the invisible bridge.

By this point, everyone had gathered around, except Stella, who wailed like a specter in the background. Sylvia returned her hand to Camilla's sweating face in hope of comforting her transition through the door, to the lands beyond.

"Momma! Momma!" yelled Camilla.

"It's okay, let go, just let go! It's okay, you have many loved ones waiting for you there. Be with them." Sylvia squeezed her mother's hand.

Camilla started convulsing so much that Emlyn and Ms. Cord had to hold her down until finally she relaxed. Her breathing steadily dropped and dropped, then subsided until there was nothing at all.

The yellow ribbon trembled along with Sylvia's hand as she slowly reached up and used its surface to close Camilla's eyelids. The Morri did not grant her request. So much pain at the end of her mother's life. She wished Gods could have curses placed upon them. What did she do that they saw fit to punish the crossing? Sylvia let herself go then, producing a low, sorrowful wail, and placed her head on her mother's stomach.

If anyone was comforting her, it was not felt, as she shuffled back through her memories in a trancelike daze. They were not all perfect. What woman could say that they had a perfect relationship with their mother? Still, Camilla taught her so much and was always there when she needed her. Now everything her mother had been was no longer tangible. Snuffed out as if her flame existed precariously atop a wick. What Gods sought fit to take her? What creature from the underworld desired to torture her family so? The thread was cut, and it was too late to mend. So much was left unsaid.

* * * * *

The showing took place a week later. Camilla lay in the foyer, preserved on a bed of ice. White lilies surrounded the box, and beneath was a curtain of black lace. The face was so cold, so lifeless. No more platitudes, no grand entrances, no more advice. Camilla's curious nature, her knowledge and steadfast iron will never to be seen again.

Stella received permission to retire to the estate with all the rest of the retired Gwens. She did not want to spend an entire week near that box. Sylvia easily granted the request. Something noticeable had broken in the martial, who before leaving started wandering around the insula like an aimless apparition.

A who's who of high patrician society came through the showing room, paying their respects and offering their condolences. Camilla had kept up with these people, Sylvia had not, but they talked fondly of her mother just the same. If Emlyn did not whisper in her ear saying exactly who each person was, then she would have found herself lost on who these strangers were entering her island.

The immediate family came next. Julia and Bevin Rhydderch approached. Like every mourning woman, she wore her hair down and disheveled with no cosmetics and like every mourning man, Bevin wore a hood to cover his head. They both had donned the black robes sewn by the gilla of the house. As they came within a dozen feet, Julia had trouble holding back the tears, then as she stood before Sylvia and grasped her hands, she let them flow out.

"I am so sorry," she sobbed. "I've known Aunt Camilla all my life, and to think that she's gone . . . Oh, but you must be devastated—your brother, your father, now . . . I'm sorry, I'm making a fool of myself." Julia wiped at her eyes with a cloth handkerchief. "If there is anything you need, anything at all, do not hesitate."

Sylvia tried to smile but only managed a smirk. "I will, cousin."

The Rhydderch clan were bloodkin to Camilla. Julia was the first daughter of Camilla's older sister and had inherited the estates on the other side of Vernondin. She was closer in age to Camilla than to Sylvia, and she assumed that was the main culprit of why she never got to know her well. Upon reaching womanhood, if she had been a proper lady, then visiting bloodkin would have been a normal affair.

"Come up and see us and stay as long as you wish. I can't imagine wanting to stay here," said Bevin. Strawberry carried a tray, and Bevin grabbed a stemmed drink as she passed by. "I do not think you have seen the estate. Seeing how well you manage your own, I believe that you would enjoy our garden and small zoo inside."

Sylvia nodded. "Perhaps, Uncle. We'll see."

Toward midday, Sylvia felt numb and excused herself for the rest of the afternoon, citing a headache. No one seemed to blame her for retiring so early.

Some stayed overnight, and she had to make attempts to sideline their curiosity upon her well-being, as if they had to ask such an obvious thing. She achieved this by staying in her room and locking the door. Sitting on the bed, she did nothing but focus on her memories, and before she knew it, it was time for sleep.

In the hours leading up to the funeral, unable to steer clear of the family any longer, tradition and ritual called her to duty. The immediate family walked beside the carriage. Six wore the loose black robes, and they kept their heads down in reverence. The women wore their hair long and disheveled, and the men covered their heads either with a hood or a scarf. Their martials, all Gwen or their Olevanti kin, wore black as well and walked together a few paces behind the family. They stopped in front of the main gates leading into the catacombs. The gates were black iron and taller than two full grown men. The bars stood like ancient Macedonian spears piercing through a metal relief of the procession of death, showcasing the war Goddesses Bé Néit and the Morri. Among them walked the black hound. The martials lifted the pallet off the carriage and carried the linen-wrapped body between them. Two attendants came up to the gate. The hinges were well greased and barely made a sound as they opened inward. The mourners came through and stood at the threshold to the steadily descending steps.

They kept themselves shoulder to shoulder inside the entrance, not daring to fully enter. Candlelight bobbed and weaved as the flames ascended the stone stairs. Two priestesses in hooded black robes came into view with their lanterns held before them. Another priestess glided past the other two with a plain wooden bowl held firmly out in front of her. Red diamonds glittered and fell away as light cast upon the surface of the liquid within. They stopped their ascent two steps away from the line of bloodkin, who immediately prayed entry.

The one with the bowl raised a hand in greeting. "We of the druidi greet you on this day of sadness." She then placed the tips of her fingers in the bowl and marked bloody circles upon the foreheads of the bloodkin. "The Gods have seen fit to grant your entry."

Sylvia and the rest kept their eyes downcast as they all filed down the stairs one by one in order of closeness in blood to the deceased.

The two priestesses, who remained silent, took brass censors from their belts and lit the incense within so they could cleanse the path of any malicious spirits. Then they beckoned the family to follow in the wake of the heady stench.

The Chronister portion of the catacombs was temple-like in its enormity, covered in the house emblem, clean from any speck of dirt, and covered in white marble. It was enormous, but the architecture was simple, a rectangular room with five Roman columns in line down the middle. The niches where Sylvia's ancestors lay along with numerous Gwens were covered in heavy black marble slabs. The slabs contained names and dates. Many had blurbs about their life, or quotes. Most had squares of cobalt-blue glass above the words with etched depictions of the occupants in life, typically in profile. A few had blue marble busts instead, those were the more recent ones, and her mother and father were captured exact within the stone. Andreas and Camilla's slab was off its niche and propped sideways beside it.

The martials carried the body held between them over to the open niche and carefully placed her beside Andreas. The martials retreated to the corner. Sylvia went into the tomb, following behind the lead priestess. The priestess poked two fingers into the blood bowl, reached into the niche, and made a line across Camilla's forehead.

Sylvia still had the ribbon wrapped around her hand. She slowly undid the ribbon around and around. Memories from when her mother did this for her father surfaced, making her lip tremble. She placed the ribbon on top of her corpse and stepped back.

She fell to her knees and began her prayers. And as she said them, the priestess walked behind her and crumbled the ash into her hair. The blood bowl was placed before her. She gently dipped each hand into the blood. She got to her feet without touching anything, then stood to the side. Each family member came up and placed a favored item beside Camilla's body, then dipped their hands in the bowl and waited.

The slab was put back in place by the attendants, then secured. Sylvia put her hands against the cold slab and kept them there. "Goodbye mother."

Everyone had their turn. Whatever her estranged family prayed about, she paid no attention. Her part in the rituals were over and she just wanted to go home.

* * * * *

The hot water streamed from the porcelain bowl, quickly filling to the brim. Sylvia submerged her hands and watched as the half-dried blood flaked away into the pool.

"Mistress?"

"Ah, Tabby." She put her hand to her forehead. "I'm sorry. Please tell our guests that I am retiring for the remainder of the day. Tell Bramble to pack; he's going with Julia. Let the other gilla know that I require nothing of them until tomorrow morning. They can spend this free time in leisure. That goes for you as well."

She sat down at the end of the couch and relaxed into the silence. Beyond cleaning her hands, she had not bothered to shower, so her hair was still unkempt. Nor did she bother to change out of her mourning robe. What was the point? She stayed like this for hours, barely moving a finger.

A hard, impatient knock battered the door. It was lucky that she was sitting in a side room near the main entrance, or unlucky. She moaned, frustrated that someone would bother her so soon. Lamenting the fact that she dismissed the gilla and servants for the day, she sighed and forced herself up. She would bid courtesy, bid the well-wishers farewell, then return to her seclusion. A seclusion that seemed more important than ever.

CHAPTER TWENTY-THREE

She expected to see well-wishers with flowers and mourning gifts, but it was much worse. Ened stood before her, wearing a fancy dress in full black and with an irritating smile that made her want to give her a good smack across the face. Five enormous men with hard stony faces stood to the sides and behind her. Sylvia eyed all of them with contempt. She took a step back and gripped the door.

"Ened, you know you're not welcome here."

"Oh! that breaks my heart!" she mocked. "I hoped that my dear niece had just forgotten my invitation, since she has so much on her pretty little mind."

Sylvia brought a hard chill into her voice. "What are you doing here?"

"Simple, I am here to reclaim what is mine. You look confused. I'll explain it slowly so you can understand. Your father took my inheritance. My place in society! And now that he and your trup mother are dead—"

Sylvia interrupted. "You're not in the will, if that is what you're after! Now leave! Go back to whatever sewer you crawled out from before I call Emlyn." She tried slamming the door, but a meaty hand and a scuffed leather boot acted as a doorstop. Before she could scream, that huge hand clamped over her mouth, and just as quickly the man had her pinned against him. The next thing she knew, they were all inside, along with a folder being waved like a flag in front of her face.

"I have something you must simply see to believe."

Sylvia was pushed along back into the side room. Ened sat down first on the couch and tossed the folder on the coffee table.

"Have a seat and take a look. If you scream or refuse, then I have copies ready to send to certain journalists and members of patrician society. Don't be a fool."

The man pushed Sylvia down onto the opposite couch. She situated herself. Screaming came to mind, but with Emlyn being on the opposite end of the insula, she would not arrive in time. She gritted her teeth.

Noticing that Sylvia was making no attempt to escape, Ened nodded. "Good, you made the right choice."

Sylvia stared at her aunt, wondering what this could be about. At a glance the men looked dangerous; a few had scars on their faces. No doubt each and every one of them had seen more than a few fights, probably murdered one or two people as well.

She leaned in and tentatively slid the folder toward her. She sat back and flipped it open. Her eyes looked as if they were about to pop out of her head.

"Do you like them? I think that blonde of yours has a vocation, a natural talent for capturing the body."

Sylvia flipped through numerous pictures of her and Emlyn making love at different areas within the garden. Many of them showed her pleasing Emlyn, and they were all stamped with a time and date, giving the impression that what appeared in these photos happened regularly.

She gulped and spoke, slow but steadily. "So, I can deal with a little gossip. They gossip about you all the time you know."

Ened was a bit taken aback. "You will be shunned, not only by patrician society, but no one will want to work with you after this!"

Sylvia leaned to the side against the couch arm. "Yes, I spent many hours thinking about a situation such as this. Do you really think that anyone would turn down my vast sums simply because I like having intercourse with my martial? Why should I care about anything else? I do not involve myself in patrician society, and I have little regard for them." She tossed the folder back on the table. "If you do not have anything else to threaten me with, then please leave *my* home."

That irritating smile returned to Ened's face as she crossed her legs and sat back with unsettling confidence. "That Mira girl, I have her you know."

Sylvia squinted her eyes. "Why should I believe you?"

"Because two weeks ago, you and Emlyn drove into the country with that gilla in the back seat, but the girl did not come back with you. I did my own investigating after that, and I have her. And she is willing to tell me everything, like how you were trying to help her escape. Trying to pass her off as a free person. This is a serious crime. I'm sure you know that."

Sylvia's mouth twitched. If Mira said who she really was, then Emlyn, Cord, and herself would find their necks in a metaphorical rope.

Ened hissed. "Yes, it is true."

"You—you had people following us. That was you?"

Ened laughed. "Indeed I did!"

"Why . . . did you do that?"

"Let's just say that I owe some powerful people. In exchange, they get a quarter of the Chronister fortune. I get revenge from the so-called family who abandoned me and ruined my life!"

"You did that yourself! You did not need any help from us!"

Ened's upper lip twitched, muscles tensed, and she spoke through clenched teeth. "You will declare that, due to the death of your mother, you have become incompetent at handling your family's assets. You will name me the inheritor. You can stay here, of course, and eat my food. It would look bad at this time to throw you out on the street."

There was nothing Sylvia could do. It was obvious what this was, plain and simple blackmail. Ened had her against a boulder and ready to pounce like a leopard. But her aunt would not receive the satisfaction of gorging on her flesh, not if she could help it.

Sylvia glanced at each of the men again. They all looked hard and immovable, but if Emlyn could get the drop on them, she believed the martial could take them. The longer they were here, the bigger the possibility. She straightened her back.

"Could one of you fine gentlemen pour me a glass?" The two standing behind Ened looked at each other. "Over there, it is a drink cabinet. Open it, will you?"

She pointed to a piece of furniture sitting under the window, much like a ready table. It had two doors underneath and the top surface was white marble. One of the men went, bent down, and opened the doors. Inside were glasses and a decent array of liquor. He reached for one.

"No, not that one. Not that one either. Keep going."

"You're trying my patience, Sylvia."

"Am I, am I really? I think we could all use a drink. A woman forced her way into my house threatening my person, and I'm trying her patience? The tonic water will be fine. Take some for yourselves."

The man poured her a glass and set it down roughly on the table next to the couch, making the tonic splash up and over the rim. Sylvia paid no attention but was disappointed when the men did not partake of the liquor. She gulped the tonic down.

"I am not playing this game of yours, Ened, so I refuse your hideous proposal. Now take your thugs and get out of my house!"

Ened gave a disappointed nod, and before Sylvia realized what was happening, those huge hands closed on her mouth again. Another of the men rushed over. The hand left her face, but before she could scream, some sort of balled-up cloth in her mouth. Then brought out a length of cord and tied it around her head, keeping the cloth in place.

She was lifted and thrown over a broad shoulder. She tried to scream then and fight, but to no avail. Her punches on their backs meant nothing and were probably only annoying at best. When they got to the foyer, she was able to reach out and swat a vase over in hopes of creating noise, but Ened caught it mid-descent.

"Tie her hands."

They did so, and she was unable to give them much trouble after that.

Ened seemed to remember the house well and went straight to a side entrance facing Verndi Street where the auto would enter the insula. No one would walk by or notice. Sylvia hoped that they would turn the corner and come face-to-face with Emlyn, but that hope never blossomed.

A horse and covered carriage waited outside, and she was quickly shoved into it like one would toss a potato sack. Two of the men sat on each side, and Ened sat in front of her. The carriage lunged forward. The wheels clicked and clacked on the cobblestones.

Ened looked at her for a while with that smug, satisfied face, as if she had won some great prize while trying in vain to remain humble. Sylvia did not take her gaze away from her aunt. Fury permeated her eyes, and she hoped Ened could feel every bit of it.

Her aunt reached into a satchel sitting at her feet and pulled out a paper clipped to a wooden board, then flourished a pen and held it out for Sylvia. Recognition fluttered across Sylvia's face. It looked official, stamped with the national seal showing Dé Brigantia and Dé Ard with a wolf in front of them, standing vigilant.

The thug sitting next to her cut the bonds on her wrists. She flung her hand out, knocking the paper and its board to the floor before trying to grasp at Ened. But the two men grabbed her before making a connection to her aunt's jaw.

A nod and a victory smile was the only reaction Ened had. "If you're going to throw a tantrum then, gentlemen, do it at your leisure."

The men grinned hideously. One held her arms while the other stretched her out on the seat. To her horror, he started lifting the skirt of the mourning robe. His hand held both ankles while the other snaked up the right leg. She tried to will her body the ability to overpower them to get away but could only manage a squirm of protest. The fingers reached her undergarments and tore them away. Terror made her still, she watched as he took his hand away from her leg, wetted his lips and undid his belt. He brought it out, and Sylvia found she could break the petrification and squirmed again, but achieved the same pathetic results. The man let her ankles go, but before she could kick, he was between them. She did her best to scream through the gag.

"Hold. I think she has something to say. Do you have something to say?"

Sylvia nodded. The man behind her undid her gag and took the cloth out of her mouth. She sobbed out, "I'll sign! I'll sign!"

The one who had intended to rape her leaned back into the cushions with a disgruntled huff. She was allowed to sit up and take the pen and paper in hand.

She hesitated, so her attempted rapist grabbed her wrist and kept it there.

"Sign or I'll have him finish, then I will send those photos. And that criminal gilla girl that you saw fit to abandon, I'll use her against you. That could be enough to ascertain your incompetence by itself. Sign, and your reputation . . . and dignity will remain intact."

The pen wobbled, but she could not bring herself to sign. "No."

Ened's snarl was primal, as if she was about to rip Sylvia to shreds. "Sign it! Now!"

When Sylvia failed to respond to this, she nodded to the rapist. But before he could lay another hand on her, she signed. Ened forced her to sign the next three pages too. Her aunt knocked on the side of the carriage and handed the driver one of the copies.

Sylvia didn't see what happened with the rest of the papers, only heard one being rolled up and the satchel being rummaged through. She hung her head down in disbelief as her cheeks colored with the shame of what she had done. The carriage slowed and came to a stop. Ened opened the door and stepped down onto the cobblestones. They were once again on Verndi, in front of the side door.

"Keep her here . . . and have some fun."

The two men smiled with glee.

Sylvia screamed out, "You promised!"

A hand covered her mouth and kept her there as Ened closed the door.

* * * * *

The day went by rather slowly. The feeling of loss permeated everything. It was the same when their brothers and fathers died, all of nature seemed somber through the dour eyes of mourners. Emlyn was now the only martial in the insula, and she felt like an island in the middle of the sea.

There had been so much loss over the last ten years that the more she thought about it, the more it seemed that some God had indeed cursed them. One thing she knew was that sitting around in the old, closed-off section of the insula was doing no good. She had no clue that lunch was almost six hours ago. Now the clock was closing onto dinnertime, and the growling in her stomach disrupted her thoughts.

As she passed into the halls of the used part of the insula, the hairs on her skin stood up. Never ignoring such a thing, she knew something was wrong.

Emlyn made her way to the kitchen. But as she got near, the clink of utensils emanated from the main dining room, where light escaped from the edges of the closed door. As she glacially opened the door, Sylvia became visible sitting down at the head of the table, Camilla's spot. For a moment Emlyn wondered why her mistress was using the grand dining room when there was no one to entertain. Then she spotted the rest of them. Five sizable men in the way of height and muscle with the look of professionals. She placed her hands on her weapons, ready for any action they might take. Sudden movement was not on the table since her mistress's life seemed at stake. It might have been different if they had not seen her, but as it was, they were all staring her way and just as ready to attack. What truly surprised her, though, was a voice that rang out, one that was hard for her to forget.

"Please come in!"

Ened was cutting a rare steak on the plate. The knife scraping against the porcelain echoed throughout the room. She ate a piece, not caring about the bloody juices running down from the corner of her mouth. She laid the utensils down and wiped her lips with a napkin.

"Emlyn! How wonderful it is to see you all grown up! And I must say, you look formidable, the very picture of a female martial!"

Emlyn tightened her grip on the handle of her knife.

"Oh please, your mistress's life is in no danger, for truth, it is the opposite! I am making life much simpler for her! Please sit!"

Emlyn went toward Sylvia, who seemed still and tense like a spring. But she slowed through a sense of dark airs engulfing the mistress. The men kept a close eye on her as she kept walking steadily.

She pulled out the chair next to Sylvia. "Mistress?"

No response. As Emlyn reached her hand out, Sylvia recoiled, never raising her head. She had not even touched the full dinner sitting before her. Emlyn had a notion that Ened would be capable of a poisoning. So she could not blame her mistress for refusing to partake even though she looked deathly faint.

Sylvia spoke up in a whisper. "Be careful." Otherwise, she did not move.

"You have grown to be a fine gilla from what I hear." Ened ate a piece of steak and dabbed her mouth with the napkin again before continuing. "I'm glad you have accepted the station to which you belong. The last time I saw you, it seemed you'd have a hard time with such a thing. So eager to run away and have your adventures."

"You kidnapped me."

"Oh, I did no such thing! You wanted to go, and you came willingly. This place was, in a manner of speaking, suffocating you, if I remember your expression correctly. But get used to it you certainly did!"

Your childhood was based on a lie, perpetrated by this . . ." She waved her fork in the air. "So-called family."

Emlyn leaned on the table, knowing where this was going. "You threatened me."

"Only after you had a change of heart. You know, I received two years in the clink for that act of kindness."

"You should have stayed in the rot where you belong," said Emlyn.

Ened's face became cold, eyes stern and piercing. "Careful how you speak to me, gilla. I am free, and you will address me as appropriate to your station." After a moment of tense stillness, Ened asked, "Well?"

"Yes . . . Mistress." Emlyn had to force it out like a snake regurgitating its supper.

"Good, good." Seeming satisfied, Ened relaxed.

Emlyn sensed that the hated Chronister relative would not want to take the chance of asking for complete obedience.

"That hole in the wall you call a bedroom is no longer yours, nor will you stay within Sylvia's room. I have switched you to the blue master chamber in the east wing." This room was opulent with a king-sized bed, and as Ened said—blue.

"Are you satisfied with that?"

Emlyn nodded hesitantly.

"You and Sylvia may no longer be near each other without my permission. There will be no . . . cuddling up together."

Ened scowled in Sylvia's direction. "To touch a martial in such a way . . . it's disgusting! Why would you do such a thing, Sylvia?"

Sylvia made no move to respond.

"And you, Emlyn, is it not your job to . . . not only protect your mistress from threats, but also give her counsel? Why did you not advise her to use some other gilla? You both disgrace your family names, and I will not have it in this house!"

The irony at the end of that statement was not lost on Emlyn.

The dinner went by in silence. Only the utensils could be heard screeching as their tips hit the ceramics. Ened snapped her fingers, and a trembling and bruised Strawberry walked through the side door leading into the kitchen. She took the plates and silverware from the table, managing not to drop any of the items, until she heard Ened cough. If Strawberry had not spent so much time learning how to serve at a table, then she would have spilled the lot of it. She turned.

"What is this?" asked Ened, pointing a finger at a red wine stain next to where her plate had been. Ened had placed her fingers in the wineglass and flicked it on the delicate white lace of the tablecloth after the poor gilla had turned to leave.

Strawberry performed a shallow curtsey. "I-I'm sorry, Mistress."

"Yes, you will be sorry, but that will be for later. Now, take care of this." Tabby, whatever you do, refrain from attacking them.

Strawberry curtsied again, trying to keep her bottom lip from quivering. "Yes, Mistress," she blurted, then made an inelegant dash through the door.

As the servant door slammed closed, Ened exclaimed, "That is how you tame a gilla! Be severe with them, or they'll walk all over you!" Ened drummed her fingers on the table, eyeing them both, then stood. "I believe we have an understanding?"

Emlyn nodded slowly, while her mistress dug her nails into the wood of the chair.

* * * * *

The air in Sylvia's top-floor bedroom was heavy. The starkness of the space now seemed suffocating instead of comforting. Emlyn was pacing back and forth, lost deep within her thoughts. Sylvia gave her time, just watching and trying to suss out what the martial was thinking. It was all she could do; what was there to say really? They were damned. She would be treated as an idiot child, a ward with no right to herself, almost a gilla. What would happen to Emlyn, there was no telling.

After a while, Emlyn stopped, and they looked into each other's eyes. Sylvia felt almost locked within those amber rings. A mixture of love and fear bubbled up.

"Mistress, what did they do to you?"

Emlyn sat on the corner of the bed. She tried to touch her shoulder, but Sylvia jerked away and scooted back to the head of the frame.

"Never mind that," said Sylvia, quickly exhaling the words.

Emlyn held her hand in the air before placing it on top of the white bedsheet. "Why not refute the signature?"

"Mira is a registered gilla, a traitress, a criminal. I let her go. That would be a cyclopean mark against me. I might as well be crazy for doing such a thing. Then there is the fact that I signed my name three times." Sylvia abruptly cut herself off and swallowed, finding her mouth suddenly dry. "Tabby, whatever you do, refrain from attacking them."

"I can kill them all easily."

"You had to have seen as well as I, these are not simple thugs. They are hardened men trained to fight. Seeing how you had trouble with three assassins . . . They have the advantage over you in numbers, and as we speak Ened is hiring more men because of what you are and what you might do."

Emlyn pleaded, "Please, Mistress, let me make up for my lapse of duty."

"That was my fault, Tabby. I made myself vulnerable, and Ened took advantage. Do not blame yourself. I deserve the blame."

Emlyn's eyes went wide. "But your honor has been—"

"I told you to forget that!" said Sylvia, grimacing.

"Why? Why won't you try? And if you can't, then why won't you let *me* take the risk? It is what I was trained for."

Sylvia looked to her lap. "I've lost everyone I cared for. If I lost you too . . ." she trailed off.

Emlyn tried to touch her shoulder, and once again she found her mistress recoiling. With a heavy sigh, Emlyn stood up and walked to the door.

"Tabby?"

She stopped.

"If you have anything up your sleeve, keep in mind that it could become much worse for me. Do not give them an excuse. I will come up with a plan, trust me. Hold back your anger. Do as I say, okay?"

Chapter Twenty-Four

Being a recluse had its merits in Sylvia's eyes, but now that Ened had taken everything, it became a curse. No one would think her absence as strange, and oh how she wished it could have been different. She had to remind herself that these thoughts were only hindsight and ultimately a waste of time. Still, the hired thugs had her locked in this room most hours of the day at the will of her abominable aunt. It was easy to just lie on the bed and drift off into many different fanciful notions detailing what could have been.

Ened did indeed treat her as if she were a brain-dead child, and with her silence, she might as well be. Whenever the door clicked and swung open, those thugs would manhandle her, all the while comparing her to a dessert as she struggled and hurled insults back at them. What else could she do? She was never taught to fight—those lessons were for Emlyn. Compared to these men she was just a twig. They would bring her to dine with her aunt at the same time every evening. Ened was the definition of punctual. The men would not harm her beyond what Ened would allow, so she did not attempt any response to her aunt's insults about her, her family, and practically the entire world, all the imaginary enemies beyond the gate ready to swindle her out of everything she *earned*—a word Ened seemed to favor to an unhealthy degree. Sylvia only regurgitated the usual required responses—no, yes, as you say— just to placate the unbelievably cranky woman.

Thirty-seven days, twenty hours a day, this room, this damned room, was getting old. She closed the book on her lap. Tomorrow they would allow her in the library again for fresh reading material. She had finished the classics first. The one on her lap was the last of them, *The Bacchae*. In a morbid sense, she thought being rend asunder like in the book might improve her situation. Oblivion did not sound as awful as it once had.

A rap at the door made her drop the book. She caught her breath, then answered. She had not seen Strawberry except when the girl served dinner. The poor creature beyond the threshold held little resemblance to the one she had known. With puffy bags under her eyes, swelling bruises on her cheek, and hunched over in a posture that could only have resulted from a fear of retribution.

"Strawberry? What are you doing here? How did you get a key?"

"I-I picked it, Mistress," Strawberry said while timidly looking down the hall.

"You what?"

Strawberry produced a hairpin and what appeared to be a nail file.

"I see. I thought you were a pickpocket before you were apprehended?" said Sylvia.

"That was just for extra cash, my main line was burglary."

"Still full of surprises. So, what is the purpose of this?"

"To escape," whispered Strawberry.

"What is your proposal?

"I . . ." Strawberry thought for a moment. "I don't know, Mistress. It's just not right what she's doing."

Sylvia rubbed the bridge of her nose, but having come to a conclusion, she nodded. "Very well."

They made their way down the hall quietly, like a pair of creeping thieves. Strawberry led, signaling for her to follow when the way was clear. All was still besides the sound of their breathing. When they talked, it was only at a whisper.

"How is everyone?" Sylvia asked.

"Master Fagan left. Olier took his position but is tryin' to get him to come back."

"How does he view your treatment?"

Sylvia could sense that she girl was thinking about some terrible incident that must have occurred.

"Not well," she said forlornly before perking back up. "Ms. Cord is still here, at least she takes no guff. They leave her alone. Asks about ya often."

At the end of the hall was an archway, and beyond that they had to choose right or left. Sylvia crept to the left while Strawberry attempted to go right.

"Where ya going?" asked Strawberry.

"The blue room is in that direction. We need to take Emlyn with us."

Before she could move, a hand tightened around her forearm. "No, Mistress! She's not in the blue room anymore!"

"Then we must find her!" She made to go, but Strawberry held firm.

"Mistress Ened is terrified of her—she won't admit that, but she is. That's why Emlyn is under constant guard."

Sylvia sighed, feeling her heart drop. "We would be a wave crashing against mountains."

"Yes, yes that's it," exclaimed Strawberry. "Please, Mistress, follow me."

They soon came upon a false light cascading out from an open room. Strawberry froze.

"What is wrong?" asked Sylvia.

The girl's eyes were as wide as saucers, her chest beat hard, and beads of sweat revealed themselves on her forehead. "That's her room, Mistress Ened. She's awake, oh Gods, she's awake. We'll be caught for sure!"

"Settle down and be quiet. Stay here if you must."

Strawberry grabbed her arm, but this time Sylvia wrenched it away and gave her a sour look. "You were not afraid to unlock my door, so why are you so petrified now?"

Strawberry did not respond. Sylvia turned away, sacrificing a look around the doorframe. An ornate lamp lit up the room in a soft glow. The entirety of the area was dressed up in opulence. Brand new bedsheets the color of lilies, silk pillows, curtains threaded with gold worth a veritable fortune by itself. She looked to the left and found the light dancing across the cold faces of a rather impressive collection of porcelain dolls. Some had broken faces revealing empty recesses. She remembered these dolls from the attic, her father told her that they once belonged to Ened. He had caught her trying to play with them, then forbade her to play with the dolls as he closed the crate lid and locked it. Now she wished to finish breaking them just to see Ened's ire but reminded herself of the noise an action like that would create.

She turned to the nightstand, which carried the weight of the viny pewter-and-gold lamp. Underneath were two drawers. The top drawer was opened to its fullest extent. She looked to the bed and realized the sheets were not turned down. A thought flashed across her mind: this was too convenient. But curiosity won out. Ever so slowly she inched her way to the drawer, carefully placing each foot on the hardwood floor, hoping that no creak would spring up.

The contents were nothing much, numerous talismans, most of which held no clear meaning to her on their purpose. They were rather ghastly, rooster feet. Wrapped, painted red bones of small animals, blood vials, and little figurines of foreign, monstrous Gods. Then right there, displayed prominently, was a vial that stood out from the rest. She carefully brought it out and held it to the light. It was filled with dark bluish liquid. Her heartbeat pulsed in double time.

"Mistress."

Sylvia felt as if she jumped ten feet in the air. She sucked in her breath to keep from screaming.

She took a breath and whispered, "Do you have any idea what this could be?"

Strawberry took a close look. "If I'm not mistaken, a poison, called Sap's Lie."

A disturbing thought marched across Sylvia's mind. It pounded, louder and louder, like oxen stampeding down a hill. She knew a headache was coming.

"What are its symptoms?"

"I'm not sure, Mistress. I've never seen it work."

". . . Right." She palmed the vial. "I'm going back."

Strawberry had a look like a foreign speaker who was trying to understand Kymbrian speech.

"You go and head back to bed. Forget tonight." She put the vial back into its place.

"But, Mistress, we should leave. We really, really need to leave."

* * * * *

The next day, under guard, Sylvia was let into the library. Immediately she began her search looking carefully at each title. At midday she found a collection pertaining to poisons, these were a series of short, cheap books that laid out symptoms. Finally, in the last book, she found it. Sap's Little Lie, made from about a dozen herbs, most of which she had no idea of their purpose, but put together it was clear through the symptoms, and those symptoms were exactly what she feared. This was a poison that took its time to kill and produced bleeding blisters all over the body. Then slowly burnt out the brain with fever. Akin to the red sickness.

Her mind flipped a switch, and a pulsing red flooded her vision. She sat down like a fallen boulder on one of the leather chairs.

"You done yet?" said one of the thugs harshly.

"Yes, I have found my book."

Sylvia clenched her fist until her knuckles ached. No one else had caught the sickness. Her own aunt poisoned her mother. Why else would she have that vial? But why? How?

She schemed, considered consequences, laid plans. Emlyn was rarely seen. For Sylvia, the constant absence of her martial felt as if an arm had been cut off. The longing for her flooded in sometimes, causing her to bawl into the pillow. Was Emlyn being treated well? Was she moved to the estate? Gods, was she being bred to some luckless martial? The thought made her stomach churn and dive. It was unlikely, of course, but it sat on her mind nonetheless.

During her musings she realized that Strawberry would be the only possible conduit. There had to be a good way to communicate with her. A plan started to form. A plan that hinged on Strawberry's resourcefulness.

CHAPTER TWENTY-FIVE

The doorknob jiggled and clicked a few times like candy against teeth before turning in one final click. It slowly opened with a creak that rhymed well with the thudding in her chest. Beyond was a hall pierced by a beam of moonlight, illuminating the portraits of ghostly apparitions peering out from a dozen paintings. The length seemed to stretch. She shook her head.

Sylvia wondered how many times Strawberry used this skill since she had arrived here in the insula. She silently thanked the girl for taking what time she could to sneak to the bedroom and teach her the finer points of picking locks. She shoved the lock-picking tools into her pocket and stepped into the cold hallway.

There were no guards present as she went. It was decided that Strawberry would distract them. Sylvia hated to think what that meant. Ensnared by her sudden willingness no doubt. She shivered and promised that once she was rid of Ened, she would do her utmost to free the girl and set her up for the rest of her life.

A drawer screeched open. She froze and pressed herself against the wall. Her heart thumped like a hammer against stone. The noise was coming from a washroom on the other side of the wall that her back was now against. She slowly slid down, attempting to make herself small.

Waiting, closing her eyes, she dared not look around that corner. Whoever it was, their footsteps went into the adjacent hall and were headed her way. She remained perfectly still and prayed silently to all the Gods. Pleaded for help to keep from making one iota of noise. She wanted to run, to bolt; in what direction it did not matter. Her whole body wanted to move, but she forced her mind not to panic and continued to pray. Only when the footsteps clacked by her, oblivious to Sylvia hiding so compactly in the shadows, did she cease praying and let herself breathe again.

Her heart felt like it could blow at any moment, but she was safe for now. She kept to that spot, making sure to completely calm down before moving on.

She came out under one of the archways and into the garden. She could smell the coming rain. If they get stuck in the mud...it did not matter, it was far too late to turn back.

Auto battery charges hummed in the garage. The building used to be a stable, able to house two horses; but it was converted many years ago to shelter two autos. There in the open portal was Emlyn checking on the charges. Emlyn spotted her, smiled, and waved her over to quickly come out from the open garden. Sylvia stopped in her tracks. She opened her mouth to speak but found that she suddenly had nothing to say.

Realization came, this would be the last time . . . *The last time I will see her with that smile.* She managed to push herself forward.

"Strawberry delivered the note to you."

"Yes, Mistress. But one kept his post. I took care of him. He's resting, trussed up and gagged." She patted her weapons, "Took these bac from him."

It was obvious that Emlyn expected her to be jovial about that information, or at least to smile. Sylvia was in no mood to do either.

Emlyn's half grin fell. "Mistress, do you have a plan?"

"Is the auto ready?"

"Yes—"

"Then get yourself into the passenger's seat and we will worry about the rest later, hm?"

* * * * *

The auto sped past the city limits. The motor hummed in unnatural discordance to the foggy countryside. The rain had been strong, but thankfully brief, so their journey was not impeded too much.

The wheels suddenly turned off the main roads, splashing mud as the tires hit the damp back trails.

"Is this . . . part of your plan, Mistress?" Emlyn asked while raising an eyebrow in Sylvia's direction. But she gave no sign of hearing a single word. So Emlyn just faced forward and waited.

As Sylvia drove further into the absence of civilization, the darkness became a blanket blocking the outside world. The headlights acted as a carving knife, piercing through the dense fog. An illumination threatening to be devoured at any moment by an intangible monster. Waiting for the moment when they would step out of the auto before chomping them into little bits.

Emlyn looked over her shoulder out the rear window at an abysmal void exuding pure malice. She turned her head to look at Sylvia. Her mistress's fingers threatened to leave a permanent indentation on the leather steering wheel. Her face held a worrying look that stood in front of a consciousness that was no longer present.

No change protruded in that dire countenance lit by the sick yellow glow of the headlights. Emlyn felt a chill, an unnatural protrusion creeping up her spine that had nothing to do with the weather. It told her that something was wrong—very wrong. She wished to know what it was. Why did mistress insist on driving? Why were they so far away from the city house? From what she could tell, they were well within the borders of the Crown forest, about an hour and thirty minutes west of Londinium. At least it was somewhat *near* the country estate, but the knowledge of where she was did not keep a suffocating gray from clouding over her mind.

"Mistress?" She was paid no mind. "Mistress!"

As Sylvia rammed her foot against the brake pedal, the tires splayed mud in all directions. They lurched forward, but the seat straps kept them well secured. She turned her head to look at Emlyn, who saw disturbed, watering eyes. It froze her to the core.

"This is as good a place as any," said Sylvia through gritted teeth.

She pulled up the brake stick, then thrust open the door, launching herself off the leather seat without turning off the auto. She marched out to the extent where the headlights lit up the night. Her expensive leather boots slurped and sloshed into the mud.

Not looking back, she firmly planted herself there, gazing out into the blackness at nothing, and crossed her arms. She felt like hours had passed instead of minutes as the familiar incoming dread of loss threatened to overtake her.

The passenger side door shut, making Sylvia give a slight jump.

"Mistress, what are we doing here? It's not safe here."

"Tabby, come here, please."

Sylvia could hear Emlyn's boots slurping in and out of the mud coming ever closer like an abominable creature sucking meat from a bone. A creature she helped to create.

"Mistress, please. What if you fall? What if you catch a cold?"

"I do not care about dirty clothes and colds."

Who would care after what she discovered? Emlyn reached a hand out to lightly grasp the mistress's shoulder. "Mistress."

"Don't call me that! Don't call me Mistress!"

She jerked her shoulder from Emlyn's hand. "I've hated it ever since I was made to accept the dreadful title!"

Emlyn let her hand fall to her side. She did not understand what to do or say. There was only confusion.

Sylvia turned to her. Her face contorted like she was in a great deal of pain. "Emlyn, stay here."

Emlyn watched as her mistress trudged through the mud to the side of the auto. The further apart they became, the harder it was for her to remain silent.

"M-Mistress, why . . . why're you doing this?"

Sylvia stopped next to the front tire , but she did not turn to face her. She flexed her fingers.

"Please, what did I do? Did I anger you? Please, I beg for your reason! Whatever it was, let me earn forgiveness!" Emlyn pleaded in a flurry of desperate responses. It came from a deep place, and Sylvia's heart felt like it would drop to her bowels.

She turned. Not since the breaking had she seen such an outpouring from her . . . old friend. The rug was being pulled out from under her, so Emlyn had to know why. Sylvia leaned against the left headlight, blocking its beam, allowing Emlyn to see her silhouette.

"You would give your life to protect me from degradation. Would you not?"

"Of course, Mistress!"

"Please, Tabby. Don't call me that."

"Yes—" Emlyn swallowed hard, keeping back that ingrained response.

Sylvia stepped closer. "It's impossible to legally free you, and I'm sorry that your collar has no key . . . ugh." She ran a hand through her hair. "There's no point! I've no control! I need to confront her! But I have no idea what I'll say or do, but I do not want you to sacrifice yourself for me, Tabby! This is the only way I see that will guarantee that outcome!"

She stared into Emlyn's frantic, searching eyes.

"I don't want to be free!" pleaded Emlyn.

The words seemed to signal something deep within Sylvia, fracturing that pumping organ.

"Yes you do! You will run for the rest of your life, but it is better than this. Anything is better than this, and if there is anyone who can dodge and trap a hunter, then it is my Tabby!"

"I don't understand! Why will you not let me protect you?"

"They made you this way, and I . . . I went along with it. I helped kill my friend." Understanding did not flicker in Emlyn's eyes.

Sylvia started breathing heavily, flaring her nostrils. She resigned herself and knew that this could not be avoided, the thing she wanted to tell her all those years ago. The thing she could not put into words. Even now, she could not find them, but she sure as Lofn could express it in action. So she did what she had never done before. It was familiar, but this time it would be true. To Emlyn's astonishment, Sylvia was right in front of her. The thick mud did nothing to slow her down. She put her hands on the sides of Emlyn's face, then kissed her full on the lips.

The kiss lingered. Sylvia grasped the back of Emlyn's head, pulling her further into the embrace. She willed all her love, everything she felt towards her over the years into this kiss.

She did not care that Emlyn was not responding, not taking her in her arms like in so many of her fantasies. What did it matter now? And for that she was glad her fantasies had not become the truth. If they did, she might have never peeled herself away from Emlyn's still lips, from those shocked, confused eyes. She finished the kiss and promptly marched to the auto carefully to not slip on the well-tread mud. It was as good as any march of death, her own bridge to the final door.

"Mistress!"

Sylvia hid her eyes as she turned to the auto. In quick succession, she planted herself on the leather seat and slammed the door, sending an invading echo into the silence. Emlyn winced as if she were a little girl who had just been scolded.

Sylvia refused to look up out the windshield—oh no, she would not be able to stand it if she did. This needed to happen, and she was confident that just a glance at Tabby would erode her resolve.

Emlyn could not see her mistress with the headlights threatening to blind her. She stayed, always obedient no matter how far away. She reached up and touched her own lips, tasting the lingering raspberries of

Sylvia's lipstick along with the remnants of salty tears. *Mistress kissed me many times before, but that was lust, was it not? This was different, perhaps a farewell. Yes, a goodbye . . . abandoning me.*

She was being left there like a mangy dog, no longer wanted. Her teeth ground, brow furrowed, showing a small raging whirl of hate and despair sweeping up and over her. She wanted to dash ahead, force herself back into the car . . . *And what? What then, hurt my mistress? Maybe. Perhaps she deserves it as much as her aunt.*

Shock and surprise shot through her mind. Thinking that way seemed a sacrilege to everything she was taught, everything that was trained into her.

She started running after the auto, but it was backing away, faster and faster, being swallowed by the surrounding darkness, further and further every second. The ground was so muddy, too slippery. She fell and was able to turn just in time so as to not hit face first. Watery mud splashed up around her, washing the anger away and dirtying her clothes to a great degree, but she did not care. She just wanted to be near her mistress, to keep her safe, to know what she planned to do with without her.

Without me, she pondered. *She's leaving me here, just leaving me here as if I were some unwanted animal. Am I not useful, important?*

"Damn her, *damn* her! May the Morri rip her to shreds! And if they can't manage it, then may all the shades of the underworld and the black hound hunt you till your death!" Fear crept in for a moment, for she had thought of Ened at first, but the thought ended with an image of her mistress. And martials should never think that way.

She got to her knees and did not blink as the headlights disappeared completely. She stayed in that spot trying to will her mistress to come back, but to no avail. Lost in the shroud of night, visibility did not exist, only blindness. The feeling of the ground under her knees was the only thing that seemed to anchor her to this world. To keep her from floating into some nameless void. She could not stay here.

She had to move, had to have a destination. But where to go, where to start?

Not to the country estate. That is the first place catchers will search after the city insula. I'm a gilla. Should I not be caught? Mistress does not want me, so if they catch me, I can't go back to her . . . Do I really want to? Would I go to Ened, to another Chronister? Can't be sold on the block either . . . Then I would be a broodmare for martials . . . She shook her head. *I cannot do that. I just can't!*

She pumped the mud with her fist, making an angry, desperate indention. Her nails dug into her palm. Her heart pumped a fast, leaping rhythm.

I need to go back, help her, even if she does not want my help. It's . . . what I was born to do.

She flung herself back into the mud as if she were shot by an invisible bullet. It splashed up around her, covering her like a wet blanket.

"Born to do!" she shouted.

She placed a palm on her forehead and laughed maniacally. "Oh, you stupid fool! Idiot, they made you what you are, all of them, every single one! All built on one *little* lie!" She swallowed upon a realization. "But it's all I know."

Emlyn reached a hand out into the blackness, but she could not see her own flesh.

* * * * *

"What did you do with her!" screamed Ened.

Sylvia could feel the drops of spittle hitting her head, but she would not look up, in fear of losing herself to rage. A hope ran through her that the vein pulsing in this vile woman's forehead would burst, then she'd drop dead. She said nothing in response; in fact, she had said nothing since arriving back from her little sojourn with Emlyn.

The dinner table was awry. Broken plates, forks, spoons, knives, servers, and various food items littered the floor. When Ened threw a fit, by the Gods she threw it well. She had an expert hand at throwing pots—especially plates. Ened never chucked one at her, but she threatened again and again. But Sylvia never responded in the slightest. Only stared at the floor, barely containing the boiling pot in her mind. It swirled, gathering strength with each hurled barb.

Eventually Ened became too exhausted and ceased the tirade. She sat and leaned back into her dining chair while placing her fingertips on her forehead as if a sudden headache had overwhelmed her. Sylvia wished for the power to reach out an invisible hand and push the old crone over. Maybe she would crack the back of her skull.

"I wish you could understand how important it was for Emlyn to stay exactly where I placed her! You did it now, you stupid, idiotic girl!"

Sylvia looked up after what seemed like ages. Her neck cracked and became sore, but she did not look toward her aunt. It might not have been the best time, but holding back was no longer an option, impossible, even if she wanted to. The metaphorical pot was rattling the metaphorical lid.

"I found a vial in your room." She took a deep breath. "Did you kill my mother?"

Ened stopped rocking and slowly inched the front legs of the chair back to the floor while giving her niece a long, measured look. The edge of her mouth slithered up at a snail's gait.

". . . Yes."

Sylvia tensed. Her eyes went wide, and she trembled. "Why? How?"

"Why? You know why, idiot. As for how, well I suppose it matters little if you know; I used a certain high patrician who came into your life not long ago."

"Lucius?"

Her aunt produced that infuriating crooked smile that she remembered so well from her youth. Ened only used it when she had achieved something over someone else. One might call it a victory grin. She would not have needed it if she had gotten her life together, stipulated by Grandfather Augustus; instead the woman, from what Sylvia understood, went in the opposite direction.

How far Ened had her tendrils snaking around the underworld, she did not know, but her aunt owed somebody, and owed big.

The Chronister house was next to destitute four generations ago, a secret they tried their best to hide. But Augustus was a true visionary, seeing the coming flood of electricity before anyone else and investing what little they had into the new technology. All that man built, his son and granddaughter maintained. Now it was threatened once again, this time by one of their own. Connections that she thought would have been impossible, or downright silly, a few months ago seemed to come together.

Ened leaned back in her chair again and gave her another long look while reading those connections coming together in her niece's mind, never letting go of that grin. "Do you think those were some random bandits between here and the estate?"

Sylvia's eyes bulged, disbelieving that something like that would be admitted. "You killed Daddy, your brother?"

"Well, not directly, I just told some unscrupulous people where to go."

The grip on the carving knife tightened. Sylvia had sneaked it into her pocket during Ened's tirade. None of the thugs had seen it, thinking of her as cowed. The two thugs in the room paid more attention to their smokes than her.

Her hand shook as red overtook her vision. The thought of betraying her ancestors by spilling family blood passed her mind. *Losing my virtue would have been betraying them, signing the papers too; so what does it matter if I do it again?* She breathed out long and slow. *Why am I worried about this when Ened spilled family blood? My ancestors, my mother and father would applaud revenge. I'd be doing the Morri's work.*

Ened kept talking, but Sylvia did not hear. Out of the corner of her eye, she stared down at her pocket. All the world seemed to be on the outside. Only this moment existed—herself, her hand, the pocket, and the knife.

A bubble in her mind's eye burst. The scraping of her chair against the marble floor, followed by shouts that, to Sylvia, might as well have been in a different language.

None of the thugs were fast enough. They could not stop her as she jumped at Ened, making them both fall back in the chair and hit the floor with a resounding thud. The shock in Ened's face only subsided when she let out a scream as the carving knife found its way in the side of her stomach. Then another burst of sharp, hot pain no more than two inches away from the previous wound.

By then, the thugs were able to grab Sylvia and pull her back, but as they did, she slashed wildly. The blade laid a deep trail down Ened's face, all the way to the chin. Blood splayed out, gushing like a squeezed cherry, a red flower in immediate bloom.

Sylvia's hand was caught, and the knife wrenched from her grasp. She screamed in rage and spat at Ened. "Exactly what you deserve!"

More thugs rushed in, and one stepped in front of her and punched her squarely in the jaw. The world swirled with amazing speed, and the lights faded to blackness before the entirety of her retreated into nothing.

Chapter Twenty-Six

Emlyn made very little headway. The darkness was all encompassing, not only with the starless night, but her mind seemed to be surrounded by dark thoughts, dark moods, and old nightmares. The mud inside and out was thick, keeping her frozen in place for hours until the first light of a deep orange dawn when she could finally see a way out. Carefully she moved away from the heavily muddied back trails and into the thick line of trees looking like some drawn-out monster stepping in long strides. It was a cold morning, and the mud caked all over her body acted as a conduit. She could not keep from shivering.

Her mind ran like an infuriating squeaky wheel trying to make sense of it all over and over again. Everything was built on a lie. But it had meant something. It led to something important. Something old, perhaps even timeless. Tradition was important. It was what made her feel special, that she was a part of this long bloodline reaching all the way back to the great Lucanis, the founder of Kymbri. She could remember the names of every ancestor even from the time before they were martials. But to carry on such a legacy . . . she was happy to do so . . . or so she thought.

After her breaking, who she was as a child seemed silly at best. This was propped up by her family, by the Chronisters, and everyone else in this damnable place. Just a martial hiding beneath the veneer of a free child. But the murder case . . . hunting down Batt, seeing what he had become, it frightened her. He was a decaying mirror held up in all its sickening glory. He was what she could become. What if she lost her mistress in the same way? Look what happened to Stella, such a shell after Camilla died, she no longer had a purpose. Goss and Grandmother Cali revealed themselves to have no inner light, no soul that belonged to them. It left with the death of their owners. Did she truly want to be like them? Was that what it was all leading up to?

Emlyn thought about these things as she traversed the woods back toward Londinium. What could she do but what she was trained for? Find her, protect her from . . . Eneddia, and whatever machinations she had concocted against her mistress.

She washed her clothing and herself in a stream. Hunted game using her revolver. Stuck to the woods until she reached the outskirts of the city, where she stole a thick ratty brown blanket from a wash line and draped it over herself like a hooded cloak. She hoped to remain inconspicuous. In the least it seemed the best way at hand to hide her collar.

Finding Finicus was top priority. He and his gang would know the best places to hide while she did her bloody work. At least until it was done, then she could give up, and gilla affairs could execute her in any way they deemed fit. It did not matter as long as she accomplished the goal.

Emlyn pretended to be a crippled beggar with a bum leg to gain a few fennis or be ignored entirely. The fact that her face was full of dirt and grime, that her clothes were torn and frayed, added to the effect.

She spent days wallowing in her own stink, in the filth of the streets, always asking softly for Finicus. Asking too much or sounding demanding might have tipped someone's hat that she was a runaway. If they asked why, then she'd say she had a job for him, and from there they would either nod solemnly or laugh, seeing only a beggar with nothing to offer.

* * * * *

"That's a good way ta get caught, gilla lady. More folks than I are interested in who ya are."

He stood imperious, looking down at her with his hands on his hips and a rueful smile. Emlyn had just sat down in a corner of one of the alleyways to take a bite of a half-eaten meat pie, along with whatever insects had managed to worm their way in, but stopped before it reached her lips and tossed it to the ground.

She moved the makeshift hood back and looked up at him. He had a new flat cap on in yellow plaid resting uneven on his scalp. The clothes he wore were grimy but new; they had no holes or patches yet. But what struck her upon closer inspection was the absence of his collar.

Finicus's eyes went wide. He remembered.

Emlyn had felt a kinship toward the boy. When she had invited him into the insula, she thought it was just the sorrow at his plight and the rhythm of his candor. But Emlyn admired him in a way. It did not occur to her why that might be until now, he was another mirror representing a truth. She gulped at the realization.

"Emlyn!" He breathed it out low. "Oh Gods." His head swerved to look at the street, making sure no one was watching.

"If Colmane caught me with ya . . . or any catcher."

"Do you plan to turn me in?"

"If I knew what was best for me I would!"

"But you will not." Emlyn could not help but grin.

"No . . ." He rubbed his chin in thought. "Do ya know what happened?"

She shook her head.

"Best to show ya. Might sound a ruse comin' from me."

He led her to a newsboy. Finicus snuck up in the boy's blind spot and swiped the paper on top of the stack sitting to the right of the boy's feet. It happened so fast that it looked like he was just walking by like anyone else. He kept looking around the entire time until he made it back to the alley.

"Page two."

After handing it to her, she opened it and sat, resting her back against the wall. Right there in bold was the headline: "Eneddia Chronister Speaks: Exposing Last Week's Surprising Incident!"

It was an interview with the hated shrew. "Eneddia Chronister was in better spirits after being slashed across the face by her niece, Sylvia Chronister." Emlyn looked over the paper at Finicus in shock. Her mistress did such a thing? It seemed an unreal notion.

She read on, finding out that Sylvia was being held under heavy guard. "Heavy guard! My Mistress of all people!"

Reading about the extensive injuries, she silently cheered for such decimation upon Ened's person. She folded the paper and looked at Finicus with a determined but pleading gaze.

"You must help me, Fini."

"Ya kidding me? If Colmane finds ya with me, then I'm done for! Utterly done for!"

"Fini . . . please."

He turned his head to look at the crowded street and bit his lip. Of course, no one was paying attention, Fini was rather paranoid with her around. But he needed that moment to consider without being influenced by her sorry state.

"Okay, but you'll have to be careful. More careful than you've been. Stop asking questions of strangers and stay out of view, I mean it! Out of sight, out of mind! If ya need somethin' I'll get it. Understand?"

Emlyn nodded.

"So stay where I put ya!"

"Help me find where my Mistress is being held."

"No! No." He kept his voice low but stern. "Helping you commit suicide isn't on the schedule! I'm gonna get ya cleaned up, then I'm getting ya out of here! This was the stupidest place to return to. I thought you were smarter than that!"

Emlyn let him berate her as she followed down the twisting alleyways. "No good martials, obsessed gilla drones! Freck cumbers!"

She knew that each and every insult was right, so why bother denying his assertations?

There was a faucet poking out from behind a shop. Easily accessible within the alley. Emlyn disrobed and washed her clothing as best she could without soap. Then washed herself quickly, trying to ignore the chill of the ice-cold water before the owner of the shop, who heard the water running through the pipes, came out brandishing a baton and yelling, "Get out of here! I'm gonna call gilla affairs if you don't stop using my water!"

Emlyn grabbed her clothes and gun belt. Finicus grasped her wrist and led her quickly down the twisting alleyways to who knows where. They stopped so he could catch his breath.

"How . . ." Emlyn made a gesture toward her neck. "How did you get your collar removed?"

He sat on the ground and put his back against the old brick wall. "I'll take ya to him tomorrow. I need ta earn today."

Fini took her to the place where he usually bedded down. "Now stay here, right? I'll be back at the last chime." Meaning he would be gone until midnight.

There was not much to it. It was a tiny little alcove hidden by a few wooden crates. It was deep, a narrow stream of water came out of a pipe, flowing into a small round drain leading into the sewers at the back. Surprisingly, it was cleaner than expected. He must have stayed there regularly and was probably the safest place he could think of.

The hours passed by excruciatingly slow. Emlyn had nothing to put her attention to except her thoughts. She reviewed everything that happened up to this point and nothing made sense, not in the slightest, but it had to do with Ened. A darkness washed over her. The thoughts of killing Ened rolled around her skull like bees in their hive. She didn't like to kill, and before this she could at least justify her killings because they had put her in danger. And Batt, well, he needed to be put down, though thinking about it now snagged like a hook ripping through her brain. He was a reflection, of course, one that was difficult to look at. A dark, insane reflection that she shot in the head. But Ened . . . she deserved the Morri for betraying blood. But was that Emlyn's to give? To shoot her cold without any justification. What did she do? Treat the mistress badly? This sobered her thoughts for a few moments, but the bees kept buzzing, and her anger grew to a boil, overwhelming any rationality.

Emlyn found herself on Verndi Street, a street that was little better than an alley. But it was the back entrance for the autos coming in and out of the Chronister insula and an easy way to get in if she picked her moment. There was a true alley down one side where the insula came up against another building, but there were no entrances and the windows there were covered by bars. It was the perfect place to hide and wait for an opportunity. So she crept into the darkness of the alley, put her back against the wall and waited, poking her head out every so often to check for movement.

It was well into the night when a door next to the auto entrance opened and revealed a feminine cloaked figure followed by two guards and one very large foreigner just as shadowy in the dimly lit street. That was Ened. Emlyn knew by the way the figure walked. She pressed herself against the wall as they passed by the alley. Her eyes narrowed, intent on what had to be done. Then she slowly drew out her knife and revolver and stepped one foot out when a hand clasped her shoulder. She spun around, slashing the air. Her revolver cocked, and its barrel was pointed at the head of Finicus, whose blood drained from every inch of his face.

He gulped. "Emlyn . . . don't," he whispered. "They'll know it was you."

She lowered the gun. "I have to."

"They'll kill you."

"My life does not matter. I need to make up for my lapse of duty." She turned to continue. She could still catch up. But he grabbed her arm. She could have wrenched away, but instead she stayed still.

"Pish! Duty, she abandoned ya! Besides, ya think your mistress would rather have Ened dead than see you alive an' well?"

No, Sylvia would not want her involved in this, did not want to see her hurt by Ened's machinations. The mistress knew Emlyn would try to protect her in any way she could, and that was why she made the choice to abandon her.

Emlyn looked into aged eyes, and something cracked behind her own.

"Think on it. You're a bird whose cage has been opened, yet you're too 'fraid to leave. The outside world's a scary place, and that cage offered you safety, I get it. But you were free before being put inside. Sure, maybe it was a lie, but it was there. Did ya not feel it, even once?"

He stared into her eyes as she stood like a petrified tree as if some God was passing judgment on her.

"Ya said that ya had no goal to be anything. I thought it a load of bunk. So I'll ask differently; if you were always free, never put into the collar, what would ya have done? What would your . . . um, ambitions have been? Is somethin' ta think on, right?"

When she didn't respond, he gestured at her to follow, then held out his hand to her. "C'mon, let's get out of here."

Emlyn could only nod before holstering her revolver and followed the kid on a long silent walk back to his alcove where they settled themselves in for the night without a word.

* * * * *

It was far past midnight, yet Emlyn could not sleep, not because the blanket she had stolen made a poor pillow, no, she was giving his question her full attention. Mulling it over again and again, tumbling it about to reveal a polished stone of veracity. She loved those adventure books as a child, longed to see far away lands and always felt that the insula was too small.

"I would have gone to foreign lands," she sputtered out.

"What?" asked Finicus, fully awake.

"Not just one destination but many. Sounded nice when I was young. That's what I would have done if I was given the chance."

He smacked his lips. "Nothin's stopping ya now. You're free. Flee. Enjoy it."

"I can't forget her though."

He sighed, and she could hear him sit up.

"Can't imagine what ya must feel for her, as close as ya are. She was a good woman, maybe a good mistress. Sure ya thought she was the best. Cac! If I didn't care so much fer my freedom, I'd have taken her offer. But she's a jailbird now and will prolly be for years. So ya have to put her out your mind."

Forgetting about her seemed such a silly notion. How could she when her entire life revolved around Sylvia?

"Get some sleep. I can hear your gears grindin' from here."

For the next few hours, Emlyn slept only lightly. Her mind kept running, and she fought with herself to not get up, march back to the insula, and slit Ened's throat while she slept. But that would be the notion of a cumber. Even if she made it back out, her chances of survival would be miniscule. Leaving was the only option. To go as far away as she could to see how much could be forgotten.

*****

"This guy, he's a stoic. Doesn't like the collar institution. He'll set ya up! Hates Colmane."

Finicus brought her to the back door of a mechanic. It was still early in the morning, and the sign out front said that the shop was closed, but Fini went around back and knocked on a white door with red flowers painted on its border.

The door swung back, ringing a little bell somewhere on the inside, and revealed a tall, broad dark-haired man wearing an apron stained in oils and grease. If he was an adherent to the stoic philosophy, then his mannerisms told the same story: stout, impassive, serious, like how Emlyn was supposed to act within her capacity as a martial.

"Finicus. What are you doing back here? Did Colmane send you?" His voice had a deep gruffy baritone and sounded like they were wasting his time.

"No, I came by my own accord, Mr. Henris."

Henris did not seem amused. "I thought I made it clear that I did not want to see Colmane, or *you*, ever again."

"As glass, Mr. Henris! But I know how ya feel about gillahood, an', well . . ." He pumped a thumb over his shoulder. "This is Emlyn."

She pulled back her makeshift hood, revealing her head, neck, and collar. Henris's face went white with shock, quickly replaced by rage. He stepped out and shut the door behind him.

"What are you doing bringing a runaway to my door?"

"Her collar needs a break."

"Boy, have you lost all of your marbles?"

"You helped *me*, Mr. Henris!" pleaded Finicus.

"That was entirely different! You work with gilla affairs, Colmane gave the nod! Is she working with you two?"

Finicus just looked to the ground and kicked a stone lying on the pathway.

"I thought not," said Henris, looking down at Fini with a Sneer.

"Please . . . sir. I must get out of the city," interjected Emlyn.

He looked at her and seemed genuinely sorry. "If I take that thing off your neck and you are caught, they will interrogate you, torture you to find out who removed your collar. You would give them my name, and I'd lose my business. Understand me? I've got a wife and newborn to think of."

He studied her before his brow furrowed with worry. "Okay, I cannot remove your collar, but you look like you can handle yourself." He tapped his chin, considering. "There is a merchant ship leaving early tomorrow. They will hire you on the spot. Get as far away as you can from this place."

He bade them to wait while he went back inside. A few minutes later he came back out with a bundle of folded clothing in his hands and placed the items in Emlyn's arms, then placed one full kint on top.

"You look dreadful. Go grab yourself something to eat."

* * * * *

The white shirt with the plain brown jacket were loose and looked a bit odd as the breeze hit the folds. As Emlyn walked onto the dock, the smell of the ocean salt hit like a bullet. Leaving the dark alley into the blinding sun made her stop for a moment and squint.

Emlyn shrugged, adjusting the strap of her duffel bag, and couldn't help but feel awkward. She spent most of the night awake, trying to get her voice to sound as masculine as possible, and practiced how to move and respond to people as a man would. While women on ships were not unheard of, it was always as a passenger or guest . . . or as cargo. They did not like working next to a woman, though, and considered doing so bad luck.

Finicus left her at the docks, or at least he pretended to. But she could sense in his voice that he would keep watching from the shadows until the moment she walked onto that boat and disappeared into the horizon.

Emlyn stepped forward and spotted a grouping of birds flying out across the channel, over a recruiting table partially blocking the gangway to the steamship. An older man with a snow-white beard sat behind it watching her cautiously approach. He extended his hand, gesturing for to her to come forward.

"C'mon, lad, no need to be shy."

Emlyn stepped up to the table and let the duffle bag hit the ground in front of her. The old man looked up to study her face. His bushy moustache jutted out from right under his nose and twitched side to side like a bell ringer.

"Name? Aedan, huh?" He wrote the name in a leather-bound book. "No last name? That's fine. What are ya runnin' from—wait, I don't want to know. We'll be goin' round the medi, so we're bound to run into danger. Pays poorly for a mercantile. If ya don't mind that, then just sign at the bottom here." He pointed to a spot at the end of the paper for a signature. Emlyn had a flowery script and had to consciously change how she would put her name down. With the pen in her hand, she hesitated.

"An X is fine, son, just need ya to put hand to it."

"I can, just not well."

"Ya look a tough buck!" The voice came from behind, startling her.

She swerved her head. Her gaze rested upon a man, muscled, sturdy, and slightly taller than herself. He had brown hair that curled at the ears and eyes the color of the ocean below, along with a roguish grin that seemed to grow ear to ear.

The man taking the signature brightened up. His old eyes seemed to lift, followed by a smile. "Bryn! Glad you decided to come back!"

Bryn shrugged. "Only thing I'm good at. This a newbie?"

The older man nodded. "Yeah, green as grass by the looks of him."

Bryn clasped her on the shoulder. She looked at the hand, wondering if she should brush it away, and decided that it would be in her best interest not to.

"Follow my lead, newbie. I'll show ya the ropes."

CHAPTER TWENTY-SEVEN

The heavy chain connected to her cuffs rattled and jingled with each step. She viewed it as entirely unnecessary, seeing how there was no intention of escaping, and anyone would think the cuffs were a bit much on her small frame. At least they did not deem it necessary to shackle her ankles.

Two men kept her between them. The one in front was an older gentleman with a pepper beard, quick to trust, a very salt-of-the-earth type. The other was younger with a dour countenance, more high-strung and slow to trust. They had been guarding her for two months now, switching shifts. Or sometimes sharing shifts when someone important stopped by like a reporter, or Julia, who promised to house her after she served her sentence. Five to ten years max in a cushy jail for high patricians.

The doors to the courtroom opened with barely a creak. The hinges were well oiled, everything seemed well oiled. The floors shone, and the numerous golden emblems of two fighting wolves were almost blinding in their polished glory. At the other end of the walkway, a podium stood like a monolith, accessible by the short flight of stairs behind it. Behind the podium were five chairs for various druidi keepers well versed in the country's laws. There were a few reporters sitting in simple folding chairs around the edge of the room, furiously writing in their notepads. This room was thankfully closed to the public. The reporters were enough. It would have been embarrassing to be mocked by a crowd.

They came to the middle of the room, about ten paces before the podium. There were no tables to stand behind. This was open and shut, so there was no need for any defense.

The older guard, named Fruge, stepped in front of her. "Lift your hands."

She did so, chains rattling.

"About that job . . ." He smiled warmly.

Sylvia smirked. "Yes, it's still yours after all this is over."

It had taken Fruge a long time to spill what was on his mind. He wanted to take his family out of the city, and she was more than happy to facilitate this by getting in touch with her uncle.

The key clicked in the lock. "Good."

He took the cuffs off and placed both the chain and cuffs in the hands of a male gilla who quickly grabbed them and ran back to his spot in the corner. Fruge was a good man, easy to talk to, easy to know. His younger friend, Septon, had more walls than all of Londinium, but nothing worked better for tearing down walls than excruciating boredom. He eventually regaled her with tales of his seven-year-old son's adventures in Iria park, and she eagerly listened. He was surprised she was genuinely interested in his life. It helped to change his opinions on patricians, at least in her case.

The cell they kept her in was isolated, with a small one foot by one foot window near the ceiling. The only other way to see out were the iron bars of the door. Her only contact with nature was the one hour every other day alone with her guard in the walled courtyard. Over a month of incarceration seemed such a long time to wait for a trial, but it was a high-profile case afterall.

Fruge handed her a newspaper a few days after being put in the cell, and on the second page, the headline called the incident: a scandal. Of course, they painted her aunt as the true victim with Ened claiming that her niece was such a nice but disturbed girl, that she was just so bewildered why her younger brother's darling daughter jumped up and attacked her with a knife with such brutal abandon. Her aunt speculated on her niece's slide into insanity after the death of her brother, father, and mother, and her constant reclusiveness. She said that Sylvia should not be in a prison but in a mental house where she could truly get some help. Sylvia was at least glad that her liaisons with Emlyn were not present in this distortion.

Fruge shared as much information as he could about how Ened had sunk her claws into patrician society, holding lavish, widely talked about parties for charities, even the Teyrn came to one. Of course, she was trying to set herself up as a philanthropic aristocrat who would remind everyone just how much she resembled Augustus Chronister in generosity—only generosity, not his business savvy. Sylvia wondered how anyone could take her aunt seriously. But she knew that money spoke louder than anything else.

Ened accepted responsibility for all Chronister assets. She would control everything not belonging to extended family: the electric contracts, the house, the country estate, and gilla. Hearing this boiled her blood, still did. But she spent long hours deliberating with herself: This was a new opportunity. She could leave it all behind, say goodbye to the family legacy. And the more she thought on it, the more appealing the idea became. Now she could not wait to get this over with and move on to a new, simpler life.

She refrained from telling her side of the story. There was no proof, so why bother? They would give her five to ten in a very cushy cell, then she would be out, free to go to her uncle or to Julia and gather capital to travel overseas and establish a small homestead somewhere.

The door to the side of the podium opened, and out walked the arbiter, who could only be described as overly stretched. He wore a stylish long cream-colored vest, but an outdated stark white shirt underneath that became puffy toward the cuffs. He climbed the stairs to his podium as five white-robed keepers filed in holding their gigantic books and then sat in the chairs that were set up behind him. They rested their tomes on their laps almost as one.

The arbiter flipped through pages from a book resting on the podium. He peered down at her like a giant who just noticed an ant. He adjusted his glasses.

"Sylvia Chronister!" His voice resounded with a smooth baritone. "Miss Chronister. You are accused of attempted murder upon a family member, a one . . ." He flipped a page. "Miss Eneddia Chronister. The records say that . . ."

He adjusted his reading glasses again as he looked at another paper held up in his hand and began to read. "You were conversing with your aunt during dinner when you grabbed a knife, lunged yourself at her, and stabbed her twice in the stomach before being pulled away by her bodyguards. Do you deny any of this?"

The judge was so high up that it was straining her neck to look at him. "No, sir, I do not deny any of it."

He peered over his rounded silver glasses at her. "Do you have anything to say for yourself?"

She cleared her throat and held herself in all that dignity could afford while wearing a simple gray, floor-length dress. "I have no excuse for what I did. However, I plead your judgment be lenient. That you consider all I have contributed to our nation over the years."

The judge took his glasses off and quickly cleaned them with a cloth. Sylvia thought he could use a stronger pair instead of a cleaning.

"Very well. I will personally sacrifice so that the Morri will not hound you for your ill-intent against blood."

Sylvia nodded. That would not help her in the least. As much as she hated Ened, the Morri made no distinction. She was blood, and that was all that mattered. They would punish, especially when you fail to carry out their will. She was sure the Morri would curse her in some way or another, maybe, who knows. The Gods were fickle, after all.

"Sylvia Chronister, I hereby sentence you to five years at Filci."

Sylvia knew the sentence would be light, but she was expecting seven to ten years. She sighed in relief. Getting this over quickly was exactly what she wanted.

Septon and Fruge got close to her, ready to escort her out. The arbiter was about to close his book, signaling an official end to the case, when the doors opened. A young gilla ran in, and all eyes followed him as he hurried to the keeper on the far left.

"Catch your breath, then tell me why you have seen fit to disturb these proceedings."

The gilla took a moment to do just that before whispering in his master's ear and handing him a note. Sylvia watched the man's eyes go wide and wondered what could be important enough to storm into the middle of a hearing. He looked at her in a way that brought a cold chill to the back of her neck. Then he turned to the colleague next to him and started whispering. His colleague strained a bit to open the heavy, leather-bound book on his lap and flipped a few dozen pages.

The arbiter became impatient. "Instead of taking up this court's time, how about you come up here and tell me what the problem is?"

The keeper climbed the stairs to the arbiter and whispered in his ear. The arbiter opened the note and shot up an eyebrow. Then rubbed his eyes aggressively with his thumb and index finger before taking another look at what was written there.

"We require a recess. Gentlemen." He pointed at Fruge and Septon. "Please bring Miss Chronister to my office."

* * * * *

His office looked more like a library and felt just as stuffy. Sylvia was seated in a red-cushioned reading chair nestled within the corner. Her two guards stood on each side of her. Arbiter Dial entered the room looking agitated. He sat behind his mahogany desk and did not look up at them.

"Listen, Arbiter, me an' Septon, we're past time. We both have families to get home to."

"I am well aware, gentlemen. Do not fret, you'll be paid for your time. And I have a feeling you will want to stay for this."

Sylvia spoke up. "Excuse me, Arbiter Dial, we *have* been waiting a long time. If it is not too inconvenient or against court proceedings, may I know what this is about?"

He gave her a long considered look.

"Cac! Might as well! You're still a patrician until, well, you know." He whirled a finger in the air in the shape of a circle.

"No, I am afraid I do not know. Please enlighten me."

He reached under his desk and brought out a cordial in a crystal decanter, then brought out two glasses and started pouring. "This will most likely be your last hours of freedom, so have a drink."

"What do you mean, I'm going to jail."

Arbiter Dial shook his head and spoke reservedly. "I'm afraid not. It's gillary. You will legally become a gilla."

The shock emanated from everyone in the corner. Fruge ran his fingers through his peppered hair and put a steel grip on the brim of the round hat that he held down at his side.

"Brigantia's name!" Fruge muttered in his surprise.

Septon stared at her like she had disappeared before his eyes.

Her awareness seemed to shrink, and for a moment she was completely unaware of the reality around her.

"W-What?" She sat forward in disbelief, forearms resting on her thighs. "Is this some sort of joke?"

He swirled the liquor in his glass and stared into the ripples. "Seems there is a very old law that allows the victim of attempted murder to reduce the assailant to gillary—as long as bodily harm had been committed. I'm having my assistant bring the paperwork. I am sorry. In lieu of this unique situation, and to preserve your dignity until you are collared, I have decided to give the official ruling in private."

Sylvia blinked a few times, trying to process this information.

"How could a law like that still be on the books, and who would evoke such a thing?"

"We are not a land of a few simple laws. Any number can fall through the cracks and be forgotten about."

"Who, Arbiter?"

He scrunched up his face in disgust, "Your aunt."

She squeezed her hands into a fist. "It . . . It's an archaic law, surely I will be able to fight this in the high court?"

"Oh, I believe you could have, and won."

"Could have? Speak plainly." She demanded.

He poured another glass of the amber cordial for himself and drank it in one gulp. "I do not believe that any high patrician should be made a gilla. It goes against our values. And blood owning blood . . . that is sick." He sneered at the thought. "So while you waited, I made a few calls, and . . . well, I'm sorry, Miss Chronister, but even with my influence, no defender on my list is willing to work with you."

Sylvia stood up, feeling more than a little high-strung. "Please, allow *me* to make a few calls."

"Be my guest." He nodded toward the phone on the corner of his desk.

She called every defender who worked with the family in the past, and every single one of them hung up on her. She slammed the phone back on its receiver and breathed like she was on the verge of losing that ability.

"I am very sorry," said Arbiter Dial.

"She's a murderer. She killed my father and mother, possibly my brother. Now she wants to make me her gilla."

The arbiter's eyes shot up. "What? Can you prove that? Do you have evidence? If you have any, then we can reverse this ruling!"

"No, no, I've nothing except her own confession before I stabbed her!"

He sighed and let out a slight frustrated growl. "I am afraid that's not nearly enough. Unless there are other witnesses?"

She thought of the guards that were present, but they were paid to keep silent and might not have been paying attention at the time. It was their lack of attention that allowed her to attack Ened.

Sylvia put her palm to her forehead; she reached for the glass of cordial. The liquor sloshed all over the place, and by the time she got it to her lips, there wasn't much of it left.

The glass dropped, but being thick, it only chipped on the mahogany desk. She gripped the edge to steady herself. "Ened, the harpy!"

Her eyelids became heavy, and her legs wobbled violently before buckling and sending her to the floor. The soft red carpet was the last thing she felt before the darkness overtook her.

* * * * *

Her eyes fluttered open into slits. The memories crawled to the surface one by one as she slowly became aware. The ringing in her ears cleared. Voices were arguing, flurrying like bats flying to and fro in her skull. She placed a hand under her, feeling the softness of the carpet, and for a short moment, it was comforting. Then she remembered why she was there. She managed with some difficulty to open her eyes—yes, it was that red carpet, blood red, like the gash she placed on Ened's cheek.

Sylvia could feel the cool air from a fan on the windowsill behind her. She glacially moved her head down. Yes, naked as any babe . . . or new gilla. The discomfort at her neck became noticeable as her skin pressed against cold steel.

"No, no." She managed to say in a whisper. Her muscles seemed to be unable to work in unison, so she relied on her eyes and found herself no longer near the desk. Instead she had been placed in the opposite corner of the room. There, in front of the arbiter's desk, was the woman she hated the most in this world.

"I implore you to hand her over to my office."

"Why would I do such a thing after I went through so much trouble to make this happen?"

"It's not right—"

The woman's voice interrupted. "Says who? What, does it go against your ethics? Are you some sort of stoic philosopher denying gillahood? Is it a wretched thing to you?"

Sylvia recognized the arbiter's voice, and Ened's was as shrill as ever. Her vision cleared, and she could see them fully; Dial was still behind his desk but standing with his hands placed firmly on the slick top, never taking an eye away from her aunt, who was pacing back and forth. For the most part he seemed calm with only a tinge of frustration sliding across his face.

Ened continued her mounting tirade. "Of course you are! You kept me from entering this room and denied me the emotion of putting the collar on the girl by drugging her!"

"She fainted."

"Cac!" Ened swiped her hand across the desk, knocking about some documents and making the cup Sylvia drank from fly and shatter against the wall, just below the window.

This made the arbiter growl in anger. "Lowering a high patrician is bad enough, but putting your own blood to gillary is madness!"

Ened stopped her pacing and looked directly at him. "She might have my name, but she is no bloodkin!"

"Do you have any proof of that claim?" he said sternly.

"No, but she resembles no Chronister in our family line! Look at her!" They both looked in her direction. Ened produced that crooked smile, now marred by the long vertical scar curving down from the right side of the nose to half an inch away from the corner of her mouth, deep like a crag in a mountain. "Ah, the thing's awake!"

Ened marched over to her with a gleam in her eye, looking quite triumphant. Sylvia found her collar being pressed against the front of her throat, making her cough and gag. She tried her best to grab it in a desperate attempt for relief. Someone strong had control of her and brought her up to her knees, then forcefully down to Ened's boot. She stopped the forward motion by rigidly placing her arms on the carpet, glad that her muscles were now working.

"New gilla should greet their owners by kissing their feet!"

Sylvia kept firm. She would never kiss a boot, and these particular boots were covered in mud and who knows what other foulness from the streets. The unknown hand wormed its way into her hair, and she was forced down so hard that her elbows buckled, sending her mouth crashing onto Ened's toe.

"That's enough! I will not abide this . . . insanity in my office!"

Sylvia was let go, and she began spitting out the foul grime.

"You can have more money than Plutus, but you do not own this room or my court! You are a foul and petty woman! Now get out!"

Ened's smile faded. She walked slowly to the desk and placed her hands on top, mirroring the arbiter, invading his space to get face-to-face with him.

"After I have settled *my* new gilla in *my* house, make no mistake, I will ruin you!"

She turned her head and gestured for the mysterious man in the corner to follow. Sylvia's collar was grabbed from behind and lifted up again, making her choke. She had no choice but to go along with the motion and find her footing.

As soon as she was on her feet, she took a moment to hack and wheeze before being pushed forward. She looked fully about the room, seeing that her guards were long gone. The man from behind stepped in front of her. If she thought the thugs that Ened hired were big, then this man was a mountain, full of angles. There was no softness about him, and he was obviously from the east. She wondered if he was Hanren, but judging by the stature and his long black mustachios tied up by a cord into a bun just under his chin, he had to be Liao, a large nation of nomadic peoples neighboring Zarmatia. He was dressed in western style except that it was all black. It was the only thing about him that did not stand out. He stared down at Sylvia, making her shiver in fear, and the shock finally wore off. "No, no, you can't do this! It's wrong!"

"What's wrong, dear, is denying me my due and ruining my face!"

Sylvia dropped to her knees. The movement wrenched her collar from the Liao's grasp. She scrambled to the arbiter's desk, grabbed the edge, and pulled herself up.

"You can't let them do this! Please, do something!"

He gave her a once-over, considering. What he was thinking of, she could not tell. The Liao grabbed her collar and pulled her back, making her choke and wheeze again.

Recovering from this quickly, she spoke with some trouble. "Please, she'll kill me!"

"Silly girl, that would be a waste!" declared Ened.

Arbiter Dial looked away, embarrassed by whatever thought he had.

"I wish there was something I could do, but even if I could find some way, it's too late. Unless Miss Chronister here wants to free you or sell you . . ."

Sylvia felt like the world stopped for a moment at the thought of someone having the ability to sell her.

The arbiter rubbed his forehead. "I will . . . look into what you have told me, but for now you are legally her property."

"No! This is not happening! It's a dream, this isn't real!" In her hysterics, she kept pulling away, jerking her neck and bracing away from the Liao as much as she was able. Like a marble statue of a foreign God, he did not seem to notice her struggles.

Once he had her under control, Ened stepped up to her and grabbed her collar. She reached behind and only unlocked it for a second, then slid a new tag to the front, resting it in the hollow of Sylvia's neck.

Facing Ened, she spat out, "You had this planned all along!"

Ened gave a nod, and the Liao backhanded Sylvia and let her crumble to the carpet from the force. She tasted copper, promptly spit out the blood, and realized that her lip was cut.

"You will address me as Mistress!"

"Enough! Leave this office!" said Dial.

The next thing Sylvia knew, she was being hoisted up and over the Liao's shoulder.

* * * * *

There were no words spoken on the way to the insula. Not much to say when one was face first on the floorboards of an auto with boot heels digging cruelly into her back. At first she used that time to think on what got her to this point, all her failures to be more vigilant, to get out and participate in patrician society, being too upset to see Ened's plan, freeing Emlyn. No, if there was one thing she should not regret, it was letting Tabby go. Ened had said that she had plans for Emlyn.

Heels dug into her back, and Ened chuckled again and again at her humiliation. Sylvia seethed in an escalating spiral of anger.

"Are you in the least bit interested about the name on your tag? Not speaking? It says: Bide, property of Eneddia Chronister. Do you know what Bide means? No? I'll tell you, it means fool. A fitting name if I do say so."

By the time the Liao sat her in the familiar peach-colored lounging room, she had no hope of hiding her anger. The silent Liao sat across from her and showed no emotion as he stared back. The stillness of the gaze was unsettling, almost like looking into a martial's eyes. It was fine. Sylvia was used to looking martials in the eye, and this foreigner was no different. She could swear he gave a faint smirk, and it made a shiver permeate her skin and pierce all the way down to her bones.

Suddenly he stood up, making her jump. Before Sylvia could blink, he was on her. The first thing she thought was that he was going to use her. Instead he lifted her off the couch and put her face first on the ground. He took a cord of some sort from his belt and tied her hands behind her back. Then did the same to her ankles. He grabbed her hair and leaned her back, putting her on her knees. It happened so fast, it took a moment for the pain to catch up.

He kept his fingers in her hair, and she found it difficult to move. Through the door came Ened with something smoking in her hand.

Sylvia's eyes bulged because as Ened came around the couch, in her mitted fist was a handle attached to a wedge clothes iron.

"I think a little payback is in order."

She waggled the iron in front of Sylvia's face, the heat made her wince. She struggled in her bonds, but the Liao bent down behind her and placed a gigantic hand on her throat, keeping her still.

"I don't plan on taking your eye, Bide, so don't you move. There, such a good girl."

Sylvia's eyes were wide and wild as the hot piece of metal came closer to her skin. The iron pressed and seared into her cheek. Smoking, stinking. She screamed and screamed and tried to violently move away, but the grip held firm and the iron pressed cruelly.

"You made me ugly! I'll do the same to you!" yelled Ened. She relented and took a step back.

Her cries started to subside. She was pushed to the floor. "I—Wha, what did I do to you?" She tried to scream it out, but it made the pain even worse. "What did I do?"

"Well, nothing really. Not that you were planning to give me my due or anything. But you look so much like your mother that whatever I do with you, well, I'll be doing it to her. Now, are you ready to kiss my feet and beg for forgiveness?"

Sylvia opened one eye and looked at the boot placed in front of her face. It was clean, but that made no difference. She forced herself to remain still. She locked eyes with Ened.

The old crone's smile faded as Sylvia managed to suck back and then spit onto the boot. "May the Morri find you and rend you asunder, betrayer!"

Ened's rage shone. "You little bitch! The family betrayed me! *Me!* You and Andreas thought you were rid of me?" Ened's insanity became more and more apparent as she started calling Sylvia Camilla. And this more than anything else scared her. It showed that her aunt was capable of anything, even beyond branding her face with a hot iron.

She kicked Sylvia, luckily on the unburnt side on her cheek, but it did not lessen the pain she felt, only enhanced it to an almost unbearable degree.

"Get her up!"

The Liao got her by the collar and did so, getting her back on her knees. "Hold her there!"

Ened kicked her in the stomach. "Kiss my boot!"

Sylvia smirked. "Go suck a bitch's tit, you old shrew!" She would have never cussed like that before, but she was no longer a high lady or any sort of lady.

She heard men laughing within the room. Some of the thugs must have come in to watch, and now her one good cheek glowed as hot as the other from numerous incoming smacks from her aunt. One man called out to Ened on not being able to control a gilla. The Liao left her. There was a scuffle, then a sickening crack somewhere from behind. She did not want to imagine what the sound could have been.

Ened screeched and kicked her again. She was allowed to fall this time since the Liao was no longer behind her. Ened continued the assault on Sylvia's chest and stomach. "Tell me I'm your mistress. Do it now! Kiss my boot! Now!"

Sylvia did nothing except laugh.

Ened soon stopped her temper tantrum, having exhausted herself. Out of breath, she said, "You will not talk to me that way!"

An idea seemed to occur. Ened looked wildly at the gaggle of thugs. "Call a surgeon here, I want her vocal cords cut, and if he cannot do that, then I want you to remove her tongue!"

Sylvia stopped laughing. She could hear the men in the room hold their breath.

Her aunt produced a skull-like grin after hearing her niece moan out a weak "No." Sylvia's growing desperation produced a wickedly delighted expression of glee from Ened.

"Ah! Now you shut up! But you know, I like the idea of you being mute. I mean, you sound nothing like Camilla, so why do I need to hear your voice?"

Sylvia looked up at her with a shocked expression.

"You might be thinking that giving in now would placate me. But it's far too late for that. I'll ask you to kiss my boot again after the surgery, and at that point, you will heel to me. Maybe then you will realize that Emlyn is not coming to save you. No one has your back, no one is standing in your corner, no one except me. I will treat you well, that is, if you're a good girl."

Ened bent down and twined a few strands of Sylvia's black hair around her finger. Sylvia stared at the digit. Her heartbeat was the only sound in the room, pounding like a fist ramming into her chest over and over again. The finger came close to her face, and she craned her neck and struck as fast as a viper. There was a crunch, and a satisfying scream. She smiled as blood trickled from her lips. She kept smiling, until something heavy came down upon her. There was a sudden flash, then the only thing left to her was the familiar void.

GLOSSARY

Ap- Yes.

Aic - A brief greeting, or a positive expression.

Ambax- Personal guard.

Arbiter- A high judge.

Axel- Caelland/Zellian for gills.

Arva Arress- Southwestern Lucanian lord/lady.

Auloa- Long Double pipe instrument.

Bloodlined- A gilla who will be bred, resulting in the offspring being born into forced servitude.

Brigada- Battalion.

Broathan- Born without the presence of a father.

Bunk- Not real make-up.

Cac- Old Roman word for feces now back in fashion.

Campy- Ancient war-horn with a long skinny neck and bulbous head fashioned after a boar.

Catcher- Catches runaway gilla.

Cated- A sonata.

Citara- An instrument with its origins in they east with 5 to 7 strings. Usually played with a pland(pick).

Cumber- Of little mind, useless.

Cumberwith- A stronger version of cumber.

Dalarwain- The right hand to a leader.

De- Deity/deities.

Decanus- The head of a large group of Peacekeepers.

Dep or depad- Stupid.

Drib- Some, a little bit.

Fluet- Single pipe instrument.

Geisel- A prohibition or demand placed on an individual, usually given by a Magistrate, Arbiter, or Druid-priest, sometimes by a Decanus.

Cobb- A small gilla, mistress or sex toy.

Golden Sickle- In reference to the Druid cutting mistletoe with uncorrupted metal.

GLOSSARY

Ae- Yes

Aio- A type of greeting, or a positive expression.

Ambax- Personal guard.

Arbiter- A high judge.

Asel- Gaelland/Gallian for gilla.

Atyr/Atyress- Southwestern Lucanian lord/lady.

Aulos- Long Double pipe instrument.

Bloodlined- A gilla who will be bred, resulting in the offspring being born into forced servitude.

Brigada- Battalion

Brosthun- Born without the presence of a father.

Bunk- Not real, made up.

Cac- Old Roman word for feces now back in fashion.

Carnyx- Ancient war horn with a long skinny neck and bulbous head fashioned after a boar.

Catcher- Catches runaway gilla.

Cened- A senate.

Citarra- An instrument with its origins further east with 5 to 7 strings. Usually played with a planch(pick)

Cumber- Of little mind, useless.

Cumberwhirl- A stronger version of cumber.

Dalarwain- The right hand to a leader.

Dé- Deity/deities.

Decanus- The head of a large group of Peacekeepers.

Dep, or deppid- Stupid.

Drib- Some, a little bit.

Fluet- Single pipe instrument.

Geissi- A prohibition or demand placed on an individual, usually given by a Magistrate, Arbiter, or Drudi priest. Sometimes by a Decanus.

Gobb- A sneaky liar, insincere suck up.

Golden sickle- In reference to the Drudi cutting mistletoe with uncorrupted metal.

High Patrician- Ultra rich aristocrat with a hierarchy unto themselves. Most possess very old, highly respected family names.

Jib- Flattery, a lot of talk that means nothing.

Kymbri(Kymbrian)- Country name and language.

Legrix- Military rank equivalent to a Lieutenant.

Lick of the tongue- Cure, cured.

Low Patrician- Rich families, usually new money with little history to their names. To gain low or high patrician status, your entry has to be documented.

Magistrate- A local judge.

Nodens- Celtic deity associated with healing, the sea, hunting and dogs. Still considered a separate deity on some parts of the isle.

On stutter- Electric machinery that has malfunctioned.

Overrun the cup- Too much.

Peacekeeper- Uniformed people who patrol the streets for criminality.

Peacer- Slang term for Peacekeeper.

Pig-haves- Derogatory word against the rich.

Pleasure palace- A place where pleasure gilla live and work.

Rib tickler- Joke.

Rutta- A short string instrument played with a bow.

Seven doors- Doors of the afterlife: Reincarnation for the good, reincarnation for the bad, House of Dawn, House of Twilight, The under, The otherworld and Oblivion.

Steel screw- Another for a workhouse.

Teyrn- King/Queen.

The stints- Poorest area of Londinium.

Torix- Military leader equivalent to a captain.

Trup- Harlot, or derogatory word for woman.

Tyswir- Western Lucanian lord.

Venti- Zarmation for gilla.

Vigiles- Firefighters.

Wahyr- Goodbye, farewell.

Wain- Leader

The Blades of Emlyn Gwen

2022

Morgan L. Potts is a storyteller dressed in black, native to the piedmont of North Carolina with a penchant for coffee and mixology. She possesses a fascination for the underdogs of history along with the many permutations of radical power dynamics.

light-of-kymbri.com
morganlynnpotts@gmail.com